THE

MYSTERIOUS ALEXANDRA TARASOVA-YUSUPOV

A Novel of a Woman who was, as Churchill said,
"a riddle, wrapped in a mystery, inside an enigma…"

BY
CARL DOUGLASS

ISBN Number: 978-1-59433-829-8
eBook ISBN Number: 978-1-59433-830-4
ISBN Numbers, Library of Congress Number, Publication Dates,
Publishers Information

Manufactured in the United States of America

DISCLAIMER

This book—*The Mysterious Alexandra Tarasova-Yusupov*—is a novel, a fiction. None of the persons ever actually lived nor did the events described take place in the way they are described although there are known historical figures and events included. There are familiar places in the book such as Moscow, Vladivostok, Victoria, Australia, and Shanghai. An effort has been made to describe those places as they might have been at the time the author sets the story. The principle character, Alexandra Tarasova-Yusupov, is very loosely based on a real person who lived at the time in both the Russian Empire and in Australia. She came to the author's attention through the work of Marvin and Kay Rust, former missionaries for the Church of Jesus Christ of Latter Day Saints in Melbourne, Victoria Province, Australia. The Rusts and others donated their time to Victoria to update and digitize the provincial records. In the course of their work they discovered a beautiful Russian woman who moved to Australia—with scant history before that–where she prospered. After several decades in Australia, the woman returned to Russia mysteriously, and was never heard of again. Her Australian husband applied for a probate of her estate a decade or two after her disappearance but was never granted a death certificate or any control of her sizable assets for equally mysterious reasons. Beyond those skimpy facts, the woman has slipped away into the mists of time.

The Yusupov family, alluded to in *Alexandra*, is legendary in pre-Soviet revolutionary empire history as one of the richest families in the world, decidedly the richest family in Russia–even wealthier than the tzars. Their influence was comparable to that of the imperial family. The characters based on the Yusupov family are briefly mentioned by name, but the principle protagonist—an important scion of the family—is entirely a product of the author's imagination. Considerable license has been taken in describing actual events and dates in China, Australia, Russia and the Yusupov family's histories but actual events and places are included that are part of history and lore for the purpose of creating a realistic setting for the actions of the novel. Changes from history (such as some dates and places) to serve the story are included unapologetically at the discretion of the author.

ACKNOWLEDGEMENTS

The author is indebted to Mr. and Mrs. Rust and their fellow missionaries for their assiduous efforts to discover any and everything possible about the woman who has morphed into the main character of this novel and for their insistence that I write a book about their fascination with the mysterious woman. They worked with a number of other expert archivists from the LDS church and the State of Victoria to update and to scan in the treasured archives before they are lost to the elements and various invading creatures. To name a few of those tireless and generous contributors who have saved Australia millions of dollars: Delbert and LaRae Dillingham, Jim and Marilyn Freeman, Daniel Wilksch, Lupe Pulu, and Dee Madden.

It was of interest to this author to see the passion of these dedicated missionaries not only to their work, but to the concept that the person whose name and brief factual history they had unearthed was a real person who lived and who cries out for her life to be so fully discovered that she can take her place with other "saints" whose factual identities will be preserved in the remarkable genealogical archives of the Church of Jesus Christ of Latter-day Saints. That church library exists for the benefit of anyone who might develop an interest in any one of those identities so preserved. This author regrets that this book must be one of fiction since there is not enough information available to permit more than a footnote to the life of this undoubtedly remarkable woman.

The author is forever grateful to Evan Swensen and his publishing company, Publication Consultants, for the generous help to craft this book into one acceptable under his stringent writing and publishing requirements. He is owed a similar debt of gratitude for the previous books published under the author's name by Publication Consultants. The friendship and advice of members of Author Masterminds is also greatly appreciated.

The author obtained invaluable historical insight from the following publications, to name a few:

Aleksandr Solzhenitsyn, *One Day in the Life of Ivan Denisovich, 1962,* The Gulag Archipelago 1918-1956, 1973
Count Lyov Nikolayevich Tolstoy: *The Cossacks,* 1863, *War and Peace,* 1869, *Anna Karenina,* 1877), *The Cossacks,* 1863, *Family Happiness,* 1859, *The Death of Ivan Ilyich,* 1886

David Cordingly, *Under the Black Flag: The Romance and the Reality of Life Among the Pirates,* Random House Paperback, May 9, 2006
Fyodor Mikhaylovich Dostoyevsky: *Crime and Punishment,* 1866, *The Idiot,* 1869, *The Brothers Karamazov,* 1880

Geoffrey Blainey, *A Shorter History of Australia,* Vantage Books, 1994
Homer—Translated by Robert Fitzgerald: *The Iliad, The Odyssey*
John R. Bernasconi, *The Wordsworth Guide to Antiques and Fine Arts, Wordsworth References,* 1971

Josh Provan, *Ching Shih, The Pirate Queen of the China Sea,* Hong Kong Maritime Museum
Nicholas V. Riasanovsky and Mark D. Steinberg, *A History of Russia,* Oxford University Press, 2004
Philip Gosse, *The History of Piracy,* (Dover Maritime) Paperback, August 2007 ,31 (original, 1932)

Phillip Knightley, *Australia: A Biography of a Nation,* Vantage, 2001
Rear Admiral Samuel Eliot Morison, USNR, *The Constitution Gun Deck,* a Naval Historical Center Publication
Robert Hughes, *The Fatal Shore: The Epic of Australia's Founding,* 1986
Robert Service, *The Last of the Tsars, Nicholas II and The Russian Revolution,* Macmillan, 2017

The Editorial Committee of Chinese Civilization: A Source Book (Author), *China: Five Thousand Years of History & Civilization,* Paperback, April 30, 2007

The Military History of Tsarist Russia, Editors: Kagan, F., Higham, R., Palgrave Macmillan, 2002

DEDICATION

To Alexandra Sokolova Nakis, may she know that she is loved.
Lest we forget.

[Alexandra Abramovna Tarasova-Yusupov Bradshaw] "is
a riddle, wrapped in a mystery, inside an enigma..." To
paraphrase and to take liberties from Churchill's famous
quotation regarding Russia.
 —Winston Churchill, BBC radio broadcast,
October, 1939

BOOKS BY CARL DOUGLASS

Neurosurgeon Who Writes with Gripping Realism

FICTION

Last Phoenix-A Novel of Betrayal and Revenge, A Story of the CIA's Phoenix Program
Gog and Magog—Yawm al-Qiyamah, Yawm al-Din, The Day of Judgment
Sheep Dog and The Wolf-A Story of Terrorism and Response, and the Sheep Dogs Who Protect

Trojan Horse in the Belly of the Beast, **Three Books:**
- *Though They Come From the Ends of the Earth-Book One*
- *Dancing with the Devil-Book Two*
- *Trojan Horse in the Belly of the Beast-Book Three*

Finders Keepers, Losers Weep-A Novel of Innocence Betrayed and the Search for Restitution
Gog and Magog—Yawm al-Qiyamah, Yawm al-Din, The Day of Judgment

Saga of a Neurosurgeon Series, **Six Books:**
- *Young Coyote-Book One: Garven Wilsonhulme's Way to Success-No Quarter Asked and None Given*
- *Anything Goes-Book Two*
- *Heaven and Hell-Book Three: Garven Wilsonhulme Takes on All Comers in the Jungle of Modern Competition*
- *Long Climb-Book Four: Young M.D., Garven Wilsonhulme, Engaged in a Social Poker Game of Winner Takes All*
- *Academia: The Law of the Jungle-Book Five: Surgeon in Training, Garven Wilsonhulme, Fang-and-Claw Competition for Glory*
- *The Vulture and the Phoenix-Book Six: Neurosurgeon, Garven Wilsonhulme, the Final Great Fight*

All in Jest-Renowned Neurosurgeon in the Fight of Her Life

NOVELLAS (Twelve)

Sybil Series	McGee Series
1st Novella-*The End of the Beginning*	1st Novella-*Friends at Homeland Security*
2nd Novella-*Uncharted Country, Uncertain Future*	2nd Novella-*Crossing the Cult*
3rd Novella-*Secrets*	3rd Novella-*Wednesday's Child*
4th Novella-*Secrets and Scandals*	4TH Novella-*Death on a Pale Horse*
5th Novella-*Decisions*	5th Novella-*The Boss's Daughters*
6th Novella-*Running with the Big Dogs*	6th Novella—*Another Whistle Blower*

NONFICTION

On Evolution, The Origin of Selection, Order, Progression, and Diversity–out of print

Something About Religion—out of print

BOOK ONE

CHAPTER ONE

A Scion is Born

There are only three events in a man's life; birth, life, and death; he is not conscious of being born; he dies in pain; and he forgets to live.

—Jean de la Bruyere

Arkhangelskoye Estate, Moscow, Russia, June 22, 1852

A squalling, red-faced baby was born after his twenty-year-old mother had been in active labor for twenty-eight hours, and the family feared for her life. His final emergence into the world was considered to be an omen by the peasantry and nobility alike–whether for good or evil–no one was certain. His name–already determined by his authoritarian father–the robust nine-pound boy–upon his first cry— became one of richest members of the richest family in the empire and the entire world for that matter. As soon as he was able to walk and talk, he would begin to have divine right authority of life and death over the family serfs, to command legendary sums of money for his every whim, and would be ranked in the upper five of the empire's eligible bachelors. He was christened Prince Boris Nikolaiovich Yusupov when he was baptized with three immersions at three-days-old by the venerable family priest, Episkopos Johannes Ivanovich Vasiliev. The most important witness of that ceremony was not his princely father or mother but his godfather, Grand Duke Paul Alexandrovich son of Alexander II Tzar of all the Russias. Thus, was tiny Boris linked for all of his life to the tzars of Russia.

The baby's mother, Princess Tatiana Alexandrovna de Ribeaupierre Yusupov–a lady-in-waiting to the Empress–waited until the baptism ceremony was over, then she took her husband's hand and led him a short distance away for a brief private conversation.

"Niki, there is something we should discuss; and today is the appropriate time since Grand Duke Paul Alexandrovich is here in our home."

"A problem, Tati? Surely not today?"

"Not a problem, my dear Niki, just something to discuss."

"And something of a mystery, I take it."

"Not really…not at all, in fact. My young ladies' group discussed modern health issues and especially obstetrics and infant care this past month since three of us were with child and late in our terms.

Niki's response was a brief affectionate laugh, more of a snort.

"Don't belittle them–my dear husband–they are ladies of the most important families in the empire, and the best educated women in all of the Russias. Let me finish what I wanted to discuss with you. The ladies, Especially Countess Helene Charlotte Louise von Phalen, who serves as a lady of the state and the painter, Maria Baehr, are very knowledgeable about what should be done. Both of them studied in Friedrich-Wilhelms-Universitat, the greatest school for the sciences in all of Europe.

When she finished that inflated sentence, Prince Nikolai, gave her one of his irritating and patronizing avuncular smiles and asked, "Tell me, dearest one, what did you learn?"

She was aware of his prejudice against learning that women participated in and especially which they taught as science. In fact, he often quoted the Chinese dogma from next door Manchuria, "women's virtue is without talent", a particularly odious statement to Irina and her friends—not that she would ever criticize her husband for saying it.

"The latest safety measure, which is catching on all over the world, is circumcision of baby boys."

He started to speak, but she put up her hand to stop him.

"Wait until I finish, my prince," she said, "I am assured that babies have fewer infections, and later on in life, their women get fewer infections as well. You will be pleased to learn that male potency is also enhanced, but I hesitate to mention a subject so delicate as that," she smiled.

He could not restrain himself to just a disdainful smile, and he laughed heartily.

"Hogwash! You know where that bit of lunacy comes from don't you?"

"Besides the university, no; but, I assume you are about to inform me."

"I am indeed, Tati, and to save you embarrassment. The professors there in Berlin are Jewish, and you are learning Hebrew scientific nonsense—about the same as their alchemy of yesteryear. To be blunt, circumcision is as Jewish as their prophet, Moses. We–and I mean you– have to regard any such silliness as being just another effort by the sheenies to elevate themselves."

"That is just anti-semitism, isn't it, Niki?"

"Not at all. Sheeny just relates to the fact that they think they are *schön*. I believe that is a reference to their perversion of men loving men. It is just a fact. They are *untermenschen*, and it is a silly passing fancy to give credence to their supposed scientific research. Circumcision is Jewish. We are Russians, not Jewish; and no Yusupov prince is going to have some butcher cut on his generative organ. This discussion is over. And above all else, the Grand Duke is not to hear such heresy in our home. Do you understand, my dear?" he asked softly.

"Yes, my prince. Of course I do," she said as meekly as she could muster up.

"Perhaps, you need new friends," he stated with finality.

When the head of the Yusupov family made a declaration, no one– not even his wife–had the temerity to advance another idea after he gave his glance of finality.

As the evening was drawing to a close, Prince Nikolai, took a momentary opportunity to present a consideration for the new baby's godfather.

"Grand Duke, I have a request of you as little Boris's godfather."

"Of course, my boy, whatever I can give."

"It is not a material request, Paul Alexandrovich; it is even more important than that. My first born should pursue a military career, one the tzar can find appropriate. I ask that, at the appropriate time, you put him forward to enter the General Staff Academy."

"An excellent and timely request, my boy. The day of his birth is the most appropriate day of all to begin molding that robust little boy into a strong man and eventually into a loyal officer of the Tzar's forces. I will be honored to be his "rabbi" as the Jews say for someone who puts a younger protégé forward."

He laughed at his use of the Jewish honorific. Prince Nikolai joined in and thanked his Maker that his silly wife had not gone to Grand Duke Paul Alexandrovich before he could intervene.

CHAPTER TWO

THE MAKING OF A HORSEMAN

"The wildest colts make the best horses."
—Plutarch, CE 46 – CE 120

The *Yusupov* Palace on the Moika River, Saint Petersburg, March 4, 1863

Eleven-year-old Boris Yusupov conspired with the senior equestrian trainer in his father's stables to have the man teach him how to ride like a cavalryman—"like one of Ivan's Cossacks"—was the exact reference. Boris wanted to be able to give a flawless demonstration of his expert horsemanship for his father on the occasion of his upcoming twelfth birthday. Boris was already quite skillful, having been placed in a small saddle on a tough little Dagestanskii Pony when he was just two-years-old and had graduated to riding the most spirited of father's fine stock of Cossack cavalry horses.

Boris was a prepubertal youth, slender and lithe from his vigorously active life, taller than the other boys in his age group, and devoid of the coarse features of the slavs in the countryside and fortunately lacking any hint of the Yusupov Turkish bloodlines of which his father was so proud. Boris had curly blond hair hanging down to the top of his shoulders and deep-seated Wedgewood blue irises–generous gifts of the Viking ancestors who had so liberally sprinkled their DNA into his gene pool over the last six hundred years. Knowing that he was going out for a hard day's ride and would have his legs clinging to his large horse's lathered skin all of the time, he wore an old pair of serf's baggy brown knee-length trousers and a pull-over shirt laced up at the neck. The shirt was made of the same cloth used for flour sacks—rough, coarse, and utilitarian. It was long, extending to just above his knees, and was tightened at the waist by a rope knotted in front. The only nods to his superior landholder's status were the heavy and valuable muslin jerkin hanging loosely on his broadening shoulders, and his fine, knee-high polished black Hessian boots with a foppish tassel at the knees.

Today he was mounted on Kryzhu, a tall muscular chestnut, the largest of the estate's stallions. Father Prince Nikolai retained the strong masculinity of the Polish word Kryzh, even adding the stronger -u to emphasize the love Russian aristocrats had for the powerful Polish horses preferred by all officers for their personal cavalry mounts. Boris was accompanied by his favorite dog—as he always was—an Asian dhole, a dog but one with its own genus. That genus is characterized by more teats and fewer teeth than Canis, and whistles more than it barks or howls. They live in the forests and steppes of Russia. The puppy was brought by Cossacks to Prince Nikolai when Boris was eight years old and named—appropiately—Donoschik [whistler]. It became Boris's dog in short order.

It was still early—first light had not yet dawned—when the retainer and the boy set out through the rear entrance of the stables. Vladimir–the trainer of horses and men–led the way as precisely as if he could see in the dark. Boris held his horse's reins loosely; so, the horse could follow safely, relying on the age-old wisdom of horses and of men who rode from the youngest age when they could remain in the saddle.

By the time it was light enough to see a hundred meters, they were trotting along the ridge of the hills on the eastern border of the Moika estate and opposite of the river. Vlad seldom spoke to his betters when others were around; but today, he was voluble, taking his role as a teacher seriously. He was well aware that if his young charge were to be injured during these training rides, the blame would fall on him–not on the horse, not on the boy, not on the lay of the land. He was also well aware that Prince Nikolai expected his son to be a superior horseman by the end of the summer and that the boy, Prince Boris, held him to a higher standard—that of a man who became one with his horse and able to ride hands free to hold his Cossack weapons.

Vlad signaled a stop with a curt hand gesture. He swiveled in his saddle and surveyed the hilltop area.

"This is a good place to practice, Boy," he said. "Take the pike in your left hand and ride from here to the pile of rocks to our right. Walk, do not run; do not trot. Your father left strict instructions for me to have you understand that in all matters related to the education in riding his horses, you are to obey me to the letter and immediately. Do you understand, my Prince?"

"Yes, Vlad. I will obey."

He was anxious to begin the day's serious riding. Kryzhu was champing at the bit. The stallion could feel the enthusiasm of his light young rider.

"Go," Vlad ordered. "Remember, this is not a race. If you cannot obey me in this, then, we will return home where you can think about what you will do on another day when I think you are ready to try again.

Boris nodded, and squeezed his knees against his horse's sides, taking care to keep his heels away from the large animal's flank and his stifle. Kryzhu started at a slow walk, just as the boy's knees had ordered. After twenty meters, Boris gave a quick extra push against the horse's flank, and Kryzhu moved into a fast walk, short of a trot.

"Good boy, Kryzhu," Boris said to his powerful companion.

They walked crisply to the pile of walks. Boris used his knees to direct Kryzhu to make a full about face, and they walked briskly back to where Vlad stood waiting besides his horse.

"Good, lad," Vlad said. "I know it was hard to go slow, but the first thing a Cossack must learn is to keep his horse in check to conserve his energy and to keep him in line with the other mounts."

Boris nodded his understanding and said, "so what's next, Vlad?"

"Walk for twenty meters, then trot the rest of the way to the rocks. After that, stop your horse; allow him a short breather, then turn and come back at a good canter. Lay your reins on Kryzhu's withers. Understand?"

"I do."

Boris had never ridden a horse without using the reins before, and he worried a little about humiliating himself by falling off. But he made a concentrated effort not to show is concern to the tough old Cossack. At the precise place, Vlad told him to make the change, Boris gave Kryzhu a light heel kick in the posterior flank, and the horse quickened his stride into a three-beat gait perfectly between a trot and a gallop.

That task went off exactly as Vlad had ordered. Both he and Boris were pleased with the progress he was making. Boris made the sign of the cross in thanks for Mary keeping him in the saddle. The next task was more daunting.

"Get down from Kryzhu; give him a drink; give his muzzle a rub and speak softly to him."

Boris nodded and complied.

"Now, remount; give a short pull back on the reins followed by a kick in the flanks with your heels. Shout for him to go. And, Boy, hang on for dear life!"

"*Beg!*" Boris shouted, and the magnificent creature hurtled forward so suddenly that Boris rolled over backwards and somersaulted over the saddle's gullet, seat, cantle, the horse's back, hindquarters, croup, and loin, and landed in a flail on his own rump. It all happened so fast that Boris registered no pain. In a second, he was overcome with humiliation, especially because Vladimir, a servant, was laughing uproariously at him.

"Whistle for him, Boy," Vlad yelled, "or we'll be chasing him all day."

Boris's whistle was usually fairly weak; and now, with his loss of breath, it was little more than a squeak which prompted another bout of uncontrollable laughter. Donoschik imitated Boris but to no effect. Vlad put two fingers in his mouth and emitted a high-pitched commanding whistle which stopped the horse in his tracks. A second, quieter whistle caused Kryzhu to turn about and walk calmly back to the man and the boy.

Boris was fighting back tears of embarrassment and turned aside; so, Vlad would not see.

"I was so stupid," he croaked. "I don't think I will ever be able to stay on without using the reins," he said.

"The horse knows what to do whether you use the reins or not, Boy. But, your problem—just so you know and never forget—is to keep your toes in the stirrups. You seemed to forget that your orders were to keep your hands off the reins, but you were not told to keep your feet away from the stirrups."

Boris expected to see a disapproving frown on Vlad's face, but the older man was smiling. Worse, he started to laugh again, pouring salt into Boris's wounds. Boris gritted his teeth and choked back the urge to put the servant back into his place.

"Have you courage enough to try again, Boy?"

"Certainly. Come here Kryzhu," he commanded the waiting horse.

Kryzhu was eighteen hands high and stood with his withers and shoulders nearly a meter above Boris's head. Boris took a small gulp and bravely swung himself into the left stirrup and over into the saddle. Vlad gave him an approving nod, and Boris used his knees to move the horse into position for the next trial.

Boris took a deep breath and shouted, "*Beg!*"

This time, Boris had both feet planted securely into the stirrups and his knees lock against the horse's lower shoulder areas. When he gave the sharp heel kick–and Kryzhu took off again as if shot from a cannon barrel–Boris leaned forward and clung on to the mane. He relaxed his white-knuckled death grip on the mane by the time he reached the pile of rocks and kept his hands sedately in his lap as Kryzhu galloped like a cannon shot back to Vlad.

"Better," Vlad said with an expressionless face. "This time keep your hands off the mane. That is a child's way to hold on. Use your legs."

It took Boris two more circles to dare finally to let go of the mane. He exulted inwardly when he did it without falling off.

"Better. Are you tired, Boy?"

Boris shook his head. He had decided that he did not like being called "Boy" and that at the end of this day, he would merit being called Prince Boris, or at least, Boris.

The next four rounds required Boris to hold the lance pointing forward in one hand, then the other, then pointing down, then pointing up. It took eight rides for him to be able to keep his back up straight.

"Enough for now, Boris. We will eat."

Vlad watched Boris dismount and secure Kryzhu to a bush. He was very pleased when the young prince removed the saddle and saddle blanket and wiped down the lathered horse and poured some of his canteen of water over the foamy sweat of Kryzhu's back. The servant and the boy found a small amount of shade and lay down to eat a ration of salt pork and pemmican and a canteen of water. Both threw a few scraps to Donoschik, and the dog gobbled the offerings as if he was starving. Afterwards, Vlad made Boris learn how to do Cossack squats and a few other stretching exercises, then they took a short refreshing nap.

Vlad stood up, stretched, and gazed over the hillsides stretching below them intent on choosing where to conduct the next exercises on the inclines and declines. Boris followed his lead and scanned the area around him. Vlad was gazing west, and Boris looked to the east. Vlad had a calm face which did not convey emotion. The fissures etched into his brown skin gave evidence of long rides in open country looking into the sun. A saber cut scar on his left cheek gave him a somewhat dangerous demeanor. His brown eyes habitually squinted against the sun—accentuating the Asian oval shape of his eyes–even when the sun was not there. They were keen and perceptive and told of an extensive intelligence regarding things that matter. He wore a faded old Cossack uniform–Prince Nikolai, the master, affectionately called it the uniform of a bandit—consisting of a lambswool *papukha* on his completely bald head, a faded and patched *cherkeska* tunic–that had once been bright red–encircled with a broad red leather belt from which dangled a long dagger in a silver tipped scabbard within easy reach, black trousers with a gold stripe down the side of each leg ending in knee-high black boots which Vlad had long since stopped polishing.

Boris's intense young eyes rested on a small herd of horses a couple of kilometers down in the valley. As he focused in on them, he became aware that the herd was staying unnaturally close to one another. He squinted his keen blue eyes and focused more intently. Then he saw horsemen keeping the herd of Prince Nikolai's prize horses in a tight set of lines. It took a few moments for him to recognize the significance of what he was seeing. Donoschik alerted and pointed in the direction of the horses.

"Poachers!" he hissed loudly to Vlad.

The older man curled his forefinger to create a tiny hole to look through—as near to a telescope as he could manage. He watched for less than a minute.

"Good lad! They are indeed thieves. If we ride back to the palace for reinforcements or into the city for the constabulary, those *gnilyye zlodei* will never be seen again."

Boris spoke with all the fervor of the righteous when he agreed with Vlad that they had to do something drastic about the rotten thieves. Vlad looked for a moment at his young charge, then made a very serious decision.

"Are you brave enough to go after the *loshadinyye shorty* with me?" the older man asked, a worried furrow in his brow.

Boris did not answer but let his determined facial expression speak for him: he would not allow the horse rustlers to escape. It would be a stain on his honor as a Yusupov, as a Russian, and as a man.

Vlad nodded and smiled. He would have to protect this boy at all costs, but he could never go back and stand in front of Prince Nikolai and tell the master that he had cowardly left the field and had allowed the man's son to be an accomplice to his cowardice.

"I will carry two guns, and you carry the bag of ammunition. We will ride in the trees until we are a little behind them. When I raise my right hand, we will ride straight down off the ridge and arrest them… whatever it takes."

Boris solemnly nodded his acquiescence. He knew that falling off his horse was no longer an option. Today, he had to be a man. The two rode away from the brilliant sun, which they knew would be in the eyes of their quarries—four men. They kept to the trees, pausing occasionally to gauge where the *loshadinyye shorty* were in reference to their own position among the white birches. When the horse rustlers were in a position ahead of Boris and Vlad to be directly below them when they rode at an acute angle down the grassy hillside, the older man put up his right hand. They stopped and surveilled their current position, the rate of forward movement of the horse thieves, and made a rapid calculation of their speed of their trajectory down the decline.

"Now," whispered Vlad.

Boris glanced at the horsemaster who nodded, then the boy shouted to Kryzhu, "*beg*".

Vlad yelled at his horse, and the two men and their horses swept down through the grass. They fitted their horses so well that an onlooker would have thought them to be centaurs—front part horse and rear part man.

The rustlers did not see the unexpected Cossacks flying down at them until they were fifty meters apart.

A teenage boy, dressed in rags, saw them first and shouted at his father who was dressed in a tattered old army uniform. The horses they were stealing were noisy and difficult to manage. His beard flapped into his face as he whirled, stopped, and reversed to keep the horses in line and going the way he wanted them to.

"*Imperatorskiye kazaki!*" the boy called out again, mistaking the old man and the boy for Imperial Cossack irregulars at that distance.

Before his father could gather his wits and mount a defense, Vlad was upon him. He bashed the unprepared man in the face and dropped him from his horse. Boris plunged into the line of horses and almost rode down one of the two men on the opposite side. The man's horse reared and dumped his tired rider onto the rocky valley floor stunning him. The final man did not have time to judge his pursuer or to tell if he was a boy or a man. He pivoted about and began flogging his horse in the opposite direction from which he had been going. His horse was no match for Boris's Kryzhu. The horse knew exactly what to do. He was no stranger to combat.

Boris on Kryzhu easily overran the fleeing thief. The man attempted to extract his Nepalese *kukri* with an inwardly curved blade–similar to a machete–from his belt scabbard; but Boris jammed the end of his French *Chassepot* breechloader into the man's back and fired, killing him instantly. Seeing that Vlad had killed the father of the boy and was leading the boy with a noose around his neck towards a small copse of mountain ash trees, Boris decided that he had time to collect a few souvenirs of his first battle encounter.

Boris leapt from his horse and shot his quarry once in the back of the head to ensure no mistakes resulting in the man coming back to consciousness and attacking him and Vlad. He cut off a filthy braid from the man's hair, put the kukri in his belt, and removed the man's boots and tied them to straps on the sides of Kryzhu's saddle. He ran Kryzhu at a low gallop to where Vlad and the boy stood silently beneath the spreading branches of one of the large mountain ashes.

"What took you so long?" Vlad said with a broad smile that revealed his three missing front teeth.

"Bigger man, faster horse," Boris said and laughed.

"But it is obvious that you had the better horse, and you never hesitated. You are a brave young Cossack, Prince Boris. Your father will be pleased with you."

Boris blushed and was embarrassed about it, but he gave Vlad a courteous salute—one imperial warrior to another.

Vlad led Boris's gaze to the boy he was holding on his rope. The boy was probably one or two years older than Boris. He was terrified and had wet the front of his trousers. His hands were tied behind his back, and his ankles were lashed to the Cossack horseman saddle's by a long narrow strap leading to the stirrups. He did not make a whimper and seemed resigned to his fate.

Vlad said quietly, "Prince Boris, do you know the penalty for murder of a serf?"

Boris answered, "No, but it should be severe, I would think."

"It is a fine—the amount depending on the value of the serf who was killed."

Boris shook his head in surprise.

"Do you know the penalty for stealing a horse, independent of the value of the horse, who owns the horse, or who stole the horse, my prince?"

"I suppose it must be a lighter fine or maybe a few lashes," Boris answered attempting to find the judicial logic.

"Death," said Vlad flatly and laconically.

"Are we to take this young boy back to the magistrate in Saint Petersburg?" Boris asked.

"Depends."

There was a pause.

"On what?"

"The owner's choice."

"Can the owner choose to reduce the sentence?"

"No."

"What form does the execution take, Vlad?"

"Hanging."

"So, my father must order the hanging, then?"

"Not necessarily."

"What does that mean?"

"As scion, you are also the owner of the horses, Prince Boris."

"I can decide then?"

"Here and now, I think is the requirement of the scion."

Boris gulped briefly realizing his responsibility. He knew that he could not appear to be a silly boy or a weakling in front of this peasant. He summoned up his courage once again and reached inward for the hardness that he knew was part of the Yusupov character.

"We shall hang him here."

Vlad nodded, and asked, "What type of hanging, my prince?"

Boris did not know that there was more than one type of hanging.

"What types are there?" he asked.

"In cases where many horses were stolen, or the thieves put up great resistance when they were arrested, slow strangulation might be in order. In cases where a dollup of mercy is deemed to be appropriate, such as in the case of the very young, or with females, or with old ones, a heavy hangman's knot can be used on the side of the neck, and the thief is made to drop a considerable distance; so, the neck is broken; and death is swift and painless."

Vlad paused, waiting for Boris to reply, hoping that he would be as firm a Russian officer and powerful landlord as his father.

Boris read Vlad's mind and issued a clear simple order.

"We will hang him here, and it will be the type of hanging with the large heavy knot."

Vlad asked, "do you know the knot?"

"No, please teach me."

That pleased the old Cossack. He had Boris practice the knot ten times before pronouncing the boy to be an excellent hangman. Boris placed the end of the rope around the boy's thin neck, circled it the required thirteen times and left it just loose enough that there would be some give which would allow the large knot to snap against the neck of the falling boy and fracture it just below the junction of the head and the neck. Vlad pronounced it to be perfect.

Boris wrapped the other end of the rope around his waist and climbed the tree to the second lowest branch. Vlad brought the boy on his horse and stood him just under the line of the dangling rope.

To the boy, Vlad said in a coarse Cossack order, "Stand on your saddle, Thief."

The agile boy did as he was told and stood there uneasily, his whole body shaking.

"Fix the rope there, Prince Boris," Vlad directed. When it was done, he said simply, "Good."

Boris scrambled down from the tree and looked at his handiwork.

Vlad led Boris behind the horse.

"Slap his rump."

Boris held his short quirt in his right hand, drew the hand all the way behind him, and whirled his arm forward striking the small horse across its rump. The horse leaped in the air and bolted forward. The hapless boy dropped like a sack of potatoes directly towards the ground. A satisfying, or sickening snapping sound came from the boy's neck—depending on whether or not the onlooker approved of the hanging. The sound caused Donoschik to let out a loud whistle. It was over in a fraction of an instant.

"Good job. We will leave him here to rot as an example to other *gnilyye zlodei* who might come this way and be tempted to steal horses from Yusupov lands."

It took two days to return to Moika Palace with their newly retrieved horses. As soon as they arrived Boris and Vlad reported to Prince Nikolai. Vlad was the spokesman. In his laconic way–and speaking Russian, his second language–he recited the events accurately in five sentences, giving all praise to the boy.

Hiding his immense pride in his scion, Prince Nikolai, pronounced, "Good work. Each of you may choose a fitting reward."

He gave the proud family dog—Donoschik—an affectionate pat on the head and scratched behind his ears. It was a time of good family bonding.

CHAPTER THREE

COMING OF AGE

"If I advance, follow me. If I retreat, kill me. If I die, avenge me.
It is better to be a lion for a day than a hundred years as a sheep."
—Il Duce, Benito Mussolini

Wild country around Saint Petersburg, July 29, 1863

School, tutors, and religion, bored Prince Boris to distraction. Already at the age of twelve, he was developing a wander lust and hunger for action of any kind that was unusual for most boys his age and outright concerning for his parents—mainly, his mother. She found him more and different tutors, and he learned extremely rapidly but was never satisfied. Boris seemed to suck the educational blood of his teachers, none of whom were particularly well qualified in mathematics, horsemanship, cavalry tactics, history, or world politics which interested Boris. They seemed to have mastered the courtly graces—the minuet, the waltz, the mazurka—which were all too tame and stifling for the agile and hyperactive prepubertal prince. Even the quadrille with its complicated but active *chassé*, *jeté assemble*, and *entrechats* steps, and the frenetic polka, failed to keep Boris's attention for more than a few minutes. He liked girls well enough, but the stilted atmosphere of the ballroom even made contact with those mysterious and alluring creatures not worth his time.

From Vlad, Boris learned the most prevalent of the Cossack languages—Kuban—which was the at-home and local business language of Zaporizhia in the Ukraine—the Don Cossack State–on the river Don. From formal tutors, Boris learned French, the diplomatic language, and was as fluent in it as the diplomats. He had an excellent tutor in German and could keep up with his master at telling jokes, describing technical matters and military tactics, and even in the use of slang. From the English linguistic master he added English language, Latin, and Greek, to his repertoire so that he could compete with the other nobles in reading classic, historical, and philosophical literature from the west, especially in the original languages. Latin, Greek, and the Slavic languages were difficult for him, and he could not find any real use for them. His father ordered him to be able to speak fluently with any nobleman from a foreign country who came to the house and with any soldier or servant who spoke one of the lesser languages such as Bulgarian, Croatian, Swedish, and Italian—all of which sounded like the chatter of monkeys to Boris. Thus strongly encouraged by the *paterfamilias*, Boris doggedly did his work albeit without enthusiasm.

What Boris did love to learn related to the out-of-doors. After considerable pestering, Prince Nikolai secured a military tactics tutor for his scion and assigned Vlad to the full-time task of teaching the boy Cossack maneuvers. Together, Vlad and the boy spent much of each day galloping around the countryside of Saint Petersburg. They explored beyond the suburbs, beyond the communal serf villages, beyond the verdant fields, and out into the wooded hills and rough valleys to test themselves and their horses. Kryzhu was the equal of every test, and Boris loved him. Donoschik never even seemed tired after running all day. Thus far during his twelfth year, the instruction in Cossack tradition was all seen from horseback, and the best part of the boy's days were consumed in getting Kryzhu to charge, to wheel, to gallop, and to stop suddenly, to pivot, to jump, to endure the men's mock foraging and realistic and joyful pursuit or the yelling of the most otherworldly howls, cursing like the vilest of troopers, and enthusiastically brandishing their various weapons. Most difficult of all was to stand quietly at the ready.

Vlad found large open areas and savannas where he could teach Prince Boris how to mount his horse with lightning speed from a recumbent position, how to thrust and to cut with a straight and curved saber and lance, and how to carry and how to fire his carbine and pistol at a full gallop. These were the advanced horse borne cavalry tactics usually taught to recruits who were over eighteen or more often over the age of twenty. Boris was honing his skills on horseback before the recruits and even the officers he met later even saw such remarkable feats. Vlad was proud of Boris and never ceased to sing his praises to Prince Nikolai.

Once–in late August–the paterfamilias accompanied Vlad and Boris on one of their practice runs in the countryside. Vlad had prepared by feeding his and Boris's horses wheat for several days in advance to provide protein energy and by running them up and down hillsides full of hedgerows to jump and trees to avoid at full gallop. He secured the essential cavalry weapons—saber, lance, carbine, and pistols—for the young prince and himself. He arranged for the three of them to leave the palace before first light as he and Boris had practiced many times in the past few weeks. This was an unfair tactic designed to get the elder prince tired before the demonstration of young Boris's Cossack skills even began in case he wanted to test the boy himself. Nikolai was a hero of the War in the Caucasus against the Avarians which resulted in the young captain being instrumental in the surrender of Imam Shamil and the annexation of North Caucasus into Russia and not a man to shrink at any military challenge.

The Princes Yusupov sat motionless on their mounts after a long morning's set of maneuvers—all at a gallop. Vlad had quietly left their sides and disappeared from their view. Suddenly, from above and to the right of them, Vlad galloped full speed ahead towards the princes. He had the advantage of being above them on a fairly steep decline and coming at them; so, they had to look into the approaching noonday sun to find him. Prince Nikolai was entirely taken by surprise and fumbled to turn his mount to be able to face the opponent. Boris was fully ready by his and Vlad's planning, and he wheeled Kryzhu to the left to be able to meet Vlad side on with his saber directed straight forward. Vlad's pace was too fast for him to slow and turn to meet Boris, and the boy came within inches of colliding with the old Cossack. Boris made a carefully calculated thrust of his saber, intentionally missing Vlad by inches. Vlad participated in the bit of family theater by acting as if he had been wounded and falling off his horse and rolling to the ground. He lay in the grass giving a convincing performance of a dead man.

Prince Nikolai took a minute to realize fully what was transpiring and to get his adrenaline driven blood pressure and pulse rate to settle down. His arrival at the scene of the one-on-one combat was ludicrously late, and he began to laugh heartily when he was sure that Vlad was not injured in the least.

"Well done, my boy, very well done!" the proud father exulted.

Boris sat sternly in his saddle relishing his victory but keeping a patrician unemotional facial expression as he glanced haughtily at his puffing father. That made Nikolai laugh all the harder. He leapt from his saddle and ran to the boy.

"My young prince, you have had a true Cossack education; and you passed with flying colors. I have decided on a reward: Kryzhu is now your own horse, and I will give you four more. In addition, you shall have four serfs of your own, young men with vigor and fire. As your prowess continues, I will grant you several more over time as you earn them. As for you, Vlad–you wily old rascal–from this day forward, your debts are forgiven, you are a free man. You may stay with the family or leave as you choose. You are awarded sixteen hectares of good farm land for you and your family."

Vlad bowed low, and said tersely, "I am in your debt, Great Prince. I choose to remain as the right arm of young Prince Boris."

"You shall take your place as part of the family, my good man. Now, let us enjoy a great feast in the field like brothers-in-arms."

By the age of sixteen, Prince Boris was a tall, lithe, strong, young man with his Nordic blond hair worn in a long mane. By dint of considerable fortitude, he mastered the studies insisted upon by both of his parents and by his relentless daily educator, Vlad, the Cossack. He could now fight on the ground hand-to-hand, bare handed and with knife, pistol, and short curved saber. He was fully capable of directing and taking his place in on-the-ground Cossack attacks and retreats. He could dismount and remount on the fly with mystifying agility and speed. His father announced to Boris's mother that the day had come when he had to go away for further schooling since the family and the estate no longer held mysteries to conquer.

"If we do not corral his energies, our precocious son will get himself into trouble. There is a foment about for change in the imperial rules and policies. Perhaps there is something to be said about making the lot of the peasants and serfs better, even one day abolishing serfdom all together and building a strong empire of willing Russians—people who have different religions and ethnicity, different languages and customs, but all of whom are deep in their collective souls true Russians. That day is not now. Such talk is seditious, even though one day, it will be part of the fabric of the empire. I am determined that our son will receive a traditional conservative education. I am going to approach his godfather, Grand Duke Paul Alexandrovich, to get our fine son into the Imperial Military Academy in Saint Petersburg. Although it is my decision, will you support me in this venture?"

"Haven't I always, my husband? And, Niki, I am in full agreement with the choice even though I will shed some tears. He is a wonderful boy, and I will miss him severely. By the way, so will any number of *fräuleins* and *krasivyye molodyye devushki*, if you haven't noticed."

"Of course, I have noticed Tati. Maybe that is a good reason to get him into a world of military discipline and cold showers, and away from all those pretty young girls," he laughed.

"It is your duty to inform him, you know," Tatiana said, with some mischief in her smile.

Prince Nikolai drafted a carefully worded letter to the Grand Duke requesting an audience with him at the Imperial Military Academy. Grand Duke Paul's response came by return mail.

"It will be my pleasure to receive you my friend. Will this Saturday for lunch be convenient?"

Nikolai sent an affirmative RSVP that day, and the meeting was set.

The most elaborate carriage owned by the Yusupov family—the four-seated Berline–was brought out, given a thorough cleaning, regilding, and polishing. Prince Nikolai's best dress uniform–complete with his medals–was cleaned and pressed; his boots polished; and, at his wife's orders, his hair and beard were trimmed in the latest fashion.

Pronounced perfect, the paterfamilias set out in his gold encrusted Berline pulled by six identical large, pure white, carriage horses. He and his servants took four days to travel to Moscow so that the Prince would not appear to be overtired, overanxious, and needy—all of which could be considered accurate descriptors. They had bracing cold showers and a hearty German breakfast and arrived refreshed at the academy gates which fronted a magnificent park. It was meant to awe and inspire Russians, and Prince Nikolai was duly impressed. It was also meant to awe and frighten opponents of the imperial army and the tzarist government. Nikolai was proud to be part of such a remarkable empire and to have the opportunity to move his scion into the highest circles of the imperial army. He had prepared for this day for sixteen years.

He left his coachmen and servants in the carriage and walked across the long stone pathway and up the twelve stairs. He paused with something that bordered on reverence as he gazed at the six gleaming white pillars of the portico set against the imperial yellow of the buildings walls.

Prince Nikolai was admitted into the hallway where the general staff offices were situated. He waited for half an hour—a highly unusual demonstration of humility for one of the foremost princes of the empire—until an infantry captain in full dress uniform marched out and announced,

"Prince Nikolai Borisovich Yusupov."

Nikolai stood and saluted.

"Follow me, the Grand Duke is expecting you."

The office was sumptuous with ornate imported exotic woods from around the empire, original portraits of the Romanov family, Tlingit souvenirs from the Battle of Sitka and other skirmishes during the family's colonization of Russian Alaska. There were elegant two-hundred-year-old hand knotted carpets from the Russo-Persian and Russo-Turkish wars, victory swords from the Anglo-Russian wars and assorted battles of the Napoleonic wars, vases and statuary from the Greek War of Independence. The Grand Duke displayed his medals from the Decembrist Revolution of 1826, the Polish Insurgency of 1830-1831, the Imperial Order of Saint Alexander Nevsky, the Order of Saint Vladimir with a bow, the Order of Saint George for Military Merit, Gold Cross, a Crimean War Campaign Medal, Gold Class, and the Imperial and Royal Order of the White Eagle given by Tzar Nikolai I himself. The grand duke, therefore, held among his many titles the right to be known as Knight of the Order of the White Eagle.

There was a set of back wall glass enclosed weapons from friends and admirers in the military, courtiers, and his hunting companions. He had a dozen swords of honor accepted from defeated enemies and as awards for personal valor: an Italian hunting sword, Karabela, Szabla, and Shashka cavalry swords, a spadroon (*épée anglaise*–English sword), and eight ceremonial swords awarded from his far-flung commands and as gifts from foreign dignitaries with whom the grand duke had served.

The furniture in the Grand Duke's office was awe inspiring, as it was intended to be: matching Italian neoclassical console tables, four *Bergère à oreilles* chairs in flamed birch with mounts of gilded bronze padded with green silk embossed with Russian Military Army Imperial Eagle Crest emblems. The chairs faced a huge rectangular desk of *doré* bronze and malachite green top. The Grand Duke's gilded and blood red velvet throne chair bearing the coat of arms of Imperial Tsarist Russia faced the four chairs. On opposing walls sat two matching Louis XV style settees. In the center of the room was a glass enclosed uniform and helmet of the imperial prince.

Prince Nikolai Borisovich stood stiffly looking at the swords, pistols, and rifles in the grand duke's collection as he waited for the royal prince to grace the room. The sheer power of the room awed him, and he was annoyed at himself for having succumbed to the blatant demonstration of imperial power.

"Ah, Niki, how good it is to see you, my friend," the booming voice of Grand Duke Paul Alexandrovich Romanov exploded in Nikolai's ear causing him to jump.

"Sorry to startle you. Do you like my collection?"

"It is nothing short of marvelous. You have had an illustrious career, my Prince. How proud your family must be."

"I would hope so. Family is everything, don't you agree?"

"Completely. In fact, that is why I came to see you."

"Is this about my fine godson, Niki? I hope there is no problem. He hasn't had an accident training with his wild Cossacks, has he?"

"No, no, nothing like that. He is advancing very well and seems to be completely tireless. With due humility, I can say that he is able to keep up with his Cossacks very well."

"A drink, Niki, before business?"

"An honor, Grand Duke."

The grand duke stepped back and pulled on the heavy tassel of a silken cord. Immediately, a lieutenant of the guard appeared, clicked the heels of his mirror shined boots, and bowed.

"Dimitri, would you fetch us some cognac, please. Pour one for yourself."

The lieutenant made a sharp about-face and exited the room for three minutes. He reentered carrying a silver tray bearing the imperial coat of arms imprinted on its surface with three half-filled Russian cut crystal cognac snifters. Grand Duke Paul Alexandrovich shifted the *Bergère à oreilles* chairs; so, the three men could face each other.

"Please be seated, gentlemen," he directed. "Nikolai Borisovich, would you sit next to me. My hearing is not what it once was—all that artillery for all of those years, you know. Dimitri Sergeiovich, please sit across from us. Your young ears won't miss a thing."

"I asked Dimitri to join us. He is in his first cadet year; if he performs satisfactorily; and I am sure he will, I will make a place in next year's entering class of cadets at the Nikolai I General Staff Academy. He is a bright young man and can fill in any blanks I may leave out. Dimitri is the grandson of the leader of the Moscow Black Hundreds who have given such staunch loyalty and service to the tsarist government for all these decades—even centuries. For all of that fine family status, Dimitri has proved himself to be a fine scholar, horseman, artist, and military historian. He has lived up to his promise during his first year here."

Prince Nikolai smiled and gave Dimitri a quick friendly salute.

"The Grand Duke is too kind," Dimitri demurred and lowered his head for a moment.

The three men slowly sipped the fiery deep amber fifty-year-old Hennessy cognac and spent half an hour talking about world travel, the empire's difficulties in securing the sea ports that the tzar and his court demanded, hunting, and court gossip, about which Dimitri was a veritable fount of knowledge.

After the appropriate period of small talk was completed, the grand duke gave an almost imperceptible nod, and Dimitri stood and announced that his presence was required on the parade ground. Paul Alexandrovich smiled, shook his hand; and they exchanged formal salutes.

"Now, to business, my friend," Paul Alexandrovich said, and leaned forward to engage Nikolai Borisovich.

Prince Nikolai took in a deep breath.

"My Prince, I have come to speak to you about your promise to your godson, Prince Boris Nikolaiovich. Do you recall that day?"

"Indeed, I do. How old is the boy now?"

"Sixteen."

"A bit young to be making application to the academy, wouldn't you think, Niki?"

"Ordinarily I would presume so, but I have really come to you to ask what he can do to advance himself? Without boasting, I can assure you that he is quite a remarkable young man."

"Well asked, Niki; and I will answer you in the same vein. I presume he has become a master horseman?"

"He certainly has, and he has mastered the field maneuvers and tactics of the Cossacks. You would be proud of your godson, Sir."

"I am sure I would. Has he had a command?"

"Not officially. I have given over command of the serfs and Cossacks in our employ. He has outfitted them into a well-functioning and handsome cavalry force. They worship him, and they will follow him to their deaths if ordered."

"As it should be. Has he seen battle, my friend. You know that every applicant to the academy must have acquitted himself in battle, especially with a position as an imperial army officer."

"I do know that, and since he is only sixteen, and the empire has been a bit short on wars during his brief life, my son has not had the opportunity. I came hoping that you might be able to find him just the right position."

"We always have a war someplace," the grand duke laughed. "I'm sure those heathens–the Ottomans–will stir up their poverty-stricken minions to some violence somewhere in the near future, and it will be just the assignment for my fine godson to cut his teeth on. You know, Niki, and your beautiful wife, Countess Tatiana Alexandrovna de Ribeaupierre, must also realize, there is real risk in such adventures. I cannot make guarantees, although, I obviously can exert some influence to keep him out of the worst trouble."

"That is a wonderful offer, my Prince; but Boris will balk at that. He will insist on being in the thick of it all and on making a genuine contribution. He will earn his rank, and he will earn any medals that come his way. He is a soldier's soldier, and he has not even reached his majority yet."

"All right my friend, here is what I will do. Bring him to the academy in a week, and I will get him trained enough in imperial lore and tactics to be able to hold his own. As soon as the Ottomans prove true to form, I will get him a commission as a stabbs captain and will sic him on those dogs. If he performs satisfactorily–and I am sure he will–I can make a place in next year's entering class of cadets at the Nikolai I General Staff Academy. Keep him out of trouble until then, Niki."

"You have my word. Thank you very much, my liege."

Nikolai smarted from the Grand Duke's demeaning off-hand comment that he would make Boris a mere Staff Captain and that the scion of the Yusupov family would have to earn his way up the ladder to become a Full Captain, then finally to become a Captain of the General Staff—a rank available only to members of guard regiment.

"*We'll see about that,*" Nikolai said to himself as he left the Grand Duke's office. "*Being a Yusupov has its benefits and skipping ranks to Captain of the General Staff will be the least of those moves. I look forward to the day with relish when Prince Boris Yusupov receives his general officer's stars. I have the tzar's ear, and a hold on his purse strings. We'll see what that kind of leverage I have to use when I need it. Staff Captain, indeed!*"

CHAPTER FOUR

DISCOVERY

**"It is much better to do good in a way
that no one knows anything about it."**
—Charlotte Brontë, *Jane Eyre*

National Archives of Australia, Victorian Archives Centre, 99 Shiel Street, North Melbourne, Victoria, Australia, May 15, 2013

When they first arrived in Australia to start their remarkable mission for the Church of Jesus Christ of Latter-day Saints a little over six weeks earlier, Elder LaRen and Sister Katherine Durrell were new missionaries—"newbies"—new to Australia—"pommies"—and new to Australian digital record gathering and filing—"sparkies". Technically, a pom or pommie is an Australian transplant from England; but the locals were generous to lump Americans into the generic term for outsiders from the English-speaking world. A couple of times they had been called "freshies", the implication being that they were newbies to Australia; but did not stick because the real meaning of "freshie" or "saltie" is fresh water or salt water crocodile, not an altogether complimentary appellation.

But–after six weeks–the Durrells were no longer newbies because four more new missionaries came to join the original six—two couples and two single senior sisters. They had earned respect by their diligence and proficiency enough to be recognized as Americans, in the better sense of the word; so, they were no longer pommies, and the term "sparkies" seemed too far out even for the slanguage-loving Aussies—which they call 'strine'; and they dropped it. The Durrells and their fellow archives missionaries were now so competent that coping with the Commonwealth departmental records–those of the statuatory bodies, royal commissions and such varied areas as the recordings of naval vessels, lighthouses, migrations, defense, trade affairs, veterans' affairs, and Aboriginal interactions with the latecomer English for more than a hundred years. The record finding, keeping, and digitalizing had become a matter of rote; and the missionaries had to hunt for small diversions to keep up their enthusiasm.

Elder Smith from Ogden, Utah was the mission humorist and source of most of the interesting–and sometimes only quasi-appropriate–diversions. He was a retired farmer; and he and his wife had twelve children, all of whom had left home making the Smiths empty nesters. He was easily bored; and on this particular Tuesday, the heat in the record room was somniferous, added to by the white noise humming of the digital cameras, photocopiers, scanners, and printers.

"Hi, everybody, I hate to disturb you or to distract from your fascinating work, but something important has come up from my research."

"I hate to disturb you"…was always the entre for a bit of whimsicality on Elder Smith's part, and all useful work halted for a few moments.

"Get a drink and be refreshed for the revelation I am about to share with you."

Sodas and juices in hand, the missionaries all turned to look at Elder Smith.

"Marianne and me found a very interesting person in the ships' ledgers this morning, and we followed her into customs and immigration files after lunch. Her name is—was—Alexandra Tarasova Yusupov—sounds Russian, we think. Seems from her immigration photo that she was a real beauty, even in those funny old outfits they used to wear. She apparently settled down in Melbourne—he used the American hard "r", because he thought he would sound funny if he said, "Melbun" like the Aussies did—and looks like she might have made something outta herself. Marianne and me have some nice old photos and copies of records you'd outta see. I propose we take her on as a project, find everything we can, and get her into the church. From now on, she's Sister Yusupov to me. Anyone else wanna help resurrect her?"

After looking at the sepia photos and documents weathered with age to a venerable yellow, everyone signed on. The mysterious Alexandra Tarasova Yusupov became the official distraction of the small klatch of missionaries, and they dabbled in research about her whenever they could find a spare moment. It was P-day [preparation day], always on Monday; and it was the only day mission rules allowed them to leave their duty posts and to do their washing, shopping, recreating, and communicating with family and friends. It was important to all the missionaries that they make the most of their precious time off. The close-knit group of senior missionaries made a pact that they would see some bit of Australia— Melbourne and Victoria, really—each P-day.

Today they voted to see their way around the city center. They had only a little more than half a day; so, they worked their careful plan. They took the free City Circle Tram—one mode of transportation which allowed them a few minutes for each of the main sights: The Princess Theater, the Grand Windsor Hotel, the "Paris" end of Collins Street, St. Patrick's Cathedral, and a naughty peek into Young and Jackson's Pub to see its infamous painting of *Chloe*. To complete their adventurous afternoon, they took afternoon tea at the Grand Windsor Hotel and overindulged themselves from a table filled with chocolate delights including Chocolate Indulgence, Death by Chocolate Cake, and Chocolate Mousse. They politely declined any kind of tea; that would be a definite violation of their Word of Wisdom; and not a one of them was tempted in the least.

CHAPTER FIVE

A Little Problem

"Look after your clothes when they're spick and
span, and after your honor when you are young."
—Russian Proverb

**The Yusupov Palace on the Moika River, Saint Petersburg,
August 14, 1863, morning**

An attractive brunette girl with lightly bronzed skin, and a clean shining single thick plait of braided hair hanging down her back almost to her waist, stood quietly and respectfully just inside the entrance hall of the Moika Palace. Her face was inscrutable; she was clean; her eyes intelligent and curious. She was dressed in a simple yellow headscarf, a somewhat too large yellow blouse with light blue stripes, a drab, obviously hand-me-down jumper, and flat open lace up sandals over very dirty feet. The most striking thing about the girl was that she was obviously in the late stages of pregnancy. She held a small just-picked bouquet of wild flowers in her right hand.

The middle-aged housemaid who answered the door had tried to shoo the girl away, but she was adamant. She had come to see Countess Tatiana Alexandrovna de Ribeaupierre on a very important matter, and she would not be dissuaded.

"The princess is very busy. She schedules appointments to see the peasantry and commercial persons on Thursdays. Leave me a note, and I will schedule you in then."

The girl hesitated.

"Can you write, girl?"

"I can, but I have to see the…princess now. My father will kill me if I don't. Please."

Her face spoke volumes testifying that she was telling the truth. She was being brave and strong, but a naughty tear dropped down her right cheek.

The housemaid had been a girl once–a peasant girl like this one–and from somewhere inside her a vein of compassion arose.

"I will do my best, my dear. Please sit on the settee and wait. It may take a while."

The girl sat, looking pathetic as she tried to curl her dirty feet under her and out of sight.

"Are those flowers for the princess?"

"Yes."

"Give them to me, and I will put them in a vase with some water."

Again, the girl was hesitant; but finally, she handed them to the maid.

Princess Tatiana listened to her maid and was inclined to have the girl sent away until she heard the maid say, "with child." Even without further explanation, Tati felt a shiver of dread streak down her straight back.

"I will see her for a few minutes. Bring her to my office, Mary Ivanovna."

The peasant girl was painfully shy and overawed by the grandeur of the imperious woman facing her. She looked at the floor and became pale as if she was about to faint.

"Sit, my girl, tell me your problem. Perhaps I can help," the princess said soothingly.

The girl backed to a chair, awkwardly curtsying the entire way.

"Now, what is it?"

"I…I…I am with child, your majesty," the girl stammered as if that was all the information necessary to explain her presence in the great house.

"I can see that. What is your name, my dear?"

"Anna. Anna Evgenovna Petrove, your majesty."

"Please, Anna, call me Princess Yusupov. Only the imperial family are addressed as 'your majesty'."

"Forgive me Princess Yusupov, I am unschooled."

"Can you read, my dear?"

"I can. My mother is educated."

"Now please do not be so shy. You have something to say, and it was brave of you to come to the Moika Palace to meet with me. It must be something important."

"It is, my princess. I have come to have you arrange my marriage to your son, Prince Boris. It must be soon, as you can see."

Tatiana blanched, being able to fill in all of the blanks. The girl's simple truthful face was undeniable. The impact of the realization was terrible and intensified by the situation regarding Boris's pending entrance into the Nikolai I General Staff Academy.

"*That foolish boy*," she screamed inwardly.

"Have you some sort of understanding about marriage with Prince Boris, Anna?"

"Yes, I am with child."

"You know it is from Prince Boris?"

"I was a virgin. He is the only one."

"I am sure you are a good girl, but I am also sure that this marriage can never happen. You are aware of the difference between your family and this one, Anna?"

"My mother told me. My father told me that I should have kept my legs together, and it is my fault. He will kill me if I am not married to Prince Boris before the baby comes."

"*Dieu a paradis!*" Tatiana muttered to herself.

"What are we to do?" Anna asked pragmatically as if it were now Anna Evgenovna and Tatiana Alexandrovna against the world, against all the norms, against all tradition.

"We must first speak to my husband, the prince. Then, we will find a solution," she said more hopefully than she felt.

Tatiana left Anna to cool her heels in the most sumptuous room the girl had ever been in and hurried to find Nikolai. He was in his library studying reports on the drought in central Russia.

"Sorry to interrupt, husband; but we have a serious matter to attend to."

"Your face looks serious. Is someone sick? Has there been an accident?"

"Neither of those, Niki, but just as bad."

"Tell me."

"I have a peasant girl named Anna in my office, Niki. She tells me that she is with child, and the father-to-be is none other than our first born."

"Our child has made a child! Can this be possible?!" Prince Nikolai growled, making a concerted effort not to shout at his wife, knowing that she was not the problem.

"It would seem so. Now what?"

"Do you believe her?"

"Oh, yes; and so will you when you see her. She is too simple and innocent to be lying. I am sure of that."

"What does she want? Money? Land? What?"

"She is deathly afraid of her father. She says he will kill her if she is not married before the baby arrives."

"And I suppose that is also believable, Tati?"

"I am convinced. We cannot let that happen."

"Of course not, but what can we do. I need your common sense."

"Although she does not really know what all is involved, she wants to marry Boris and in a matter of days, if not hours."

Nikolai steepled his fingers against his forehead and was lost in thought for a few moments.

Frowning, he said, "There is no good solution; however, this is one time when our power must provide the answer. You deal with the girl. I will deal with our errant son and the girl's parents."

He walked to where the servant's cord hung and pulled on it twice, an indication that the need was pressing.

In less than a minute, two young men dressed in Yusupov livery—a handsome classic Greenwich style knee-length frock coat of scarlet red and military style detail. The cloth was of evenly died moleskin and lined with satin. The gold cuffs and full-length collars had golden buttons set in red darts. The men wore black trousers and soft slipper-like opera shoes. They had brilliantly white long blouses and lace edged neck ties. They bowed stiffly and awaited orders.

"Ivan, you are to accompany the princess and find out where the young girl's father and mother are and bring them to me as quickly as possible. Have them clean up as well as possible."

"Georg, you are to bring Prince Boris to my library; and under no circumstances is anyone to see him enter the palace. This is of paramount importance; do you understand?"

"Yes, my Prince," Georg replied promptly.

"Questions, Ivan ?"

"One, Prince Nikolai Borisovich. Am I authorized to use force?"

"Only if absolutely necessary. Take two Cossacks but keep them in check."

"I will."

"Go, then; report to me when you return. Be quick about it."

In three seconds both men were gone.

"Now, Tati, we will go to see this Anna who has brought such a stir into the household."

Anna sat primly on the settee in Tatiana's office, and had fully regained her composure and sense of purpose. When the prince and princess entered the room, she quickly stood and made her best imitation of a curtsey.

"Anna, this is Prince Nikolai, the head of the house of Yusupov."

"Your majesty," Anna said, "it is an honor."

Boris was not in the mood for any idle chatter.

"Anna, the princess tells me that you are with child, and that you believe the father is young Prince Boris. Is that right?"

"Yes, your majesty."

She was so resolute and yet so innocent looking him in the eyes and calling him "your majesty" that he had to control himself from laughing.

"When did this happen, my girl?"

"Several times, but the one that made the baby was eight months and a half ago. It took place in the forest near my family's house."

"Do I understand correctly that your parents know about this?"

"Yes, they do."

"What do they want from us? What do you want from us?"

"I am to be married to Prince Boris before the baby comes. That is what all of us want. If I am not a married woman when I have the baby, my father will kill me and my child. My mother is afraid of him and will not protect me."

Nikolai groaned inwardly.

"*Obviously,*" he thought, "*I cannot let this happen. This girl must be protected, and there cannot be any marriage into the Yusupov family.*"

Tatiana tugged at Nicolai's sleeve.

Nikolai looked down at his wife's earnest face. She motioned to him to come with her.

"What is it, Tati?" he asked.

"Just come."

"All right. Anna, the princess and I will leave you for a few minutes. When we come back we will have a solution."

"Good," the peasant girl said in a tone that bordered on being brash.

Nikolai would never have tolerated a member of his household or a peasant he encountered in the countryside to have used that tone with him; but, for some reason, he rather admired her courage, and let it go.

Fifty feet down the hall, Tatiana stopped him, and said, "Niki, I believe I have a solution that solves all of the problems this girl presents. Please hear me out before you interrupt."

"By all means, give me a solution. I always trust in your wealth of common sense, Tati."

"First, you have the parents coming to the palace. You can speak kindly to them, or you can treat them as serfs with you as the master, whatever is necessary. You offer them a sum of money enough for them to buy a larger parcel of land near our estate in Moscow and forgive any taxes in perpetuity. Second, you tell them that you will arrange a marriage to a successful servant in our household in Moscow. Third, you tell them that there will never be another offer or an additional offer, Niki. We cannot allow ourselves to be blackmailed. Fourth, they sign a document in which we and they promise never to reveal what has taken place. If they do divulge the secret, all of the gifts we offer will be rescinded, and they will be banished from our land and sent to Novonikolaevsk or Vladivostok for the rest of their lives. Their daughter will be sent to work as a char woman in the Novodevichy Convent."

"I can make all of that happen."

"For my part, I will find her a husband in Moscow before the week is out."

"Good. You tell Anna, and I will meet with her parents. Our boys should be back with them any minute."

Anna wept bitterly, but she was an intelligent and pragmatic girl, enough to know that no girl without any title—who was going to have a baby with no father—would have a chance in the world. The offer made by Princess Tatiana was the best that could ever happen…but only if her stubborn father did not refuse. Every peasant in Russia knew that people like the Yusupovs could have their family killed without any repercussions. It was the reality of life. She agreed to cooperate, and Tatiana agreed to help persuade her parents and to find her a suitable husband.

Prince Nikolai sat impatiently in his library waiting for the confrontation with Anna Evgenovna's parents. The coach bearing the two parents, the two servants, and the two Cossacks raced up to the rear entry to the library; and the entire entourage barged into Nikolai's library—something that could not have happened on any ordinary day.

Nikolai remained seated, and the servants escorted the roughly dressed peasants over to where the lord and master of the household—it might as well have been the universe, so far as the Petrovs were concerned—sat on the Yusupov throne.

"My Prince, this is Yvegeni and Sacha Petrov."

"Yvegeni, Natasha, I am pleased that you have come to see me today," Nikolai said, using the formal name for the woman, which pleased her.

"We had no choice, Prince," growled the brutish man, obviously angry and did not care who knew it.

Ivan, the liveried servant swatted the insolent man sharply across the side of his head.

"Try again, fool," Ivan ordered.

Yvegeni ground his teeth, but he controlled his temper, "thank you for seeing us to discuss our problem. Both of our problems, my Prince."

He gave a small reluctant bow.

"Good of you to do so. Please tell me simply what your problem is."

It was very unusual for any business matter to be brought up abruptly, much less one between a serf and a master; and Yvegeni was put off guard by the prince's directness.

"Uh, hmmh…Sir, your Lordship…we have a problem with our daughter which is now a problem that involves your son, Prince Boris; so, you also have a part of this problem."

He paused trying to determine what to say next, knowing that his life may depend on not only what he said, but how he said it.

"Sir, our daughter is with child and will have the baby very soon. It would be ruination for our family if she were not to be married when she does. Your son and our daughter…uh, hmmh…need to get married… quietly within the week…Sir. If you please."

"My wife and I have talked to your Anna, and she appears to be an honest girl. We believe what she says, and I will deal with my son in my own way today. However, you are no fool. You are well aware that such a marriage can never happen."

Yvegeni started to speak, but Nikolai held up his hand to stop him.

"Please let me finish. This condition your daughter finds herself in may not be such a bad thing as we all might think at the beginning. She and my son have committed a grievous sin, but it need not bring harm to them or to their families. I can make this into good news, if I can count on your good sense and your realization of how I can benefit you as a friend. I am a bad enemy, as you might imagine, Yvegeni. I implore you to come to agreement with me."

"How long do I have to decide?"

"Here and now."

Yvegeni nodded in the affirmative, but his face showed his disinclination. He held his piece.

Nikolai presented the plan Tatiana had suggested in full, and the Petroves listened with ill-concealed pleasure. When Nikolai finished, he knew he had won by what Yvegeni had to say.

"How much?"

Nikolai suppressed a smile, waited a moment to organize his thoughts, then made a nonnegotiable offer of 1000 rubles, ten hectares of fertile land, freedom from taxes for life, and a stipend for Anna and the baby of 100 rubles a year for the remainder of their lives.

The offer was princely, but Yvegeni had the mind of a peasant.

"Our family is growing, my Prince, we will need more land to support them than ten hectares, Sir."

Ivan drew back his hand as if to strike the greedy peasant, but Nikolai stopped him.

"Speak your mind, Yvgeni, but be mindful of what you ask so that I do not come to believe that you have come to my home to…shall we say…steal from me."

"Oh, no, Sir. I would never…I was thinking another ten hectares would help us to get by."

"You know, Yevgeni, I was quite impressed by the strength and courage of your Anna. Agree to a total, one time offer of twenty-five hectares, and an agreement between us that no one outside this room— and Anna, of course—will ever know of our arrangement. I have people everywhere who keep me informed. Do not treat Anna or her new husband with cruelty…ever. I will know of it. If you do, you will come to understand that you have just made the worst mistake of your entire life. If you maintain a good farm, and bring the girl, her husband, and their children into your family in good faith, you will find me to be a generous friend. *Ponimayu?*"

Yevgeni nodded that he understood, and Ivan and Georg took the Petroves out the way they came in with assurances that Prince Nikolai of the Yusupovs was an absolute man of his word.

After they left, Nikolai had his secretary arrange for the State Commercial Bank in Moscow to make the payments as promised and to organize the purchase of a twenty-five hectare plot of good farm land near the Yusupov estate within the Moscow *gubernia* [administrative province]. Tatiana telegraphed her instructions and her generosity to the manager of the Saint Petersburg estate via electromagnetic telegraph which resulted in a marriage in the family church there two days before the delivery of a healthy baby boy. She and Nikolai thanked God for Baron Pavel L'vovitch Schilling, the inventor of the machinery that enabled such remarkably rapid modern communication.

The day was only half over; and now, it was Boris Nikolaiovich's turn to pay for the little problem caused by his indiscretions.

CHAPTER SIX

A LIFE-CHANGING DAY

"Taking a new step, uttering a new
word, is what people fear most."
—Dostoevsky,
Crime and Punishment.

The Yusupov Palace on the Moika River, Saint Petersburg, August 14, 1863, afternoon

Boris was having a great day riding with Vlad around the hillsides east of the Moika Palace, hooping and yelling like a battle crazed Cossack. He was sweaty, happy, and content. His future as a military officer was assured, and he could scarcely contain himself long enough to get into a combat officer's role. With the troubles stirring on the Crimea, he knew it would not be long before his ambitions would begin to be realized.

It was only a little discomfiting to see a hard-riding Cossack boy racing towards where he and Vlad were taking a well-earned cat-nap under the birches.

The boy halted from a full gallop and ran to Boris yelling, "Prince Boris, you are ordered by Prince Nikolai to come to see him in his library at once. Vlad, sir, you are not to accompany the prince."

That was highly unusual and put something of a damper on Boris's enthusiasm for life he was enjoying up to them. He mounted Kryzhu and raced off towards the Moika Palace behind the Cossack boy. Sensing urgency, Boris walked swiftly to his father's library.

"Father, you sent for me," he said to his father who was standing with his back to the entryway gazing at the row of latest European science books that arrived the previous day.

Boris knew he had been heard; so, he waited.

Prince Nikolai turned and looked at Boris, his expression as inscrutable as a *natriyevo-vzlomshchik* [soda-cracker].

"Take a seat."

Boris sat in front of the huge desk. His father took his seat behind the desk instead of sitting beside his son as he usually did.

"Boris, my son, you have disappointed me," Nikolai said quietly.

It was liked being stabbed with an ice pick.

"How, Father. I truly do not know."

"Yes, you do, Son. I have met with a peasant girl named Anna Evgenovna Petrove and her parents, Yvegeni and Natasha. Do you recognize the names?"

A bridge collapsed on his head, and it took a moment for Boris to clear himself from the wreckage.

"Only Anna. I know only know Anna, not her patronymic or her surname or the names of her parents, Sir."

His eyes fixed on the seams between the hard wood planks of the floor.

Nikolai spoke very quietly, almost in a whisper.

"You do not even have the decency to know the names of the mother of your child or anything about her background. You disgust me."

"I...regret...I...I... mean, I am sorry, Father, so terribly sorry to have brought shame upon the House of Yusupov."

"At least you have the decency to recognize the gravity of what you have done, foolish boy. Your fine mother and I have taken care of the problem. But you must pay."

"Anything, Father. I will submit to anything you order."

"Yes, you will. This is what will happen to you, and it will happen today. I will assemble the family and our serfs. You will be tied to a stake and lashed for your sin and for your foolishness. I will apply the whip. Then, you will face all the men you have been training in the Cossack military arts and confess in every detail why you have been whipped like a slave. Then you will beg their forgiveness and release every one of them from your personal service. Finally, you will beg them to come back to your service because you and any men you can muster will leave for the eastern region of Crimea at sunrise tomorrow. It seems that there has been another wicked riot in the ancient city of Kersh by Crimean Tatars. You will quell it under the orders of your godfather and general, Grand Duke Paul Alexandrovich Romanov.

"Should you succeed, you will regain your place, be made a permanent captain, and begin your education in the Tzar's General Staff Academy. Should you fail, you will never be heard from again, and there will be no record of you as having ever been part of the House of Yusupov. Now, get out of my sight. Stand on the rear porch at five o'clock and watch the construction of the whipping post."

Princess Tatiana clenched her teeth and observed the punishment meted out by her husband. The worst of it was the humiliation in front of the serfs. Her son was demeaned down to their level.

Boris did as his father ordered. He stoically endured the pain of the whipping and never uttered a sound. After the acute pain was over, he maintained a flat expression and without begging or whining or making excuses, he debased himself to the family servants. It was growing dusk when he finally got to the point of asking for volunteers from among his would-be Cossacks.

"After what you have witnessed today, you know that I have no right ask you to respond to my request that you follow me into battle for the empire. There is a battle to be fought in the Crimea, and I will be on the train for Moscow tonight. I ask any and all of you to go with me, but should you choose not to go with me, there will be no recrimination against you. If I have to go alone, so be it. I will fight for the empire and the tzar."

Vlad stepped forward and stood at attention. He spread his arms out at his sides and waited. In a few seconds, the serfs who had trained under him and Prince Boris formed ranks beside and behind him. They saluted. Not a single man stayed back; in fact, fourteen men who had not been part of the training joined the others.

For the first time that day, Boris feared that he would humiliate himself by crying.

CHAPTER SEVEN

THE WARRIORS

"To be prepared against surprise is to be trained.
To be prepared for surprise is to be educated."
—James P. Carse,
Finite and Infinite Games,
A Vision of Life as Play and Possibility, 1986

The Eastern Front, Kersh Peninsula, Crimea, September 18, 1863, Dawn

The trouble began in the Kamysh-Burun Iron Ore Plant of Kersh when workers complained about low wages and poor living conditions. Agitators spread the unrest to the Zaliv Ship Building Factory within a day, and by nightfall another in a seemingly endless series of riots in the Crimea was underway.

For the first week, the unrest was barely what could be called a riot. Then the Crimean Tatars under Mullah Ismail Noman Seydamet used the riots as an excuse to launch an all-out battle. In the Crimea, the Tatars were a force to be reckoned with since they constitued the majority of the population, and they were among the fiercest fighters in the empire. When Prince Boris and his Cossacks arrived in the Kerch Strait by ship during the night of September 25, a fierce wind made further sailing too dangerous to attempt in the misty darkness. The Bosporus Imperial Naval Ship's captain settled on a landing on Tuzla Island, a very narrow sandy spit in the middle of the strait. The imperial marines and the several noble family sponsored militias made camp under miserable conditions and staked down their horses which were in danger of being blown into the roiling waters of the strait. The storm abated overnight; and by dawn, visibility was excellent; and the waters were calm.

Boris and his Cossacks were dispatched to the Azor; three other militias were dispatched to establish a camp on the shores of the Kerch Peninsula on the west; and another two other militias were sent to the Taman Peninsula on the east. The main force of imperial marines was put ashore and force-marched into the city of Kerch and to an encampment on the high slopes of Mount Mithridat. The arrangement of the imperial forces thereby created a pincer to squeeze the Crimean Tatars and the rioters to death if they did not cease and desist from further aggression.

Imperial marines and the militia funded and commanded by the two sons of the ancient House of the Princes Argutinsky-Dolgorukov were in position to control the Krasnodar Krai and its Taman Bay. The imperial naval contingent and the militia of the House of the Princes Javakhishvili–Dzhavahovy Zhevahovy–led by Spiridon Ivanovich Zhevakhov were in command of the attack from the Taman Peninsula from east to west. Despite his youth, and because of his family status, Prince Boris of the House of Yusupov and his militia were charged with holding the critical position in the Azor region and of attacking from west to east and down into Kerch itself. The marines were under orders to clear the rabble out of Kerch and to reestablish order in the city and its suburbs.

Tatar spies informed Prince Boris of the easterly movement of Mullah Seydamet's Crimean Tatars overnight.

The oldest of the three spies told Boris, "Mullah Zhevakhov has collected a large force of men from the factories and his own Tatars in the forest to the east of the city center. We learned from a friend that the mullah plans an attack at dawn two days from now. The rioters and Tatars will set off under cover of darkness tonight and will force march to the Azor coast. Pardon me, Great Sir, but they have been informed that a mere boy holds the coast and beyond for the empire. They consider it the weakest point in the imperial army's defense forces."

Boris ignored the implicit slight with difficulty.

"Do they have a large force of horses?"

"Too noisy, I heard them say."

"Have you other intelligence for the tzar's forces, my friend?"

"No, as it is we barely escaped with our lives."

"Does the mullah know that you were spying for us?"

"No, Great Sir, we were very quiet and very smart about our work for his great majesty."

"It would do you well to hope that such is true, my friend. And of course, I trust you fully. But, just to be clear, are you aware of the fate of those who betray the Cossacks?"

"I have heard, Great Sir. We would never do that."

"Of course not. That would be too terrible to imagine. And your families would be hunted down and treated the same way. Or–more certainly–you will receive great riches on the morning three days from now when the mullah's forces have been routed. Do we understand each other?"

"Yes, but…"

"But, what, my friend?" Prince Boris asked, fixing his steely Wedgewood eyes on the brown eyes of the spy.

"Our contract was that we would be paid now since we have brought you the news that will lead to your victory."

"That is a misunderstanding. I will personally pay you double what you were promised while we watch the mullah and all his men suffer the punishment set aside for traitors. And, we will keep you safe here in our camp. You will want for nothing."

The spy thought better of saying what had come to his mind. He had underestimated this boy.

"We will be grateful for your kindness, Great Sir," he said instead.

"As well you should. Now, as you go to enjoy the comforts only the House of Yusupov can provide, I must attend to the business of going to war."

Boris turned sharply and walked away from the three thoroughly cowed spies. As his Cossacks joined him, the very malevolence of their persons made the spies religious. They plead with Allah to make their information the truth.

Boris and Vlad quietly went from man to man and had them walk with their horses and weapons out of the main camp in scattered groups to avoid the attention of potential spies. He left a message with his servant boy to be delivered to the commanders of the marine forces and the militias to be opened when Boris and his Cossacks had had time to establish their ambush sites.

It was a long night of forced marching. The horses were kept in the rear and staked out in an area of rich grass to keep them quiet and free of restlessness. At first light, Boris called a halt and had the Cossacks hide themselves in the deep forest for the daylight hours.

Mullah Zhevakhov was not so certain of the ease with which his plan would work that he took unnecessary risks. Movement of his ragtag troops was made slower because his men could only imagine traveling or fighting on horseback. They grumbled and purposely slowed the march; but, fearing deadly reprisal, they remained silent except for a few curses as a few of them fell or were struck by branches as the stumbled along in the pitch blackness of the northern night.

The mullah and his senior officers took stock of their progress and found that they were not going to make it to the agreed upon battle ground unless they traveled during the daylight hours. He had the men move with the greatest stealth of which they were capable through trees, rocks, and deadfall. He was furious at the level of noise they were making but knew that he was not going to get anything better from them. He longed for the days of Ghenghis Khan and Timur the Limper when a battle commander had only to whisper a command and his perfectly loyal and capable soldiers would obey instantly and to the letter.

Boris's spies reported sighting the Tatars on the early morning of the second day. That confirmed that the spies who reported the attack had been loyal and correct. Boris silently vowed to reward them beyond anything they could imagine. The other value of the sighting was that he now knew exactly where his enemies were located, how slowly and clumsily they were moving, and had some idea of the numbers he would face. He smiled at the fact that not a single horse had been seen or heard.

"Vlad," he ordered, "send ten men back for the horses. Muzzle the mounts and keep them absolutely quiet. Have your sons move half of the force to the area we think will be the battleground. It looks ideal from the traitors' perspective. The other half will stay with me and shadow the mullah's army."

"Hardly an army, Prince Boris, from what I hear. Many of those traitors have only sticks and rocks for weapons, and the greatest part of the horde is nothing but a bunch of factory workers who have never seen a battle or held a sword in their hands. It should be easy, My Prince," Vlad said with a wicked smile.

"Don't underestimate your enemy, a very wise warrior once told me," Boris said and smiled at his aging ally.

Vlad nodded his head in both agreement and acknowledgment that he was the source of that bit of pithy wisdom.

"Once we have defeated them, what do you want done with the prisoners?"

"I should say, as you always warn, 'one thing at a time'; but I am of a mind to make a very memorable example of them all. What do you think, Vlad?"

"What can I say, My Prince, it is the Cossack way."

"Then we are agreed, Vlad."

It was said with Cossack terseness and brevity.

The rioters and Tatars struggled hungry and thirsty for two more days—half a day longer than the mullah had demanded. Finally, the scouts returned with the message that the battle ground was only a few kilometers march away from the main battle contingent. Most importantly, they had not sighted any enemy scouts, imperial soldiers, or camps; and they were almost to the shores of the Azor.

"The men are exhausted," his chief aide said to the mullah, "they will be in no condition to fight, if we don't give them rest and meat."

"They are Muslims, servants of Allah. They will find strength. I have received a call from God that tells me that we are on the brink of a great victory. ALLAH AKHBAR!" he said with passion, and somewhat more volume than the aide considered safe.

"Of course. I have no doubt in them. We will proceed, but with caution. Nothing must cause problems for Allah's will."

The chief aide went his way encouraging, cajoling, and cursing the rabble he had been ordered to make into fighters. His opinion was that they were peasants, cowards, and complainers; but it was not his place to question the man of god. Nevertheless, he moved carefully the last few kilometers. He had been overly successful in his efforts to buoy up his men's spirits and to kindle their passions for battle. He sent out orders for the ranks to maintain silence, but he was not successful in the least.

Spies from all around the slowly moving army reported in to Boris and Vlad. The mullah's forces would be in position in less than half a day.

"They will take up positions and be ready to launch an ambush in no more than six hours," Vlad estimated.

"We cannot be ready before then, Vlad. We have not seen the horses, and we cannot launch any kind of an attack without mounted Cossacks."

"Oh, ye of little faith, as the priests say," Vlad laughed, "you have not seen the horses, but that does not mean that they are not here. You underestimate my Cossacks, My Prince."

Boris gave Vlad a dubious look.

"Come walk for me—no more than half an hour's time."

Vlad led Boris deep into the woods. They climbed over a massive dead log and looked into a narrow valley full of horses and of men saddling and bridling them. Weapons leaned against trees at the ready. Boris laughed at himself, and he and Vlad signaled their great approval of the stealth with which the Cossacks had moved an entire cavalry into a ready position.

"We still have a serious problem, My Prince," Vlad said soberly.

"We do. What is the nature of the Tatar ambush?"

"Indeed. I have conjectures and hope but no knowledge. Belief is not worth a tenth of what a sentence of real information would give us."

"More spies?"

"I fear to do so, My Prince. The Tatars are no fools. If they see even one of our men, they will guess the rest. We must wait."

"And worry."

"Yes, but more importantly, prepare own surprise without becoming fools by believing in their diversion."

"Vlad, give me your best idea of what that diversion will be," Prince Boris asked.

The answer to that question was something the scion of the House of Yusupov would pay a fortune to know, but all he could do was to watch and wait.

"Our scouts have seen a few Cossacks in the larger of two valleys ahead, Great Mullah," the aide reported, "the best news is that they do not have horses—too difficult to move them through the forests, as you so wisely determined as we left Kersh. There can not be many of them; and without mounts, they are like rabbits without legs."

"Did I not predict? Did I not tell you of the wisdom Allah—the one god–planted in my humble brain?"

"I can no longer doubt. I am a faithful Muslim and a warrior without reservation. This will be a great day!"

"Send out the ambush force. Held the rest back until the Sons of Dogs give chase. I will lead the main force to annihilate the curs of the left hand. Let the plan we have worked so hard on begin now!"

CHAPTER EIGHT

FIRST BLOOD

"Storm'd at with shot and shell,/ Boldly they rode and well.
Into the Jaws of Death,/ Into the mouth of Hell/ Rode the
six hundred."

—Alfred Lord Tennyson,
The Charge of the Light Brigade, 1854

Forests on the Azor Shores, Kersh Peninsula, Crimea, September 22, 1863, First Light

Vlad and young Prince Boris watched from their perch high in a large branched coniferous tree as Tatars begin to circle the valley below. It was remarkable to the two men that none of them was mounted. In a matter of minutes, the valley floor was filled with men carrying an assortment of improvised weapons. Suddenly, the invaders began to scream out their battle cries and to run pell mell towards the shoreline.

Vlad looked intently at Boris's face.

"Not yet, Vlad. Not quite yet."

The horde rushed into the trees to the east and were soon out of sight.

"Now, Vlad. Send the best runners after the Tatars. Have them make a large noise, but do not have them engage."

Vlad hurried down the branches and along a hidden path.

He gave orders to the leader of the young Cossacks, and they rushed out behind the fleeing Tatars. The only sound was the yelling of the

Cossacks as they pursued the Tatars. In slightly less than half an hour, the Cossacks now ran back, fleeing in terror from a larger force of oncoming Tatars and ragtag rioters.

Boris quickly moved down and out of his perch and ran as hard as he could to cross in front of the apparently fleeing Cossacks. When he reached a point just inside the treeline, he was met by a trio of excited Cossacks who helped him to his seat atop Kryzhu. He wheeled about holding a sword in his right hand and a spear in his left. The fleeing Cossacks split into two sparse columns and opened a space in the center. Boris kneed Kryzhu into a full gallop.

"*Beg!*" Boris shouted at Kryzhu, and the powerful horse leaped forward like a ball shot from a well-maintained cannon.

Kryzhu had learned to be ready for the command to leap into full action as soon as he heard the command, and Boris had learned to be ready for the explosion of horseflesh power that would otherwise fling him backwards onto the hard rocks on the ground and to have to endure the humiliation of sitting shamefully on the ground as his mighty horse raced off to battle.

Boris was twenty meters in front and all alone when a disciplined Cossack cavalry galloped into formation behind him quickly filling the gap between them and Boris just as Boris was gaining ground every second between him and the decoy Cossacks. The mounted Cossacks flew to within fifty feet of the running Tatar ambush decoys, and then they split into two columns to flank the runners. They followed their orders not to engage.

Mullah Zhevakhov shrieked with joy as he saw the Cossack dogs fall into his ambush. He had his aide raise attack flags to launch the final stroke of genius of his complicated ambush. A massive force of rioters and Tatars ran screaming out of the trees to the west and flung themselves headlong into the sparse smattering of running Cossacks. Just as the irresistible force came within a spear's throw of the Cossacks, the cowardly Russians turned sharply and began to run into the trees on either side of the narrow valley corridor.

"Filthy kaffir sons of dogs! Cowards!" he whooped as he saw that his Tatars had broken the will to fight on the part of the falsely vaunted Cossacks before the first sword slash or stabbing by a spear had taken place.

His surge of immeasurable joy lasted only a few moments. A cold chill ran down his back as he turned to the west at the sound of an army of banshees bursting into the mouth of the valley heading east. They were mounted! It was not possible. They looked every bit like the paintings he had seen of Cossack cavalrymen bursting into a battle and altering the enemy's capacity to fight in less time than it took Mullah Zhevakhov to take a full breath. The painting came to life; the dream became a nightmare; the thrill of success became a painful shock running down his spine.

Boris and Vlad galloped as the twin heads of spears aimed at the heart of the Crimean Tatar and rioter rabble forces followed by a battle-cry screaming and supremely disciplined cavalry battalion.

Mullah Zhevakhov could only look on in astonished horror as the decimation of his fine troops began to occur. He watched with fury as an old Cossack, and a young blond boy on a giant war horse threw themselves into the center of his confused foot soldiers. His perfectly planned and executed ambush and been turned against him. Cossacks were nothing more than wild men—disorderly and bloodthirsty, and totally lacking in discipline—this could not be happening. It defied everything he had ever been taught by his Tatar masters. Yet, here he was watching his skilled, brave, disciplined, and unbeatable Tatars falling like wheat being cutdown by countless scythes.

His army was in shambles; hundreds of men were being slashed, stabbed, and trampled to death. The survivors turned the battle into a rout as they threw down their weapons and fled aimlessly for the trees. The Cossacks formed up into three columns and encircled the hysterical Tatars and rioters who were now falling to the ground and begging for mercy.

Mullah Zhevakhov could do nothing but turn-about and to flee in the same craven cowardice that he had been cursing his army for displaying. His only thought now was to get out of this hellish place and to survive, by any means to survive.

He shed his kaftan and his weapons and threw on a cloak he tore from a dead rioter. He was sure that the bloodthirsty Cossacks would not chase what had to be seen as nothing but one more poor nameless conscript running for his life.

He was wrong. The young golden haired lordly rider reined up in front of the mullah and leaped from his horse. Three Cossacks reined up and leaped from their horses surrounding the mullah.

"Do not kill him. Keep him alive!" shouted the boy over the din of the battle. "He is worth far more alive than dead!"

The frenzy died down, and Vlad led his two sons to the mullah and trussed him up like a pig going to market. They procured a riderless mount and unceremoniously threw the grand mullah across the empty saddle. They secured his hands to his feet below the horse's belly and rode off to the slaughter ground.

Boris rode close behind the Cossacks, and they met a squad of marines and naval combat veterans.

Captain of Marines Sergei Antonovich Karpov began herding the Tatar and rioter prisoners towards the center of the valley and signaled for his corporals to bring the enlisted men in towards the center with their sabers at the ready. Sergei Antonovich stepped to Prince Boris and offered to relieve him of responsibility for Mullah Zhevakhov. The alternative to Boris and his militia controlling the leader of the mutinous mob was to be found in the ever-shrinking central area of the valley.

"No," said Boris and proceeded to have a stare-down contest with the tough and battle hardened marine officer.

Sergei Antonovich went ahead with his collection of prisoners for the educational exercise about to take place in the center of the valley as he had not heard Boris.

Boris put his body between Mullah Zhevakhov and the enthusiastic marine.

"No," he repeated.

The marine's hand went to the grip of his sword and moved it a fraction out of its scabbard. His marines and Boris's Cossacks were shocked by a lightening quick move by the prince. Before the marine could blink, he was facing a razor-sharp and still bloody cavalry saber wielded by an obviously earnest young aristocrat.

"So, you who believe that you are the Son of Somebody, are about to interfere with me doing my duty. Step aside and live, Boy."

"No," Boris said for the third time, and this time delicately rested his sword's edge on the marine captain's neck, just enough to produce a few drops of the man's blood.

The marine paled, now aware that he had made an unfortunate miscalculation of the courage and capability of the young man, and that he might just *be* the Son of Somebody. Even if he were to best the brash boy in a fight, he knew how the world worked in the imperial armed forces. It would not turn out well for him.

He snarled and adopted a surly expression. He made a move to back away and pulled at his sword's handle. That was a mistake that resulted in a slightly deeper red line being drawn on his throat, and considerably more bleeding. The next mistake on the part of the marines that day was that a young corporal unsheathed his saber and hurled himself at Boris. The result was that the young corporal was dead before he fell to the ground, and Boris's sword edge had returned to the captain's throat before the officer could complete his intended sentence.

"No."

The now terrified marine officer quickly turned his eyes towards a group of four marine enlisted men in what he thought was an eye glance equivalent of verbalizing "no". In a matter of seconds three Cossacks attacked the hapless young marines who had never before seen battle or a dead man. Before Boris or Captain Karpov could intervene to prevent the horror of an internecine conflict, all the marines were dead of sword thrusts except for one who was decapitated.

Sergei Karpov leaned over and vomited. Boris had just enough composure left to scream in Ukranian Cossack, "СТОП", which ended the fight. Apparently "stop!" was better understood than "*Het!*" [no].

"Get the mullah back to the ship, then join me and the militia in the center of the valley before we become witness to a slaughter of defenseless men which will stain the honor of the imperial armed forces for generations," Boris ordered Vlad.

Young Boris was not aware that the slaughter of vanquished opponents was standard practice by imperial forces for time infinitum and in most cases by other less honorable military victors. For him, honor was crucial; and for that day, it was hailed as the motto of the empire and would become the only memorable aspect of the entire unfortunate incident.

On a practical level, the rescued Tatars were imprisoned for a short time then sold as slaves to the Ukrainians; the highly chastened factory workers of the Kersh peninsula returned to work at longer hours and lower pay and were happy that that was as bad as it became. None of that became part of the chronicles of the Crimean Troubles as handled by the tzar's forces over the decades.

CHAPTER NINE

A STEP AHEAD

"Forget yourself and go to work."
—Bryant S. Hinckley to his son,
future LDS president Gordon B. Hinckley

National Archives of Australia, Victorian Archives Centre, 99 Shiel Street, North Melbourne, Victoria, Australia, June 11, 2013

The two preceding weeks had been particularly fruitful for the Mormon missionaries working in the archives in Victoria, Australia. So much so that the state published a two-page article extoling the great work done by the church and its missionaries for the people of Australia and for succeeding generations. For the Church of Jesus Christ of Latter-day Saints, the most positive outcome was that the anti-Mormon rhetoric rife in the country now came to fall on deaf ears; and the Church began to see fruits of its very costly program in the form of polite inquiries about the Church's remarkable genealogical program which came to be recognized as a great free gift to all of the people of Australia. The equally costly volunteer missionary program began to see more genuine interest on the part of nonmembers, more convert baptisms, and greater assimilation of the LDS people into the regular life of Australia.

For the missionaries toiling away in the basement of the archives center, several good things resulted. First, they were treated to a dinner with the Rotary Club and asked to speak about the good work they were doing for the country. Second, the missionaries and regular members of the church found themselves being invited into neighbors' homes for lunches, dinners, and afternoon chats. A somewhat lonely and cloistered existence there in the basement began to expand out so that the missionaries could be what they really were–regular good people with a lot to give. Sister Smith and Sister Clyde were even invited to give a quilting demonstration and to start a class for younger Australian women who were beginning to take an interest in some nearly forgotten crafts and skills like quilting, macramé, and bread baking.

The most important small victory was announced by Sister Durrell.

"Elders and Sisters, Elder Durrell…"

"Otherwise known as her husband, LaRen…" blurted out Elder Smith, the group's self-appointed class clown.

"Please, Elder Smith, you know about the rules on first names. It's a mission rule, and so it is a sacred thing," Sister Nichols—the generally accepted parliamentarian of the tight-knit little group—scolded. "I just don't think you should joke about sacred things, that's all."

"Oh, good grief…" Nephi Smith started to protest and was promptly shushed by his long-suffering wife.

He rolled his eyes but saved his wife's tender feelings as the group's peace-maker—by keeping his lips zipped.

"As I was starting to say, Elder Durrell…"

"Oh, my goodness, Sister Durrell, go ahead and take credit you deserve," Elder LaRen Durrell said insistently.

She blushed and went on, "I have found a little something related to the mysterious Alexandra Yusupov who got some interest going among us a while back."

"Good. I'm hoping you have a usable piece of genealogical evidence, Sister Durrell," said Sister Nichols.

"Here, I have an authentic birth certificate from Balagansk, Far Eastern Russia, dated five April, 1861."

CHAPTER TEN

SENIOR STAFF MILITARY SCHOOL

"He needed the warmth of the sun to take
away the chill of foreboding that grew in him."
—Francine Rivers, *A Voice in the Wind*

Nikolai I General Staff Academy, Moscow, Imperial Russia, December 8, 1863

Stabbs Captain Prince Boris Yusupov reported as ordered to the registrar of the General Staff Academy. His acceptance into the premier military academy in the empire came as no surprise since his father had learned of his heroics—at least the escapades that had grown wings of their own since they took place and became the stuff of near legend for an aspiring young imperial army officer. What Boris lacked in professional schooling, he more than made up for by his daring-do, the saga of his leadership, and, of course, by having his name become synonymous with honor insofar as it related to a Russian army officer. Without family influence, Boris's commanding officer placed the young prince's name on the list of honors for the past year. He was awarded the crosses of Saint Stanislaus and Saint Anne—second class, an unheard-of set of honors for one so young.

It helped that his father had forgiven him for his dalliance with the peasant girl, even though Prince Nikolai was not ready for his scion to darken the Yusupov doors just yet. The richest man in the empire and the most influential—second only to the tzar himself—had once again approached Boris's godfather, Grand Duke Paul Alexandrovich, sixth son of Alexander II, Tzar of all the Russias, a full general in his own right, and the commandant of the General Staff Academy. To no one's surprise, Boris was given a warm reception by the Grand Duke and was accepted into the ultimately prestigious academy based on Grand Duke's formal recommendation. Prince Nikolai's vanity was thoroughly heightened by having a son who was the youngest man ever accepted to the academy—not yet seventeen—an obvious harbinger of an illustrious career, presumed Nikolai.

Boris was allotted living space for himself and three servants, and each of his two apartment mates were given the same privileges. There were rules against having young women in his living quarters, but no prohibition against having a cook and a couple of scullery maids. For all of his worldly experience, Boris was rather shy around girls; so, his older and more world-wise roommate, Alexander Soloviev, found a handsome Nordic woman who could cook. The other roommate, Andrei Zhelyabov, went Alexander one better and brought in two teenage Slavic girls whose looks were such that none of the men cared overly much whether or not they were good at cooking or cleaning. The Yusupov quarters soon became the party center for the academy's aristocratic students.

Boris—despite his military experience and sophisticated manners—was still a seventeen-year-old boy and rather vulnerable to being manipulated or seduced into accepting ideologies that were popular but not appropriate for the conservative scion of one of the most conservative families in the empire. Alexander, Andrei, and Andrei's girl-friend, Sophia Perovskaya, were falling under the spell of Mikhail Bakunin and his Land and Liberty reformers party. The group published literature demanding that the land in Russia held by the government and the church be granted back to the poor landless people. The group, their meetings, and their publications were secret; and Prince Boris's aristocratic set would have been aghast if they had learned that the one-day-to-be head of the House of Yusupov was consorting with such rebels and near-traitors to the tzar.

Perhaps that is why Boris found his roommates and their satellites so fascinating: they were against everything his father and mother and their imperial friends held holy. Their discussions were exciting, all the more because they were necessarily secret; and they were so iconoclastic.

Had he put more thought into what was going on, Prince Boris would have realized that the icons which were being threatened were the very ones on whom Boris had to depend for his career, comforts, and the maintenance of his luxurious life style.

Two months into his first year of studies at the academy, Boris was having difficulty plowing through the heavy tomes required for his additional studies course in the science of war. The course was of obvious importance because it was core to his chosen career but also because–if he passed the course with a satisfactory recommendation from the colonel who taught it–he was all but guaranteed a place on the general staff of the army and a generalship at a young age. He was now ambitious enough to believe that that was his destiny.

Alexander sat on the large soft cushion chair with Ingrid Swenssdatter, the cook, cuddled on his lap reading Bakunin's book, *Statism and Anarchism*.

"Listen to this, Boris…Andrei…Sophia, this is what I mean when I say that Bakunin needs to be the next Russian leader—not, tzar, but real leader of the people."

He thumbed back through several pages until he found the passage he was looking for.

"They, [referring to the Marxists, Alexander emphasized] maintain that only a dictatorship—their dictatorship, of course—can create the will of the people, while our answer to such rhetoric this is: No dictatorship can have any other aim but that of self-perpetuation, and it can beget only slavery in the people tolerating it. Freedom can be created only by freedom, that is, by a universal rebellion on the part of the people and free organization of the toiling masses from the bottom up."

It took Boris a few seconds to remove his mind from the science of war and over to the religion of radical politics—anarchism. He came to his senses as he realized that these people were not just eccentric thinkers, they were dedicated enemies to everything he held dear. What a foolish boy he had been. He was in a dilemma, but he knew what he had to do, however difficult.

"Alexander, I presume you fully realize that we are sitting in an apartment set aside by the tzar and his government in order for us to become officers his imperial army. It is one thing to have an interest in what is going on in the country, but it is quite another to be flirting with anarchy and possible insurrection. We will have to choose whether to fight for or against the tzar, and I certainly choose the tzar and the great Russian imperial government."

"While the tides of history are turning against dictators all over the world? Wake up, Boris. This is the real world, the new world. We have a chance to rid ourselves and the world of such dictators, oligarchs, and despots. Revolution is in the wind. Change is inevitable. However dangerous, we must be part of the change. Surely you can see that. You can't be entirely blinded by those relics of the past in your family and their corrupt governmental connections."

Alexander was red in the face, angry, and passionate. There was no potential for compromise in this young ideologue. Why hadn't Boris seen that before?

"You speak sedition, mutiny, and anarchy. I cannot be associated with you any longer. Leave these quarters. Take all your belongings and find a new place to live. Take your friends while you're at it. That includes you, Andrei and Sophia. Do not mention my name in any of your conversations since you know that I will never agree with you!"

Boris worked to control his temper and his passion. All he knew for sure was that he had get himself away from this anarchistic and seditious pack. They would ruin him. That much he was as certain about as the existence of heaven and hell. The passage from *Revelations* 21:1-27, flashed into his mind: "Then I saw a new heaven and a new earth, for the first heaven and the first earth had passed away, and the sea was no more.." He actually trembled at the thought of how dangerous his foolish boyish antics had been.

CHAPTER ELEVEN

PROOF

And now as I said concerning faith—faith is not to have a perfect knowledge of things:

therefore, if ye have faith ye hope for things which are not seen, which are true.

—Book of Mormon, Book of Alma 32:21

Faith is an island in the setting sun, but proof is the bottom line for everyone.

—Paul Simon

National Archives of Australia, Victorian Archives Centre, 99 Shiel Street, North Melbourne, Victoria, Australia, September 30, 2013

The day had been one of the most productive any of the missionaries could recall. Maybe it was because the days were becoming a bit cooler. Maybe it was because this was Friday; and there was a long weekend full of senior missionary fun—two dinners, one with the mission president and his wife, and one at the home of the Durrells–a pot luck as usual. And, they had an excursion planned into the outback led by an old time Aussie bogan. He was eighty-five, had a beard down to his belt buckle, and wore clothes with holes in them—"the raggedy man who worked for pa, the raggedyist man you ever saw"–Elder Tanner said about him.

Elder Smith burst into the photography section with his usual hyperbolic grand entrance, and said in his basso profundo pseudo-Mussolini voice, "I have found the first and grandest piece of evidence. Congratulate me everyone," he guffawed.

"Hey, Kramer, take easy. What's up?" Elder Durrell said reminding the rest of how much Elder Smith looked and acted like one of the characters on their favorite rerun show, *Seinfeld*, whose entrances were guaranteed to be hilarious and outlandish.

"We-eel, lookee here!" Elder Smith said and spread out photocopies of documents on the empty table top.

There were four copied pages, excellent facsimiles of a birth certificate. It was written in Cyrillic characters which might have been Martian for all anyone could understand.

"I only recognize one thing for sure," Katherine Durrell said still squinting at the copies. "This document is about our mysterious Alexandra Tarasova. I presume the Yusupov part came much later."

"Right you are, young detective. You're are on the right track. I– suspicious as I am–had this translated at the Consular section of the Embassy of the *Russian* Federation in Canberra last week. Here is that translation into real letters and words."

The eight missionaries crowded around the translation.

"Citizen: Last Name-Tarasova,

First Name-Alexandra, Patronymic-Abramovna

Was born on: April 1, 1861 the first day of
April eighteen hundred and sixty-one

Place of birth City,

Village-Baranskaya

District -Irkutsk Oblast

Region Vladivostok, Far Eastern

And the record No. 19338

Book of Registration on April 1, 1861

-Nationality Russian, Buryat

Father-First name and Patronymic-Abram Timurovitch

-Last name-Tarasova

-Nationality- Buryat

Date of Issue -April 1, 1863

Mother-First name-Irina

-Last name-Inkjinoff

-Nationality-Buryat
Place of registration

[Name and Location]

-Irkutsk Office of Vital Records

-Irkutsk Imperial Executive Committee

-Empire of Russia

Date of Issue -1 April, 1861

Official Seal of the Office of Vital Records

Head of Office [Bureau] of Vital Records

Signed:

Vladimir Omanovich Yewstrophsky

Official Seal of the Office of Vital Records

CHAPTER TWELVE
BIRTH OF A PRINCESS

Deep in every heart slumbers a dream, and the
couturier knows it: every woman is a princess.
-Christian Dior

Balagansk Prison Infirmary, Balagansk, Irkutsk Oblast, Far Eastern Russia April 5, 1861

A last-of-season blizzard howled outside the walls of Balagansk Prison while delicate little Irina Ishmaelovna Inkijinoff Tarasova underwent a fairly easy delivery of her fourth child and first daughter. The baby was larger than her other children at delivery and unusually so for a girl. The new daughter was a lusty red-faced squalling bundle of energy from the moment her head peaked out into the world. Irina placed the baby's mouth just below her right nipple and watched with pleasure as the infant crawled and squirmed to find the nipple and to get her first bit of nourishment outside the uterus. Father Abram Timurovitch Tarasova jumped up and down with pride and excitement when he saw the vigorous baby fight her way into the world. From that moment, she would always be his favorite, his princess.

Balagansk was founded in 1654 on the left bank of the Angara River opposite to the mouth of the Unga River by a Cossack detachment led by Dmitry Firsov in the course of Russian colonization of Siberia. The choice of that location for baby Alexandra Abramovna Tarasova's arrival was occasioned by the fact that the best physician in Far East Russia was assigned by the imperial army to the Balagansk Prison infirmary, a cleaner and safer facility than the more prestigious Far East–Vladivostok Naval Hospital of the Pacific Fleet located in the rapidly growing larger city. Abram could afford the best the region had to offer and studied the facilities carefully before making his decision. As it turned out his methodical decision-making practice paid off with a healthy, happy wife and a daughter that was remarkable and precocious—and a genuine beauty from the moment of her birth.

By the age of three–owing to naturally occurring immersion in a polyglot society–Alexandra spoke Russian almost like an adult as well as the native languages of the Irkutsk oblast: Buryat, Siberian Tatar (Volga Tatar), and Mandarin Chinese. She caught on to the languages of trade and amused traders who frequented Abram and Irina's fur trading emporium with her attempts to mimic French, English, Italian, and Chosŏn speakers. By the time she was six she had mastered Russian, Ukrainian, French, German, Chinese, English, and Chosŏn as well as Buryat—at least to the extent that she could keep up a moderately complex conversation.

She no longer just amused the shrewd and calculating traders and titans of commerce in the far eastern Pacific but had to be reckoned with as a shrewd and careful trader always acting in the best interests of her family. Her activities at the market interfered with her formal schooling but did not keep her from excelling. Alexandra Abramovna Tarasova took prizes in French literature, Russian and Siberian history, calligraphy, Latin translation, and mathematics. In the latter subject, she exceeded the knowledge and capacities of her teachers, and Abram had to bring in a tutor from Germany for her and her brothers. The tutor added ancient Greek and Roman history, and the history and current affairs of modern Europe.

All of that was of little more than passing interest to the precocious little girl. What truly fascinated her was trade, and especially trade outside of Russia which required ships. She nagged her ever-patient and forbearing father constantly to be allowed to travel on one of his ships to Shanghai, Seoul, Tokyo, and someday to Europe and maybe even the Americas. He finally gave in–much to Irina's displeasure–when Alexandra was eight.

Despite her mother's subtle mix of native and Russian Nordic ethnic looks, by the age of eight, Alexandra was a striking, curly-haired, round-faced, cherubic, Viking girl, betraying every bit of her Rus inheritance. Her hair was so blond as to incorporate the tones of silver. It was fine and unruly, and Irina despaired of her daughter ever having one of the currently trendy hairdos. Most of the time, Alexandra's locks hung down in enticing ringlets. She was taller, sturdier, and more athletic than even the boys in her school and was the equal of her brothers who protected her with lion-like ferocity. Heaven help any miscreant who gazed too long on her fragile porcelain beauty or might even accidently touch her alabaster skin. Her smile made her friends of the indigenous peoples, her fellow students, the expatriate Russians interned in the Far East, and the Chinese, Japanese, English, and German traders, even those whom she bested in contests and trade deals.

The good ship *Tarasova Fur Enterprises* left Vladivostok Port for its regular run to Shanghai and Tokyo, and Alexandra's first time at sea on July 13, 1869. The waters of Golden Horn Harbor were unusually calm that sunny day, hopefully, a portent of things to come. They sailed smoothly past verdant little harbor islands, the coasts of Chosŏn and China, and into the South China Sea. For the first time, Alexandra saw people significantly different than her: dark hairy Ainu on Hokkaido Island, bearded moon-faced Chinese junk sailors, haughty British naval officers, and ill-tempered monocled German traders. The ship's goal was to make port in Shanghai, located in the East China Sea, on a major estuary of the Yangtze River, and for Abram and the ship's officers to meet with the taipan, James Matheson.

"What is a taipan, Father?" asked Alexandra, never one to let an opportunity to learn slide by.

"Big business man. Mr. Matheson heads the hong trading house of Jardine, Matheson and Company. They manage and control trade throughout the China Seas, and from inland China. Nothing gets moved, bought, or sold without these foreign-born masters-of-commerce controlling the to-or-from policies regarding Japan, Chosŏn, China, or the Philippines. We have to go see the man before we can unload our freight and trying to make some money."

"What does he do for us, Father?"

"He gives us a certificate of custom which allows us to buy, sell, and transport. With his signed approval, we can go anywhere in the region without paying local taxes, or having our goods impounded. You understand what that means, don't you, Princess?"

"Yes, Sir, I do. That doesn't mean that I think it is right, though."

"Neither do I but we must keep such thoughts to ourselves if we want to remain in business. We also need his money. Promise me."

"I promise."

The port of Shanghai, Guizhou Province, was the grandest place Alexandra had ever seen or imagined. Ships thronged the harbor, coming and going from Great Britain moving opium, tea, and silk. Chinese cotton, silk, fertilizer, and gun powder, were being transported as far away as Polynesia, Persia, and Europe, and as nearby as Japan and Chosŏn. Alexandra was amazed by the great number of ships bearing the flags and emblems of the British East India Company which seemed to dominate the harbor. Father pointed out the various different settlements: Chinese, French, British, and American—the more western European half of Shanghai and the more eastern Chinese half. Each had its own grandeur and mystery, and for the young girl seeing them for the first time, a great measure of wonder.

The most wonderful thing of all was the home of the Tai-pan. Abram and Alexandra rode in a jin-rickshaw up a winding gravel road. As part of the Bund, the framers of the International Settlement created China's first Public Park–a place of peace and beauty–which was, of course, off limits to the Chinese, as was the rest of the International Settlement.

Abram stepped off the cab seating portion of the rickshaw and helped Alexandra to step down. He haggled briefly with the rickshaw puller, then–with a heavy sigh–gave in and handed the man several round coins with square holes in the center. The man looked deeply offended; so, Abram gave the man two more coins and waved him off. The puller took the coins from the palm of his hand and placed them in a small purse he kept inside his pants. Then, he spat on his hand and left with a surly face.

Alexandra laughed and that made her father burst out laughing as well. They were in a good mood when they climbed the long stone stairway to the front door of the big house. Four men stood lazily leaning against fountains, statues of dragons, and one of them on a wagon full of fertilizer.

"Guards," said Abram. "Do not cause them to be nervous about us. They would just as soon kill us as look at us."

Alexandra nodded gravely.

The two great bronze doors opened unexpectedly. Each was held open by a uniformed man holding a Sharps New Model 1863 repeating rifle made in America. None of them smiled or nodded.

A uniformed maid showed them in and had them sit on uncomfortable silk covered settees while she left to inform the the taipan's staff of the arrival of the Russians. Half an hour later—as Alexandra sat fidgeting—a tall, powerfully built man with short cropped hair, a monocle, and a conspicuous scar on the right cheek, walked up to them.

"*Kommen sie mit,*" the stern man said brusquely.

Alexandra wiggled her face to mimic the man's expression.

"*Ja wohl, mein herr,*" she said as sternly as the butler.

He seemed confused.

"*Sind sie Russen?*" he asked, thinking he was talking to the wrong visitors.

"*Ja,*" said Alexandra.

The butler was beginning to think the older man with the girl was a mute. He made a smart about-face and started down the parquet hallway without looking to see if he was being followed. Alexandra and Abram trotted obediently behind him.

"*Der taipan werden sie jetzt sehen.*"

He said it hopefully, not yet quite sure that the interlopers spoke or understood *hoch deustch*.

Alexandra marched confidently into the palatial office and right up to where an imperious thin elderly man sat behind a heavy Philippine mahogany desk. Taipan Sir James Nicolas Sutherland Matheson, 1st Baronet was not a large man, to Alexandra's surprise. She had expected a powerfully built gruff man like her father. The taipan had sandy hair, bushy eyebrows, and mutton-chop mustache—what her mother called ginger. She had heard of it but had never seen such hair before, even in paintings or photographs. His skin was very white and spotted with freckles. His eyes were robin's egg blue and would have been very attractive on a woman; but in his case, they were hard and unfeeling. He wore what Alexandra presumed was the latest fashion from England, or maybe Germany—close fitting tweed morning coat and matching five button wool vest, starched white shirt with cufflinks bearing the emblem of the house of Jardine-Matheson, a black bow tie, light brown pleated wool trousers, and side button burnished brown boots polished to a high sheen.

He shot his cuffs and said, "Top of the mornin' to ye," in a thick Scottish brogue. "The famous fur man from the wilds of Russia, I take it, and his pretty lassie. Come girl, tell me your full name."

Alexandra curtsied, smiled, and said, "I am Alexandra Abramovna Tarasova, Sir."

"And how *auld* er ye, me tidy lassie?"

Alexandra hesitated for a moment trying to translate the strange sounding sing-songy dialect into the King's English she had learned and practiced.

"I am eight-years-of-age, Sir. Thank you for asking."

"Wull me lassie, yur *pure barry* to be able to know so much at yur tender age."

"Thank you, Sir. My father and mother have worked to make me educated."

"And successfully, I wid sae. Most of the people yu'll meet have *heids* full o'mince. Not worth wastin' taem on."

"I beg your pardon, Sir. But I don't know what *heids* full o'mince, means."

The taipan extended his head back and guffawed, a hearty, completely genuine, and affectionate laugh.

"It means they have *heids* full o' mush."

"I never heard it put that way, but, now that you say it, I know plenty of people like that."

"But not you, me lassie, yur too *braw* fer athat."

Not altogether sure what the important man had just said; Alexandra, nonetheless, extended her head back and laughed heartily enough to shake her gleaming blond ringlets.

The taipan decided that there had been enough bantering with the precocious child; so, he turned his face to Abram.

"Eno' o' *bletherin'* Aye suppose," he said, "lets *get tae* business, what da ye say, my friend?"

"I came to ask the help of the House of Jardine Matheson to make my commerce larger and stronger. I need financial help to build more and better ships, to expand the types of goods I buy and sell, and to widen the range of my business locations."

"Aye like yur directness. That's *braw* fer me. But why should Aye put me money into yer enterprise. How do Aye know that you not a *right chancer*, lookin' ta *chore* mae outta loan money?"

"You are a Scotsman, and as such your word is your bond. So is mine. I would never cheat you; first, because it violates my moral code, and second, because it would wreck my chances to do business in the

China seas. I am in business for the long haul, and I want the support of an honest partner. I will do what I promise, and I will return every farthing I borrow with interest. You will prosper from a deal with me same as I will, Taipan."

"A nod's as guid as a wink tae a blind horse," Matheson said, his face all business now.

Abram had heard the phrase before from Scottish ship's captains; so, he knew the taipan wanted a no-nonsense, crystal clear communication about the Tarasova Fur Company's carefully crafted business plan. He reached into his weathered leather satchel and pulled out the documents of the plan crafted by his lawyers which omitted nothing. It suggested a fairly modest profit for himself for the first few years and a larger profit margin in later years. The Jardine Matheson Company would have an iron-clad contract detailing the nature and extent of the Tarasova business and the best projections for future growth of the company and the partnership of Tarasova and Matheson.

"Yae seem as clear and smart as yer fine lassie, mae friend. Let us start low and go slow—*mony a mickle maks a muckle.* I will get yae the finances, but I have one condition that 'tis critical."

Abram's enthusiasm sagged, "what is that, Taipan?"

"Aye will have one of mae people aboard each ship and on each expedition and major commercial enterprise. There's nae negotiating on that. Aye hope that is *braw* fer yea as well."

Abram hesitated for less than a second, "Aye, Sir. That would be good business."

"*Guid* fer the both a us," said the tai-pan.

The men shook hands, and the taipan gave Alexandra a wink.

"Now that we have a business enterprise together, Aye look forward to seeing this *bonny* lassie on some of yer ships. And, Lass, tha mun cum tay visit me in my wee cottage here anytime."

CHAPTER THIRTEEN

DEBUT OF A BUSINESS TYCOON

"...Love can give you the most exhilarating wonderful highs at times...
...Then there will be dives that will take all you have just to hold on...
— Elizabeth Funderbirk,
Love Torn Asunder, from the *Title Page*

Aboard the Jardine-Matheson-Tarasova Brigantine, *The Far East Transporter*, **South China Sea between the Chosŏn Coast and Hainan Province, September 12, 1873**

Twelve-year-old Alexandra Abramovna Tarasova sat in the captain's quarters of the brigantine *Far East Transporter* pouring over the bills of lading, description of inventory, and scrutinizing the documents relating to customs and port requirements of the fifteen ports of call for the trading ship on this it's fifth voyage. After four years, the Jardine-Matheson and Tarasova partnership had been successful beyond the greatest expectations of any of the partners. Trust among the partners had been proved over and over again; and now, there was an easy interdependence among them. Young though she was, Alexandra had established a friendly and respectful relationship with the nephew of the Matheson clan, Hugh Matheson, and was fondly referred to as the Tycoon of China by Hugh's youngest son, James II. James was twenty-one; and–like Alexandra–he was all business and was–at the moment–studying the recent reports of piracy in the East China Sea. A worry line furthered his young brow.

"What's troubling you, Jamie?" Alexandra asked.

"Probably nothing," he said. "There have been an increasing number of reports of pirates attacking commercial ships in the south, and East China Seas region. One of the worst problems is that the pirates are not so much interested in stealing the merchandise, but they take hostages for ransom. We lost one ship and crew to the Red Flag Fleet and have had to go to the expense of outfitting all our hundreds of ships with security measures and an armed force of former British marines to counter any attacks. I'm not really worried; but, still, we need to be cautious. Don't worry your pretty little head over it."

He laughed as he saw the young girl's mock angry face.

"Sorry," he said, "you know I marvel about your accomplishments at such a young age. I fear that you will be an opponent to me when my father, Hugh, dies. Maybe even earlier when Uncle James passes on."

Alexandra laughed and stuck out her tongue.

She became serious and asked, "Tell me, Jamie, what do we know about the woman pirate, Zheng Shi, and her Red Flag Fleet?

"You know, Alexandra, she's more of a threat than the Chinese government, the British, and everyone in Jardine-Matheson lets on in public. Our spies tell us that she has a thousand ships carrying out her piracy all throughout the Chinese, Indian, and Philippine Seas. She is probably the richest person in China; and no one, and I mean no one, will turn state's evidence against her. That would be certain suicide. She has bribed, coerced, and blackmailed, dozens of police officials and government people who protect her from legal consequences of her criminal enterprise. No ship–and certainly not this one–is safe from her pirates. I have begged for greater security, but our skin-flint parents think that they are saving money by taking chances that our ships will not be hit. The idea is—really–that even if we get attacked and lose a ship and cargo or two or three, it won't add up to what the extra security will cost. It's worth the risk."

Zheng Shi sat on the foredeck looking through the best telescope money can buy. Her fondest desire was to find one of Jardine-Matheson-Tarasova's heavily laden treasure ships and to force the smug owners to pay a king's ransom to get the crew and any passengers back. She would make them grovel and snivel—to humble their arrogance kneeling in front of her to beg for mercy. She laughed to herself at the thought of forcing them to make her a legitimate partner in their hugely successful capitalist gang.

Zheng Shi thought about how far she had come in a man's world. She started her adult life at age twelve as a prostitute and learned early how to manipulate men. She inveigled them into alliances that eventually benefitted only her. When sugar and spice failed to work, she used deadly threats and blackmail. When–in the rare instances–when that did not work, she was quick to resort to torture and murder—even of innocent wives and children—if that is what it took. Now–at age thirty-five–Shi had an extensive and well-organized criminal business which functioned smoothly. One of the reasons for her success was that she paid loyal underlings well, promoted them when they proved themselves, and never broke her word. On the other side of the coin, she made mutilated and horrifying examples of those who failed her, cheated her, or attempted to usurp her command; men and women alike lost their ears and noses, were flogged mercilessly, or were keel-hauled as reminders of the cost of violating the code of the Red Flag Fleet.

She was philosophical about her own role in her criminal enterprise. She admitted—only to herself—that she was at fault for the current decline in the profits of the Red Flag Fleet. She had overextended when she financed heavily to build four hundred more and faster ships. The principal reason she needed to take some of the Jardine-Matheson-Tarasova's treasure laden ships was to keep her creditors from uniting against her and getting the East India Company, the Chinese government, and the British and Portuguese governments, to join in a witch hunt to take down all she had worked so hard for.

Alexandra and James II sat drowsily in the captain's cabin discussing ways to circumvent increasing controls by the Chinese and British governments, to limit the vexing successes of the East India Company, to counteract the seemingly unstoppable hemorrhage of silver from Hong Kong, Shanghai, and Macao, and how to get a better grip on the opium trade that was being threatened by misguided officials of the Chinese empress's shaky government. As the two young hubristic entrepreneurs set about solving the problems of the world, Zheng Shi set eyes on their ship through her beautiful telescope.

Shi carefully scrutinized the mast head of the ship in the distance: "*The Indo-China S.N. Co., Ltd* at the top of a large grey rectangular sign mounted on the ship's port side bow. At the bottom it read, in larger print, *JARDINE, MATHESON & CO., LTD, Jardine House, HongKong, 575 Nathan Road, Kowloon.* In the middle of the plaque was painted a flag with a white cross on a blue background. From the flag rays pointed to captions indicating the countries served: Japan, Hong Kong, Australia, Tasmania, and New Zealand. There was no doubting the ownership or the undoubtedly princely valuable cargo.

Although, Zheng Shi owned nearly 2,000 junks and 50,000 pirates and could attack major cities successfully, today she was alone in the calm South China Sea with a prize almost beyond calculation, she had none of great fleet and fleet marine at her command at the moment. She paused to assess the odds of risk versus failure, and greed overcame caution.

"Take down the red flag," she ordered. "Set a course directly for the Jardine-Matheson ship off the port side bow. All Chinese below decks and put men and women in western dress on the decks. Keep weapons out of sight. Keep quiet; prepare to board the ship. Spare as many as possible for ransom. Now, look alive!"

Shi quickly raced to her cabin below decks and changed into a European man's suit which she hoped would fool the silly Europeans long enough to allow her junk to get close. Anyone who looked at Zheng Shi from as great as fifty meters away—even on a galloping horse—would get a laugh out of seeing the beautiful pirate admiral trying to pass as a man. She was tall for a Han Chinese and wore her shiny black hair down to her knees when working at seduction and up in a tight, neat bun with side curls when she went into action. Unlike her Han sisters, Shi had a slender high-cheek boned face—none of the moon shape of the girls around her. The bun and curls were held tightly in place by combs, pearl headed hat pins, and a roguish red bonnet as her signature appearance. The man's costume she wore was ludicrous up close because it did nothing to hide her ample and alluring bosom, and it overemphasized the womanly curves of her hour-glass figure throughout. She wore a white shirt, black tie, and a deep black suit with pants fitted to her long strong legs. She returned to the foredeck and laid her wide pirate's belt with its daggers, pistols, and sword against the bulkhead near the wheel, ready for battle.

The sleek pirate junk caught a good wind and began to race towards the prey ship. All hands felt the excitement of battle and booty approaching. The ship's crew would receive twenty percent of the take with the remaining eighty percent going to Zheng Shi and the community coffers. No one complained about the disparity in the dispersal of the treasure; everyone would be rich as Croesus as soon as their day's work was over.

The experienced seaman atop the crow's nest on the mains'll mast of the square-rigged three-masted Jardine-Matheson-Tarasova brigantine caught a glimpse of the pursuing Chinese junk. He waited for a few minutes to determine if the junk was flying any colors of the various pirate fleets or if there were men dressed in the raggedy disheveled clothes of the roguish pirate types. He could not see anything specifically suspicious, but there was no good reason for a large junk to be this far north or to having so much sail yardage. He acted on the instinct for a high index of suspicion.

"Junk, ho," he yelled and pointed towards the starboard afterdeck.

James II leaped from his chair, ran out out of the cabin and up onto the foredeck. It took Alexandra a minute to clear her brain from the mind-numbing stupor she had settled into. She raced up to the deck to join James, the captain, and the first officer. They were all squinting at the sails of the junk and trying to see anything that would identify the ship as friend or foe.

"Naught to be seen there," the captain said and continued to stare through his telescope.

"That's just the thing," Alexandra said, "there're no company or government markings, no indication of nationality, and no one on deck except a few men dressed as gentlemen on a day's outing. Doesn't fit."

James II nodded in agreement, "but it does have closed cannon port holes. Now why would any peaceful junk have need for so many cannon?"

Captain Brilinskov listened to the young man and woman for a moment then made his decisions.

"Full sails, all hands on deck and armed, prime the cannons. Full speed ahead. I think we can outrun 'em."

Alexandra did not think so, but she kept that feeling to herself. The junk seemed to be gaining on the brigantine gradually but surely. A pang of fear ran down her back.

"Let us get the young miss below decks in case trouble gets a brewin'", the first mate said and gallantly took Alexandra's arm.

"No, man. I will stay above decks and know what is going on. I have serious responsibility for the partnership's investment in this ship and cargo. I will want a say when or if the time comes."

Her resolute face dissuaded the first mate, the captain, and Jamie from further intervention. If she demanded to stay, then let her stay.

The pirate junk continued to gain on the company ship. As the sun began to set in a red ball sinking into the ocean to the west, the junk was gaining distance enough that now, Alexandra could see the captain of the ship standing in plain sight on the foredeck. She came to the realization that she was looking at a woman masquerading as a man, and she could even make out a supply of small arms stacked discretely against the bow rails.

"I think the captain of that ship is a woman, and I think that ship is one of the Red Flag Fleet," she said.

"Gorblimey," the bosun's mate said, "I think the young lassie may be right."

The captain swore.

"Get yer bleedin' weapons to the ready. All hands prepare to be boarded. Know that you will fight to the death, or you will meet a fate worse than death if that ilk takes us. Fight for yerselves, yer company, and yer country, mates. Let's show 'em what we're made of!"

The first mate and the chief bosun's mate raced around the deck getting further rigging and sail yardage headed aloft. The speed of the company ship picked up, and they began to move slowly ahead of the oncoming junk.

As the distance between the two ships began to increase, Zheng Shi knew that the Europeans had guessed what her ship was up to, and she shouted at the men on the deck, "All hands on deck in full combat and boarding gear. Open the portholes for the cannon and prime every last gun. Gunners ready the first fusillade."

The chief gunner yelled, "Fire number one gun to test for range!"

On the brigantine *Far East Transporter*, the crew watched in fascination as they saw a starboard porthole open and a cannon roll into view. There was a puff of smoke, but no sound for a few seconds. Then, the sound of the cannon's fire could be heard, and the on-racing fireball could be seen and followed with the naked eye.

"Hit the deck and cover up, men!" shouted the security sergeant.

Alexandra and Jamie disobeyed and watched the cannon ball approach their ship with a deadly compulsion holding their breath. The ball fell harmlessly into the wake of the company ship causing only a small splash. It was off by more than fifty yards.

The sun sunk into the western horizon, and the sea began to mount as clouds closed in. The junk drew back further and further until it could barely be seen, and then it was lost in the clouds.

"Hard to port!" the captain yelled at the steersman.

"Aye, aye, Sir!"

And slowly the large brigantine began to heel to the left.

"Trim the sails to starboard and keep the port sails full rigged!" the captain ordered.

The turn to port increased, and they began to disappear into the gathering clouds and the gloaming.

Zheng Shi stared until her eyes hurt, but finally she had to admit that she could no longer see any trace of the ship that had looked like such easy pickings.

"They're out of sight," she muttered to her first mate. "I know that they aren't that far ahead, but the darkness and the clouds are our enemies. I don't know if they are going to port, to starboard, or straight ahead."

"Or coming about to attack," the first mate said cautiously.

Zheng Shi hated to admit it, but that was a real possibility.

"We'll go straight ahead for two hours; and, then, if we can't find them, we'll turn about and head back to Hainan Island for security."

It galled her to say it.

In two hours, the brigantine *Far East Transporter* was in complete darkness, and they were sailing with instruments alone. Orders for all lights out made for inconvenience and even a low grade chance that they might plow right into something in the night. All hands knew it was the best course, and no one whined or complained. By morning, the growing storm clouds dissipated; and there was no sight of the Chinese pirate junk. The crew and the company officials heaved a collective shy of relief.

Two days later they pulled into Shanghai harbor, off loaded their entire cargo, and watched as the stevedores loaded up a massive cargo of furs, machine parts, and bundles of packed rice. Alexandra reported to her father by telegram, and James went directly to his uncle's mansion and told him about the encounter with the pirates.

"Och, laddie, 'tis a *bowfin* day when the likes of that gingin hoore takes ta ship; but we canna be *feart* o' hier. Thankee fer the *guid* work and the bad news. Leave it to me, Ae'll see tha' 'tis rightly handled."

"More security and guns aboard our ships, then, Uncle? She may be a disgusting whore; but she is smart as a whip; and she has a fleet as large as England's to fight her battles."

"Ya *goat* tha' right, and we'll be atakin' the fight to them blighters. They'll know wha' 'tis lak to rile up a Scotsman!"

Abram Tarasova's first response when Alexandra got home was, "I can't tell you how happy I am that you weren't hurt or worse. No more ship's adventures for you, Princess. I hate to admit it, but your mother is right again—as usual."

"I am fine, Father. Don't make a big thing out of this. It is good that we got waked up and can prepare against the next time. And—incidentally– I will be sailing regularly. Just see to it that security is secure."

The *Far East Transporter* set sail two days hence and made its way against stormy seas and pouring rain—a right *dreich* trip, as the taipan would say. Alexandra chose only to remember what she had learned about commerce, pirates, and sailing ships and to ignore the drab and gray weather that was common in the South and East Chinese seas at that time of year.

With Jamie's and the captain's help, Alexandra began to learn the finer nuances of haggling with world-wise and greedy foreigners. There was more at stake that when she negotiated over a bundle or two of furs. The profits, the friendships, the respect, that came from those tedious bargaining sessions were of intrinsic value; and she and James did well. Alexandra learned turns of phrase in several languages that were utilitarian in the haggling process, and also that she could be fooled and out bargained, a painful, but educating lesson. She determined that she would not repeat her mistakes in future voyages. She was so determined that she kept a journal chronicling what she had learned—both the uplifting and the unflattering.

She looked for special items that she and her father could sell to the visitors from all around the world to the Port of Vladivostok. In Japan, she bought muskets with ornate conch shell inlaid stocks, hundred-year-old Samurai swords worth a small fortune, vividly embroidered kimonos and obis, and cartons of paper celebration lanterns. In Chosŏn, Andrea had crates filled with special foods, *kimchi, bibimbap and tangpyungchae,* and hundred-year-old eggs, musical instruments that were becoming popular in Vladivostock—saxophones introduced from America, and Chosŏn stringed musical instruments including traditional six-stringed zithers, twelve stringed *gayageum* zithers, *haegum* single stringed fiddles and *ajaengs*. Because she enjoyed the peculiar high-pitched sounds, she included a crate full of *daegeum* and *piri* flutes.

Alexandra had a great day visiting silk factories and bought directly from the manufacturer. They were excited to accommodate the young Russian girl, especially after she demonstrated a knowledge of good silks, a real skill in negotiating, and excellent facility with their difficult language. The men of the families who sold her the silks carted shipping crates full of the best bolts of fine silk with exotic and complex designs, pre-made Joseon period brides robes, exquisite Kisaeng/Gisaeng art images for wall hangings, elaborate silk wall paper—enough for one hundred rooms. A telegram would be all that was required to obtain another shipment. It was a heady experience for Alexandra to sign her name to invoices for tens of thousands of Chosŏn yen.

The voyage home took four weeks because the *Far East Transporter* encountered a strong *taepung* storm halfway between Tokyo and Vladivostok. The first week of the passage from Seoul saw the ship in calm waters and sunny skies with a friendly wind which portended a comfortable, swift, and safe journey. As it turned out, the voyage was none of those things.

On the ninth day out, the skies became leaden; and the winds began to kick up the waves. In eight hours, rains began to hit the *Far East Transporter* like millions of tiny needles. Soon the torrential rain did not fall so much as it came at them horizontally. The wind's direction changed every few minutes. For a while it would come from abaft, then aport, then astarboard. The storm controlled the ship and determined whether or not the men and one girl would live or die.

"Typhoon! and again *"taepung"* for the Chinese hands," screamed the captain over the din of the howling of the wind and the crashing of the ten-foot waves against the outboard bulkheads of the ship.

The first mate yelled from abaft, "All sails ahull, lash the spars to the deck rails."

Every man and even Alexandra ran to furl and to get the helm lashed. The main mast tops'll ripped apart, but none of the other sails suffered any damage. The work to affix all the spars to the deck rails was dangerous, and every man who went up a mast knew that this could be his last voyage–his last day. One man fell from the foremast and broke his arm, and another was catapulted from the port yardarm of the mizzenmast and into the boiling sea. He was never seen again.

Finally, with the sails all furled, the chaotic movement of the helpless ship began to diminish, and the tremendous rocking and pitching grew less threatening. A deck hand lashed Alexandra to the mainmast against her wishes and her protestations.

"Ye'll have some chance to survive iffen we still have a ship when this blows over," he shouted, but she could not hear over the harsh, discordant racket from the assorted and seemingly endless noises.

Alexandra gave in and sagged to the deck and wrapped herself around the mast. She was freezing, soaked, and exhausted. She found enough strength from deep inside herself to hang on for dear life for what seemed to be an eternity.

The ship slammed into house sized waves coming from every direction with booming noises adding to the insane cacophony. Men were screaming from injuries and panic; the pigs brought along to provide fresh meat for the voyage had all been broken out of their pens and were running hither and yon in a mindless panic. Eventually, most of them were washed overboard squealing and screaming. Alexandra envisioned the ship as a helpless sinner being punished in hell, and she prayed that God would forgive her of her transgressions.

"*I will never curse or sneak a taste of rum again, or steal from my brothers, if you will spare the ship and me. I promise,*" she said quietly to herself with no real faith or hope that she would live to be thirteen.

CHAPTER FOURTEEN

LOSS OF A SHIP AND A GREAT LESSON

"There's always a siren, singing you to shipwreck. Some of us may be more susceptible than others are, but there's always a siren. It may be with us all our lives, or it may be many years or decades before we find it, or it finds us. But when it does find us, if we're lucky we're Odysseus tied up to the ship's mast, hearing the song with perfect clarity..."
— Caitlín R. Kiernan, The Drowning Girl

Aboard the Jardine-Matheson-Tarasova Brigantine, *The Far East Transporter*, South China Sea between the Chosŏn Coast and Hainan Province, Japan, Russia, October 24, 1873

The typhoon persisted for three hellish days; and when the winds died down, the torrential rains kept on for another three days. No one on board had any idea where they had traveled or where they were. The sky and the sea were black, and visibility was no more than a few feet in any direction. At last—on the sixth day of starving and freezing—the storm left as quickly as it had arrived. The sun broke through the fog and mist at noon, and the captain called out their location. It was as if God had heard all their prayers.

"God be praised. Hallelujah! Golden Horn Bay off the port side. We are saved, my friends, saved!"

Alexandra wept with relief and utter weariness. She was too hungry, too cold, and too weak to be able to stand for several minutes after one of the sailors untied her from the mast. Alexandra's self-esteem, and cocksureness, her faith in her own abilities, and her very self, were shaken by the sustained terror she had experienced. She felt like a little girl, a little twelve-year-old child; and she wanted her mother. As soon as she could get away from the overly solicitous ship's hands, she ran to the aft of the ship and down the ladder. She hid in her poop deck stateroom and had a good cathartic cry. There, she slipped under the covers on her bed and began to weep. She cried for more than an hour—a noisy, voluminous outburst that vented all her fears and rage. Now that the force and destruction of the storm was gone, the tumult of her emotions began to abate. At first, she felt that she had lost her self-esteem and its attendant chutzpah—her inextinguishable sense of destiny. She became a weak, frightened, pre-teenage girl, who wanted her mother.

I will never step foot in a ship again, so help me, God!" she moaned to herself.

Slowly, she began to think more objectively and to recognize that she was a survivor of the worst the sea had to set against her. She accepted the fact that the monstrous natural typhoon had passed, and eventually her personal hurricane had abated as well. When she felt more like the girl she had been before the storm struck, she knew she had to venture back out on deck. She was not so sure about the survival of the crew of the ship, and she became ashamed of her selfish joy at being alive and not caring about the other human beings on the ship—or about the great ship, *The Far East Transporter*, itself.

Her tears dried up; her courage came back; and her sense of responsibility for the men and the ship and the business became of paramount importance to her. Alexandra stiffened her resolve and retraced her steps up to the weather deck. She was embarrassed, but not displeased when the officers and the crew broke into a spontaneous standing applause. She had become the ship's mascot and a good-luck albatross to them all.

It took only a few moments for the joy of the fresh air and sunshine, the exhilaration of being cheered by the crew, and the feeling of the solidity of the weather deck to subside. She looked around her and saw with dismay the terrible destruction the sturdy ship had suffered. Masts were broken, sails torn into jagged tatters, holes broken in the bulkheads above the sea level, and cargo strewn all around the usually pin neat decks. Bolts of precious silk were unrolled, ripped, and filthy. The worst thing was the awful look on the faces of the captain and the crew. There was a look of despair on brave men's sun creased visages; some simply stood and stared out to sea, looking at nothing–a thousand-yard stare. There was a sense in many of the men that there was nothing left for them, and a profound gloom hung over the battered survivors.

At Alexandra and James's insistence, Captain Brilinskov took the two young owners on a damage reconnaissance tour of the ship. The damage was far worse than they had presumed from their first view on the weather deck. Below decks, furniture had been thrown around and multiple holes the size of large dinner plates had been punched into and in some cases through the bulkheads so that daylight was clearly visible from the inside. The farther below decks they went, the worse the damage. One deck below the poop deck, the ladder was broken to pieces. They made a detour. There was debris scattered all over the next deck and a hole was broken into the cabin below. In the aft cargo hold, debris was sliding back and forth as the ship rocked from side to side.

It appeared that none of the carefully packed crates remained intact. Alexandra's carefully packed treasures were broken and ripped. They moved forward toward the bow on the deck above the cargo hold and opened the hatch leading into the hold just ahead of the main mast. Water mixed with whiskey from smashed kegs was sloshing ominously around the deck as the ship rocked from side to side. The precious rolls of century old hand knotted carpets were torn open, and the rugs floated on top of the gathering water, obviously ruined.

Alexandra fought to hold back her tears. Jamie looked at her face and nodded his agreement.

Captain Brilinskov looked forlorn; his face sagged; and he said, "Come now. We've seen enough. Nothin' left but for the insurance sharks to fight us over. This is a mighty loss for the lot of us. This great ship will be on the bottom of the ocean before night fall."

He was right. The captain was a master sailor and managed to get the *Far East Transporter* to a sandspit at the mouth of Golden Horn Harbor before she listed aport and lay forlornly half in and half out of the icy sea. Alexandra, James, and the ship's officers saw to it that every man was off the ship and on dry land before they clambered over the broken railing and into the knee-deep freezing water to get onto the land spit. They waited anxiously for Captain Brilinskov until he finally completed his inspection of the dying ship and became the last man to leave the ship as was his duty.

He instructed the first and second mates to run into Vladivostok to reach the insurers office before other salvagers could take what was left. He dispatched two of the strongest crewmen to run around the banks of the harbor until they came to someone with a boat large enough to fetch the crew home before they all froze. Only then did he sit wearily down and stare at his boots. No one was interested in speaking.

It was dark when Alexandra was dropped off at the Tarasova fur commercial offices. She knew her father would still be up and working on the next ship's agenda and already spending the money he was going to reap from the returns of the treasures of the *Far East Transporter*.

He leaped out of his chair when he saw Alexandra come into the light of his office. He wrapped her up in a strong bear hug.

"I didn't expect you until a week from now, my girl. I'm all the more the happier to have my princess back. Sit and tell me of your adventures and your treasures. I can hardly wait to hear."

"Father, I have to give you the worst news first. We were struck by a typhoon and nearly sunk. We were battered around for three days, and the ship was very badly damaged."

Abram started to speak, but Alexandra raised her hand to have him wait.

"And, the ship sank just at the mouth of the harbor. We lost eight hands and all the cargo. My great success is now like ashes in my mouth."

CHAPTER FIFTEEN

FORCED TO BEGIN LEARNING THE FAMILY BUSINESS ON LAND

"Joseph shall return to Canaan, grieve not. Hovels shall turn to rose gardens, grieve not. If a flood should arrive, to drown all that's alive, grieve not. Noah is your guide in the typhoon's eye, grieve not."

—Khaled Hosseini,
A Thousand Splendid Suns, 2008

Tarasova Fur Company Headquarters and Trading Center, No. 71 Svetlanskaya Street, Vladivostok, Russia, December 9, 1873

Abram Timurovitch tried to hide his shock and grief. It was not possible that his ever serious and bright princess of a daughter would make a joke out of such a terrible thing. He mulled over what to say. If this had been one of his grown sons, he would have given him a beating, laying all of the blame on him. If this had been a ship's captain who brought him the news, he would have had him flogged and his career with the company terminated and had him black-balled. Had the ship simply been lost at sea, he would have raged and then wept. But this was his daughter. He could not think of anything but great joy that she had survived.

"That is terrible news, Alexandra," he managed after a lengthy pause as he ran over the great losses in his mind, "but you are here and not harmed. I thank our seamen's patron Saint Nicholas the Miracle-Worker that our family has been blessed by your safe return. Please now tell me all about it if it is not too terrible for you to do so, my love."

Alexandra chocked back a small sob then began, "We had great success in our trading efforts. I was able to achieve very good discounts in Seoul and packed millions of rubles worth of goods into the holds. They would have been worth tens of millions when sold from here in the trading center."

She went on making each occurrence into a fascinating story. The story of the storm was almost more than her father could bear, and he moved to her side and put both of his heavily muscled arms around her as she continued to the end of her harrowing tale.

"Have you lost all faith in me, Father," Alexandra asked plaintively. "I feel it is all or at least mostly my fault. Will you ever let me go on another commercial sailing venture?"

Abram laughed at his daughter's altogether genuine distress and said soothingly in his rich deep voice, "My girl. I am most proud of what you did. You are not *Iisus* or *Bog Otets*. You are just a human like me and cannot control the winds and the waves. Only the Son and God the Father can do that."

"I love you, Father."

"And I, you, my princess. So much so that I will keep you by my side for some time to learn the business and to keep you safe. You will have your day as a Tarasova captain, but you must let your old father have a time to get over this terrible near miss."

"I will obey you, Father; but I will not always be a girl. I will be a woman soon. You must promise that I will be able to travel all the China seas and even around the Pacific. There is so much world to see, and I want not only to see it but to be an important competitor as a captain of the Tarasova commercial company. I will one day succeed you. That is not a boast; it is a fact. I have every confidence. My brothers can be my equals, but I will not walk or sit behind them. That may be all right for other women, but I will never kowtow to a man."

Abram laughed heartily, "I would expect nothing less of you, Princess. Just don't take over while I am still able to run the company."

Then they both laughed.

CHAPTER SIXTEEN

MORE EVIDENCE

"There is nothing more deceptive than an obvious fact."
—Arthur Conan Doyle,
The Boscombe Valley Mystery, 1891

**National Archives of Australia, Victorian Archives Centre,
99 Shiel Street, North Melbourne, Victoria, Australia,
December 15, 2013**

The Mormon senior missionary couples had developed a firm bond over their several months of service in Australia. That bond enabled them to work with an efficiency none of them would have imagined five months ago. In part, their burgeoning success in digitalizing the Victoria Archives Centre's hand-written records came from the fact that all of them were professionally proficient in performing the complex and difficult electronic tasks of changing old, long-hand, penscript, and barely legible yellowing records into easily accessible digital photographs and computerized documents. Another element of their success was the missionaries' genuine affection for one another which translated into a love for the work they were doing. A further element of that affection was their genuine conversion to the church in which they had believed all their lives and now saw its practical goodness in ongoing operation. Finally, they began to have fun doing their work; the most fun came from their united effort to solve an enticing mystery.

"Brothers and Sisters, we have another breakthrough in our quest to prove who the mysterious Alexandra Tarasova was. I declare humbly, that I found a great document; and I am graciously willing to share this priceless nugget with you," Sister Marianne Clyde announced with an impish expression on her cherubic face.

"We're certainly glad that you have done all of this marvelous work and a wonder in appropriate humility," joked her husband, Moroni.

"Out with it, Marianne," insisted Sister Lisa Taylor. "No more suspense. I, for one, could use a bit of uplifting."

Marianne gently removed a yellow parchment document and a newspaper front page which appeared about to crumble. She placed the papers on a parchment paper lining of the collating table.

The writing on the document was in Cyrillic calligraphy which was a handsome example of the best of Russian handwriting. The meaning was completely obscured by the foreign language and alphabet and required considerable explanation. The newspaper, dated 05, April, 1876, was too long and complicated to permit a full translation; so, the missionaries had to make do with a synopsis kindly provided by the Russian born janitor of the archive centre.

Marianne began, "The gist of the pretty hand writing is that it is an invitation to a debut and birthday party for one Alexandra Abramovna Tarasova. Perhaps you have heard of her?" she said with an impish smile.

"Tell us the rest, Sister Clyde, and hurry up about it," insisted Sister Taylor again.

"It is on letterhead parchment stationary from the Tarasova Commercial Trading Centre in Vladivostok, Far Eastern Russia. It must have been a very important and very formal occasion given the expensive paper used in the announcement, and goodness only knows how many invitations went out. The newspaper article tells about the grand party and the dignitaries who attended, including captains of industry, an admiral, multiple probably important businessmen and their wives, the commandant of the Balagansk Prison, and two headmen from the Buryat tribes—one local to the Vladivostok area and one from well to the north."

The missionary couples poured over the documents and made their own scanned copies. It was considered by all of them to be an invaluable piece of their puzzling mystery. It was P-day, and by prior arrangement, the band of senior missionaries set out for another day of low-grade, appropriate, adventure and a quest to learn more about Melbourne. By now, all of them were comfortable with the correct pronunciation for their adopted city—

"Mel bun".

This time they decided on a vigorous walking tour and started at Southgate to visit the Victorian Arts Center, then crossed the bridge to Swanston Street Walk and on to Collins Street. They quickly took in Bourke Street Mall and did a little cursory shopping. Then, they made the climb up the hill to the State Houses of Parliament. They were not permitted to enter the parliament buildings; so, they went back down to Russell Street and took a tour through the Old Melbourne Gaol. Afterwards, they went back to La Trobe Street and walked through the magnificent State Library, their putative employer.

Sister Lisa Taylor suggested, "Let's do lunch—as they say in California—I've heard of this nice little pub right here by the library. We can have authentic Aussie food."

The group was rather uncomfortable entering a pub, but one of the men explained that pubs were not like American bars. The Queen Victoria was a nice quiet place, and they quickly lost their misgivings as they enjoyed the pub fare: free bread and cheese, chicken wings, pork slider, deep-fried, breaded calamari, and potato wedges with sweet chili and sour cream. They declined an arm load of pints of Foster's Lager and had to settle for Diet Coke even though several of them were mildly uncomfortable about the possibility that caffeine drinks were in violation of the Word of Wisdom.

The following morning, they returned to work reinvigorated to continue their official and unofficial searches.

CHAPTER SEVENTEEN

A FEAST FOR A PRINCESS

Don't get up from the feast of life without paying for your share of it.
—Dean Inge

Tarasova Fur Company Headquarters and Trading Center, No. 71 Svetlanskaya Street, Vladivostok, Russia, April 2, 1876

Nearly sixteen-year-old Alexandra Abramovna Tarasova was almost as giddy as a child awaiting Christmas as the day for her birthday/debut/and ascension in rank approached. There were four more days before the actual birthday, and five more before the official celebration—April 1ˢᵗ—was to take place. Alexandra had been the model of patience, propriety, and willingness to learn so that her father, Abram, would not be able to find the slightest fault that could keep her on the land and away from the family's commercial trading ships. She seldom brought up her desire, but let it be known in subtle ways that she was getting an education in everything that would make her an important officer in the family business.

Abram said to his wife, Irina Ishmaelovna Inkijinoff, on the twenty-eighth of March, "Irina, do you think Alexandra is still dreaming of going to sea as a serious business woman?"

He asked the same thing each day for the next two days and got the same answer, "You know as well as I do, Abram, my blind husband. You will act the fool if you do not accommodate her. Apparently, the two of you made a contract of some sort that she would learn everything there was to learn about your business that can be taken in on the land. She has done that and more. She is far smarter than her brothers or any of the other businessmen in all the Far East. Even a few of them will admit it."

"But, Irina, she is my little girl. I am afraid to let her go out into the world of sailors, Chinese, Russian aristocrats, and cunning traders. Please help me to persuade her."

"You jest, Abram. You can order her, but you cannot "persuade" her. You will lose her if you even hint that you are thinking of going back on your deal."

"Why are you always on the girl's side?"

"Because I am afraid of her. She is too smart, too strong-minded, and too able to fight, for me to handle her. Even you are no match for her. I think you should stop worrying about your poor little girl and start planning for the contest she will pose in a few years to take over the company."

He gave a heavy and defeated sigh. Not a particularly sad one, just one of resignation because he knew that his daughter was a tough genius, even though she was just a female. He knew he would have to accommodate her mind and her drive and that it would be advantageous for the company and for the family, in-all-likelihood. He determined to begin planning in that positive direction rather than to find that he had followed a machismo dominating attitude towards his remarkable daughter and thereby maneuvered himself into an unnecessarily lost cause.

Four weeks of planning, shopping, rehearsing, and cleaning the company building preceded the day. Mountains of food and drink were imported from Japan, Chosŏn, China, England, Germany, and from everywhere in Russia where luxury goods could be obtained. Abram good-naturedly complained about the costs—that he was going to be a bankrupt pauper—but he was assured from the advice of his family, friends, and business associates, that the soirée would be the best marketing advertisement his far-flung business could ever have.

Irina calmed her husband by assuring him that the positive results for the family business empire would be incalculable. She wrongly thought to reassure his many doubts and misgivings by saying that this party would be exceeded only by the one they would have when she married.

"Irina, the thought of Alexandra going on sea voyages is enough to give an old man like me a heart spasm. Don't bring up the dreadful idea that our princess will one day find a man to marry, and he will take her away from me."

Irina laughed, "Abram, you are not an old man; and you will be able to scare off the weaklings and dummkopfs for a while; but one day, some magnificent young prince will sweep her off her feet; and nothing you can do will get in the way of our princess when she has found her man and made up her mind."

Abram groaned in recognition of his eventual defeat. He smiled as he did.

The Russian Far East in the waning years of the nineteenth century and the first half of the twentieth was lacking in several crucial factors enjoyed by the Europeans for their debuts—coming out into society—so much a part of the coming of age of the rich. First of all, there were not that many rich families in Siberia or the Far East. Secondly, the only aristocrats living in Siberia were ones whose families had fallen far out of favor with the oligarchy and had been deported to the most thankless place in the world. Thirdly, the other group of young gentlemen available for marriage were members of the military, especially the imperial navy. The naval officers' backgrounds and behavior were suspect; and to complicate that problem, they were often in port only briefly—hardly enough time to strike up a relationship, be vetted sufficiently to be acceptable to the prospective bride's family, and to get into society with its debuts and marital celebrations with all of their elaborate and costly planning and execution.

Abram shuddered at the prospect of finding a husband for his difficult, even sometimes unmanageable daughter. At least for the time being, all the family had to do was to get through half a dozen or so fancy parties. Siberian formal society was not quite what English, French, American, or even Moscow and Saint Petersburg society was. The Far Easterners had to make some exceptions to the complex and mandatory sets of rules governing polite society in those more sophisticated societies. Because of the availability of more young men from rich and otherwise acceptable families in other European and American countries, the proud Siberians had to forego many of the elitist cultural customs surrounding coming-out into society.

Most of the other countries required that a girl wait until she was at least seventeen, preferably until she was eighteen or twenty. Alexandra was not quite sixteen. To ensure the all-important virginity of the

English, French, Austrian, and German debutants, many of them were schooled in religion, etiquette, and proper comportment during the debut period, as well as the restrictive religions of the several countries. In those countries casual meetings between members of the opposite sex were frowned upon and avoided as much as possible. Older ladies tended to run the process. Mothers, aunts, older married sisters, and even well-intentioned male family members and friends worked, connived, and often provided financial inducements to eligible bachelors of well-to-do commercial families or landed gentry. In those countries, the appropriate choices for young ladies and their families were somewhat limited and clearly defined. There were not such institutions in the Far East.

Things were different in Siberia and the Far East. Many of the members of what passed for high society in those regions were considered minority peoples in the West, including Moscow and Saint Petersburg. Abram held trading conferences with chieftains of the Buryats, Altai, Chukchi, Evenk, Khanti, Mansi, and Nenets who were more closely related genetically and culturally to the indigenous peoples of the Americas than they were to native Russians or their predecessor Vikings.

At least two headmen of each tribe and their wives and oldest sons were invited. The headmen persuaded their wives that attendance at the Tarasova girl's parties would mean introduction into the society that was only lukewarm to their presence and would give them an edge in commerce that had long been denied them. Several dozen indigenous couples made firm plans to attend and not to be outdone in their gift giving.

Irina took on the task of persuading the elites of the European transplants and visitors to Vladivostok and the rest of the Irkutsk oblast. Her methods were near copies of the social agenda used in the rest of Europe: presentations to the Tarasova family, presentations to the governing leaders of the imperial navy, marines, and army as well as the mayors and provincial governors. Irina held more than a dozen supper parties and persuaded other notable women to do the same. The response from mothers of younger upcoming daughters was enthusiastic. The costs were extravagant, but Irina loved the galas she produced. Hundreds of ladies persuaded their husbands that they would go to Alexandra Tarasova's debut, and they would like it because that was where the power and the influence resided.

Alexandra's two brothers, Veniamin and Valéry, were sent on separate voyages to combine commerce and diplomacy. Turning a profit from their bales of furs was important, but persuading the elite of Chosŏn, China, and Japan to attend the Tarasova daughter's debut was paramount. Along the way, they succeeded beyond their parents' expectations: they were able to coax young American, Austrian, German, English, Asian, and French diplomats and business gentlemen to make a commercial voyage to Vladivostok and to attend the celebration.

The European and American purpose for the debutantes' coming-out seasons was largely to bring acceptable choices in young gentlemen and ladies together to begin a serious vetting process for eventual marriages and the establishment of strong commercial, oligarchical, and exclusive dynasties. Abram and Irina's motives were less distant in character: they wanted business alliances now; and they were not the least troubled by inviting people of color, exotic origin, or differing cultural attitudes and practices. They had less interaction with the far-away world of Europe than they did with nearby Chosŏn on the south, China on the west and south, and the islands of Japan. The intention to build stronger bonds with the Asians was a serious driving force in decisions about who would be invited and who would be flattered and accommodated than any other cultural considerations The European circle of ruling old ladies had no real place in this frontier region because there were very few of them. This was a young people's world. Neither Abram nor Irina neglected the potential that one of the young men invited to the balls and dinners could become an appropriate and successful suitor of their daughter, and at the same time, a new partner in the burgeoning Tarasova industries.

In the frenetic period of preparation for the many celebrations planned for the coming-out of their highly eligible daughter included the construction of a huge new warehouse-sized addition to the original Tarasova Fur Company building. It was completed two days before the grand entrance ball scheduled for the evening of Alexandra's actual birthday. The result would might well have fitted the society of Moscow or Saint Petersburg for all its luxury and grandeur, if not the actual people they would meet at the celebration.

The food—enough for a thousand people for four days—included local and imported foods: a variety of smoked, salted, and marinated fish—trout, carp, zander, sturgeon and starlet (Tzar Fish) with barrels of the favorites, salmon and smoked herring; *crêpes;* red salmon and black sturgeon caviar; Irini's mother's favorite homemade "herring under a fur coat" (*shuba*, salted herring in a salad covered by layers of grated boiled vegetables, beets, onions and thick mayonnaise.), seven varieties of borsch with meat, potatoes, dill, and Smetana, the favorite Russian sour cream; black rye bread, garlic toast with melted cheese with a myriad of choices of the cheese, creamed mushrooms, and *blini*—the Russian variation on the French *crêpe*. The Russians have been creative with their *crêpes*— buckwheat pancakes, and white flour for sweet toppings and fillings (a dozen local jams, sour cream, condensed milk, and caviar).

Knowing the carnivorous nature of their expected guests, Irina sent inland to Central Asia for *tartareis*—a vegetable lamb dish, varieties of roasted lamb, chicken, beef, venison, and fish on skewers, a Russian variation of the *shishkebab* served with a spicy tomato-based sauce, Russian pickles, and thick, heavy unleavened breads. The other meat contribution to the princess's feast was *pelmeni*—Russian dumplings. They were lovingly created by the Tarasova staff and filled with lamb, pork, beef, salmon, creamy minced onions, and mushrooms, served simply or in a broth.

The Tarasovas contracted with an Irkutsk bakery to make mounds of *pirozhki*–same fillings as the *pelmeni* but placed in pastry and languorously baked in the several families' 15th century brick ovens—a favorite in Moscow but considered a luxury in Vladivostok because of the cost of the construction materials and the difficulty of finding a true expert builder. No Russian aristocrat or rich businessman's wife would even dream of having such a feast without the worldwide favorite Stroganoff. Irina personally supervised the preparation of the dish, made smoother by its Russian cream, and tastier by its large variety of mushrooms, and more filling by the ample portions of rich venison, beef, and pork meats.

The Tarasova ships brought the best of German products for Alexandra's special day: *spaetzle* and *käsespätzle*–thinly sliced beef, veal, pork or minced meat around a filling of bacon or pork belly, chopped onions, pickles, and then browned and braised in broth dumplings– served with Rouladon meat gravy, mashed potato with savory chunks of sausage cooked into it, and barrels of cooked red cabbage the Germans called *blaukraut*. For the guests staying over after the first festive day, the Tarasovas imported barrels of ingredients for *eintopf*—the one pot stew made of broth, fresh vegetables, pulses, and a variety of meats and fish. Abram had grown fond of several *eintopf* varieties: He was amused as much by the name of *lumpen und fleeh*–rags and fleas–as he was of what was simply Irish stew, and a Thüringen lentil soup known as *linseneintopf.*

Irina arranged with the Austrian vegetable monger, Klaus und Franken, *Eingearbeitet,* to provide ample pulses: baked beans, red, green, yellow and brown lentils, chana beans, sweet garden peas and black-eyed peas, runner, fava, kidney, butter, cannellini flageolet, pinto, and borlotti beans—enough for a small army, and augmented by bales of dried *Kartoffelknödel* ready for the addition of water and cooking to produce the all time favorite German dish, potato dumplings. She also ordered special boxes with ice on the bottom to hold her personal favorite *Schnitzel Wiener* and a large sampling of many of the 1500 kinds of *wurst*–*Bratwurst* made of ground pork and spices, *Blutwurst* and *Schwarzwurst*–the two blood sausages–*Currywurst,* Bavarian *Weisswurst,* Nuremberg grilled *Rostbratwurst,* and *Thüringer Rostbratwurst* accompanied by dozens of tubs of *sauerkraut.*

Two French ships–the *Vive la révolution,* and the Brig *Cargaison de France*—carried ships' larders packed with the essentials for *Soupe à l'oignon,* including the appropriate brandies and sherries; *Coq au vin,* including the alcohol appropriate for the French regional variations, *coq au Riesling* from Alsace, *coq au pourpre* or *coq au violet*—the Beaujolais nouveau–and *coq au Champagne*; *bœuf bourguignon* from Burgundy; duck meat marinated in salt, garlic, and thyme for up to two days and kept on ice for the Tarasova extravaganza's *Confit de canard.*

It took the servants two hours to unload the beverages for the evening, and the diversity, quality, and quantity of the selections would have suited the Romanoffs. There were a dozen teas from Asia and India—hot and cold—spicy hot *sbiten,* coffees, sweet fermented honey *medovukha, ormors* made of a mixture of the juice of several kinds of berries and birch tree juice, black rye bread *kvoss* with its low alcohol content, vodka bottles standing behind boxes of shot glasses, French brandies, wines, and champagne, German and French Armagnac and cognacs and other brandies smuggled in from Cornwall, England, Slivovitz plum brandy, and surprisingly good sake, absinthe (green fairy), American whiskeys made by relatives of Daniel Boone in Nelson County Kentucky, Bourbon—so-called red liquor—sour mash Old-Crow and Old Pepper Whiskey which were stored in charred oak barrels made by white and black slaves in the Americas, and rye whisky. There were five bottles of

Duret Cognac 1810 which originally came from a single precious barrel carried by a French naval ship, reserved for the very carefully chosen *crème de la crème* of the guest list. There was no gin, of course—too cheap for the discerning palates of the Tarasova guests.

Finally, for those gluttons not completely surfeit from the gourmet fair, there was a table of cheeses from around the world: fromage poises: pungent to the level of odiferous and not for the dainty characterized by their funkyness, smoothness as velvet such as Époisses, a cow's milk cheese from Burgundy, washed in brandy to a custard-creamy texture which have meaty, salty, charcoal, butterfat, grass, truffle, and briny flavors; semisoft and buttery smooth Fontina Val from Italy; Spanish basque smokey Idiazabal, a hard sheep's milk cheese. Goat's milk Leonora, another Spanish cheese, but this one hard as a stone in the center and bright yellow and creamy near the rind. It tasted of pepper and the sap of local Spanish pines; southern French Ossau Iraty, a very firm raw sheep's milk with a unique blend of tastes: butter, nutty, caramel, tropical fruit, chamomile tea, and mint sweetness. A favorite of the French guest–but no one else–was Selles-sur-Cher goat's mild cheese with a rind dusted in ashes which detracted from the almond, hazelnut, and copper pennies.

For the true gourmands there were truffled cheeses–truffle tremor, made with black summer truffles in whipped goat's milk paste with a tangy and earthy mushroom flavor. Yarg from Cornwall, England was fairly unappetizing to look at—lacy mold on nettle leaves. The taste was something like citrus and mushrooms, belying the rather unpleasant rind's appearance. To prove that the pungent, very strong cheeses becoming popular through Russia during the nineteenth century were not just luxury imports, Irina brought in exotic cheese from Siberia, the Mongolian steppes, Moscow, Saint Petersburg; and Russians were becoming experimenters with the moldy, smelly, and particularly strong cheeses. The affluent were acquiring a taste for them. The Russian varieties were set apart by being big long logs. Irina had them kept in glass cases to provide a positive Russian cachet. Besides the commonly known korall and quark, she included bries, cheddars, parmesans, and camemberts, which had fallen out of fashion in courts of European and the mansions of America. The Russian guests were aware of Irina's effort to tout Russian products and flocked to the Russian section of the cheese display.

The Russian steam corvette, *The Amerika*, was in port with Grand Duke Paul Alexandrovich Romanov—the sixth son and youngest child of Tsar Alexander II of Russia by his first wife, Tsarina Maria Alexandrovna, on an inspection and vacation tour. The royal couple was gracious enough to accept the invitation to Alexandra's sixteenth birthday celebration. That such a grand figure in the Russian empire should deign to come to their humble home shocked and thrilled the Tarasovas, who considered themselves to be rustics in comparison to any Romanov. They were accompanied on their voyage by the Count and Countess Igor and Annika Yusupov. Not withstanding the grandness of the two couples who came from Moscow to enjoy their party, they were satisfied that their spread would be appropriate even for members of the fabulously rich Yusupovs and even the tzar's family. As soon as the guests were seated for the splendid meal, Abram and Irina were blissful at the obvious success of their incredibly expensive endeavor.

CHAPTER EIGHTEEN

AN EVENING TO REMEMBER

*This is the power of gathering: it inspires us, delightfully, to be
more hopeful, more joyful, more thoughtful: in a word, more alive.*
—Alice Waters

Tarasova Fur Company Headquarters and Trading Center, No. 71 Svetlanskaya Street, Vladivostok, Russia, April 2, 1876, late evening

The dinner of dinners and evening of evenings drew to a close with the guests nibbling at exotic cheeses, drinking more French and Italian wines than they should, taking a few more bites of a*pfelstrudel, flamiche,* chocolate *soufflé,* and *medovik* and becoming overfilled and inebriated. Alexandra managed to live up to her billing as "The Princess of Vladivostok" even though she was seated between Grand Duke Paul Alexandrovich Romanov and Taipan Sir James Nicolas Sutherland Matheson, 1ˢᵗ Baronet. Both the Russian duke and the Scottish tycoon found themselves wrapped around the little fingers of the sixteen-year-old girl, much to the amusement of her doting parents who surreptitiously took in every nuance from their seats at the head of the table. It was pure joy to watch their nearly grown daughter work her feminine wiles and demonstrate her business acumen for two of the most important men in the world.

As the French waiters cleared the last plates; and the majority of the guests were helped to their carriages by the house staff, Irina turned to Abram and said, "A success, no, my dear?"

"In more ways than one. We will never be able to put a bridle on our girl. She will outdo us no matter how we try. I predict that the house of Tarasova will be mentioned regularly in the same breath as the Romanoffs and the Mathesons by courtiers and the titans of trade and industry before very long."

"You might even include the house of Yusupov, Abram. I note that Annika Yusupov treated us and Alexandra like old friends, and Count Igor took more than an avuncular interest in our nubile daughter."

Abram laughed and said, "Nubile—marriagable—maybe. And maybe this is the beginning of her acceptance into the society of the nobles. Who knows, maybe she could find a marriageable *Dvoryanstvo*, maybe even an von Antre or a Belosselsky-Belozersky."

"Or even a Romanoff or a Yusupov," added Irena, "who knows. We might as well aim high."

They both laughed at their temerity and to the fact that they had probably had too much *medovukha*, since they both enjoyed the honey flavor of the authentically Russian liquor more than they liked to admit to themselves.

Abram, Irina, and Alexandra sat in huge chairs near the great fireplace which had been lit to ward off the chill of the early spring winds. The only remaining guests were the taipan and his son, James.

After a brief chat, Taipan Matheson, who was unused to late night social activity, came to the point of why he and his heir had come all the way to Vladivostok.

"Great *soiree*," he said, "and a marvelous way to attract business, my friend. Aye have cum ta a decision, this evening, Abram. We shuld capitalize on the success of the gathering and send out business offers ta the guest list."

"Offering what, Taipan?"

"Expansion, Laddie, expansion. Let's tell the lot of 'em that we want their help to bring down the East Indian conglomerate and to make all of us richer and more powerful than we have yet bin able to imagine. Aye propose that we increase the fleet by a dozen ships this year and another couple of dozen next year. Aye propose that we send those ships to England, Germany, France, and maybe even Australia and America.

Finally, Aye suggest that we start a commercial war with those East Indian blighters—pardon my French, Ladies—and take over their interests in every one of their ports, starting with *Heung Gawng* [Cantonese for Hong Kong–fragrant harbor" originating from the scent coming from the sandalwood incense factories in Canton]."

"How would we do that, Taipan?" asked Alexandra to the surprise of her parents.

"Och, Lassie, glad ter hear yer sweet voice. I'll tell ya how. First, we keep it in the family. By family I mean the Mathesons, Jardines, and the Tarasovas. Second, we put a family member on each and every one o' the ships—a person familiar wi' the sea and its hazards and one able to stand up to the pirates of the business world. Third, Aye want to see new products, new services, new protections to keep our business on top o' the world of the Pacific."

"Father, if I may…"

"'O course, Jamie, me boy, let's get yer pint o' view. Ye've had a barrel full of experience despite yer youth."

"I know where we can obtain two ships as soon as we can get to Hong Kong. That will get us started."

"We dinna ha' captains and crews yet, me boy," the taipan interrupted.

"But, we do. I can captain one, and Alexandra, here, can be in charge of the other. Between our two families, we can come up with two crews without a bit of trouble."

Abram spoke up, "Getting a crew for a ship is easy. I have a few men sitting around fairly idle. We can teach them to be sailors in a month. But, my daughter being captain…, that's another thing altogether."

Jamie said, "This is her debut into adulthood, is it not? I have seen her face problems of business, the sea, and even pirates, and to handle them with aplomb. She's a natural. A quick learner, and we have captains and crews who can teach her anything she needs to know. Abram and Irina can teach her the business if she is not already entirely capable. I can help her over the rough spots. Keep it in the family, you said. Well, here's a good place to start."

Irina Ishmaelovna looked shocked and entered the conversation excitedly, "But Alexandra is but a girl. Is our girl ready for the business end of things, Abram?"

Irina deliberately used diminutives to describe her daughter hoping to be influential in forming the men's opinions.

"I have to say yes, my dear. I have taught her all I know. She is indeed young, but that only means that she has longer to learn more than all the rest of us put together. Watch out—all of you—or she'll be the head of the Jardine-Matheson-Tarasova company before you know what has happened."

Everyone laughed.

Alexandra said simply, "I am capable. Let me prove it."

CHAPTER NINETEEN

STAFF OFFICER

Not every day is Shrovetide, in time it will be lent.
—Russian proverb

Nikolai I General Staff Academy, Moscow, Imperial Russia, May 19, 1871

At graduation from the General Staff Academy, Prince Boris Nikolaivich Yusupov was promoted in rank to Full Captain. He was more pleased with the honor granted him to realize his life's goal, that of joining the elite Guards Regiment. He was most pleased that his father and mother attended the ceremony; and above all that, at last, his taciturn father said to him,

"Well done, my son, you have made our family proud."

That was the highest praise Prince Nikolai had ever pronounced, and Boris was inspired by it. Boris wore his full-dress uniform including his Saint Stanislaus and Saint Anne—second class medals and looked splendid. He and his family were able to have lunch with the new academy commandant, General mayor Ivan Dragorovich Strabinsky, his wife, Grushenka, and Grand Duke Paul Alexandrovich and Marienka, his godfather and mother. Lunching with such key senior officers, his influential family, his exploits in the 1863 Crimean conflict, and his acceptance into the Guards Regiment, all but guaranteed that he would be accepted into the general ranks before his career was over. All-in-all it was a highly portentous day.

After his parents departed for Saint Petersburg, and Boris was alone in his apartment, he was surprised to hear a knock on his door. He opened the door and was taken aback to see General mayor Strabinsky standing stiffly in the doorway.

"Please come in, General mayor. To what do I owe this honor?"

The taciturn mustachioed general stroked the dueling scar on his chin for a moment before answering.

"Captain, you have had honors aplenty today and enough of them. I am here to convey a serious warning to you—to tell you to take to heart what I say and beware the rest of your life."

Boris was perplexed and crestfallen but strove to avoid showing it in his face.

The general continued, "I only lately became aware of your association with some undesirable elements."

Boris's confusion registered on his face.

"You should have made better choices, young man. Early in your years here at the General Academy you associated with and, in fact, allowed individuals with very questionable political beliefs to room with you for a period. Do not look at me as if you are not aware of who these people are. Let me refresh your memory, young man: Sophia Perovskaya, Andrei Zhelyabov, Gesia Gelfman, Nikolai Sablin, Ignatei Grinevitski, Nikolai Kibalchich, Nikolai Rysakov and Timofei Mikhailov."

Boris paled, and he took an involuntary gulp.

"Yes, that bunch of plotters who call themselves the laughable name of the People's Will. Loris Melikof–Head of the Okhrana–has informed the tzar that this foolish group has planned one assassination attempt on the life of our beloved tzar which failed and are actively planning another. The tzar is furious; this is not only an attack on his person but upon the very core of Imperial Russia which you are sworn to defend."

"I have had nothing to do with any such plans or actions. I never agreed with any such ideas. When I heard them expressed, I expelled them from my personal circle; and, as I recall, they were expelled from the academy."

"I believe you, Full Captain, but you are tainted by your brief association. However, you cannot be so naïve that you were not then and are not now aware that your group of friends fell under the spell of Mikhail Bakunin and his Land and Liberty reformers party. The group published literature demanding that the land in Russia held by the government and the church be granted back to the poor landless people. The tzar and the Okhrana might have been indulgent, but after the assassination attempt, they have no tolerance. An empire-wide dragnet is in force to bring these traitors to justice. They will be imprisoned and likely hanged."

"I repudiated their beliefs and their organization. I have had no contact with any of them since those very early days. I continue to pledge my allegiance to the tzar and to the imperial army without reservation, Sir. Please believe me."

"What I believe is of little consequence now in this superheated atmosphere. Were it not for the fact that you are a Yusupov, you would be under arrest now, and your career ruined. Both your father and I will contact the tzar's inner council and stave off any action towards you, if that is possible. You are on thin ice."

"But, I have done nothing wrong, General mayor."

"Right now, that is beside the point. Suspicion is rife, and you are caught in the net."

"What can I do?"

"For now, become invisible. You are assigned to a guards unit. You can keep your head down, do not make noise, join no groups. Do the silly things like card playing and chasing girls that the guardsmen do during peace time. All around the empire, there are rabble rousers who foment trouble. Pray that one of those groups gets out of hand enough to warrant a guards unit being sent to quell the disturbance. The Ottomans are constantly making a nuisance of themselves and will do so until we finally have a war and obliterate those Mohammadan heathens once and for all. I will get you there any way I can and as soon as I can. Keep a very low profile, young prince, lest the Okhrana or the tzar's hunters catch wind of you."

"Yes, Sir. I will camp out with the guards unit and be ready at a moment's notice to leave for battle with the Ottomans or anyone else who challenges the empire."

"That is enough said, then, Full Captain. Await orders and keep your head down."

Boris gave the general mayor a crisp salute then cleared his quarters of anything that might incriminate him or link him to the infernal People's Will fools. The first thing he did was to burn all the letters from his previous roommates and his copy of Bakunin's book, *Statism and Anarchism.*

Although his orders did not require him to report to his guards unit for two weeks, he departed the academy and rode hard to the unit's headquarters. His arrival in the Moscow headquarters of the 1st Cavalry Brigade, Horse Guard Regiment, went unheralded, as he should have hoped it would be; but it was, nonetheless, rather a disappointment. The sergeant-major examined his papers, stamped them, and directed him to his bachelor officer's quarters—a drab utilitarian set of three rooms, metal furniture, wood floors, and an indoor toilet—the only significant amenity.

The newcomer quickly settled into the exasperatingly easy routine of the officer's community which was as distinct from the lesser ranks as if they were men of different colors or from different planets. Boredom was Boris's major enemy; all his physical needs were attended to by a horde of sycophantic orderlies; and all military activities and even paper work were dealt with by the omnipresent spit-and-polish sergeants-major. All Boris had to do was to attend contrived officer social events and a few community leader affairs presided over by starched shirt bureaucrats. There were a scant few women anywhere near the encampment, only a few readable books, and a rare military parade, to cut the pervasive sense of ennui.

CHAPTER TWENTY

OTTOMAN INCURSIONS

"Storm'd at with shot and shell./ Boldly they rode and well./ Into
the jaws of Death./ Into the mouth of Hell/ Rode the six hundred."
—Alfred Lord Tennyson,
The Charge of the Light Brigade, 1854

Headquarters 1st Cavalry Brigade, Horse Guard Regiment, Moscow, Russia, May 19, 1875

B oris held his vint cards loosely, hardly caring whether the other
bored officers at the table in the *sobranie* were bothering to
peek. His morning had been spent in the officers' club playing
billiards—a pass time which he was ashamed to admit, had resulted in
his becoming an expert player. He had eaten both breakfast and lunch at
the officer's mess and had only his upcoming evening's ride on Kryzhu
to divert him from the feeling that he was a useless aristocrat officer like
all the rest of his companions. He was dismayed that nearly five years of
such idleness had slipped out of his life hardly noticed.

At 1300, Sergeant-Major Ivan Andreiovich Skavar strode into
the *sobranie* uninvited and unannounced and spoke in a loud voice:
"*vnimaniye!*" [attention].

It was the first time in his five year stay in the headquarters camp that
Boris had ever seen an enlisted man in the officers' club and certainly the
first time that one had commanded attention from the assembled officers.

"Command orders all first cavalry officers and enlisted to report to the parade grounds at 1600 sharp for an important announcement. That is all."

Skavar whirled in an about face and marched stiffly out of the room without further explanation.

Presuming that the summons was so out of the ordinary and preemptory that he should appear decked out in his dress uniform—red coat with gold buttons, blue trousers with gold inlays along the side of the legs, his gold cavalry helmet with the white plum, and his regimental sword.

Captain of the General Staff Dragon Sergeivich Oblensky entered the *sobranie* and stood stiffly by as the sergeant-major barked out the command, "*Vnimaniye!*" then exited. Oblensky then spoke in the terse, clipped tones of a commander:

"The guards will muster tomorrow morning at 1100 hours ready to embark by train for a mission to Bulgaria as ordered by the tzar himself. Each officer will be allowed three packing trunks and is expected to include two dress uniforms and enough field uniforms to last the duration. Dress swords and parade boots are mandatory and field equipment including your sabers are an obvious requirement. I strongly recommend that you bring more than one. Muskets and hand guns and sufficient ammunition for a month are required. I strongly recommend that you bring along the gear to make your own ammunition should events require.

"The sergeants-major will instruct the lower ranks on their needs. Those officers with their own corps of trained fighters will report the numbers to SM Skavar tonight; so, we can have an accurate tally of the lower ranks to provide transport cars and provisions. Gentlemen, the Ottomans have bullied our Bulgarian allies long enough. The tzar expects us to take care of the problem once and for all.

"Any questions?"

There were none.

Prince Boris immediately rode out to the tents where Vlad and the rest of his Cossacks were billeted and told them tersely to prepare for war. They were leaving for Bulgaria before noon the next day. He was greeted with whoops and broad smiles. These men did poorly during periods of idleness. War was their *raison d'être* and bred into them from their mothers' knees. As Boris left the encampment, he heard the rattle and clatter of packing, collecting arms and saddle tack, and rounding up his unit's horses and their fodder.

Batak and Perushtitsa, Bulgaria, June 7, 1875-December 10, 1877

The Imperial Guards battalion rode into an area which was in a state of pandemonium. The ragtag Bulgarian irregulars were ostensibly preparing to do battle with a far superior number of Turkish Ottoman regular troops—the Nisam—and irregulars—the Redifs, Bashi-bazouks, Bulgarian Muslims, and Crimean Tatars imported from the Caucasus. Boris and his Cossacks rounded up a few dozen of the toughest looking Bulgars and made attempts to teach them disciplined cavalry tactics. The attempts were futile; the Bulgarian fighters saw the issue as a personal rebellion against the Ottoman atrocities. They were adverse to obeying orders from leaders of their own clans, to say nothing of obeying Russian interlopers.

Boris and his fellow guards officers were able only to convince the insurgents to adopt guerilla tactics of attack and vanish and to abandon their villages which could not be defended. Boris was dubious about the likelihood of his Russian counterparts being able to convey even that simple strategy. For the next year, the Cossacks and the brave Bulgars carried out annoying and costly raids hitting ammunition dumps, food storage depots, train tracks, and small encampments of Ottoman Janissaries and Yayas spread out across the Bulgarian plains and mountain valleys. At best, Boris and his unit were able to keep the advancing Ottoman army at bay and to delay their advances down the peninsula.

In the spring of 1876, word came to the Russians and the Bulgarians—who had come to accept that Russia was their protector–that another uprising had erupted in south-central Bulgaria in conjunction with rioting in Bosnia-Herzegovina. Boris considered this to be the opportunity they had been waiting for and convinced his superior, *Polkovnik* Baritsky, that now was the time to strike and to catch the Turks while their attention was spread out to multiple fronts. Boris and his Cossacks and his few trained Bulgars rode out of Batak and Perushtitsa on May 28 and made a series of punishing raids on small Ottoman units scattered out for a hundred miles around the two small Bulgarian cities.

Satisfied that he had inflicted enough damage on the poorly disciplined Turks, Boris ordered his men to cease their looting and to make their way back to their base cities. They rode into what was left of Batak and Perushtitsa on June 8. Of the towns themselves there were only a handful of buildings left standing, and they were charred ruins still smoking. There was not a single woman or child left in either city, and the few survivors described a nightmarish scenario of Ottoman atrocities which had seen as many as twenty thousand to possible thirty or even forty thousand Bulgarians slaughtered—murdered—including every last man and boy over the age of twelve.

The Russian government reacted with fury. Perhaps the Ottomans believed that such savagery would quell any further resistance, but they had not counted on the effect the atrocities had had on the civilized Russians. Colonel Baritsky sent messengers to Sofia and Plovdiv where they sent emergency telegraph messages in Morse code to all the Russian military installations in Russia and to the capitals of Europe. The response was dramatic. The Ottomans were considered to be uncivilized barbarians before the events in Batak and Perushtitsa, but afterwards the entire civilized world deemed them to be ravening sadistic monsters.

Tzar Alexander II was particularly incensed by the savagery of the Ottomans, but he was also a pragmatist who saw the events as an opening for his imperial army to recover the territorial losses suffered during the humiliating Crimean war and as an opportunity to establish Russian bases on the Black Sea to enable his empire to have an exit into the Baltic Sea and the Atlantic Ocean. He spread the word throughout his empire that this coming war should be considered the rival of the Great Patriotic War of 1812 when the Russians drove out the invading French under Napoleon. Religious Russians saw the upcoming campaign as the divine mission to unite all Bulgaria, Romania, Serbia, Montenegro, and Russian Orthodox, under the Russian flag and the Russian Orthodox cross. The nonreligious Russians saw it as a once in a lifetime chance to save Bulgaria and its downtrodden and abused people and to rid the world of the heathen Muslim Turks.

Alexander raced to get his armies to Bulgaria before any of the other European powers could arrive and claim credit. Since Boris was on the scene, he was given a two-step increase in rank to *Polkovnik* and Baritsky was advanced the same day to K-4, General mayor, in anticipation of the major influx of troops which would come pouring in within a matter of a few weeks.

Boris could hardly believe his luck. He had expected to be reprimanded or even punished for having drawn troops away from the unfortunate Bulgarian cities; but instead, events had gone the opposite way; and he was promoted on what would likely lead to a rapid rise to the field general status he and his father dreamed of. He treated his men to champagne the evening he learned the almost incredibly good news.

From that day forward, the new colonel drilled his Cossacks and as many Bulgarian horsemen as he could round up in cavalry tactics, swordsmanship, riding into battle with a lance, and hand to hand combat with saber and daggers. They were tired, and they griped; but they had a level of esprit de corps none of them could have imagined the month before when they first looked at the devastation of Batak and Perushtitsa. They were ready for the large battles to come, both horses and men literally chomping at the bit. Boris was deeply proud of his men, and rewarded them liberally with medals, drink, and time off.

Kizil-Tepe, Turkey, June 25, 1877

For all its good intentions and enthusiasm for the war against Turkey, the Russian Imperial Army moved with glacial celerity as it always did when approaching battles. Boris and his Cossacks thought they would go mad as the higher brass dithered, planned, made logistic decisions, then redid the whole thing again and again. Boris recognized the need for the 100,000-man Russian army to establish itself, but he could also see the Ottomans pouring into central and southern Bulgaria from the Turkish border. When the order finally came to march, a full year had been wasted. The target of the Russian force was a timid effort to lay siege against the Ottoman Fort Kars in Turkey. He wanted to gallop his cavalry unit all the way to the objective, but he was instructed—ordered—time and again to damp down his ardor and to pull back.

Finally, on June 25, the Russians surrounded Fort Kars and issued an ultimatum: surrender or be destroyed or starved out. The response from the Ottoman commander was insulting. The sultan stood on the parapet near the main gates and laughed out loud, then turned his back on the Russians and disappeared back into his fortified city. The Russians launched attack after attack during the entirety of an exhausting hot day—all to no avail. Boris was beside himself sitting on his massive chestnut horse Kryzhu waiting for the call to arms. It had to come after the walls were broached, but that never happened. Late in the afternoon, the fresh and enthusiastic Turks exploded out of the front and rear gates of the city and appeared out of nowhere from the surrounding hills and valleys and routed the Russians and Bulgarians in an ignominious defeat. It became apparent that the Russians had woefully underestimated the size of the Ottoman hordes commanded by Hussein Pasha arrayed against them.

It was not until the next September when Boris was able to bloody his sword. At long last, the major force of the imperial Russian army crossed the Danube, linked up with the Yusupov and Baritsky forces, and began an attack on the highly fortified city of Nikopol. The Turks recognized the great significance of Nikopol to their continuing survival as an empire and ordered the renowned Ottoman general, Osman Pasha to race to Nikopol. The Russian IX Corp got to the city first and bombed the garrison of the city into abject submission before the Ottoman general could get there and make his bid to save the city. Osman Pasha retreated to the city of Plevna, and awaited the Russian attack which they knew was inevitable once Nikopol fell.

Again, the Russian Imperial Army paused, but this time only for a few days until the Romanian Army could assemble with the Russians for the march to the south to begin the siege of Plevna. It was in the battle that ensued that the newly minted *Polkovnik* Prince Boris Nikolaiovich Yusupov made his name. The Russians fought foray after foray for five torturous months without making significant progress. During the fourth month of the advance, his superior, General mayor Baritsky led an infantry and artillery attack on the Ottomans who were ensconced in a rugged narrow mountain pass. He ordered Boris and his guardsmen and Cossacks to ride to the ridges on both sides of the pass, and to gain the advantage of elevation over the well-armed and determined Turks hiding among rocks and firing artillery at will from fortified caves.

Boris ordered his cavalry and his infantry guards unit to move as quietly as possible up the steep slopes of the ridges on the opposite side of the valley where the major attack by Baritsky's forces were very slowly beginning to advance up the bottom of the valley, suffering terrible losses of men, horses, and equipment. Boris drove his men to near exhaustion until they were above the Ottoman positions and behind them. He sent a message by courier to Baritsky:

My esteemed General, it is my pleasure to inform you that we have gained the vantage point over the heathens and are ready to attack at your command.

Your obedient servant,

Polkovnik Boris Nikolaiovich Yusupov

The reply came from *Polkovnik* Grinevitski, the colonel second in command to Baritsky in the main forces in the valley. It was a terrible shock to Boris:

Polkovnik Yusupov. It is my sad duty to inform you that our esteemed general has been killed in action by treasonous Bulgarian Ottomans. You were second in command, and in a dispatch sent by *General roda voysk* Ivan Borisovitch Gagarin and confirmed by the tzar himself and Prince Carol of Romania, you are now the commander of this mission. Further, Sir, I am to congratulate you on having been given a field commission to the rank of General Mayor. The Branch General instructed me to convey the congratulations of your Father, Prince Nikolai Yusupov, and the tzar. I await your orders, Sir.

Your obedient second in command,

–Polkovnik Leonid Brodinsovitch Grinevitski.

Boris took several minutes to absorb the shocking news from headquarters. Then he had a period of intense grief because he had loved the late general as an uncle and esteemed advisor. He then experienced a moment of conflicted emotions. He had attained his life's goal, and his career would have no limits from this time forward. He was quietly elated. He felt guilty that his ascension had come from the death of his general and friend. Vlad and the Cossacks looked to him for orders. He asked for a piece of parchment and a pen and ink.

He sat on a rock and very slowly and thoughtfully composed a directive—one which would either make or break him as a Russian Imperial Army general.

Polkovnik Rasputin: Convey my shock and sorrow at learning of the death of our great leader. It is fitting that he should die a hero in combat, but nonetheless sad. We must carry on, nevertheless. Continue to bombard the valley redoubt manned by the cursed Ottomans, but take great care not to suffer losses on the part of our great army for the time being. I will attack the heathens from above and behind them in an all-out attack. As soon as you see that we have made full contact, move the bulk of your forces up the valley under artillery cover fire. God grant that we meet at the summit of the valley as victors. If God does not grant us victory, let us die as courageous imperial army soldiers, true to our oath.

– General mayor Prince Boris Nikolaievich Yusupov

Boris turned to his officers and sergeants major, "On my command, ride down both sides of the ridge and into the valley. Fix bayonets; put protectives on your horses, and ride to glory or to death in the name of the tzar."

He sent his swiftest horseman to carry a dispatch to his cavalry and infantry now lined up out of sight behind the opposite ridge. The dispatch rider returned and announced that the men on the other side were ready to die for him if necessary.

Boris was humbled. A thrill ran through him. He ordered his men to climb to the top of the ridge, knowing that the Ottomans would quickly become aware of their presence. When he was certain that his regiment on both sides of the valley was ready, he gave the fateful order:

"*ZARYAD!*" [CHARGE]!"

Boris and his Cossack and Imperial Guards Cavalry roared down both sides of the ridges approaching the astonished Turkish Ottoman regular troops—the Nisam, Janissaries and Yayas—and irregulars—the Redifs, Bashi-bazouks, Bulgarian Muslims, and Crimean Tatars imported from the Caucasus. The Ottoman army had to make a split-second decision: turn about and concentrate fire on the new threat from above and their flanks or continue the defense against the regular Russian Imperial Army attacking from below. They hesitated. Then they became confused and alarmed as Boris's forces swept behind them in a criss-cross cavalry drill formation ending up on opposite sides and in the midst of the terrified Ottoman forces. No sooner had they collected themselves to defend against the Cossacks and guardsmen, but the imperial forces from below made it to the rough ground directly in front of them.

The ensuing battle was a scene of violence, cacophony, clashing sabers, screams of men impaled on pikes or suffering loss of limbs or deadly abdominal and chest stabbings. An objective observer–had there been one–would have been at a loss to follow the struggle and to come to a conclusion regarding winners and losers. The course of the battle moved up and down the mountain side and the valley and laterally across and up the mountain walls.

Boris screamed orders at his men to hold the line and to remain disciplined. They did so even without his added orders and demands. Slowly the Ottoman forces began to dwindle down and to form small groups of desperate soldiers fighting for their lives. The pincers of Cossacks, guardsmen, and regular imperial army officers and men ground the knots of courageous Ottomans into the bloody earth. The world there was hellish with the screams of men and horses being wounded and killed. There was a stench of fresh blood, gun smoke, and terror.

Boris sighted a horseman he recognized as one of the tzar's court who had come ostensibly to be an observer but was now besieged by Bashi-bazouks intent on mutilating him. He was beginning to falter, and shortly fell to the ground when his horse died of spear thrusts. A dozen Bashi-bazouk scimitars raised above his head, ready to end the aristocrat's existence. Boris on Kryzhu and Vlad on his horse rode into the screaming irregulars like freight trains. The horses trampled most of the attackers as they passed through them. The Bashi-bazouks with their threatening scimitars ran from the Russian aristocrat and tried to match might and killing power with the Cossack sabers. They were overwhelmed in less than a minute. Boris and Vlad leapt from their horses and executed the few Bashi-bazouks still showing signs of life.

Boris hurried to reassure the terrified tzarist bureaucrat and would-be adventurer. It was glaringly apparent that he had soiled himself, adding humiliation to his fear and now overwhelming relief.

Boris said, "Allow me to present myself, Sir. I am General mayor Prince Boris Nikolaiovich Yusupov at your service. You are now safe and under my protection and that of my superlative Cossack officer, Vlad."

Vlad saluted and said to the aristocrat in his Kuban language, "It is my pleasure, Sir."

"I can never thank you enough, Prince Yusupov. I presume that you are of *the* House of Yusupov?"

"I have the honor to be the first son of Prince Nikolai Borisovich Yusupov."

"I am Alfred, Hereditary Prince of Sax-Coburg and Gotha, and first cousin of his majesty the tzar."

He extended his gloved hand to Boris, and they shook hands as if they were old friends or even family members who had not seen each other in years. Boris was awestruck. It occurred to him—in all humility— that this incident might well be a major stepping stone in his developing career, to say the least.

Boris and Vlad assisted the thoroughly frightened and much chastened great prince back to the main encampment at the mouth of the valley and saw to it that the man was able to rest in a sumptuous tent until the end of the battle.

Then, the two men raced back up the valley to reengage in the still ongoing vicious fray. Saving the great prince enlivened Boris and gave him a new infusion of energy he would not have imagined he would be able to summon. He and Vlad led their cavalrymen and infantrymen into the thick of the battle hacking and slashing with lethal efficiency. Finally, the enemy's center broke; and the completely defeated and disheartened Ottomans and their assortment of irregulars fled in all directions.

Boris and the other imperial officers staved off a complete massacre and managed to save a significant minority of the enemy combatants as POWs. Many of them were clearly worthy of large ransoms—enough to pay for the Russian costs in the battle. The battle and the Russian-Romanian victory was decisive enough for Russia to obtain the complete capitulation of the garrison, to decide the outcome of the short war, and to result in the liberation of Bulgaria. Russia was able to wrench a province of Bulgaria for the tzar out of the surrender agreement.

CHAPTER TWENTY-ONE

POSSIBLE YUSUPOV CONNECTION

"Challenges, failures, defeats, and ultimately
failure, are what makes your life worthwhile."
—Maxime Lagacé,
Quotes Amigo, 2018

**National Archives of Australia, Victorian Archives Centre,
99 Shiel Street, North Melbourne, Victoria, Australia,
January 8, 2014**

It had been a long cold day for summer. It had rained the night before, and the sky was still full of mist and clouds. The air felt damp. Yesterday, it had been hot. The changeable weather reminded all the missionaries of the Rocky Mountain West where change was the rule. This was the best time of day—lunch—when they could shed some of the formality of their missionary duties and become more themselves and more like a group of friends. None of them even thought of breaking the mission rule against calling each other by first names, but lunches were somewhat more relaxed anyway.

Sister Taylor was feeling nostalgic.

She looked up and said, "You know brothers and sisters, it seems like we've been here a long time. I am feeling kind of lonely for home and the grand kids and my little garden."

Sister Clyde gave Sister Taylor a little side shoulder hug and soothed her, "Try not to think of it. You'll be back in—what is it?—three or four months, and everything will be right back to normal."

"I know. Maybe it's just the low-pressure weather. I'll get over it."

"I think it would help if we could make some progress towards learning more about our mysterious Alexandra. I feel kind of stuck," said Sister Durrell.

"OMG!" blurted Elder Smith, "I da..darn near forgot."

The others laughed, and he blushed.

"It's one of my many faults," he said, "sometimes it just slips out. The way we handle that around our house we learned from our littlest granddaughter Anna Bella. I said a naughty word one time, and she looked at me very sternly and said, 'Granpa, we don't say that. We say, 'oh my goood—ness'"

He mimicked the little girl's voice perfectly and made them all laugh.

"So, I feel apologetic if I even use initials like OMG which can be considered to be like taking the Lord's name in vain. I even quit saying darn and shoot."

They all laughed again; the experience sounded very much like their own.

"Okay, Elder Smith, confession time is over. You sounded like you had some real news to share and was mad that you had almost forgotten."

"That's right, I do have a little something. All you brothers and sisters have been focusing on our Alexandra; so, I worked on finding some material on her possible husband in Russia. I researched under Yusupov, and that proved to be difficult because there was so much information on them; they were a very rich and very famous back in the day. What was difficult was finding much about any Yusupov who married a woman named Alexandra, or Tarasova, or who had had much to do with Vladivostok where we know that Alexandra was born.

"I found two things. I looked into the Yusupov family tree—which goes back at least to the ninth century in Turkey. I concentrated on the period of time when a son might have been born into the primary family, that of Prince Nikolai, Prince Boris's father. I looked under Prince Nikolai "Niki" Borisovich Yusupov and his mother Countess Tatiana Alexandrovna de Ribeaupierre. The family tree listed the issue from that important couple with nine children, but no one who sounded like a likely candidate for anyone who might have been in Vladivostok any time when a marriage could have taken place, or at any time at all until I found a little something else; I'll tell you about that in a minute.

"There was mention of a Yusupov who attended the Imperial General Staff Academy in the mid-eighteen sixties. I do know for sure that he graduated with honors. I have a copy of his diploma which lists Prince Nikolai as his father. The graduate was named Boris, Prince Boris, to be exact. Now it is odd that Boris is not listed anywhere else by the family in any family activity or photo or as having done anything remarkable or even if he died.

"I did find small mentions in newspaper articles in Plovdiv and Sofia, Bulgaria. The two mentions were short and probably written by the same reporter for the Plovdiv *Vakhan* and the Sofia *La Bulgarie*. I got a good translation for the Plovdiv paper's account. I'll read it: "The heroic victory on 10 December, 1877, which ended the Siege of Plevna and was decisive in the Russian victory over the heathen Ottmans, was won by Tzar Alexander II, Grand Duke Nicolas, Eduard Totleben, and Mikhail Sokobelev from the Russian Imperial Army, and Prince Carol of Romania for the Christians and civilization over the Ottoman Osman Nuri Pasha. The Grand Duke gave credit for his part in the battle and in particular for the saving of Alfred, Hereditary Prince of Sax-Coburg and Gotha, and first cousin of His majesty the tzar to General mayor Boris Yusupov.'

"The next maybe pertinent finding was also a newspaper statement from the Vladivostok Far Eastern, Russia newspaper—called the *Vladivostok*—that a new commandant by the name of Yusupov was named for Balagansk Prison. There is nothing more about this person or any interaction with anyone else, particularly our Alexandra. That is the sum and substance of everything I could find."

"I'd say that was quite a lot, Elder Smith," said Elder Durrell. "Gives us something to work with."

It was P-day again; the weeks seemed to be rushing by as they always do to senior citizens. As per their usual practice, the missionaries headed back into the city center to continue their pleasant day off and to further their knowledge of their mission field city. This time they took in the Athaeneum Theater and Library, the Black Arcade—which required some coaxing on the part of the men to break their wives away from the bargains—and on to the beautiful Carlton Gardens. They took the short tour through the small and simple Church of St. Francis, which was pleasing to their frugal tastes and which they enjoyed more than they did the magnificence of St. Paul's Cathedral. They wandered around in the City Museum and finished up in City Square with an agreement to meet in front of Cook's Cottage. They had a late lunch on the adventurous side at the Hanabishi Restaurant largely because it was not expensive. Also, none of them had ever eaten Japanese food; but they were game to try. They shared plates and bowls of hagi kimo, miso soup, unagi sushi, and California rolls. They passed up the cute little glasses of chilled sake—no alcohol for Mormon missionaries.

CHAPTER TWENTY-TWO

HOW THE MIGHTY HAVE FALLEN

"Nothing is so painful to the human mind as a great
and sudden change."
—Mary Shelley, *Frankenstein*, 1818

Headquarters 1st Cavalry Brigade, Horse Guard Regiment, Moscow, Russia, May 19, 1879

The first year after Boris's both heroic and serendipitous victory in the Battle of Plevna, was filled with military parades, balls, accolades, and gradual entrance into the meetings and confidence of the Imperial General Staff. He was becoming one of them, even being able to express an opinion now and then. He was all but adopted into the family of Alfred, Hereditary Prince of Sax-Coburg and Gotha, and first cousin of his majesty the tzar. The second year was largely the same, except that the absence of any military crisis made the demand for Prince Boris's services or presence diminish. Invitations to the luminaries' homes dwindled even to that of Prince Alfred and his overweight wife and his godfather, Grand Duke Paul Alexandrovich's palace. He found himself settling into the languor of guardsman life—cards, dinners, parades, and vapid interactions with local dignitaries. As one of his officer friends put it, "The Russian Military has become nothing more than generals, admirals, and bands."

Boris all but got on his knees to pray for another little war where he could shake off the ennui he was feeling and could get the blood coursing through his veins as he led troops into battle. That feeling was short lived owing to events beyond his control.

In October, 1879, the Land and Liberty insurgent group split into two factions. The majority of members favored a policy of terrorism, and established the People's Will, the most radical anarchy and revolution group in the empire. The People's Will planned to assassinate Tzar Alexander II. In November Prince Boris's old associates, including Sophia Perovskaya, Andrei Zhelyabov, Gesia Gelfman, Nikolai Sablin, Ignatei Grinevitski, Nikolai Kibalchich, Nikolai Rysakov and Timofei Mikhailov, Andrei Zhelyabov, and Sophia Perovskaya made the first attempt on the moderate-leaning tzar's life. Andrei and Sophia drew the short straws and were assigned to the assassination. The two radicals used nitroglycerine to destroy the Tzar Train. They made an historical mistake; they blew up the wrong train. The People's Will attempted to blow up the Kamenny Bridge in St. Petersburg as the Tzar was passing over it. Again, the bumblers were unsuccessful.

The attempts were reported in every newspaper in the empire. The newspaper articles took pains to add that the tzar was infuriated and planned a nationwide dragnet to find the culprits. The Okhrana swung into action and mercilessly hunted down every member of the People's Will and the Land and Liberty faction and questioned them by "all means necessary". The torture brought out dozens of more names of insurgents, hangers-on, sympathizers, and possible co-conspirators.

The name of General mayor Prince Boris Nikoliavitch Yusupov rose to the surface because of his careless of choice of roommates when he was a young student in the General Staff Academy. Seventeen people were arrested, including Boris's former roommate Alexander Soloviev, and were executed by hanging for terrorism the following month.

Boris was relieved that he had cut his ties with his old roommates a long time ago and would not be listed as a subject of interest or any kind of sympathizer. His relief was reassured by his memory of his serious conversation with Academy Commandant, General mayor Ivan Dragorovich Strabinsky, in May, 1871 on the evening of his graduation. That conversation had ended any possible suspicion of his complicity in even sympathy with the anarchists. He was sure of that. To punctuate that thought, the terror around the country seemed to calm down to the point that he no longer heard talk of it.

His quietude and relief from anxiety were premature and ended one evening a week later when the headquarters sergeant-major informed him that his father, Prince Nikolai, was waiting for him in the headquarters building.

"Hello, Father. To what do I owe the pleasure of this surprise visit?" Boris asked the grand patriarch of the Yusupov House.

"I will get right to the point, Son. I'm afraid that the visit is not for pleasure. I have been given the opportunity by way of irregular channels to inform you of a problem you have and a potential solution."

Boris blanched as he watched the solemnity of his father turn to sadness. "What is it?"

"You, no doubt, are aware of the recent attack on the tzar's life by the very people he thought would be most pleased by his economic and agrarian reforms."

"Of course."

"I presume that you are also aware that your former roommate, Alexander Soloviev and companions Sophia Perovskaya and Andrei Zhelyabov were involved, and Soloviev was hanged for his part in the plot."

"Yes, but what has that to do with me? I cut all ties with the lot of them long ago."

"Unfortunately, the tzar's wrath, and the Okhrana's witch hunt knows no limitations. Any association with any of any of the conspirators however minor, long ago, or unintentional, makes one dangerously suspect. During their interrogations—which I understand were quite thorough—your name came up as one of their associates and as one of the followers of that fool, Bakunin. That was enough for the Okhrana. Because of your family name, General mayor Strabinsky was dispatched to convey the message to me. You are declared persona non-grata, and only your name and military record save you from prison. The General mayor has come up with a plan–hopefully temporary—to save you. You must act immediately."

"I will do whatever you instruct, Father. I cannot imagine that anyone would actually suspect me of disloyalty to the tzar or could think that I would participate in such a heinous act as an attempted assassination."

"Be that as it may, my boy, and despite the fact that I haven't the slightest doubt about your loyalty to the tzar and to our family, the Okhrana rules the country at the moment. This is what you must do: Speak to no one. Pack your belongings and board the first trans-Siberian train for Vladivostok [Rus. Ruler of the East—located closer to Beijing than to Moscow, administrative center of Primorsky Krai, Russia, located around the Golden Horn Bay]. A telegram will be waiting for you to inform you of your new orders. I am assured that you will retain your rank, but you must not communicate with the general staff or the family for a year. Under no circumstances should you try to contact anyone in the tzar's family, not even your godfather. Do not try and explain yourself to the general staff: that would be tantamount to a confession. Be patient. I will continue to send you an allowance, but we must arrange clandestine sites for you to receive my help. Go with God; stay strong."

Boris was stupefied. He could only bid his father farewell and to ask him to convey his love to the rest of the family. He knew he had been duly warned; and by the next day, he, his trusted servants, Vlad, his horses, and two train car loads of essential personal property left by train for Far East Russia—a three or four-week transit of Siberia.

CHAPTER TWENTY-THREE

A NEW-WORLD AND A NEW LIFE

"When you dance with the devil, the devil
doesn't change. The devil changes you."
—Amanda Hocking,
Quote Fancy, 2018

Jardine-Matheson and Tarasova Fur Company Headquarters and Trading Center, No. 71 Svetlanskaya Street, Vladivostok, Russia, June 22, 1879

Nineteen-year-old Alexandra returned from Shanghai from her first voyage as captain of the brigantine *Far East Transporter*, one of the sixteen commercial ships of the Jardine-Matheson and Tarasova Far Eastern Russia Trading Company. She was the second woman and the youngest person ever to command a Jardine-Matheson vessel and among the most profitable of the ships' captains. Male captains all along the South China Sea coast grudgingly acknowledged her proficiency behind the wheel, at the navigation table, and in the centers of commerce—ship to ship, in trading company board rooms, and in the counting sheds. It was even rumored that she had been given high praise by the Red Flag pirate admiral, Zheng Shi, despite her tender age.

"Greetings, Captain!" her father Abram exclaimed for everyone to hear and gave her an exuberant bear hug.

She grunted as he squeezed out her breath, and barely managed to whisper, "Glad to be back."

He put his arm around her shoulders and led her to his office in the headquarters warehouse.

"Show me the profit and expense figgers," he requested without further welcoming ceremony.

The company ledgers for the voyage were altogether positive, one of the most lucrative voyages in the company's history, a fact that made the grizzled sixty-year-old beam with pride and satisfaction. Both were aware that they could count as good commercial fortune that they had not lost cargo and ship to the still powerful Red Flag Fleet.

"Well, my girl, you have earned your keep with this one. Let's get up to the house and let your mother spoil you for a few days."

Irina Ishmaelovna Inkijinoff Tarasova was standing at the top of the stairs of the Tarasova mansion as Abram and Alexandra drew up in the family carriage. In the past three years, the family's fortunes and status had enjoyed a stratospheric climb. The elegant Pekinskaya Street Russian Renaissance Revival style wood mansion was one of four grand homes in the city. From the newly paved street, it had a clean lined two-story façade and a hidden basement. From the courtyard, the façade was three stories high. The outer walls were decorated with a granite base, three balconies, and two ornate cast-iron porches. The façade was ornately decorated with filigreed wood designs applied to transverse hardwood slats. The inside the mansion was ornate to the point of being gaudy— the pretentiousness of the nouveau riche as the family's detractors carped. The house was fitted with the latest in engineering technology, which included a hollow space under the floor into which hot air was sent for heating a room or bath to circulate hot air, running water, and indoor bathrooms with chain flush handles. It was Irina's pride and claim to fame, and Abram's symbol of his success in the competitive commercial world of the Irkutsk oblast.

Even the carriage and its handsome horses testified of the wealth and influence of the Tarasova family. The carriage was a phaeton imported from France, a light vehicle with a folding roof decorated with an ostentations gilded family herald drawn by three white draft horses. Alexandra loved every bit of the display of the family riches and was determined to keep the family at a financial level above the commoners. She determined to live to see the day when the Tarasova family's name would be ranked along with the Romanovs, the Yusupovs, the Sheremetevs, the Golitsyns, the Stroganovs, and the Tcherkasskys. In her young mind–at least–the Tarasovas were well on their way.

Irina and Alexandra were both vivacious and exuberant women. They raced to each other and embraced enthusiastically with loud 'welcomes', 'overjoyed', 'thrilled to have you back safe', and 'it's wonderful to be able to embrace you, Dear'. Irina took one arm and Abram took the other, and they waltzed into the marble-floored lobby of Tarasova House.

The family enjoyed a magnificent dinner and the music of a Russian symphony orchestra that had sailed from Moscow to entertain the coastal cities of the empire and those of the Russian allies—China, Chosŏn, and even Japan. Alexandra fell into her bed too tired even to remove her clothes that night.

The next day–instead of taking her well-deserved rest–Alexandra began planning her next, and most ambitious commercial voyage thus far. After breakfast with the family and enduring the latest in lectures from her doting mother about her need to find a suitable marriageable young man or else she was going to suffer the ignominy of being an old maid; after all, she was already nineteen and pushing the age limit of being nubile and looking at adulthood as an unmarried career woman— something unacceptable in polite Russian society.

She wore practical business clothing and had the family chauffer and her personal body guard—the massive Don Cossack, Stenka Mazepa– take her to Millionka—the Chinese quarter. Millionka was a slum from its creation and remained dangerous. The rich and beautiful carriage bearing the iconic Tarasova herald, the presence of the forbidding Cossack, and above all, the favorite Russian of all those who entered the Chinese quarter—Alexandra Tarasovna—made the carriage's passage at least marginally safe. The implied threat of retribution by the Russian navy, the city's Cossacks, and least of all, but still of some significance, the Vladivostok constabulary added to the margin of security for the slender patrician girl.

Her destination was Number 19 Admirala Fokina street, home and business center of the leader of the Three Families Tong, Hou [lord or nobleman] Eadric [wealthy monarch], a name he chose for himself when he gained power in the tong—much more significant that his humble birth name Chen Xiao Ming. There was nothing particularly striking about the tong leader's house; it was much like the rest of the seedy red brick buildings with their archways, balconies and nooks, and crannies where secrets thrived. Millionka—a labyrinth of narrow alleyways–was the original gathering center for Chinese traders who opened their shops for the sale of food, cloth, clothing, trinkets, religious icons, and Chinese medicines for both the Chinese who lived there and the transient soldiers and sailors. During the latter years of the nineteenth century, there were a great many Chinese—as many as 50,000 to perhaps even 100,000— and another 10,000 Chosŏns crammed into a physical area no larger than two city blocks in a major American city.

The presence of so many Chinese, Chosŏns, and Japanese is understandable when it is realized that Vladivostok is about one hundred miles from the borders of China, Chosŏn, and Japan. Late in the century permanent red brick homes were built. Most businesses were operated out of portions of the living quarters. The quarter was known for its bustling discount commerce, but was notorious for its plethora of opium dens, brothels catering to all tastes, and ornate gambling halls. In all practicality, Chinese tongs had total control in the quarter—making it essentially a nest of crime. Police came there only in the greatest rarity.

Alexandra came to Millionka for the same reason most Russian gentry did: to solidify a criminal enterprise. Others came to enjoy the wickedness for themselves, but Alexandra had no interest in any of that. Her purpose was money.

The massive Don Cossack, Stenka Mazepa was very hesitant about entering Number 19, a dilapidated red brick building on a poorly maintained street.

"Missy," he said, "maybe we not to go in here. Not safe."

"Not to worry, Stenka, I am known here, and they want to do business with me. Be calm, I will protect you," she said with a laugh he did not share.

He looked down at the petite, clean, well dressed princess of a girl and said, "I exist for you. At least have it be I who goes in first. Who know what evil lurks here."

She laughed gently, fond of his caring for her, but she was not to be dissuaded. She gave a short nod towards the door, and Stenka straightened his shoulders and walked to the heavy teak door and rapped on the door knocker.

A small window in the door opened briefly.

A stern oval shaped eye looked out, and a guttural voice asked, "What wanted here, *Báirén fùnǚ?*"

Alexandra and Stenka ignored the slightly disrespectful characterization of her as a white woman.

"To see important leader, Hou Eadric, who has requested our presence for the purpose of doing business."

"Wait," the faceless voice ordered in gruff Mandarin.

Five minutes later, the door opened, and a small Chinese man stepped out and greeted Alexandra and Stenka, bowed deeply, and said, *"Zao"*

Alexandra responded respectfully with, *"Nín hǎo"* and bowed even more deeply than Hou Eadric.

He nodded, and asked, *"M chī le ma?"*

Alexandra replied before the more fluent Stenka could caution her, "No, thank you, I have already eaten a fine Chinese breakfast."

She was taken aback when the haughty little man began to laugh almost uncontrollably. She looked at Stenka for guidance.

He whispered, *"Nǐ chī le ma,* is just a formality like *Nín hǎo.* When he asks, 'have you eaten?' he just means it as if he were saying good morning as he said when he first spoke."

"Oh," she said and blushed."

Hou Eadric wiped his eyes, and smiled benevolently, at least as benevolently as his battle-scarred and habitually austere face could manage.

He looked her over carefully.

She did the same with him. The man was a little over five feet tall, slender with long fingers and very long painted fingernails. He wore lipstick, more than she did. He had long greying hair and an unruly long mustache and beard made his already almost skeletal face even thinner. His clothing seemed anachronistic, something out of the old Qing dynasty: a slightly A-line Manchu *Changshan* blue silk robes with a square green silk emblem sewn to the front, and a shaved head with a long queue hanging down his back which made him look like an almost comic opera throwback.

Then, he swept his right arm with a long wide ornate silk sleeve as a grand gesture for the two to enter what he called his "humble home". It was certainly that. Alexandra was glad that she had not eaten a large breakfast. It might well have come back up as they entered the large dark front room.

CHAPTER TWENTY-FOUR

BIG BUSINESS IN MILLIONKA

"Beauty is mysterious as well as terrible. God and devil
are fighting there, and the battlefield is the heart of man."
—Fyodor Dostoevsky,
The Brothers Karamazov, 1879

Number 19 Admirala Fokina Street, Chinatown, Vladivostok, Russia, June 23, 1879

The entryway of the great leader of the Three Families Tong,
would have been expected to be at least as grand as the Tarasova
mansion on Pekinskaya Street. That expectation died the instant
Alexandra and Stenka stepped foot onto the dirt floor. It was a veritable
miasma, strewn with clutter, organic garbage, dog and human excrement.
The stench was a noxious mix of feces, urine, opium smoke, alcohol
vomitus, dirt, marsh gas, and soot. Alexandra did her best not to wretch
or to put her handkerchief over her nose and mouth.

Chinese men and women—mostly elderly with drooping eyelids
and sick looking—lay around on low couches puffing on opium pipes.
A crowd of younger men and women—mostly looking dirty and
dissolute—sat around mahjong and gambling tables. There seemed to
be a requirement that the gambler had to start drunk and get drunk
enough to topple off his or her chair before he could leave the table.
The room's small cheap glass windows were covered with soot; so, no
light could get in. They were scattered around the walls with no plan for

either utilitarian or esthetic value. The room had low ceilings, and the sound of rats skittering along the beams could not be missed. Patrons and onlookers were served with small ceramic porcelain cups of weak tea or *Báijiŭ* [cheap Chinese vodka].

Alexandra determined to limit her stay in that hellish place to no more than a quarter of an hour lest she and Stenka come down with some exotic disease. He kept his eyes stoically forward, but he had to wipe the tears from the sting of the miasmic air from his eyes frequently. The only light in the Stygian room came from a dozen or so smoky candles scattered around the room haphazardly.

Hou Eadric walked briskly, robes dragging the dirt floor behind him creating small puffs of vile smelling dust. He had an unreadable flat expression, as devoid of communication as bing bread. He did not appear to take any notice of the scents wafting around him or of the collection of human dross and refuse he had to sidestep to make his way through the room. He never looked back to see if the young aristocratic girl or her menacing body guard were following him.

He led them out into a courtyard which was as different from the room they left behind as the paintings Russian monks made to distinguish heaven and hell.

"This is the Garden of Heaven," Hou said and bade them to sit on one of the stone benches lining a lovely clear manmade waterfall whose waters flowed into a small pond covered with large lily pads and in which large golden koi swam languorously about.

Hou's piece of heaven held all the elements of a classical 3,000-year-old Chinese garden: water, architecture, vegetation, and rocks, all placed and tended with assiduous care. The Garden of Heaven was enclosed by stone walls and had two ponds which looked like they had been placed there by Shàngdì–the Lord on High–imported rock works, a faux mountain, trees and flowers, and an assortment of small halls and pavilions within the garden, connected by winding paths and zig-zag galleries. By moving from structure to structure, visitors could view a series of carefully composed scenes, unrolling like a scroll of landscape water color paintings. The galleries or seasonal pavilions included a Pavilion of Mandarin Ducks open to allow cool air during the summer, and a pavilion for viewing autumn foliage. There were sections facing south, toward a pine tree-filled courtyard and plum trees. The time of plum trees coming into blossom heralds spring.

The garden—in stark contrast to the hellish interior of the house—had a light scent of lavender, *dama de noche*—night blooming jasmine—and honeysuckle. It was a delightful, tranquil place to do business with a murderous pirate.

"I have done business with your father Abram and his partners, Jardine, Matheson, even with the taipan himself. Why have you come, young one?"

"My father wishes me to handle the business with the Three Families Tong. I speak fluent Mandarin; I have commanded ships and have made many successful commercial voyages for the company; and I have fought Zhèng Yi and Ching Shih of the Red Flag Fleet and won. Not to boast, but I can command men, strike a hard bargain; and I can protect my ships, their cargoes, and my men. They will obey my slightest command. I wish to arrive at a contract with you."

She said it all with a serene poker face which belied her youth and aristocratic demeanor.

Hou could not resist a small smile of incredulity. He looked at Stenka Mazepa, the formidable Cossack, for confirmation. The stone-faced body guard nodded his acknowledgment of his young charge's statements. He was not accustomed to being considered a liar, and his entire demeanor conveyed his intention to defend his honor.

"I am most impressed. What does your esteemed father, Abram, have in mind?"

"That I be regarded by you as you would him. I will never cheat you, lie to you, or cause you to doubt the wisdom of doing business with me as an equal. That is my father's wish; and from now on, we will do our business together. I will report to him, but he will leave the decisions and negotiations to me. Are we to do business?"

Hou paused and did a little mental tallying. The girl demonstrated the qualities valued by the Chinese; she was careful to save and to give face; she showed respect to him as an elder; she was patient, polite, and modest. She also had an inner core of courage and toughness. He—of course—was well versed in her brave exploits.

He said, "It is agreed."

Then he abruptly left the garden and returned to the odious main room of his house.

Alexandra gave Stenka a quizzical look.

He said, "Hou will honor a fair contract. It is not done to sign a paper to guarantee a contract upon completing face-to-face meeting. To do so would indicate a lack of trust and would result in a loss of face from you and by him. You have succeeded. Expect a written and detailed contract to be delivered to your house within the week. You have a partner. Be careful. For all of his politeness and culture he would cut your throat for a round hole coin."

Alexandra and Stenka left the Garden of Heaven at Number 19 Admirala Fokina Street via a nearly hidden exit through the garden wall and found themselves back in the teeming throngs of coolies, sailors, beggars, and cutpockets. The narrow streets were like the bottom of a canyon, the walls of which were lined with three story theaters, taverns, gambling houses, opium dens, and more than a few flagrant brothels. Hawkers, jinrickshaw pullers, three-ball and cup enticers, and scores of scarred, battered, and threatening men—the scum of the earth—chanced to look at Alexandra with wickedness in their eyes. Those glances immediately vanished when they saw the giant Caucasian who gently held the girl's delicate arm. He was armed with a Turkish saber, a thick Bowie knife from America, a brace of flintlock pistols, and a double-barreled musket slung loosely across his huge chest. No one considered it to be worth his while to take a chance with the behemoth.

They boarded the Tarasova carriage whose driver had waited with infinite patience until they returned and looked very relieved to have them back under his care and keeping. He avoided Chinatown as often as he could and was glad to be quit of it now.

Late that evening, a coolie rapped on the door of Tarasova House, No. 71 Pekinskaya Street. Because it was late and highly unusual for anyone–let alone a ragged coolie–to call at the fur magnate's residence, two powerfully built and heavily armed Buryats answered the knock on the great doors.

"No beggars," the two Buryats said at the same time.

"So, solly, great sirs, I have not come with hands out."

He presented his hands palms up and palms down to indicate that he did not have a weapon. The hands were filthy, and his long, fingernails were grimy and repugnant, the result of an energetic avoidance of bathing, probably lifelong. He had a strange fashion anomaly–Saint Stanislaus and Saint Anne–second class medals attached to his ragged overblouse.

"I bear important paper for the missy. Please to bring her to me. Thanking you bery much."

"What is 'missy's name that you have the audacity to talk with, *tiān gōu bàilèi*?"

If being called 'gutter scum' bothered the coolie, he made no indication that it did. In all probability, he had been called that and worse in his time. What he did care about was getting paid; and the instructions from the great tong leader, Hou Eadric, were explicit. Give the document into the hands of the girl called, Alexandra, explain who sent it, and leave. He was told to have the girl meet Hou the following day with the parchment bearing her signature or sign at the Chin Wang Café on Ocean Avenue at noon. Failure, he knew meant no pay and probably worse. It gave him courage.

"Is Alexandra of the family Yusupov, great sirs. It is most serious. You are asked to let her know that I am here, and she will come at once. That is what my instructions say. Please, kind sirs. Take pity on a poor man who must do small things to keep his belly full. I mean no trouble."

The two Buryats nodded. One stayed with the raggedy bag of bones with the long, greasy queue. The other trotted quickly to Alexandra's room.

"Missy, there is a poor man at the entrance who says he has important business that you will want to see. Shall I just send the beggar away?"

"No, Omar. I will see him. I know what this is about. I will follow you to the front door."

The coolie bowed obsequiously, effusively, and frequently.

"I am honored greatly, great princess. I am instructed that I am to give what I carry to you without others being present."

Alexandra smiled at her Buryats and waved them back inside the house.

"Let me see," she said.

He reached into the front of his tunic and pulled out a parchment which was protected with a spotless linen cloth. She examined it closely, signed her name, and lit the wick to heat the burgundy sealing wax. When she had exactly the right amount of wax, at exactly the right consistency, she pressed it with the stamp which affixed the Tarasova seal.

"This will do," she said imperiously. "Tell Master Hou that I will meet him tomorrow as you instructed. Please take care to keep this paper clean and unwrinkled and take it directly the leader."

He did as she said and vanished back into the darkness.

Alexandra studied the contract very, very carefully until the early hours of the day and decided it was all legally correct and binding. It was a contract which held promise of great mutual wealth, and it could have been interpreted by a critic as being very near if not over the line of legality. She knew she had just signed a pact with the devil.

CHAPTER TWENTY-FIVE

BALAGANSK

"When we least expect it, life sets us a challenge to test our courage and willingness to change; at such a moment, there is no point in pretending that nothing has happened or in saying that we are not yet ready. The challenge will not wait. Life does not look back. A week is more than enough time for us to decide whether or not to accept our destiny."

—Paulo Coelho, *The Devil and Miss Prym,*
A Novel of Temptation, 2000

Balagansk Penitentiary, Irkutsk Oblast, Far East Russia, July 28, 1879

The *Vladivostok* newspaper carried an announcement important to the government of the Irkutsk oblast and to its society in general, especially to the Russians exiled to Siberia and the Far East. The formal announcement came from the administrative center in Irkutsk.

"Tzar Alexander II and governor of the Irkutsk Krai, announce a change of command in the Balagansk District and Penitentiary to take place 12 August, 1879. The current commandant, Major Nikita Sergeivich Yestremsky, will turn over his command to General mayor Boris Nikolaiovich Yusupov. Major Yestremsky will assume a post in the Imperial

Military Academy in Novonikolaevsk. We take pleasure in General mayor Yusupov's appointment. He is the hero of the Bulgarian campaign some years ago. The changing-of-the-guard ceremony is open to the public. Proper dress is required."

–Signed,

Altan Oyuunchimeg
Altan Oyuunchimeg
Governor, Irkutsk Krai,
28 July, 1879

Alexandra was excited by the news. Significant social events were infrequent in Far East Russia; and this might promise to be exciting, she thought to herself. She was pleased when her father and mother both announced that the entire Tarasova family would attend along with other oblast dignitaries. For Alexandra and her brothers–Veniamin and Valéry Abramovich–it would be a chance to get dressed up in formal finery and to see a genuine Russian hero. Father Abram considered it to be an indicator of Vladivostok and the Irkutsk oblast's coming of age. Mother Irina was determined to make hers and her families presence stand out above the rest of the Oblast society.

The weather was beautiful—bright sun, healthy green grasses, and white birch trees owing to the ample winter snows and spring rains, and no hint of rain or high winds in the near future. Anticipation was high.

Balagansk Penitentiary, Irkutsk Oblast, Far East Russia, July 29, 1879

Boris and his small retinue of servants and guards arrived in the small and out-of-the-way township midmorning. In truth–it was barely a town–more a work camp built to serve the needs of its principle enterprise, the Balagansk prison. The only well-built structures in the camp were the penitentiary itself, the commandant's residence, a commissary open to soldiers and prison officials and their families, a fine boy's school built two years earlier to ensure that the boys and young men learned Christianity and western civilized traditions—at least the

Russian definition of those important areas of learning–and a regional post office. The remainder of the buildings were basically log huts which served as dwellings for the lower classes, a road side inn and restaurant which barely deserved to be labeled as such, and a Russian Orthodox church and monastery which served not only the spiritual needs of the faithful but as a detention center for ecclesiastical clerics who had found themselves at odds with the tzar's regime or not in keeping with any of the myriad of new rules instituted by Alexander II for his church. The best building of this poor lot was a large log structure which served as the town administrative center. In the mid-late 1800s, thirty percent of the population of the oblast and of the city were political exiles.

There were no paved roads. The dirt roads were rutted and difficult to traverse in summer when they were dry, impossible to drive on in spring during the break-up from winter, and only comfortable in winter when troika travel was the preferred mode of transportation. Within the town, there did not seem to be any identifiable street plan and very few straight roads.

The prison itself had been thoroughly scrubbed and–where needed–repainted in preparation for Boris's arrival and for the change of command. The large grassy grounds were mowed and trimmed; bushes were shaped; and the cobble-stone main road and side paths were freshly painted white. The main prison building was not as grim as Boris had it expected it to be. It was devoid of artwork, ornamental mopboards or moldings, attractive furniture, or lighting fixtures; but it was clean, orderly, and appropriately functional. He agreed with outgoing commandant Major Nikita Sergeivich Yestremsky that the changing of the guard ceremonies should be held in the attractive garden area behind the main building.

On the appointed day, August 12, a surprisingly large and well-dressed audience of citizens appeared from around the huge territory of the oblast. Many of those attending included indigenous (native Buryat) citizens often not considered to be on the same social plane as the Russians. Most of the Russians were there because of having been exiled, and more than a few had once been internees in Balagansk Prison and had served their terms except for having to live out their lives in either Siberia or Far Eastern Russia as the final ignominy of their disgrace and expulsion from society in the west.

Abram and Irina Tarasova and their children—Alexandra, and her two brothers, Veniamin and Valéry—were accorded a special welcome and ushered to the head table where the senior military and political officials were seated. The morning was becoming overly warm, and mosquitos began to annoy the guests. The mayor of Balagansk—Dashiin Dorzhiev–left his seat and went into the prison building to get the program underway with more dispatch.

Twenty minutes later, the regiment of imperial army officers and enlisted men marched out of the rear door of the main prison building in full dress uniform. Led by their Major Yestremsky, they marched in front of the cheering crowd, saluted the dignitaries, and took their place on the right side of the raised stand holding the important members of Irkutsk– the administrative city–and the lesser cities of Vladivostok, Biryusinsk, Nizhneudinsk, Usolye-Sibirskoye, Zheleznogorsk-Ilimsky, and a dozen other smaller towns. A bugle sounded charge from the south side of the building and a company of Cossack and regular army cavalry raced into the opening shouting war cries and unit mottos. Resplendent at the head of the cavalry was General mayor Prince Boris Nikolaiovich Yusupov on his magnificent stallion, Kryzhu.

Kryzhu had a Cossack banner and an Imperial Russian flag attached to his saddle and streaming out behind him as he and Boris galloped to make their dramatic entry. Boris was in full dress battle uniform of Cossack cavalry with his full complement of medals shining in the summer sunshine. He was imperially slim in his perfectly fitting dark blue trousers with two scarlet stripes on the sides, a mid-thigh length scarlet tunic with white cross straps holding his dagger and his cavalry sword and an under blouse of blue. Around his waist, he wore a gold belt matching the trimming of the tunic's cuffs, collar, and edges. He had on a Cossack fur hat, denoting his allegiance to the Don Cossacks and his general's insignia, medals, and imperial army emblem on his fur cap showing his full loyalty as a soldier of the tzar. He wore highly polished knee-high black riding boots. In his right hand, he carried a long wooden lance with an ornate steel spear point. In his left, he held Kryzhu's reins.

The reins, saddle, and saddle blanket, were scarlet lined with gold, giving him something of the appearance of a medieval knight approaching a joust. His impressive set of medals and awards–Saint Stanislaus and Saint Anne—second class medals—Cross of Saint George, 3rd Class for gallantry in the Bulgarian war, and the Golden Sword of Honor for Valor—were a blaze of color, and the polished gold of the medals and the sword, glinted with almost blinding reflected sunlight.

Boris's cavalry column crossed in front of the audience from their right to their left—made a flourish—then dashed around the back of the stand holding the dignitaries. They raced once again across the open area between the dignitaries' stand and came to an abrupt halt with horses rearing. The bugler sounded about face, and the cavalry men on their snorting horses walked sedately into their position on the left side of the stand. Boris saluted sharply, moved his lance up and down, then let it rest with its butt on the ground.

After the dramatic entry, all eyes were on Prince Boris; one set in particular could not look away. Boris was a strikingly handsome man of Viking face, sinewy arms, and graceful build. He wore a beard that was the height of fashion—light brown with a hint of curl, a perfectly trimmed and waxed mustache with curled ends, and a goatee. His features were fine but sturdy with a straight small nose, tanned skin, piercing light-blue eyes, and a battle or dueling scar on his right cheek.

For all of her urbanity and worldly experience for such a young girl, nineteen-year-old Alexandra was awestruck by the dashing cavalry general. He was the most beautiful specimen of manhood she had ever seen. Her pulse and blood pressure climbed, and her face flushed.

She whispered to her mother, "That is the man I am going to marry, Mother."

Irina smiled indulgently.

"Yes, dear, he is a most impressive man. Maybe you should meet him first."

Alexandra laughed.

"That is my plan for the day. But, I tell you, Mother, he doesn't stand a chance."

When the ceremony was over, Prince Boris placed the medallion of office around his own neck; Major Yestremsky rode away into obscurity, not even waiting until after the sumptuous lawn luncheon. Prince Boris; the mayor of Balagansk, Dashiin Dorzhiev; the governor of the Irkutsk Oblast, Kolya Morozovich Smirnov; the mayor of Vladivostok, Vasily Aleksandrovitch Zhvanetsky; and the admiral of the imperial man-of-war, the *Lord of the North Seas*, Sergei Vladomirovich Mikhailov, milled about in the crowd, meeting and greeting. Representing the business community were Abram and Irina Tarasova.

Alexandra pushed herself to the front of the line of well-wishers and curtsied low to the Prince/General mayor. She beamed her most affable, alluring, and coquettish, smile, and looked the young general directly in his eyes. She was pleased to note that his eyes followed her as she walked down the line of dignitaries. She fell off script when she reached her parents at the opposite end of the line and stopped to take her place in the line—not at all something that a proper young woman should do. Her mother laughed, and Alexandra returned an impish grin.

Prince Boris was the major draw for the admiring crowd; but by her strategically chosen feminine wiles, Alexandra charmed most of the men, women, and children, in the line. When the last of the well-wishers passed by Alexandra bade them a fond farewell and a safe journey, leaving her and Boris standing alone.

Boris's attention was drawn to a small commotion among his horses. Alexandra took the opportunity to pinch her cheeks and to bite her lips to make them redder. Using a trick she learned from a Chinese courtesan in Shanghai, she surreptitiously reached into her bodice and gave each nipple a firm pinch, which resulted in the desired effect of making them stand out.

And just in time, because the soldier walked over to speak to her. He stammered a little, ashamed that he was acting like a young boy; and she found that it made him all the more charming. She was also pleased at the effect her facial and bodily efforts had on him. She almost laughed as she saw him reluctantly move his gaze to the area above her clavicles.

"My dear young lady," he said, and bowed his knee and body to her. She offered her hand, and he held it gently and kissed it.

She smiled and said, "Prince...General mayor...I am honored to meet you and very happy that you will be living here in the oblast."

"The honor is mine. I am sorry, but I was unable to learn your name. May I ask?"

"Of course, Sir. I am Alexandra Abramovna Tarasova. My father is Abram Timurovitch Tarasova, and my mother is Irina Ishmaelovna Inkijinoff Tarasova, daughter of Soiot Buryat knjaztsy Ishmael Bazarguruevitch and his wife, Yulia Bazarovna Inkijinoff."

"A Buryat prince and princess. I am humbled," Boris said without a hint of condescension.

"It is I who is humbled, Prince. I have studied you and your family. Not a great deal is written about you other than that you are a prince of the empire, that you are true military hero after the campaign in Bulgaria. Your family—the House of Yusupov—is renowned throughout the empire and, indeed, the world as the richest and most influential family next the tzars."

Boris became sober.

"Alexandra, I have a favor to ask, and one day I will tell you the reason for the favor. You are intelligent and wise to many of the ways of the world. You are familiar with the several reasons people are sent to Siberia and to the Far East and the main reason that the Balagansk Prison exists. We needn't discuss all of that overmuch. But please do not advertise abroad that I am one of that family or how I came to be transferred to this place. Can you understand that?"

It was Alexandra's turn to be sober and no longer the coquette.

"I do. I have lived with this kind of knowledge all my life. I have great sympathy for those of noble birth who must spend—waste—time in the prison and for all those who meet a fate worse than death to be sent to the frozen north and never to be heard from again. Your secret and any others you ever want to share are safe with me."

"You are not only lovely and bright, but I think noble. I hope our friendship will grow. To that end, would you and your parents do me the honor of dining with me in Balagansk this coming Friday."

"That would please me very much and no doubt my parents as well. I am more than flattered that you would consider me a friend."

Boris bowed again. Alexandra curtsied, and they went their separate ways. Boris's back was stiffened, and he tightened his abdominal wall to be sure no creeping fat could show. Alexandra unconsciously puffed out her already ample chest and felt like she was walking an inch above the ground.

CHAPTER TWENTY-SIX

A LITTLE MORE EVIDENCE

"And I know that the record which made is
true; and I make it with mine own hand;
and I make it according to my knowledge."
—*Book of Mormon, First Book of Nephi,*
Chapter 1:1, First English Edition 1830

National Archives of Australia, Victorian Archives Centre, 99 Shiel Street, North Melbourne, Victoria, Australia, January 22, 2014

The Secretary of the Department of Social Services of the Victoria Provincial Government met with Elder and Sister LaRen and Katherine Durrell at a small luncheon at the capitol. Mrs. Olive Hastings praised the work being done by the missionaries and by the church as being of inestimable value to Victoria Province and to the country.

After lunch, Mrs. Hastings asked, "Do you think it would be possible that your church and all of its remarkable abilities on the internet and genealogy efforts would be able to contract with the Australian government to expand the digitalization of all of the old records for the entire country?"

The Durrells were unprepared for such a major scale offer. Mrs. Hastings interpreted their pause to be reluctance.

"We, of course, could pay your church well for the efforts. We are certainly not asking for you to work as a charitable donation."

"Mrs. Hastings, we are flattered that you–acting as a representative of the government of Australia would think so highly of us that you would ask us to take on this very large assignment. You have to understand that Sister Durrell and I are minor cogs in a large machine that makes the Church of Jesus Christ of Latter-day Saints go, even as it pertains to the digitalization of records. It is an enormous work that is done for no cost to the people of the world for locating and correlating genealogy records.

"I can tell you this, though. The church is not known for doing contract work for anyone, but rather, makes contributions of the work it does when it pertains to the salvation of souls. We will seek the guidance of our priesthood leaders to see if anything can be done to further the record keeping work of the country."

"Thank you. In the meantime, is there anything we can do to hasten your work…to make it easier and more efficient?"

Elder Durrell paused as he thought about her offer.

Sister Durrell spoke up forthrightly as she always did and with no hint of timidity, "As a matter of fact, Madam Secretary, there are tools we could use to further the work. I wrote down some of them as you and my husband were talking. On the conservative end of things, we could use: equipment and software to link a number of channels for the simultaneous transmission and reception of data. The multichannel approach will improve our other types of high-frequency applications for rapid transfer and storage of wireless energy input in RFID– Radio-frequency identification—which uses electromagnetic fields to automatically identify and track tags placed in systems. We would need a company with the capacity of Siemens to be able to link many channels. To even begin to keep up with Australia's needs, we would need a new, state of the art, 5G system—which would be quite costly.

"At first–and at the least–we will need bigger and better scanning cameras, computers with considerable RAM space; second, we will need professional grade photoshop scanners to be able to quadruple or quintuple the input and output. We will need Professional PrimoPDF to do the scanning and to compile the digital results. It goes without saying that we can only do good work if we have good equipment. You are familiar with the gi-go principle, Madam Secretary?"

"Afraid not. I was lost as soon as you said RFID. So, what is gigo?"

Sister and Brother Durrell smiled; she said, "Garbage-In, Garbage-Out. What I'm saying is that we need very sophisticated high-resolution cameras connected to a completely up-to-date computer to capture images from various record sources and the scanners and photo-op equipment to make the necessary improvements, repairs, and transmissions."

"Well, I guess that means that I will have to communicate with the high priests of the Australian government to see if this is at all feasible. I know it won't be possible if we have to pay labor. Please see how much pro bono work your church can do and get back to me in maybe a month. Okay?"

"We'll do our best," Elder Durrell answered.

"Oh, I almost forgot. Last time we met, you told me about your pet project to find this person Alexandra Tarasova. My IT people did some digging and found a little piece of information you might be able to use. Here is a photocopy of an engagement announcement for a woman of that name at around the time she might have emigrated to Australia. The document is degraded so much that we cannot find the name of the groom. We have a few other documents suggesting something about his life and business. You can try to see if this is your mysterious lady. We looked a bit further but couldn't really find anything that seemed authentic and related."

"Thanks. We'll put those pieces of the puzzle into our box of documents on Alexandra. We are determined to fill in the missing pieces, if we can before our missions are done."

"However any of this pans out, on behalf of the Government of Victoria, I thank you and your choice for your wonderful contribution. God bless you."

With a little effort back at the archives, the missionaries were able to dredge up a birth certificate, communal records, and a high school graduation announcement on the man called Kyle Dewit Herman Bradshaw who might–just might–be a husband of the mysterious Alexandra Tarasova Yusupov. They knew there was a gap in the timetable which left out much of anything about the Yusupov involvement. They kept digging until noon and time to begin P-day.

They resumed their walking at the place where they left off the previous P-day—Cook's Cottage. They enjoyed the simple tour of the humble abode, built in 1755. They then walked on to Federation Square and spent nearly two hours in the grand National Gallery of Victoria

155

and even watched a short movie. They had to hurry afterwards to have the chance to walk through Fitzroy Gardens and to see the clock at the Flinders Street Station. Melbournians often use the clock as a meeting place; and the missionaries agreed that if they ever got lost that they would head to the station; so, they could be located. They had planned to go further, but they got caught up in the King's Domain Gardens which included multiple separate gardens: Queen Victoria, Alexandra, Pioneer Women's, and the Royal Botanic Gardens. They had to spend time in the Shrine of Remembrance, and the Sidney Myer Music Bowl where a concert was underway by the Melbourne-based Courtney Barnett with her back-up band, the Courtney Barnetts. It was not exactly to the taste of the septuagenarian Americans, but it was fun for one time. They were offered schooners of ale, refused, and took the opportunity to do a little proselytizing about the evils of alcohol from God's point of view.

CHAPTER TWENTY-SEVEN

BUDDING RELATIONSHIP

"Gather ye rosebuds while ye may./ Old time is still a-flying./
And this same flower that smiles today / Tomorrow will be dying."
—Robert Herrick, Esq., *To the Virgin,*
to Make Much of Time, 1648

Balagansk Penitentiary Officer's Dining Room, Irkutsk Oblast, Far East Russia, August 3, 1879

Boris was nervous and anxious about having lunch with the Tarasovas. He felt some trepidations that he might be moving too quickly in his desire to begin courting the lovely Alexandra. Even after only a week, he felt pangs of loneliness being away from her. Silly as it might seem, he felt like some of the light of the oblast had been subdued when she left for Vladivostok.

Abram, Irina, and Alexandra, alighted from the family carriage and walked up to the heavy grilled gates of the penitentiary perimeter. They were met by a soldier in his dress uniform and were escorted to the front door. He rapped twice on the heavy wood, and it was opened by a man in a spotless heavy cotton long-sleeve white jacket with two rows of knotted buttons, a baker's puff cap, and wooden clogs.

"Please come in, honored guests. The general will be down very shortly to greet you himself. He has had to take care of an administrative matter. Please sit here while we wait."

He directed them to three soft chairs which had been placed there that morning for this occasion. Alexandra was flattered and pleased.

Boris appeared less than a minute later dressed in his regular *oviki*– frontline troop uniform which fit him as if it had been custom tailored, which it had. In keeping with the tzar's desire to hold on to Russia's grand imperial past, the uniform was changed to resemble those worn by the imperial troops who were victorious in Paris in 1814—close-fitting, double-breasted jackets with gold buttons and brightly colored gold trimming on the collar and cuffs for general officers. His britches were almost skin tight, and–like his tunic–was a dark blue with broad grey-white stripes down his legs and sleeves. The shoulders had gold rank epaulets and shoulder board tassels. He wore long black boots that were so carefully polished that they caught the glint of the sunlight as he passed the rows of windows. His sword was held in place by a braided galloon attached to the leather by silver buckles. He cut a dashing figure, and he caused Alexandra's color to rise and her heart to flutter. She fanned herself, which made her mother chuckle behind her hand.

Boris–followed by the chef–marched directly up to father, Abram.

"It is my pleasure to welcome you to our facility. Surely not up to your usual standards, Sir; but we do hope you will enjoy the surroundings and the fine meal prepared by Chef Ivanovsky."

"I am sure we will, General. We are honored to be here."

"Then, without further ado, would you please follow me to the dining room."

As he turned to lead the entourage, he tipped his officer's cap to Irina and Alexandra. She was sure his gaze lingered a bit longer on hers; he saluted her two brothers.

The meal was obviously much finer than any prisoner ever saw in the Balagansk Prison. In fact, it had come entirely out of General Yusupov's personal funds. A small army of servers brought in a seven-course meal. The servants all appeared to be sophisticated about the etiquette required of them, and they moved with the precision and efficiency of long practice. They were a decade or two older than the Tarasovas would have expected. They were all dressed in white from head to toe. They all had on new sandals which seemed not to fit very well on some of the men. First course was hors d'oeuvres–Oysters à la Russe complimented by a white chablis; second was a light Consommé Olga along with strong madeira; third was poached salmon with mousseline sauce complimented by a fine dry moselle; fourth was Chicken Lyonnaise with a red bordeaux; fifth was young white Asparagus salad with champagne-saffron vinaigrette; sixth was the main course: roast sirloin of beef *forestière* with *Château* potatoes, minted green pea panettone timbales, and creamed carrots served with a strong red *beaujolais*; then there was a pause to cleanse the palates with a delicate lemon sorbet; and the seventh course was a colorful dessert of peaches in chartreuse jelly, thin Swiss chocolate mints, and *pâté* de foie gras with salty crackers imported from Germany. This final course ended with a sweet sauterne dessert wine.

Abram ate as much as a man could before admitting defeat with a self-conscious little burp. Irina made an effort to keep her portions small but largely failed. The two boys were picky eaters and ate only the roast beef and dessert, except for the *pâté de foie gras* with which they were unfamiliar and therefore did not like. They filled any empty corners of their stomachs with extra helpings of the dessert. Alexandra loved everything and strove not to commit a *faux pas* like her father by keeping her course portions small. She was full but not overly so, and she could keep her eyes and her smile flirting with Boris at just the right level of nuance.

After the royal feast, Boris chatted amiably with Abram and Irina about local customs, architecture, traditions, politics, and current events. He showed humility by asking for them to give their opinions and to share their knowledge. He showed interest by being able to respond to their answers—showing that he had studied his new posting with care and intelligence. After enough chatting, he suggested,

"Would you like to take a short walk around the facility–taking special care not to call it a prison–with me?"

"We would…" Abram started to say and then felt a sharp little kick on his ankle from his wife.

"If it is all right with you, I think we would prefer just to sit on one of the benches and take in the sun. Maybe you and Alexandra and the boys could move along a little faster if you leave us old folks behind, Prince Boris."

He was not slow to take a hint, and he sensed that he was developing an ally in Alexandra's mother. She smiled, and he was convinced.

"Well, maybe we could have a little fun."

Abram said, "Just try and keep the two rascals out of trouble if you can, Prince."

"It seems rather stiff to call me 'prince' or 'general'. I feel like a friend of the family, Mr. Tarasova. Would you feel comfortable in calling me by my name—Boris?"

"Not at all, and we are Abram and Irina...Boris."

Boris and the family walked out of the building, and Alexandra's parents found a small bench in the sunlight but facing away from its direct glare. Boris, Alexandra, Veniamin, and Valéry, walked into the town.

"Have you been here before, Miss Tarasova? To the town, I mean?" He asked Alexandra.

"Please be Boris; so, I can be Alexandra. And more please, don't call these naughty boys mister. It will give them ideas."

"All right Alexandra it is."

That bit of ice having been broken, the four of them inspected the drab and ramshackle little town. Were it not for the penitentiary, it would be barely a hamlet. Boris began to describe Balagansk and the four walked along, quickly exhausting the attention span of the two overly active boys. They disappeared down a narrow, crowded alleyway and inspected each person and thing they encountered—rats, filthy urchins, beggars, disapproving women, and standoffish men.

"They'll be back," Alexandra said, glad that they had left without having her give them obvious hints.

The town was small, except for the expanses of farmland. Alexandra and Boris could have walked the perimeter in two or three hours. The population was also small and disturbingly poor.

Boris pointed out a log structure with two gables where a group of ragged men with surprisingly intelligent faces sat with two or three books and engaged in lively discussions.

"They seem rather out of place, don't they, Alexandra? Try and picture them in clean suits sitting in banks or business offices or in schools having serious and educated discussions."

"I can almost do that because of their faces. They don't look like peasants or serfs except for their clothes and all the dirt on their hands and faces."

"That is perceptive of you, Alexandra. Why do you think they are here?"

"I think I know why. They were transported from the west because of being branded as criminals or misfits. Maybe criminals," she added as an afterthought.

"What do the people in Vladivostok think of them?"

"We know that most of them are exiles removed from their homes and former lives. There is a ghetto on the outskirts of the town where the tzar sent the Jews, just because they are Jews. They will never be able to leave. There are people called dissidents or ethnic groups like gypsies who have been sent here. Some of the aristocracy are here. I couldn't help but notice that the men who served at our lunch were refined and appeared to be intelligent, maybe even well-read."

"Alexandra, you are wise for one so young. Yes, many of those men and some of the women you didn't see are true aristocrats who one way or another got into the bad graces of the tzar or the Okhrana."

He paused for a long pregnant moment, apparently gathering his courage.

"Alexandra, can I consider you a friend?"

"Absolutely," she said, her face thoughtful and serious.

"Can you keep a confidence, a real secret. One about me?"

"Certainly, Boris. I would be honored to share with you, and I swear that I will not tell anything to anyone about what you want to tell me."

He took a long breath, then said, "Alexandra, I am an aristocrat and an exile, almost like those poor wretches in the prison. My "crime" if you could call it that, is that I had a brief time when some free-thinkers boarded with me. They became part of an underground network which I had nothing to do with or even knowledge about. They attempted to assassinate the tzar, and the Okhrana learned of my minor relationship with them. One of them–a girl I knew–was hanged. Because of my good military history and my parents' high station and great wealth, they were able to ship me off to the Far East and to get me assigned as an officer in the prison. You see, I have been trying to keep up appearances, but it is difficult."

"Oh, Boris, it could have been worse, much worse. You could have been exiled to one of the work camps in northern Siberia and never seen again."

"General Loris Melikof threatened my father that if he ever saw me or heard of me again, he would have me transferred to a far northern Katorga penal colony and placed in leg shackles for the rest of my life. He warned Father that even a family as close to the tzar as the Yusupovs would be sentenced to a camp for criminals. Before they left their homes in Moscow and Saint Petersburg, they would be crippled by being knuted, bastinadoed, branded, or by having an arm or leg amputated."

She shuddered at the horrific vision—which she could not even fathom—or how awful it would be to be scourged with a knotted rope or to have her tender feet flogged. She worked to remain stoical.

161

Boris was caught up in his emotional narrative, "He threatened Father that my delicate well-bred mother would have to work in the gold or salt mines. If she did not work hard enough, she would be flogged to death or have a heavy wooden beam attached to her leg shackles and have to work in the mines until her sentence was considered to have been fulfilled. Then the shackles would be removed; and she could go to work in the freezing cold until there was nothing left of her, and she died and was dumped into a pit with bodies of the other nameless slaves.

"My father promised on his own life that I would never be seen or heard of again by the Okhrana or the tzar. He promised that no one in the family would ever communicate with me again. He made me promise on my family's lives that I would never try and communicate in any way with my family. It was like I was dead."

He regretted having emptied his soul to a girl he hardly knew and feared that he might have made a fatal mistake. He was so emotionally overwrought that he could not fight back against the tears welling up in his eyes.

She said nothing for a while but looked at him with profound caring and sympathy wondering what to say that would not make her seem like a spoiled brat, or an uncaring snob, or, worse, a vapid and silly girl.

He spoke first, "I am sorry, Alexandra, I had no right to burden you with my story. I am sure that you would never want to have anything more to do with a criminal like me, whose family even has rejected him."

He hung his head and could not look her in the eyes.

"Oh, Boris, I am thankful that you trusted me enough to share such a terrible crime that has been done to you. I have known for a long time that many of the poor souls in the penitentiary were guilty of little more than to have spoken to the wrong person, or had the wrong opinion, or had fallen out of grace with the tzar's family. I feel that you and I have made a deep bond even though we have only just met a couple of times. Please come and see me often. I know a great secret that I will only will share with you at a certain time. All right?"

Then, she did something that astonished both of them. She embraced the much taller man, pulled his face down to hers, and kissed him passionately.

He was flummoxed. She was embarrassed to her core. They handled it in a spontaneous mutual way: they started to laugh—a whole face, whole body shaking cathartic outburst. Their future was sealed in that moment.

CHAPTER TWENTY-EIGHT
GROWING TOGETHER

"O my Luve's like a red, red rose,/ That's newly sprung in June./
O, my Luve's like the melodie/ That's sweetly played in tune./ As
fair art thou, my bonnie lass,/ So deep in luve am I;/ And I will
luve thee still, my dear,/ Till a' the seas gang dry."
—Robert Burns, A Red, Red Rose, 1794

Tarasova House, No. 71 Svetlanskaya Street, Vladivostok, Far East Russia, August 10, 1879

Alexandra's father, Abram, requested that Prince Boris visit him at his home and asked that he set aside an entire day to tour the business warehouse and the Tarasova ships. Abram hinted at a possible business arrangement. What he did not hint at was that his intention was for his daughter, Alexandra, was to be a part of any purely business arrangement whatever the two young people might have in mind about their social future-very hopefully, for a dynastic marriage. Boris responded with alacrity that he would be only too happy to come to Vladivostok.

In order to keep the early morning appointment, Boris rode Kryzhu at a fast trot all the way from Balagansk to Vladivostok and was satisfied that his fine war horse was still up to hard riding. He settled Kryzhu in the Tarasova stables near the house and walked to the front door. He gave himself a last-minute inspection to ensure that his uniform was in proper order, then rapped on the large doors. It was a hot day; so, he was sweating. He took a quick swipe of his brow with his handkerchief as the liveried Chinese major domo opened the doors and invited him in.

"The master is expecting you. Please to follow me."

Abram stood up from behind his beautifully carved and freshly polished mahogany winged griffin partners desk and walked towards Boris. He paused to take out a packet of papers from the Victorian mahogany carved drop front desk—a work of art with brass lion pulls, carved sides, drawers and lid, ball-and-claw feet and a full sail Tarasova ship carved on the lid.

"Please be seated, Boris," Abram directed; and he and Boris sat facing each other on comfortable soft matching early 19th Century Russian Biedermeier sofas made of white birch wood and padded with heavy maroon velvet. The neck and head rest area was made of rich gold tapestry material.

"I know you and Alexandra have some social activities planned, but I wanted to be able to talk some business with you and to show you our operations before you got caught in her web."

Boris laughed, "I'm afraid you are a little too late in that regard."

Abram returned a self-satisfied smile.

"Let us take a short ride over to the fur trading building. I would like to show you around."

"My pleasure."

The two men rode the half mile to the large warehouse in the Tarasova phaeton pulled by the three powerful white horses.

"Welcome to my humble workshop," Abram said as they entered the sturdy log structure which was easily as large as the main floor of the Winter Palace, in Boris's mind.

Two thirds of the floor space of the two-story building were occupied by bales of fur of all kinds, quality, and value—martens, beavers, northern spotted fur seals, wolves, foxes, squirrels, hares, Arctic fox, lynx, sable, sea otter, and ermine. Boris was staggered at the financial implications of such a wholesale treasure trove. About half of that area contained finished coats, parkas, mukluks, and fur lined winter pants.

In the other third of the floor space there was a wide assortment of retail consumer goods, accumulated by commercial expeditions largely headed by Alexandra to areas south of Vladivostok. Buyers—men, women, and children—milled about in crowds holding up dresses, coats, shoes, formal finery, toys, and a large assortment of liniments, ointments, creams, salves, cosmetics, cure-alls, canned vegetables and fruits, and an entire section devoted to expensive caviars. Buryat boys and girls hurried about the floor to assist shoppers to carry out their purchases. The retail portion of the fur emporium was the busiest in the shop and obviously the most efficient and friendly to the customers. Whole families–sometimes even whole villages–purchased the fitted fur garments from Tarasova's which they no longer had the time or the funds to make on their own. Abram had learned several years ago that the crafts were dying out and that there was both a nostalgic and a practical need for the furs. He saw the fur trade giving way to haberdashery goods brought in from China and Europe. When he offered fur articles hand crafted by his loyal Buryat employees, he soon realized that he had had a stroke of genius.

"Boris," Abram said, "this fur business right here would be sufficient to provide me and my family and all of our employees with a lifetime of comfort; you could consider it to be soft gold. I can truthfully say that we could be rich from the sale of beaver skins for American and European top hats alone. My own Russian and Buryat *promyshlennikmi* [fur trappers] are the best in the world, and I have had the wisdom to make their efforts and hardships worth their while. But, I have to say that I have always wanted more. I want to rival John Jacob Astor's American Fur Company, Simon Fraser in Canada, the British Hudson's Bay Company, the Russian-American Company, and the Russians Gregorii Shelikhov, and Pavel Lebedev-Lastochkin."

"From what I see here, I have no doubt that you can achieve it all. I applaud you Abram Timurovitch."

Boris gave a small bow and a salute.

"Thank you, Boris; but I am getting a bit older and will need some help. I would like you to think on that as we go about today."

Abram had certainly gotten Boris's attention.

Abram led Boris out of the fur emporium and back to the phaeton. With a small click of the long reins on the carriage horses' backs, they drove onto *Amerikanskaya* Street on down to the free port. Abram maneuvered the horses and the carriage through the thronging workers, sailors, military personnel, and businessmen to a fleet of six beautiful three-masters, all bearing the Tarasova herald—a bear at the helm of a sailing vessel. Guards in Tarasova livery came to attention when the master and his guest walked past. They saluted Abram as the master, and Boris as the general.

"This is another part of your world, Abram. I can scarcely believe what I am seeing."

"To be truthful, most of this is Alexandra's doing. She has a great head for business and is an accomplished sailor and ship's captain. She is in partnership with James Matheson II, the nephew of the founder Matheson of Jardine, Matheson as we are with the taipan himself. Not to boast, but our combined fleet consists of more than fifty ships; and we are moving forward to establish a monopoly on trade from Vladivostok through the South China Sea, the Sea of Japan, East China Sea, to the Indian Ocean. We control a large share of commerce with Japan, Chosŏn, Southern China, Vietnam, Thailand, Malaysia, the Philippines, and the Indonesian archipelago. We build and hire as fast as we can, but we are always some behind the East India Company. We are determined to win that race."

"Highly ambitious, Abram. Do you ever fear becoming over stretched financially?"

Abram laughed, "All the time. It is the way of the world here. Great companies, shipping lines, and commercial houses, come and go as they fall to the strength of larger and more aggressive companies. Right now, we have leveraged ourselves with as much debt–private and banking–as we dare. Frankly, we pray constantly that we will not be destroyed by a typhoon or pirates or the East India Company, or that we will be unable to meet our obligations in a lean year or two. So far, we have bulled our way ahead, but our accountants are urging caution."

"Probably this is none of my business, Sir, but does your income exceed your expenses? Whole countries have become bankrupt by failing to heed their sober advisors' cautions."

"I am going to assume that you are close enough to the family to be able to have such information. Yes, right now and for the next two years, we have every expectation of maintaining a positive balance. After that, it will be imperative that we grow in order to keep the East India Company wolf at bay."

Boris felt flattered and began to feel the worm of ambition niggling at his innards. He tried not to let his face reveal his thoughts. Did this mean that the family was strongly in favor of a match between him and Alexandra? He hardly dared to hope.

Alexandra–dressed in a chiffon bouffant summer dress which flattered her nubile figure–appeared from a walkway between two of the brigs.

"Enough business and stuffy man talk for a little while. I have a picnic fit for princes. Mother and I slaved all morning to prepare it. We will serve you," she said brightly radiating her toothy smile.

Abram laughed and said, "As if I could imagine either of you doing cooking and scullery maid service. And where are the servants to make ready this feast?"

"Oh, Father," both Irina and Alexandra laughed. "you know us too well."

Irina raised her right hand and without looking back gave a distinctly feminine wave. A small army of servants marched forward, set up tables, placed a marvelously decadent brunch out on serving tables. There was one large table for the four of them, set with fine china, the best silverware, serving ware, goblets, and napkins.

The House of Tarasova Chinese major domo bade them sit, and sommeliers brought out an assortment of afternoon wines—sweet table wines, sherry, port, claret, and sack—apple cider and pear perry served in bearded man jugs from Germany, cordials flavored with local berries and herbs collected by the Chinese and Buryats, fermented honey mead laced with secret spices, a little grain, and some fresh fruit. There were jars of Ossetra, Tzar Imperial Kaluga Huso, and Baika caviar and crackers to start.

Alexandra placed slices of heavy seeded German bread, flaky French croissants, and Alaskan sour dough on a separate table then began to build sandwiches to order. First, she slathered the slices of bread with creamy butter, garlic aioli, garlic and onion mustard, Choices included thick slices of cold roast of beef, chicken, pastrami, wurst, and sliced cheeses—gouda, Swiss with air holes, white cheddar, and Gruyere. Add-ons as it suited the men's choices included sliced fresh tomatoes, cucumbers, lettuce, onions and dill pickles.

Abram winked at his daughter when Boris was busy with his sandwich. She smiled back. They finished the meal with three different Russian wines imported from wine grapes planted at Fort Ross on the Sonoma coast of California by Santa Rosa wine makers who migrated down from the Russian Valley in the Alaskan colonies and Petrovska Beer from the Stepan Razin Brewery in Saint Petersburg.

"Alexandra, while the servants clear up our leavings, why don't you show Boris around this part of our fleet here in Vladivostok?"

"I would be delighted if you would, Alexandra," Boris broke in.

"I will be only too happy to give him the tour," Alexandra said and laughed gently at Boris's impatience.

Abram stretched out on a gentle mound of sand and pebbles and smoked his pipe as the two young people he was staking so much of his future on, walked towards the ships. He gave a little smile of satisfaction as he saw Boris take hold of Alexandra's hand.

"Is it really true that you have your captain's papers, Alexandra?" Boris asked as they walked up the narrow gangway of the barquentine *Matheson-Tarasova Fur Carrier*.

"It is true, and I earned them by going through an apprenticeship and taking a very rigorous test."

"I continue to be amazed at you and your accomplishments, Alexandra. Not many women could lay claim to such a feat."

Alexandra laughed, "There is a very famous woman admiral of a fleet in these parts. Have you ever heard of the Red Flag Fleet?"

"No, I guess I am too new here."

"You will know all about her soon enough. Her name is Zhèng Yi, and she is an infamous pirate who is alleged to have more than a thousand ships in her fleet and commands more than seventy thousand pirates. She is a huge thorn in the Jardine-Matheson-Tarasova side and in the side of the East India Company. She has thus far evaded capture and has almost free rein in the seas around us. One day, we will launch an all-out war against her."

"And you will be out there as one of the admirals, I suppose."

"Never let it be said that I'm not ambitious, Boris."

They both laughed heartily at her braggadocio.

"Tell me about this boat, will you Alexandra? Seems like it is time for me to begin to learn."

"First of all, get 'boat' out of your vocabulary. This is a ship, a barquentine, to be precise."

"What distinguishes it from other sailing ships?"

"Here comes the skipper. I'll get him to give you the details."

She introduced David Ching, a half Chinese, half British, middle-aged man with a sparse beard, a balding pate, and a florid large nose. His eyes were almond shaped but too close to each other to give one the impression of him being fully Chinese.

Boris saluted, and the salute was returned.

"Skipper, tell my friend here what a barquentine is, and how it differs from the other ships moored here."

"Sir," he said, "the *Matheson-Tarasova Fur Carrier* is a ship-rigged vessel that carries three square sails on each mast—we have three masts, but others may have four. You will note, Sir, that our ship is fore-and-aft rigged with the foremast fully square-rigged and her mainmast rigged with both a fore-and-aft mainsail (a gaff sail) and square topsails and topgallant sails. It is a medium sized carrier built for speed displacing nearly 40,000 feet and has 30,000 square feet of cargo space. The hull is reinforced oak, tough enough for cannon balls to bounce off, and the sails are the heaviest oiled canvass to withstand typhoons and a lifetime of exposure to sea water. We have fourteen guns, a well-stocked armory, and a crew of hard working hands and real fighting skills."

"You are justifiably proud of your ship, Skipper, as you should be."

"I am proud to be part of the Jardine-Matheson-Tarasova fleet, Sir."

"I see that there are differences in the five other ships of the fleet moored here. Pardon my ignorance, Skipper, but I am a land-lubber soldier."

"I am aware of your reputation for heroism, General Yusupov. It is an honor to have you aboard, and a pleasure to share what knowledge I have. Next to us is what we call a clipper ship which serves a special purpose for us in these dangerous times. They are built for speed. So, you will note the long, slim, graceful, streamlined hull, its long projecting bow—like a spear head–and the very large spread of sails mounted on three overly tall masts. Clipper ships are American in origin–built for smugglers and pirates–but also to win in the tea races here in Chinese waters. The practical purpose then and now is to bring the first tea harvest of the year to ports all over the world, and also to give us an edge in transporting our goods on short notice. Our vessel was built in Bristol, England, and others under our command were built in Harwich, London, Pool, and Southampton, merchant ports. I graduated from being master of clippers to becoming the captain of this beautiful ship on whose deck we stand.

"The next four ships, in order, are Captain Alexandra Tarasova's ship, the brigantine *Far East Transporter*. It has three masts with all of them fully rigged but the foremost. The main mast is the aft one as you can see. It is rigged with both a fore-and-aft gaff sail and square topsails and topgallants. It is probably the best ship for the Tarasova company purposes—a compromise between the barquentine and a sloop. It is actually faster and more maneuverable and is a favorite for pirates, smugglers, reconnoitering, and as a fighting ship to protect larger cargo vessels. Because of the Red Flag Fleet, the *Far East Transporter* and our other brigantines are excellent for fast maneuvering and for carrying large enough cargoes—50 to 200 tons–to be worth the expense of multiple voyages.

"The next two are oceanic Manila Galleons, the largest ships in our fleet or in the East India Company fleet. The Jardine-Matheson-Tarasova-Chang *Master of the South Seas* and the *King of the Merchant Fleet* were purchased from Spain. The ships are identical in everything but name. They carry 2,000 tons of cargo. They are large, multi-decked, and heavily armed. They have three masts with a lateen fore-and-aft rig on the rear masts. As you can see, they are built with a prominent squared off raised stern, and have square-rigged sail plans on their fore and main-masts.

"The last two ships moored here look rather like our galleons but are much smaller. They are called carracks, an old style but still useful cargo ship. They usually have three masts, but our two, the Carrack South Seas Carrier, and the Carrack Jardine-Matheson-Tarasova Express Ship, are fitted out with four masts, each with four sails. The main and foremasts are square rigged; the mizzenmast carries both a fore and aft triangular sheet called a lateen sail. For greater speed and maneuverability our ships are fitted out with a square sail beneath the bowsprit forward of the bow, and topsails are hung above the courses on the mainmast and foremast. Our carracks have bonaventures—the fourth masts—you see and carry another large lateen sail. Take note of the deep and broad hull, high sterncastle, and an even higher fo'c's'le which hangs out over the bow. The sterncastles and forecastles are larger than those on a galleon which makes them more comfortable and spacious but more clumsy in the water. I prefer the galleons, but most of the ships in our fleet are the less costly carracks."

Boris was overwhelmed with too much information and could not keep track of the many names for ships and ships' parts he was hearing. He strove not to show his ignorance.

"Skipper, thank you for your masterful and concise descriptions. I can see why you are a valued member of the Tarasova company. I can also see that I am going to sit down with a few books and pictures until I can master at least the nomenclature. I trust that Alexandra can help me."

"More than glad too, Boris," she said quietly as they continued their tour of the handsome and impeccably clean ship.

It did Boris's soul good to see the gleaming polished teak decks, the oiled and shined masts, the spotless white sails, the well-ordered brass monkeys bearing their cannon balls, and all of the brass that shone like gold—obviously polished that morning.

Alexandra pointed back at the shipyards to the south, "Captain Ching, perhaps you can give General Yusupov an idea of what we do in the yards."

"I would be proud to do so. I am afraid I have already bored you with too much ship detail, but please allow me to give just a short summary and invite you to come back one day and walk about the yards. I think you will be quite amazed.

"Where to start? In no particular order, the Tarasova Ship Yards are fully independent and employ several thousand highly skilled shipwrights and specialists who save the company millions in costs and months of time if the work had to be contracted out. We have: blacksmiths and anchorsmiths, block makers and blockers, caulkers, color makers (most are officers' wives, I might add), draftsmen, mast makers, riggers, ships' taylors...and...I am forgetting something. A little help, Alexandra, please?"

"Chain and rope makers, carpenters, sawyers, and warehouse workers, shippers and purchasers."

"Oh yes, I neglected to mention the importance of the shippers and purchasers," Captain Ching said.

They thanked the proud young sea captain for his time and for his encyclopedic knowledge. When they were back on the docks, Boris shook his head.

"What?" Alexandra asked.

"I admit that I will have to do a lot of studying and to get first hand knowledge of the fur business, the shipping, the mathematics of commerce, and the people and places that we will deal with," Boris said almost as an aside.

Alexandra's mind was made up about Boris as a future—near future— husband and partner. The way he referred to the Tarasova enterprises as something he and Alexandra were about to share convinced her that her plotting to win him was nearly in its final stages. She was almost giddy with anticipation of what was planned for the next few days.

CHAPTER TWENTY-NINE
A WHIRL-WIND COURTSHIP

Courtship is to marriage, as a very witty prologue to a very dull play.

—Anon

Tarasova House, No. 71 Svetlanskaya Street, Vladivostok, Far East Russia, August 10-18, 1879

Alexandra cloistered with her mother for a concentrated two-hour rendition of what had transpired, what had been said, and what was promised by her father's and her day with Prince Boris. They plotted, argued, planned, and conspired, as mothers and daughters do as they scheme to ensnare a suitable marriageable young man. For all her girlish excitement, Alexandra kept a level head and made notes. What resulted was a clear but complex tactical plan, and the majority of what a wedding celebration would be. There, she and Irina differed.

"But, dear," Irina tried to argue once again for her conviction that a lavish extravaganza at the House of Tarasova would be the only fitting way for Vladivostok's princess—or the nearest the growing city separated from the seats of power in the west could produce—and for the Tarasova family.

"Let me tell you my ideas, Mother. I want something different, unique, and memorable. And for that matter, a lot of fun."

"Don't be silly, dear. Marriages are not supposed to be anything silly… like…fun. They are solemn occasions, important ones for establishing ourselves. Do you remember your sixteenth birthday party?"

"Of course, I do, Mother. How could anyone forget such a bacchanalia? Princes and grandees and the rich from all over the world. More wonderful food than a city could consume in a month. Don't get me wrong. I thought my birthday and coming-out party was perfect… for the time…and for the purpose. This is different. Boris and I will be celebrating love, happiness, and, yes, fun. We want to make and keep friends, real friends. I think my ideas will be novel and interesting and will endear all those old generals, admirals, and tycoons to us. I have talked to Jamie Matheson about it. He agrees that it will be the talk of society for years."

"Alexandra, do you hear yourself? You sound like a grammar school child about to go to her first party. You are a grown-up and a successful business person in your own right. You would give everyone the wrong idea if you insist on going through this silly affair. I forbid it."

Irina knew that she had sealed her doom so far as the wedding was concerned by letting her emotions get the better of her. She could have kicked herself down the stairs for her outburst. She knew better than anyone else that Alexandra would never allow anyone to give her orders about her life. More than that, she knew that her headstrong daughter would react to her mother saying 'I forbid it' by doing everything in her power to thwart her.

Alexandra spoke calmly and coldly, "Mother, these are my plans for my marriage. First, you can invite anyone you want. That goes for Boris, for my brothers, for Father, and all of his business and shipping friends. I am going to invite whomever I want, and you do not get a veto. Second, I choose the location. That will be on our back lawn; it will accommodate hundreds. Third, I choose the menu with your help if you can catch the spirit of things. We are going to have a lawn party, a great picnic. Fourth, I am going to have modern music, not just those old people like Beethoven, Mozart, and Handel. I plan to hire small orchestras to play the folk tunes of Mikhail Glinka, music by the "Mighty Five"– Miliy Balakirev, Aleksandr Borodin, César Cui, Modest Musorgskiy, and Nikolay Rimskiy-Korsakov."

"Who in the world are those people? I never head of them."

"I am in a new generation, and one different from yours and my grandparents. The music my friends and I like is lively, exciting, and all about Russian life and folklore."

"And 'fun', I suppose?"

"Yes, Mother, 'and fun'. You need to give it a try. My wedding will be different, something to talk about, and something to remember us and our companies over. I guarantee that Boris Yusupov will be delighted, and his introduction into Russian life and that of our business partners all around us will be a most positive thing."

"You always get what you want, no?"

"When I make up my mind, and I insist, Mother. And you have to agree, I am seldom, if ever, wrong about my firm convictions because I think them through. Will you help me or make things difficult?"

"I will have to help you. My goodness, I can only imagine what crazy things you would come up with without me to put a bridle on at least a few of them. Please promise me that you will listen to reason if I have a concern."

"But, of course, Mother, I always do."

Knowing that she could never succeed in a fight with her self-willed, obstinate, and overly intelligent daughter, Irina sighed.

"One last question, Alexandra. Does the groom-to-be agree to all of this modern folderol?"

"He will, once I tell him," Alexandra replied with her patented irresistible and impish grin.

Irina suppressed a laugh and rolled her eyes theatrically.

Boris came down the stairs from his room on the third floor of Tarasova House looking freshly bathed and refreshed. He was dressed in the latest casual fashion for gentlemen: an informal tan matched three-piece wool sack suit with loose fitting Cossack style trousers which was now dominating men's style in the Victorian era, knee-high riding boots from Paris, a beaver skin top hat (which came from the Tarasova emporium), a paisley cravat tied as a bow that formed almost, a Lavallière–his only nod to the ornamental in dress of the day–and a soft white linen shirt.

Alexandra was waiting on the marble floor at the bottom of the stairs. She gave a brief little clap and an affectionate smile as he reached her.

"Like my new fashion, Alexandra?" he asked.

"Love it. In fact, it is going to be part of my plan to modernize this stuffy old place and family."

"Do you have a little time for me?" he asked.

"Always. How about a ride around the property?"

"I'd love to. Can we go the way we're dressed?"

"I need to change into pants," she said knowing that women wearing pants was strongly frowned upon.

She searched Boris's face; and when she failed to see any disapproval, she scampered off to her room to change into riding pants. He almost had to turn away when he saw her youthful form in the tight-fitting pants. He breathed out slowly to settle himself down.

The couple rode out to the carefully preserved copse of white birch trees. Alexandra dismounted by throwing her right leg over the saddle and jumping gracefully to the ground. Boris moved a little more carefully.

"I have taken the liberty of getting tickets for the opera tonight…if you would like to go."

"Which opera? I don't really care so long as we go together," Alexandra responded.

"Actually, it's something rather modern, an operetta called *Madame Favart*, by a Frenchman named Jacques Offenbach."

"Is it new?"

"New to here—maybe first presented in the late 'fifties. Apparently, it has been popular ever since—stood the test of time."

"Someday, we really must go to Berlin, or London, or Paris, or Moscow, or Saint Petersburg and see the great and new entertainments available. It always seems like Vladivostok and the Irkutsk oblast are backward and lacking modern changes," she said.

What happened next, struck Boris for some reason he would never be able to understand. He looked into Alexandra's eyes, took her right hand in his. He dropped to one knee and watched her face flush and her breathing become deeper and quicker.

"Alexandra Abramovna Tarasova," he said, his voice quavering a little. "Will you do me the honor of becoming my wife. I find that I cannot live without you."

Despite the amount of manipulating, maneuvering, hoping, and planning, she and her mother have done; Alexandra was still somewhat taken aback at how rapidly the progress to this point had happened. She paused for only a minute.

"Oh, yes…yes!" she whispered softly and intensely.

He swept her up in his arms and hugged her until she gasped for breath.

"Sorry," he said. "I am just so excited."

"You have to talk to my father, you know."

"Of course. I will do it before dinner tonight. Do think he will give us his blessing?"

"I know he will or else he will be sleeping in the servants' quarters for the next month."

They both laughed and then kissed passionately, sealing the engagement so far as they were concerned.

Boris showered, trimmed his beard, polished his boots, and put on his dress uniform. He asked the major domo to request a meeting with Abram before dinner.

An hour before the family was to be seated at the family's long table, Boris took a seat across from Abram who was dressed equally formally and sat in authoritative stiffness behind his desk.

"Prince Boris, my man said you wanted to meet with me before dinner. Please tell me what is on your mind."

Boris determined not to stammer or to allow his voice to crack, "Sir, I have come to ask your blessing on my engagement to your daughter Alexandra Abramovna. I have asked her, and she has consented."

Abram smiled, "So, I am just a formality, then Prince?"

"Most definitely not. You and your entire family have treated me as a member of the Tarasovas. I would be most disheartened if you were not to approve, but I would abide by your decision. Furthermore, I am new to the oblast, but I have means at my disposal to join you in business–if that becomes agreeable to you–as well. I can think of no way better to weld a union of marriage than for us also to be partners in commerce. I would be everyone's fool if I were to think of you or to treat you as anything less than I would my father, and I assure you that my allegiance to him is very much more than a mere formality."

"You could not have expressed it better, Boris. Of course, you have my blessing. For one thing I would fear being shot by any one of several women if I refused. Welcome to the family, my son. Tonight, let's feast and toast to the engagement. The women will plan the wedding itself. But the two of us can begin looking into having you join our growing commercial empire."

"That sounds like the best of all worlds to me. I guarantee that I will treat Alexandra as a princess, and you and your wife as king and queen. I also pledge to do all I can to further the Tarasova company."

"The Jardine, Matheson, Tarasova, Yusupov business empire which will end up victorious over the British East India Company!"

Abram reached for his decanter of thirty-year-old Macallan Select Oak single malt whiskey and offered Boris two fingers of the precious amber liquid. He poured himself a glass; they touched glasses, and Abram said, "*K dolgoy zhizni i uspekhu* [to long life and success]."

Abram summoned Irina and Alexandra to join him and Boris.

He said, "A parade of eligible young men have been sniffing around Alexandra since she was twelve…"

"Daddy!" Alexandra yelped.

"Sorry, *Dorogoy*, I have spent too much time around the rough men in the warehouse and on the ships. You are my dear one; and I will try to speak more like a gentleman, especially around our prince."

His smile belied his sincerity, and all of them laughed.

"What I was trying to say, is that Boris is the finest of the lot. He wants to marry you. Your mother wants him to marry you; and I want him to marry you. My two boys are too young to join the business, and we need a good, smart, strong man—a man who is part of the family— that we can trust and rely on to join our family in all ways. With your permission, I am going to propose a business arrangement that will bind us together and make us prosper beyond our previous imaginations."

He paused to wait for the affect that his statement would have. The usually unflappable Irina gave her approval with a slight nod of her head.

Alexandra spoke softly and enunciated clearly to be sure that she did not betray her rising excitement for the events of the day, past, present, and future, "Although I am supposed to be the blushing bride with air in her head, I want you to know that I have given a great deal of thought to the matters of business. I love Boris and want to be his wife. I would accept an arrangement in which he had nothing to do with the business if that is what you or he would want. I look at the arrangement–the business arrangement—with caution as I always do with matters of business, just as you have always taught me…I approve heartily…with all of my heart!"

Boris said, "And so do I. I will make my contribution, and I pledge my loyalty and to this fine woman who has consented to have me as her husband and to each of you for accepting me without reservation as a member of the family. I am certain that none of us will regret this decision made on this extremely important day."

At dinner, Alexandra made the announcement about the engagement which was received with cries of 'congratulations!' 'great choice!' 'to your success!' '*bol'shoye schast'ye* [great happiness]!' By mutual decision, Abram, Boris, Irina, and Alexandra, did not bring up the subject of any business arrangements.

The following morning, Boris sent a telegram to his mother—the first communication since he arrived in Vladivostok. He did not include his name in deference to his agreement with his parents.

> "Mother, I am well and prospering. Stop. I have a great business opportunity. Stop. Please release the sum of four million (4,000,000) roubles (silver based) from my trust. Stop. It can be sent to the Irkutsk Oblast Bank. Stop. Thank you. Stop. Your loving son."

CHAPTER THIRTY
A MARRIAGE IN EVERY SENSE

The goal in marriage is not to think alike, but to think together.
—Robert C. Dobbs

Tarasova House, No. 71 Pekinskaya Street, Vladivostok, Far East Russia, September 30, 1879

The wedding of Alexandra Abramovich Tarasova and General mayor Prince Boris Nikolaiovich Yusupov was talked of in the oblast and in Vladivostok that it was certain to be the greatest wedding celebration in the entire history of Far Eastern Russia. It was rumored that the wedding would exceed the grand celebration attending the young Tarasova girl's sixteenth birthday party when dignitaries from all over Russia, China, Japan, and Europe attended and brought lavish gifts. They should have gotten an inkling that things would be different when they learned that a blanket invitation was proffered to everyone in the oblast, as well as the foreigners from as far away as America.

The next two innovations should have alerted the citizens of the oblast that this indeed would be quite different from Alexandra's birthday bash, but also very different from any wedding celebration they had ever seen. The first was that it was clearly scheduled for late morning. The second was that—weather permitting—the festivities would take place in the Tarasova property's lavish lawn and gardens. Had they been informed about the entertainments that were planned, they would have come to the conclusion that this was going to be something passing strange.

Alexandra won out against her mother about the food and the entertainment. Irina outmaneuvered her daughter by commandeering the invitation list. As a result, the food and entertainments—while sumptuous—would appeal to a more avant garde crowd, and the guest list was half again as large, included more business contacts, and also would include a younger and more fashionable crowd—dandies, actors, entertainers, folklorists, and a few that Irina raised an eyebrow sternly about. They agreed that it would be a formal religious marriage ceremony—a sacrament—and they also agreed that the officiator would be a very popular, but not entirely well-regarded priest serving in the naval base by Saint Petersburg. Both Irina and Alexandra had been leaning towards would-be reformers of the orthodox church and had read several of the writings of Father Ivan Ilyich Sergiyev, better known as Father John. Alexandra was especially in favor of him performing her marriage because he had the reputation of being somewhat at odds with the conservative hierarchy by his insistence on reform in some areas of church practice.

Their hopes were enhanced when they learned that Father John would be preaching in Siberia. He had already performed masses and had given strong speeches in Novonikolaevsk, and this very week he was in Irkutsk. Alexandra had the chauffer drive her to Irkutsk where she quickly learned that Father John was conducting a mass confession and giving a lengthy prayer with a reformist theme. Alexandra ordered that she be driven to the Epiphany Cathedral, an example of distinctly northern Russian religious architecture. Father John had finished his mass and his group forgiveness for sins and was about to leave the huge crowds and retire into the interior of the cathedral when a very determined Alexandra pushed her way through the crowds and intercepted him before he could go into seclusion.

"Your holiness," she said, a little out of breath, "I must speak with you in private for a few moments…just a few moments, please, kind father."

Taking note that the supplicant was obviously a very rich young woman, and that she was most earnest in her request, he granted her a brief audience just inside the narthex–the entrance–located at the west end of the nave, opposite the cathedral's main altar.

"What troubles you, Daughter?"

"My mother and I are devotees of you and your message. I know that you will be coming to Vladivostok in two weeks, and we would be greatly honored to have you stay in our home during your visit. I humbly plead with you to perform my marriage which will take place at that time. Please, Holy Father, grant me this wish, and my family and I will be forever grateful."

"Are you a virginal, Dear Daughter? For I have sworn to perform marriages only for the pure."

"I am."

"Have you sins to confess before you take upon yourself the holy sacrament of marriage?"

"I think nothing serious, but perhaps you could hear my confession now and make your own judgment."

He nodded and led her by the hand to the nearest confessional booth. There, he heard her petty confessions of telling the occasional lie, of having lustful feelings, and have sometimes used profanity when she was among rough sailors while on commercial voyages. He made the sign of the cross with his three fingers then kissed his out-sized three-bar cross hanging from a heavy silver chain around his neck.

Outside the booth, he showered a beaming smile on her, which was accentuated by his large white teeth showing in contrast to his heavy full-face beard and shaggy, curly, shoulder-length black mane. His piercing black eyes were kindly but a bit unnerving with their intensity.

"Tell me your name and all about yourself and your family," he asked.

Alexandra told him everything about herself, her groom-to-be, and her family. She casually let drop several times that the family was very rich and influential and that the groom was a member of the House of Yusupov. Father John's interest peaked at that, and he took her by the shoulders with his very large and powerful hands.

"My Dear Daughter," he said quietly, "I cannot refuse the offer to seal you and your beloved in the sacramental bonds of holy matrimony. I will be delighted to stay with you and your family and to perform the ceremony on the day you have chosen."

Alexandra leaned forward and gave right-left-right brush kisses on his cheek and bowed low before him.

"Oh, thank you Gracious Father. You will have no problem finding our home. Ask anyone where the House of Tarasova is located as soon as you arrive in the city. Oh, I forgot to tell you that we would love to have the ceremony performed outdoors in our garden, a place rather like where you were preaching today."

He said, "I would be delighted. The greatness of God is best manifest out in nature. It is a perfect choice."

She made the sign of the cross, and he responded in like manner which was as serious as any signed contract might have been.

Tarasova House, No. 71 Pekinskaya Street, Vladivostok, Far East Russia, October 15, 1879

The day of the wedding was a radiant Indian summer day. The leaves on the trees had not yet fallen, and their color was a rainbow of resplendent oranges, yellows, and reds with a few remaining green leaves whose turn to color and then to fall had not yet come. The gardens were freshly weeded and raked; the lawns were still a rich green and appeared to have been manicured with comb and scissors. Old and new flowers lined the perimeter of the garden area like a fragrant park wall.

Abram walked through the garden with Irina and Alexandra, and they all pronounced that the site of the wedding was ready and looked perfect.

He said, "My two favorite ladies, I would like to mention something about Father John; so, none of us get surprised by something he does or that we hear of disapproval of him by the Metropolitan in Irkutsk. I hear from my people that the father is odd, to say the least. The church has heard complaints for his wife that he has refused to have relations with her and has sworn a vow of celibacy—something too much like the Roman practice. People see him walking about the streets making the sign of the cross, constantly reciting long prayers, and walking with his arms crossed on his chest. Some say this might be a sign of mental illness. He is unlike any other priest in that he serves the liturgy every day without assistants. His performance during the services is loud, and he waves his arms wildly. He regularly departs for the standard text, and more strangely, he turns his back to the altar. Like the Romans, he preaches confession and taking the Holy Communion regularly, even weekly or daily, instead of the usual once or twice a year. Finally—and the thing I find strangest of all—is that he permits menstruating women to take part in confession and communion, which—as you know—is strictly forbidden by the archpriests and the metropolitans."

"I know all of that, Father," Alexandra said, "but, the holy church, in its wisdom, has taken no action against the man. I presume they look at his differences as eccentricities and not substantial. I like him and want to have the spice he can add to our gathering and to my marriage. Boris says he could care less about any of the strangeness as long as Father John remains in good standing with the church and our marriage is valid."

Alexandra's statement was not entirely true. Boris had raised questions that were important to him about the Kronstadt Father's well-known anti-Semitism, his constant talk of humility which should be practiced by the clergy and the aristocracy, and his regular articles in the far right-wing conservative newspaper *Novoe Vremya* [*New Time*] which had not met with the approval of the Most Holy Synod because it is seen as interfering with affairs of the true church. However–since the hierarchs decided there was nothing they could do–he was willing to accept Father John as well— something well short of a ringing endorsement.

Since a wide-open invitation had been sent out to the entire oblast and well beyond, Irina planned for garden party gourmet food for several thousand people. It was well that she did because as the populace, the intelligentsia, the aristocracy, Boris's prison officers and Balagansk city officials, the local Buryat indigenous people, Abram's customers, and his and Alexandra's widespread shipping commercial acquaintances, streamed through the gates of the estate. The servants and security officers soon lost count.

A jazz orchestra brought in from Moscow played discordant notes– that none of the family recognized as music–while the people gathered. The local symphony octet played Tchaikovsky while the wedding party took their seats. The affect of the unusual music and that the wedding was more like a garden party than a real marriage in a church caused a low hum of commentary to buzz around the seated and standing guests.

Boris, Abram, and Father John took their places at the front of the party. A wedding march of sorts—it was, strictly speaking, an old Russian wedding night song–was played by a Balalaika trio. Whether or not the conservative aristocrats, determined old ecclesiastics, and stodgy mustachioed business grandees, approved, all the young people and the majority of the crowded onlookers clapped and hooted their approval. Alexandra reveled in her success.

She was radiant in person and dress. The wedding gown was made in Saint Petersburg by seamstresses vouched for by none other than Princess

Tatiana Alexandrovna de Ribeaupierre Yusupov, a lady-in-waiting to the Empress (and mother to Prince Boris)—which was to remain a secret to the rest of the Yusupov family as long as Tati lived. The gown was gorgeous and splendid: pale gold silk overlain with bobbin tape Russian lace curving back on itself and joined using a crochet hook. The designs of the gown were abstract in form. She had puff sleeves and a scoop neck which were just coming into fashion in Saint Petersburg; the scoop showed too much in Irina's opinion; but this was Alexandra's day. The sleeves, collar, and hem had ruffled lace trim. The train was rather short by usual standards in Vladivostok—only two feet long, but Tatiana had insisted that this was the coming style in western Russia.

Alexandra began her stately march down the grassy aisle accompanied by her mother and her two grand-mothers. She curtseyed to her father, her groom, and her priest, then turned and made a small bow to the assembled guests, which provoked another unseemly boisterous outburst from the young.

Alexandra had asked Boris who he wanted as his best man. He made a most diplomatic...and genuine...choice.

"Let it be James Matheson II," he said without hesitation and thereby secured the good will of the taipan and the entire Jardine-Matheson conglomerate.

Father John called out in his stentorian voice, "What man will stand here as the *koumbaros*, the man who will be the best friend in the wedding and one of the most important men in this young couple's life?"

Jamie took his place beside the groom. His father, mother, and younger brothers beamed at the wedding company and Jamie's part in it.

Father John explained, "The Eastern Orthodox wedding ceremony is a centuries old rite full of profound symbolism and meaning for the church, for the bridal couple, and for the families. Most rituals are performed three times to represent the Holy Trinity. Because of the sacred significance of the sacraments, Brother Matheson and I will lead Boris and Alexandra through all of them three times.

"We will begin with the betrothal ceremony and the blessing of the rings," Jamie said, having made a quick study of his role in the Russian Orthodox wedding ritual over the past two weeks.

Father John recited a litany of blessings and a substantial list of passages from the Bible. He held out the two rings in his hands, declared the betrothal, and pressed the bride's and the groom's foreheads three times each with the rings. Jamie, the *koumbaros,* placed the rings on the right-hand ring fingers—third finger—three times each.

As Jamie finished the ring ceremony, Father John handed Alexandra and Boris lit candles to be held in their left hands throughout the rest of the ceremony.

He said, "This symbolizes your spiritual willingness to receive God's blessings on your lives and your marriage."

He then had Alexandra and Boris join their right hands, symbolizing unity and gave a lengthy prayer for their oneness. As he finished praying, Jamie, as *koumbaros,* presented Alexandra and Boris with two floral crowns studded with semiprecious stones, shining metals, and gold threads. As they held the crowns, he tied the ends of a white ribbon to each crown and placed them on the couple's heads signifying their unity, then switched the crowns back and forth three times as they faced the altar signifying that neither could be sure which crown was hers or his; they were the same.

Father John intoned a serious requirement of the acceptance of the crowns, "These crowns are to remain with you as long as each of you lives. When you die, you are to be buried with your crown to show your lasting faithfulness."

Jamie handed Father John a gold cup two-thirds filled with red wine.

"Drink thrice each from this common cup, my children. Hereafter, you will share everything—joys, successes, riches, sorrows, failures, and times of want. Know that you are not alone: view this as symbolic of your unity giving you double the joys and half the sorrows."

Father John took hold of their hands, and they circled the table three times, their first steps as a married couple. A small chorus sang three hymns. Father John blessed each of them separately and together.

Then, in his most solemn voice, he intoned the ancient and most important phrase, "*Na zisete!*", and the entire wedding assemblage echoed and exclaimed, "*Na zisete!*" "*Na zisete!*" [May you live!].

Before Father John could say the words, Alexandra pulled Boris to her and kissed him with all her might. The entire wedding party burst out in joyful laughter.

CHAPTER THIRTY-ONE
ANOTHER DISCOVERY

> And I also command you that ye keep a record of this people, according as I have done, upon the plates of Nephi, and keep all these things sacred which I have kept, even as I have kept them; for it is for a wise purpose that they are kept.
> —*Book of Mormon, Book of Alma 37:32*

National Archives of Australia, Victorian Archives Centre, 99 Shiel Street, North Melbourne, Victoria, Australia, February 12, 2014

Elder and Sister Smith had two months left on their eighteen-month mission; the Taylors had four and a half; the Clydes had six; and Elder and Sister Durrell had eight more months. They were beginning to feel something akin to separation anxiety with the deep bonds they had developed with each other. As often as it could be expressed appropriately, they each promised to keep up their friendships when they left the mission field and returned to the U.S.; but they all had some doubts about being able to keep the contacts viable, having had similar attachments on previous missions, on cruises, or when the boundaries of their local wards and stakes were changed. That bit of concern made all of them redouble their efforts to find enough more verifiable information about their favorite shadow from the past–Alexandra Tarasova–to establish her firmly as a once living and vibrant person.

Close as they were with their co-religionists—people who shared like political views; they were all conservative Republicans, people whose lifestyles above and beyond their religious activities and traditions were rooted in the western United States, their inbred biases against people not like them such as the movers and shakers of Motown, Hollywood, and the gay marriage crowd—they all had a quiet longing to be back home. Moroni Clyde made an announcement that enlivened and enhanced their enthusiasm for the work they were doing.

"Elders and Sisters, it has been a while since we found out anything really new about our Alexandra. But, yesterday, I was thinking about what we know, which isn't all that much. She was born in Russia. Somehow and for some reason, she had to get from Russia to Australia. She got established and eventually married there, had children, then disappeared.

"I decided to check the one area we know had to have happened. So, I began to dig into the ships' passenger lists from 1890 to 1927. I have to admit that I lost track of time and didn't do my part in our digitalization efforts for Victoria Province. Anyhow, I did find something–actually two things—related to our girl that we can verify.

"Here is a copy of a maritime business contract registered in Vladivostok, Seoul, Tokyo, Shanghai, Hong Kong, and Moscow:

> "To all who shall see these presents, greetings: A maritime contract has been entered into and duly and legally registered by Abram Timurovich Tarasova and his daughter, a married woman, Alexandra Abramona Tarasova-Yusupov, her husband, Boris Nikolaiovich Yusupov of Moscow, James Matheson II of Shanghai, Junji Shimazaki of Tokyo, and Yi Chin-Mae of Seoul. The business title is the Far Eastern Maritime Commerce Corporation, and the business shall include the production, warehousing, and shipping of goods throughout the China Seas, the Indian Ocean, and the Pacific Ocean ports which honor this registry.
> Entered this eighth day of March, in the year of our Lord, 1879 By the office of the Lord of the Admiralty, Admiral Douglas Mortimorency Cotswold, Hong Kong."

The finding solidified the fact of Alexandra's first marriage, her involvement in oceangoing business on an equal footing with her father and her husband, and was presumptive evidence of her and her family being solidly affluent. Further—reading between the lines—Alexandra became an undoubtedly strong person during a time when women were supposed to be at home, barefoot, pregnant, and quiet. It was obvious that she was none of those.

"Any luck finding passage from any port in the far east to any port en route to Melbourne, Australia, Elder Clyde?" Elder Durrell asked.

"'Fraid not, but in all honesty, I haven't had enough free time to look into that aspect of her life that had to be some time into the future, and as yet unknown circumstances," Elder Clyde said, musing.

"That has to be one of the key elements in her history that needs to be discovered, I think we will all agree. I will offer to investigate that thorny question," Elder Durrell offered.

"He'll never be able to do it alone. He can't even find his glasses. So, I'll help the man keep on track," Sister Durrell said jokingly.

"Hmmf," Elder Durrell snorted, and all the missionaries had a good laugh.

CHAPTER THIRTY-TWO

HIGH SEAS COMMERCE

"All of us have in our veins the exact same percentage of salt in
our blood that exists in the ocean, and, therefore, we have salt in
our blood, in our sweat, in our tears. We are tied to the ocean.
And when we go back to the sea – whether it is to sail or to watch
it – we are going back from whence we came."

—John F. Kennedy

Golden Horn Wharf, Vladivostok, Far Eastern Russia, March 14, 1879

Prince Boris sometimes felt that he was dizzy from the frenetic life he had begun by marrying the small tornado of the Tarasova family. He had made a verbal and written contract with Alexandra and her father, Abram, and contributed two million roubles to establish the Tarasova and Yusupov Far Eastern Fur Trading Company. He, Alexandra, Abram, and half a dozen men he did not really know had made a complicated maritime contract to establish the Far Eastern Maritime Commerce Corporation which required a great deal of his time and effort to be expended at sea, where he was not altogether comfortable. His duties and commandant of the Balagansk Prison continued, and he had to spend at least a portion of each week signing papers, attending to personnel problems, and dealing with the admission and release of political prisoners—many of whom were nearly his social equals, and who were in the Irkutsk oblast for no more crimes than what had gotten him sent to the hinterlands. The most taxing and time consuming of his efforts were to keep up with his seemingly indefatigable young wife.

The wedding night started before the sun went down and the guests allowed the ardent young couple to leave the party with a cacophony of cat calls, lewd suggestions, and unsought after advice. Alexandra was anything but a shy retiring virgin. By morning, Boris had to throw up his arms in defeat and to collapse into a dreamless sleep until noon. From then on, they conducted business: signing contracts, inspecting properties, and planning their first commercial voyage together. Before sundown, in the privacy of their boudoir, Alexandra sapped his energy again…and again. By week's end, he felt as if he had lost twenty pounds, and almost his ability to walk or to lift anything heavier than a pillow. All in all, it was the best time of his life.

Two days before setting sail on Alexandra's ship, the *Far East Transporter*, more than a hundred stevedores, coolies, clerks, *gruzchiki* and other cargo handlers, swarmed aboard carrying heavy boxes, machinery, furs, and the officers' baggage. They worked around the clock until both holds were packed so tightly floor to ceiling that only a narrow aisle allowed passage by a man.

Alexandra, the captain, and Dimitri Polikov, the pilot, moved the heavily laden ship out to sea through the Golden Horn Bay. The ocean was calm, the sky cloudless azure blue, and the sun was warm and inviting. The previous night, the sky had been a deep bright red—not a hint of the usual darkness.

Alexandra leaned over to Boris and asked, "Do you know the importance of "Red sky at night, sailor's delight. Red sky in morning, sailor's warning?"

"Not really."

"Red sky at night—really at dusk–is the sun hitting dust and water particles in the high clouds, which means that a storm is moving away from west to east. But red sky in the morning means that the dust and rain are still hanging in the sky and portends a big storm."

"So, it should be smooth sailing for this our honeymoon voyage, then, Alexandra?"

"Oh, not necessarily. Maybe the whole ditty is just an old wives' tale. Never can tell."

"Well, I am going to look on the side of the old wives to start with at least," Boris said.

He was obviously buoyed up and excited for a new adventure. He had never been on a significant ocean voyage before, and the plans were for the *Far East Transporter* to be at sea for two or three months with visits to more than a dozen exotic ports. Alexandra was, as always, excited for any adventure.

The *Far East Transporter* sailed out of Golden Horn Bay with a favorable wind and unfurled all sails once outside the break water. The wind was at the ship's back for the entire first day at sea. The second day was grey and cloudy; but the waves were no more than two feet high; and the good ship—heavily loaded as she was—fairly skimmed along the surface, making between twenty-five and thirty knots an hour. Alexandra and Boris were wrapped in each others' arms when the ship's bells sounded eight bells–2 bells, then a pause, followed by 2 more bells and another pause, then the clanging of the bells repeated the same patter—indicating that it was 0800, the end of the morning watch. They made first port–Naha in the Ryukyu Islands in the East China Sea—to unload a cargo of beaver skins and ermine which was taken to Shuri Castle, and dozens of coolies refilled the ship's coal bins during the mid-forenoon watch.

Alexandra was first to observe that many of the coolies wore locked metal neck bands, and some had hobbles on their ankles which made their working progress slow, painful, and inefficient.

She pointed them out to Boris, "Look, slaves. I thought the slave trade pretty much died out when the American slave states lost their civil war."

She was angry and disturbed, demonstrating even to herself for the first time her genuine concern for poor and defenseless people.

"They may be criminals serving out their terms, much like we see in Balagansk," Boris said.

"I certainly hope I never hear of any Russian being treated like that in your prison, Boris. It is unacceptable for our civilized nation. I am more inclined to think that these poor people were abducted. Promise me that you will never treat people like animals."

"I promise. You know me, I am a member of the aristocracy; and we treat our workers and servants quite decently and have done for centuries. They are like our children."

"Good. Boris, I could never tolerate that in any of our businesses. We must be on the look-out for any kind of abuse. Well treated workers do better work, and we want all of them to feel like they have a real share in our Jardine-Matheson-Tarasova-Yusupov company."

"I agree. Let's go down to breakfast before we're too late."

They encountered a surprise storm with a strong northwest wind as they rounded Taiwan and had to furl their sails to be able to make a cautious and unplanned stop in the secluded Su-ao Harbor of Taipei. They spent three days hunkered down in their ship until the fury of the storm wore itself out. Despite the torrential rains and high winds, the accommodating Chinese restaurateurs were able to bring in five-course epicurean Chinese meals twice each day. Alexandra was very familiar with the fare and took pleasure in introducing the exotic foodstuffs to her husband, who had never seen, let alone tasted such food.

Despite his original sense of disquiet at seeing stewed dog meat, garlic stir-fried rooster's testicles, the feet of chickens, crispy smoked Indonesian fruit bats, turtle soup, and something called 'stinky tofu', presented as edibles, he quickly found that he rather liked it. Alexandra was adept at the use of chop sticks, but Boris could not become facile enough to get food to his mouth reliably and finally had to resort to using European utensils—much to his chagrin—which made Alexandra laugh good-naturedly at her husband's futile attempts.

The weather cleared, and they were able to go ashore to trade—furs and machine tools for silks. Alexandra was an old-hand at the ancient art of Chinese haggling and was patient enough to wait until she obtained premium rolls of elegant silks for a third the price they went for in Far Eastern Russia. She knew which designs were most treasured and secured bargain-basement prices for what the Chinese called the "auspicious design" some of rolls of which originated in the ancient Shang, Tang, and Song dynasties. The 'audacious' appellation for the silk came from the use of the four meanings important to the Chinese culture: Fu, Gui Shou, and Xi.

She was shown gorgeously colored Ming and Qing dynasty themes of birds, animals, blooming flowers, meaningful stones, exotic trees, fish, and insects. Because of the great meaning attributed by the Chinese to dragons as good omens for almost anything, Alexandra bought dozens of roles of brilliant red and orange dragon motifs. As a present for Boris, and without him knowing, she bought a magnificent Silktree Albizzia whose leaves open in the morning and fold in the evening symbolic of harmony between couples and a wish for more sons.

For the next six weeks, the *Far East Transporter* sailed among the East China, South China, Philippine, Celebes Seas, the Pacific Ocean, the Straits of Malacca, and into the Bay of Bengal. They spent several days at a time in Hong Kong doing business with the taipan's representatives, and several days more in Shanghai staying at the taipan's palatial home—which he self-deprecatorily referred to as "ma-bit" or as "my wee cottage"–where they were fortunate to be able to sit down with James Matheson himself and his nephew and Alexandra's good friend and partner, Jamie II, to discuss business.

"*Gaun yersel,*" the taipan said in his broad scots dialect.

Alexandra nodded her acceptance of his congratulations but held her tongue knowing that James Matheson did not appreciate idle comments.

"Here," he said, hav' yrsel a wee hauf."

Alexandra and Boris accepted a two-finger measure of fine twelve-year-old Glenfiddich and shared a toast with the taipan. Taipan Matheson had a one-track mind about business in the China Sea region: the East India Company must be defeated. Where he once would have settled for a sharing of the wealth between equals, recent events had soured him to the point that only a victory in a war would suffice.

"Ye've surely grown up tay be a handsome quinie, my dear Alexandra," he said, "and 'tis a foine man ye ha' joined wi'."

"Thank you, Taipan. He has a good head for business, and desires to get your advice about how we can do the best during this voyage. Our profits are your profits as well, Sir. What do you suggest?"

"Ay do me best thinkin' when I take a donner. Why don' ye walk along wi' me, Boris and Alexandra?"

They walked around the grounds in the cool of the evening. For the first quarter of an hour, the taipan did not speak but was lost in thought.

"First let me ask a few wee questions a ye. Wa' was yer plan after ye leave Shanghai?"

Boris spoke first, "We are thinking of going into the Bay of Bengal and doing some spot trading along the coast, maybe Bangkok, maybe Rangoon, some of coastal cities of southern India."

Alexandra added, "And maybe we can meet some of the sea traders and move some opium. We have some potential contacts."

"Let's dinna mince words, you two. Ye've been talkin' wi that sleekit Chinee bandit Hou Eadric of the Three Families Tong. Ay woulnae buy a blow rag off the swick. He's been a swick for meny yonks."

Boris gave Alexandra a bewildered look as if the taipan had spoken to him in a dialect from a distant planet.

Alexandra gave the taipan a chance to get a few feet ahead, then whispered, "Let me translate quickly. What the man said was 'you have been talking with that sly and untrustworthy bandit, Hou Eadric.' I'll tell you more later. Then he said he would not so much as buy a handkerchief from that cheat; he's been a cheat from a long time ago.' The taipan knows everything and everyone and where all the bones are buried. We should play close attention to what he tells us."

The taipan waited for them to catch up, then said, "Aye presume ye are here for mi advice and help. Aye'll tell ye that Aye cannae dae anytin' ta help ye, if ye turn to that sleekit arse. Aye think ye should go a different way for a slew o' reasons. First, is anyone Hou Eadric refers ye ta will be just waitin' to skin ye. Aye know that Boris is a solid man, but he's no match for two dozen pirates. Second, commerce is poor in the Bay these past months, yonks, if truth be told. Ye'd be better off just bypassin' Bangkok, Yangon, Dhaka, Chittagong, Rajshahi, Comilla, and the rest of them. Third, there's a foine opportunity awaitin' ye in old Ceylon, across the Bay on the tip of India. It's called Ceylon or Lakbima. It's a British Crown Colony, well administered, well policed, and commerce is on the up-and-up, for the most part. Mind, ye still have to count fingers after a handshake; but ye're not likely to lose everything like ye would doin' any kind of business with the scum on those junks, or the desperately poor souls on the coast of the bay who would sell their mother for a shilling or snatch yer heid off ye when ye turn yer back.

"Aye can gie ye a few names of guid people in Colombo, and the colonial governor is a friend o' mein. Wadda ye think?"

Alexandra held back her bit of secret knowledge, but agreed when Boris said, "We would be fools to try on our own to do what is against your knowledgeable advice. What sorts of things should we concentrate on to transport back to Russia, Taipan?"

"They have store houses full of rubber, teak, exotic kinds of tea, coffee, and spices from the Moluccas, which are part of Indonesia in the Banda Sea."

"How difficult can we expect the passage to be across the Bay of Bengal, Taipan?" Boris asked.

"Good question, Lad. Most times these months, it's passin' calm; but ye can ne'er tell about old Mother Nature. Sudden turrible sea storms kin spring up in the bat o' an eye lash. Be prepared, batten down yer hatches and furl the sails; and ye kin ride 'em out. They're usually pretty short—less than a day. Ye'll do jist foine."

With the *Far East Transporter's* larders re-stocked, water supplies brought in sufficient to last a three weeks voyage, and enough coal to make it all the way to Colombo and back without danger of being stranded mid ocean, they left Shanghai the following day. The ship was perfectly capable of moving under sail alone, and the coal was a belt and suspenders requirement of Boris's.

They outran two attacks by Bengali pirates but otherwise moved swiftly over calm waters all the way to the British Ceylon shoreline making it there in record time. When they put into the harbor of Colombo at the terminus of the Kelani River, they were greeted by a white clad military band of black-skinned Sinhalese with Ceylon's governor, John Winthrop Herbert Delaney, standing at stiff attention in front of them.

"Greetings, and welcome to the British Crown Colony of Ceylon and to its grand capital of Colombo. We boast that we are the cinnamon capital of the world, the safe harbor of western civilization among backward heathen nations surrounding us," the queen's representative said with full formality.

"We are most pleased to be here and to receive your gracious welcome, Governor Delaney. We bring greetings from the Jardine-Matheson-Tarasova-Yusupov consortium and personally from Tai-pan Matheson to you, Sir," Alexandra said.

"We are most appreciative of the escort you provided for us during our final day of travel on the Bay. We have come to understand just how unsafe travel here would be without your government's assistance. We look forward to doing business in the colony and to working closely with you and the business people you recommend." Boris added.

"Thank you, Captain, and Prince Boris. I hope your stay will be comfortable and profitable. I must tell you up front that we do substantial business with your competitor, The East India Company, and a few others of lesser standing. You should know that we do not have a monopoly agreement with East India, and we will not make such an arrangement with you. Our policy has been largely one of free trade, and we have ample commercial strength to accommodate several companies. We are no longer plagued by the Dutch and the Portuguese who fought us for the spice trade rights; so, I can assure you that your ship can return to Vladivostok with a hold full of cinnamon, mace, cloves, nutmeg, and pepper from the Moluccas with us as intermediaries at a modest handling fee, of course. You may not yet be fully aware of the value of these spices. One example which should help to convince you is that several European and South American countries still accept pepper as a medium of exchange of equal value to their money."

"We should make a formal business arrangement and then begin to load our cargo hold. We have information that tells us that your colony and many of the principalities around you value furs—at least for trade purposes for transport to Venice—and silks which we carry which are of the highest quality. In good faith, we can sell at discount prices, if we can buy with the same courtesy, Governor," Alexandra told him.

That information convinced the governor that this was a company—and certainly a young woman–to be reckoned with and who would be as good as her word, or at least as good as her contractual bond.

"It will be no problem to grant you a right to conduct commercial activities in our cities, among our populace, and on our territorial waters with the full protections of the British government. Your actual business arrangements will have to be conducted individually with the companies registered in British Ceylon. Perhaps you would permit me to schedule a dinner meeting with the most influential and prosperous company officers within our borders."

"That would be a most welcome opportunity for which we thank you in advance, Sir," Alexandra and Boris said in unison.

The dinner was held in the ballroom of the Mount Lavinia Hotel, a British Colonial Victorian style structure which had been the official residence of Thomas Maitland, Governor General of the colony, early in the nineteenth century. The handsome well maintained old building was exclusive for the crème de la crème of Ceylon Society and could boast of the most beautiful view in all of Colombo—the beachfront of magnificent Mt. Lavinia. It was resplendent with electric lamps that made a glow visible from miles around. The dinner–arranged by the governor—was splendid and expensive since almost every item on the menu had had to be imported from London and British Hong Kong. It was quintessentially British: potted shrimp, rag pudding, olio—a delicious mix, a hodgepodge, of vegetables, meats, spices, and British dumplings–pigeons, sirloin of beef roast, venison—the hallmark meat of the very rich landowners–chyne of mutton—a medieval stew laced with white wine and a large variety of spices—turkey, snipes, duck—English style, not Peking—partridge, French beans and artichokes.

Since the consumption of meat other than fish was largely restricted to the upper classes, the extravagance of having so many meat courses—and especially venison—appropriately impressed the visiting brass and coaxed their minds into a generous mood.

Alexandra sat at right hand of the governor general at the head of the long table, and across from Patrick Queensbury, the representative of the East India Company and by Sir Edwin Appleby and his wife, Margaret, among the established leaders of Colombo high society. Sir Edwin was the owner and senior director of the Ceylon Maritime Spice Trading Company and was rumored to be a millionaire many times over. Boris was seated at the opposite end by Glenleven Armitage and his august and bejeweled wife–Lady Miriam–the acknowledged first leaders of British Ceylon's expatriate high society. Alexandra's omnipresent and ever watchful personal bodyguard, the massive Don Cossack, Stenka Mazepa stood behind her.

To the left of the governor general, the only Sinhalese member of the xenophobic Colombo high society, sat dressed in the finest British custom-tailored grey wool evening suit available from the Hong Kong outlet of Gieves & Hawkes. He was the chief officer of the Bay of Bengal Company which moved goods and services from east to west, and to the north. The goods included spices and Chinese manufactured goods, Indian pottery and brass lamps and statues, furs from the north and from Russian Alaska, and—it was widely rumored—slaves from Africa and India to the West Indies, prostitutes to all of the major cities of Asia and Europe, and opium to England on English ships for which he held a crown license to engage in the lucrative trade over which England had fought wars with the Chinese.

After the first three courses of food and wine, Sir Edwin leaned over to Alexandra and said, "My dear, I have had business dealings with your father for over a decade. Am I to understand that he wishes you to take over that part of his enterprises? You are rather young, and a woman to boot, if I may say without intending to give offense."

"None taken, Sir Edwin. I think further investigation will quiet your concerns about me and about my husband, Prince Boris Yusupov, both of whose families stand behind us."

"I am acquainted with Prince Nikolai Yusupov and do some business with him. Is there any relation between Boris and the prince?"

Having been forewarned by Boris to avoid admitting any connection between him and his father or the rest of the family, Alexandra said, "I am not quite sure where Boris fits into that fine family, Sir."

"I like to get right down to brass tacks, Princess Yusupov. First, may I call you Alexandra? My given name is Edwin, but my friends call me Eddy."

"I would be most pleased to have you call me Alexandra, Eddy. Now, what have you to say about 'brass tacks'?"

"Good, right to it. The usual items of commercial exchange in and out of British Ceylon are Chinese silks and teas, Indian cottons, Arabian coffee, Indonesian spices, and African ivory—of all kinds, if you get my drift. The principle final trading destination for us is Venice. How would you fit into this long-term arrangement?"

Boris, sitting at the opposite end of the long, inlaid wood table, had a very similar conversation with his seating partner, Glenleven Armitage, and his august wife–Lady Miriam–and the owners of the famous Armitage and Winterbury Commercial House. They were widely rumored to be multi-millionaires from her aristocratic family's fortune and his business acumen.

When asked what the Jardine-Matheson-Tarasova-Yusupov consortium could offer the already established commercial pathways, Boris answered, "Let me tell you why you should do the bulk of your business with us and should encourage your influential friends to do the same."

CHAPTER THIRTY-THREE

HIGH SEAS,
HIGH STAKES COMMERCE

Creative risk taking is essential to success in any goal where the stakes are high. Thoughtless risks are destructive, of course, but perhaps even more wasteful is thoughtless caution which prompts inaction and promotes failure to seize opportunity.

—Gary Ryan Blair

Mount Lavinia Hotel, Colombo, British Ceylon, May 12, 1879

Boris faced his questioner and realized that this was an all-important test of his mettle, his acumen, his knowledge, and his negotiating ability. The man sitting next to him had proved himself in the rough-and-tumble Asian business world that held to the statement of morality as "the survival of the fittest", and the definition of success—a decades long ascension which left behind destruction of those not so fit—was "the last one standing". Glenleven Armitage showed his age, but that did not diminish the aura of toughness that hung around him. Boris had only this one conversation to establish himself and his wife as worthy business partners or perhaps—more likely–respected opponents.

"You already have some fur trade," he said to Armitage. "We can supply far superior furs in quantities you have not yet seen and of a quality you have only dreamt of and at prices you have never been able to get from other traders. You get ivory from Africa. We can supply more and faster because our ships are capable of traveling down the west coast of that continent with fewer impediments and better business relationships there."

"What about ivory?" Armitage asked starting to get to the kernel of their talk.

"We will get what we need to be competitive. I take it you do a brisk business in ivory."

"We do. It is getting harder to work in the trade ever since England banned the trade in 1833. We have to register our ships under foreign flags and to pay dearly for the privilege."

"Are you interested in contracting with us?"

Boris paused. He was disgusted by the euphemisms and hypocrisy surrounding the slave trade. Real trafficking in elephant ivory would have been bad enough on his conscience, but he had to toughen up to deal with repugnant people in a terrible travesty against mankind. He had to stiffen his spine and determine that 'business was business' if he was going to succeed way out here in the east.

"Yes," he answered tersely.

"How about moving opium on your ships?"

He was getting into bed with the devil; but he was already in for a kopek, why not go in for a rouble?

"Opium transporting is legal in Great Britain, is it not?"

Boris knew the answer but wanted assurances. Prison or the gallows was not something he wanted to be part of the risks of being partners with the likes of high society in Colombo or Shanghai.

"We fought two wars with the yellow midgets and won both of them over our God-given right to move opium. The last one—which ended in 1860—settled the question forever. It brought down the Qing Dynasty, and gave us unheard of rights to operate in China. You can stop worrying your handsome little head over such trivialities."

This was the moment of truth.

"I will talk to my wife and partner. I presume that she will agree with me, and you will have made a new partnership. Drawing up the papers will keep a dozen lawyers busy for a month."

Armitage reached out his large callused hand which enveloped Boris's more refined hand and squeezed it hard enough to cause pain. His hard, slate-colored eyes looked at Boris's softer blue eyes waiting for him to show weakness, but Boris fought successfully to avoid even a minor embarrassment or opportunity for Armitage to have leverage over him.

Meanwhile, Alexandra was carrying on her own verbal jousting match with Sir Edwin Appleby and Lashith Chathura Pathmarajah-Dassanayake–the smooth talking, perfectly dressed Sinhalese chief officer of the Bay of Bengal Company–neither of whom she trusted; and she knew that neither of them had respect for her as a business woman.

"Gentlemen, we have enjoyed a fine dinner, excellent drinks and wine, and cordial chatting. Not to seem brash or impolite, but don't you think it is time to talk business? I came to Colombo and then to this pleasant evening with more in mind than to enjoy a few genteel pleasures. I traveled from Vladivostok for business, representing the firm of Jardine-Matheson-Tarasova, and most recently, Yusupov. None of those people got to where they are today by suffering fools. My business credentials are strong despite my youth. I am a registered ship's captain and an owner and chief officer of a large commercial and shipping operation on my own merits.

"I offer, on behalf of my husband and myself, to enter into a nonexclusive partnership with you; or if that seems to be an overreach, then we can agree to honorable and binding contracts to do business with one another without concerns over cost or profit sharing."

"What do you bring to the table, Alexandra?" Dassanayake queried, a slight condescending smirk in his smile.

"Please refer to me by my title, Princess Yusupov, Mr. Pathmarajah-Dassanayake, since it appears that formality will be necessary."

"Please, Princess, I think I have gotten us off on the wrong foot. I regret having given offense. Could we start again?"

"Why of course, Lashith. I always like to do business among friends. How do you feel about that Sir Edwin?"

"Edwin will suffice. Now perhaps we can negotiate properly and come to an agreement, or we can separate on good terms."

"And I am fine with Alexandra."

"Please, Alexandra, let us know what you offer?"

"Lashith, Edwin, I am sure you have investigated my background and that of my family. You are also, no doubt, aware of the power and influence of the Yusupov family—second only to the tzar and his family in wealth and power. No one in this colony doubts the strength of the taipan and of the Jardine-Matheson Company. Boris and I bring all of that to the table as you so quaintly put it. More than that, I personally command six ships and all the sailors and marines on them. I am on a first name basis with the heads of almost every trading company in Japan, the Chosŏn peninsula, South China, and north and eastern Russia. Our trading arrangements net us all millions of pounds sterling, roubles, won, dollars, yen, Thai baht, and German marks.

"We hold substantial bank accounts in the Bank of Japan, multiple *Qianzhuang* banks in a number of Chinese cities and our principle bank in Asia—the HSBC [The Hong Kong and Shanghai Banking Corporation] located on the Bund. In Great Britain we have accounts in the Lancaster Banking Company, the Bristol Old bank, the Manchester and Liverpool District Banking Company, and the National Provincial Bank. Our banking in Germany is with Deutsche Bank, Commerz Bank, Lehmann Bank in Halberstadt, and Goldschmidt Bank in Hamburg; our two French banks are Banque de Paris et des Pays-Bas and the Rothschild bank. In Chosŏn, we bank with the Russo-Chosŏn Bank in Yongdo. In Russia we have banking accounts in Moscow—Poliakoff's Bank and the Moskowsky Zemelny Bank. In Saint Petersburg–Nicolai and Ludwig Stieglitz Bank and J.Y. Guenzburg Bank; in Novonikolaevsk—the Siberian Trade Bank, and Irkutsk—the Sberbank. We have a growing account in San Francisco in America—Naglee's Exchange Bank."

"Tell us more about your maritime interests, Alexandra?" Sir Edwin Appleby asked. "That seems to be your area of greatest interest and expertise."

"All right, let's begin inland. You are probably familiar with the world-famous immense Lake Baikal located between the Irkutsk and Buryat Oblasts. The people of Irkutsk call it the 'Blue Pearl of Siberia'; Baikal is the world's largest, deepest, and purest, freshwater lake; and the lake and its surrounding forests have an nearly untapped emperor's fortune in *nerpa* [ring seal], the great fish the Buryats call *khelma*; and Europeans know as sturgeon and its caviar, giant brown bears, and wolves, whose skins are extremely soft and thick due to the cold climate, whole underwater forests of sponges, omul fish—a white fish which is wonderful smoked—and the oily, scaleless *golomyanka* fish. There are hundreds of species of birds with beautiful plumage like the roseate spoonbill for ladies' hats. Baikal snails are found in their thousands in shallow waters flowing into the lake and around the edges of the lake. They, alone, are worth a fortune if harvested and protected properly."

"Are you exploiting those riches at present, Alexandra?" asked Sir Edwin.

"Yes, we are investing in the villages and villagers around the lake for harvesting skins, fish, caviar, and the snails. We have built twelve river going vessels that transport the goods to Irkutsk and a fleet of wagons to haul them to the railroad and then to the sea where we distribute them all around the east and south China sea region.

"We have a relatively small fleet of commercial vessels under our exclusive ownership and are partners with Jardine-Matheson in their much larger fleet. Both entities are highly lucrative."

"Why then, do you seek a partnership or a contractual arrangement with us, Alexandra? Do you just want to eat us up the way the East India Company does?" Pathmarajah-Dassanayake bluntly demanded.

"To the contrary, we know that we who are not part of the British East India Company will eventually be swallowed up and disappear. History is replete with examples. What we–and what you–need, is to become part of a large and powerful enough consortium to be able to compete successfully against that rapacious company. We have to be rich enough that Asian and European nations will be willing to buy our goods at lower prices to make a profit without having to fight a kind of war against England and its company."

"I take it you are not quite there yet," Sir Edwin said.

"True, but we are getting there. We are large but must get larger to hold East India at bay, and much larger to defeat them, which is our eventual goal. We are building heavily armed defense vessels to accompany our supply ships, and I estimate that we are about half way to fulfilling that quest."

"At present, can you fend off or escape the Red Flag Fleet?" Sir Edwin asked.

"Yes, we can and have done on repeated occasions. However, Wu Shi'er, Zhèng Yi, and Ching Shih have joined in a massive pirate empire with 70,000 pirates and 1800 fast junks and are steadily growing all the time. Frankly, with your help we can defy or even defeat them, but without it, who knows?"

"We appreciate your candor, Alexandra. We face our own problem of the Bengal pirates, but they are not as well organized as the Red Flag Fleet. I am concerned about the costs involved in joining forces with you," Sir Edwin said.

"And I do not trust the Jardine-Matheson company eaters any more than I do the pirates," said Pathmarajah-Dassanayake, "and I will not join with them or anyone who makes it a contract imperative to join them in order to do business together."

"I have the same misgivings, Alexandra," said Sir Edwin, "but I would consider having a firm business arrangement with the Tarasova and Yusupov people or perhaps even with you and your husband, Boris, separately. What level of cost do you envision us having to contribute to become partners with you and your father?"

"The rouble is presently listed on the exchanges as thirty to one U.S. Dollar, which is becoming the most stable and useful money in the world. We would need to have at least 300 million roubles or ten million U.S. dollars to be able to afford to share our profits."

"That is very steep, and it does not speak to the costs and risks, my dear," Sir Edwin said rather patronizingly.

"We have run in the black for well over a hundred years despite severe winters, labor disputes, fights with pirates and the East India Company. Every year we have become more efficient and richer and have been able to keep debt to the minimum. You are welcome to go over our books once you sign a contract which would allow you to back out if the debts versus profits are unacceptable. I think we have come to a point where further discussion will not be helpful. We can part friends now, or you can become our partners under the conditions I have outlined. Gentlemen, what will it be?"

Pathmarajah-Dassanayake was about to make a haggling point when Sir Edwin lightly touched his forearm and shook his head.

"We agree to your terms but know that we will have nothing to do with Jardine-Matheson. I have never trusted that old buccaneer, James Matheson; and I can't bring myself to accept that nephew of his either," Sir Edwin said with finality.

"Done," Alexandra said, "I will find Boris, and the two of us will sign for ourselves and our families. We will need not only your signatures but a good faith transfer of one-half of the agreed upon buy-in price transferred to our Shanghai bank, the HSBC on the Bund."

"Agreed, the two men said almost at once.

Alexandra brought her good news to Boris and found that he had some of his own.

In his excitement, he blurted, "Alexandra, I was able to get Glenleven and Lady Miriam Armitage to agree on behalf of their Armitage and Winterbury Commercial House to a full partner ship with the Jardine-

Matheson-Tarasova-Yusupov consortium. They have agreed to telegraph 600,000 roubles—twenty million U.S. dollars—to our account with HSBC tomorrow morning if we can all sign tonight. Their attorneys are drafting a contract right now. Does that suit you?"

"Perfectly. My news is positive but not as good as yours. Lashith Chathura Pathmarajah-Dassanayake of the Bay of Bengal Company and Sir Edwin Appleby of the Ceylon Maritime Spice Trading Company agreed to a contract with us but excluding the Jardine-Jameson connection. They will telegraph ten million U.S. dollars to HSBC tomorrow as well."

"Alexandra, it makes me very uncomfortable that we have to exclude the Tarasova, Yusopov, and Matheson families. We may have just jumped into deep water with a shark feeding frenzy. But, like your father, my father, and the taipan, we have to take risks if we are to end our days as the taipans of our own empire and be unassailable by attack from anyone," Boris said soberly.

Alexandra nodded her agreement.

Before noon the next morning, the principles met and went over the contracts with their lawyers. By two in the afternoon, they all agreed that the contracts were sound, and affixed their signatures with high contrast India Ink. A servant sprinkled fine white sand imported from Koh Rong Island, located an hour away from Sihanoukville in Cambodia. The die was now cast.

CHAPTER THIRTY-THREE
A BIT OF SECRET COMMERCE

"With a secret like that, at some point the secret itself becomes
irrelevant. The fact that you kept it does not."
— Sara Gruen, *Water for Elephants*

Aboard the Tarasova-Yusupov Commercial Vessel, the *Far East Transporter*, Yangshan Deep Water Harbor, Shanghai, May 30, 1879

From 1863 onwards, the American Concession and the British Settlement joined together to form the much more efficient and profitable Shanghai International Settlement. The French and Chinese remained separate. The Shanghai International Settlement included the land on the banks of the Huangpu River to Suzhou Creek and the area from Yang-ching-pang Creek to Suzhou Creek. The Chinese kept the ancient walled city and all the area of the city surrounding the foreign enclaves. For a decade, the intrepid, clever, and elusive leader of the Three Families Tong, Hou Eadric, conducted his ongoing and highly successful criminal enterprise from his safe house on Old North Szechuan Road in the Chinese sector. He maintained safe houses and his houses of commerce of all sorts on Elgin Street in Central Hong Kong named in honor of James Bruce, the eighth Earl of Elgin, credited for issuing the order to loot and destroy the Summer Palace in Beijing, and in Number 19 Admirala Fokina street, Millionka in Vladivostok.

At the moment–eleven ten a.m.–the battle-scarred and habitually austere Hou Eadric sat in an overstuffed chair in the lobby of the old Oi Suen Hotel near the Ladies Market. The man was a little over five feet tall, slender with long fingers and very long painted fingernails. He wore bright red lipstick. He had long greying hair and an unruly long mustache and beard made his already almost skeletal face even thinner and a shaved forehead with a long salt-and-pepper grey queue hanging down his back.

The location was perfect for the wary criminal leader because it was a rundown area frenetically busy with retailers hawking an incredible variety of goods at the top of their lungs day and night. There were no permanent shops in the Ladies Market itself, but stalls and push-carts selling spices, used clothing, bolts of calico and silk, fresh fish and garden vegetables, children's toys, opium pipes, festival kites, and dirty books. Hou was dressed in his habitual anachronistic old Qing Manchu *Changshan* fuchsia silk robes with a square green silk emblem sewn down its front. He had on curled-toe silk slippers the shape of a ram's horn in a non-matching chartreuse color with blood red bows at the point the front of the slippers began their upward turn.

He was reading the shipping information page in the English-language newspaper, the *North China Herald*, searching for the item he had come to Shanghai for. As his spies had told him, the item he sought was listed in the section on afternoon arrivals into the harbor:

> "the brigantine *Far East Transporter,* owner–Jardine-Matheson and Tarasova Far Eastern Russia Trading Company, Captain—Alexandra Tarasovna Yusopov, Cargo—opium, furs, skins, whale oil, and silks will enter the harbor at three p.m. and dock at 4:15 p.m. today, May 30, 1879."

Hou finished his cup of strong green chai and walked into the teeming street.

A waiting servant asked him, "Rickshaw, Master?"

Hou responded with a barely perceptual haughty nod of his chin, and the boy rushed out into the street and flagged down the first puller he saw. Hou got in and told the puller to take him to the Masonic Club on the *Waitan*. The *Waitan* was known by the round-eyes as The Bund and was the most important waterfront area in central Shanghai. The area held several important qualities for Hou: it was extremely busy and diverse; so, no one would question a Chinaman's presence there. The *Waitan* centered on a section of East Zhongshan Road which ran along the western bank of the Huangpu River in the eastern part of Huangpu District, with easy access to sail and oarsmen driven launches to carry him and his cargo out to the *Far East Transporter* waiting in the Yangshan Deep Water Harbor. His two body guards followed immediately behind in another rickshaw.

It would not have been a positive experience for Hou and his men to have the harbor patrol police stop his launch and to inspect his cargo disguised in uniform bamboo boxes marked with innocuous signs: Soaps, Perfumes, Feminine Products, and Ceylon Coffee. He knew he did not have to worry because he had paid handsomely for one of the Englishmen–who had a very large gambling debt–to be elected to the Shanghai Municipal Council with its monopolies on shipping licenses, city owned rickshaws, settlement tramways, opium sales, and prostitution. The indentured Britain was in a position to have police look the other way, for a small fee, of course.

The real outgoing cargo consisted of a multimillion won, rupee, and rouble, consignment of cannabis, cocaine, heroin, morphine with glass syringes and sharp needles, laudanum syrup, and opium in the form of blue pills, bound for Russia, Europe, Turkey, and the Americas—with the base in the U.S. city, Boston, valued conservatively at twenty million USD. It was the largest shipment the Three Families Tong had ever made, and the profit would likely be sufficient for Hou and his wife and concubines to move to Beijing and live out the rest of their lives in relative luxury. Even if he elected not to retire, Hou knew that he could supply a string opium dens he had planned throughout India and Asia for as long as he lived. He blessed the day that he had made a contract with the round-eyed young Russian beauty, Alexandra. In case he ever needed her again, he was determined to be fair in dividing up the profits and to be as polite as only a Chinese gentleman can be.

Visibility was perfect—a warm, sunny, bright blue-sky day—and the waters were calm as the *Far East Transporter* made its way into the bustling Port of Shanghai from the Hangzhou Bay entrance south of Shanghai. The port faces the East China sea on the east, Hangzhou Bay on the south and includes the river confluences of the Yangtze, Huanpu, and Qiantang. Hou's spies had described the exact location where his launch would be anchored with a small time-frame between 4:00 and 5:00 in the afternoon. The area around the central Yangpo buoy was always very busy with fast junks and lumbering coal and iron ore barges moving at their varying speeds. Alexandra was informed that the launch was to be located one hundred meters SSE of the buoy and would be easily recognizable because it was freshly painted in an auspicious Chinese fire red.

Alexandra had the helm of the *Far East Transporter's* grey painted launch, and her personal body guard—the massive Don Cossack, Stenka Mazepa—stood close by her armed to the teeth. Boris had been duped into teaching the ship's meager marine component to do Russian army close-order drills, a task which should keep him busy the rest of the afternoon. When she saw the bright red launch close by the buoy, she signaled for the crew members tasked with off-loading the launch into the *Far East Transporter's* holds.

She slowly and deftly pulled along side Hou's launch, her starboard side to his port side. The nimble ship's monkeys swung across the narrow distance between the ship and the launch and secured them together. A ramp built by Hou's men was placed across the space, and the off-loading began at a running pace. They could not be caught holding any of this cargo which was illegal every place in the world in the time period in which they were working. The work took just under an hour and a half and was secured in the *Far East Transporter's* holds hidden under large beige canvas covers and behind the bales of silk from Shanghai.

Hou and Alexandra observed the transfer and both made rapid calculations of the products to be certain that nothing and no one was shorted. Hou used his abacus deftly and rapidly after long years of practice, and Alexandra did the math in her head.

"Alexandra, you and I are about to become very rich. Just keep your head and don't let another soul see the new boxes. Let us not attempt to exchange money here. We operate on a basis of trust. I will see you in my building in Millionka when you get back. I intend to take three weeks to get there, and I presume it will take you closer to four. That will help keep us separate in the eyes of spies, pirates, and the constabulary."

They bowed in a modest *wai*, neither of them was as yet comfortable with the western custom of hand shaking for business. Within minutes the two vessels separated—Hou back into the Chinese sector of Shanghai, and Alexandra heading back out to the open ocean.

Boris was not as easily duped as Alexandra thought, and it offended him that she considered him so easily fooled. It also bothered him that he did not know what was being transferred into the *Far East Transporter's* holds and why it was shrouded in so much secrecy. Even before they got married, each of them had promised to deal with full honesty with the other; and this activity strained their trust and credulity. He vowed to wait for the right moment to bring up his questions.

The right moment did not come during the remainder of the voyage home or during the vigorous activity of unloading the cargo and doing the accounting. Any thought of bringing the subject up evaporated when Boris saw Alexandra grow pale and begin to vomit as they off-loaded a crate of foul-smelling—but good tasting—durian fruit from Saigon. It was not like her to be bothered by bad sights or odoriferous smells.

When she stopped retching, Boris asked, "What's the problem, Alexandra? You look terrible. Did you catch one of the Chinese fevers?"

"No, Boris, but my monthly curse has not been with me for two times."

"Is that a female kind of problem?"

"You might say so. It appears that I am with child—maybe for two months now."

It was Boris's time to become pale.

"Are you sure?"

"I am sure, big brave Boris. I am very sure?"

"Is it a boy?" he asked guilelessly.

She laughed, "Only God knows. We will love our baby no matter what its sex."

"That we will, my love. That we will. And whether the baby is a prince or a princess, we will see to it that he or she has a great role in an important family."

The early months of the pregnancy were difficult for Alexandra— nausea, vomiting, weakness, easy fatigability, and little interest in marital or business life. At first, Boris was understanding and sympathetic; but by the fifth month, his stay in the bull's pen began to grow tedious, then frustrating, and finally made him angry. By the seventh month, Alexandra seemed to be doing well. Her appetite had returned with a vengeance, and her food preferences were so strange that it was as if a different person had inhabited her body. Prior to the pregnancy, Alexandra was a dainty eater and always mindful of her beautiful figure. Now she was a glutton; there was no kind way to describe her, in Boris's mind. She ate pickles with chocolate, mutton with sauerkraut, cake and pie with vegetables, and all in ever increasing amounts. Her weight began to balloon which made her cry. In fact, she cried much of the time, unable to tell him or her mother why. Irina said she had the melancholy that went along with being with child, and it would pass like all bad things.

One positive thing came of Alexandra's ennui and lack of interest. Boris had to take over the business coming from their recent commercial voyage and from their involvement with Abram and Irina in the fur company enterprises. When he supervised the off-loading of the brigantine *Far East Transporter*'s holds, the stevedores and clerks took him aside to show him boxes hidden under large beige canvas covers and behind the bales of silk from Shanghai which were not included in the ship's manifest.

"We have no knowledge of these boxes. They are very sturdily built and heavy. We presume that they are some considerable value, Sir. Perhaps it would be best if you were to attend to them personally, Prince Boris," the unctuous port clerk said with a bland expression and syrup on his almost smirking lips.

"Perhaps that would be best," Boris said dismissively.

He knew that this could prove to be problematical if a secret cargo became public knowledge. He remembered rather vividly seeing Alexandra supervising the boxes in question from the red Chinese launch in Shanghai harbor. He felt anger rising in his chest.

Inspection of the boxes confirmed his worst fears which added fuel to his growing anger and to the beginnings of feelings of estrangement with Alexandra. How could she risk their family's reputation and financial holdings with such a brazen and secret deal with low-life criminals? The knowledge that she was keeping serious secrets from him was like a corrosive in his gut. But, there it was hidden under large beige canvas covers and behind the bales of silk from Shanghai: cannabis, cocaine, heroin, morphine, needles, laudanum syrup, and opium in the form of blue pills. Boris did not know the value of this illicit cargo, but his limited observations made him sure that it was in the millions. He had reluctantly agreed to ship legal opium to be able to business in Colombo. That went against the grain of everything he believed about doing business honorably. This was different; it was vile and illegal. It made him angry and afraid.

He pondered about what he should do, torn between his oath of fealty to his wife and her family and his deeply held honor. Pragmatically, he was looking at a fortune in illegal and—in his mind—dangerous goods. To be caught with this much could mean being charged with a capital crime and being hanged for it. He could not think of where he could hide it until a proper disposal could be made. It would expose him, the ship, and the company to grave danger to be caught dumping it into the ocean.

He sat there for half an hour racking his brain. One of the stevedores tapped him on the shoulder.

"Master, there is a merchant from Millionka here who wishes a word with you. He says it is rather urgent. Shall I send him away?"

Boris looked at the man standing in the light of the hatch leading to the deck above the hold. He had seen him before; he had seen Alexandra talking to him. He could not recall the man's name, if he had ever heard it; but the man himself was unforgettable, an anachronism—something from the old Chinese past. He stood with his arms folded with an imperious look on his face. Boris saw that the crew men deferred to him.

"Bring him to me please," Boris answered the stevedore.

"I am Hou Eadric," the Chinaman said and bowed deeply. "I know that you are Prince Boris of the House of Yusupov."

"What can I do for you, Mr. Hou?" Boris said and bowed even lower.

CHAPTER THIRTY-FOUR
TENSE TIMES

I know being pregnant and giving birth is the most wonderful
thing on Earth. I know that after you have a baby, there is a sense
of addiction, a need to have another. It's biological.
—Janine di Giovanni

**Aboard the Tarasova-Yusupov Commercial Vessel, the *Far East
Transporter*, Vladivostok Freeport Harbor, Vladivostok,
Far East Russia, June 15, 1879**

Hou gave Prince Boris one of those enigmatic or more popularly
called by Englishmen—inscrutable–smiles and made a defer-
ential *wai* before answering. The smugness of the man's general
demeanor and the false smile rankled Boris and added to his general
sense of distrust.

"Ah, good master, I am Hou Eadric. It is rather what I can do for
you. I don't know how much your esteemed wife has told you of our
business transaction; but since she is suffering the pangs of being with
child at this time, I thought it prudent to conclude our bargain before…
shall we say…problems raise their ugly heads."

"Are you responsible for this cargo which is not listed on the legal
manifest of the ship, Mr. Hou?"

"I am, along with your delicate and lovely wife, whom I must say is
a very astute businesswoman."

"What happens now, Mr. Hou?"

"Now, I take over; and all problems for you evaporate. Is that not a good thing?"

"Yes. However, once you take the goods, how can I be sure that my wife will receive her proper share of the proceeds."

"I am most pleased that you asked that question. In my business, we rely on trust; and Princess Yusupov and I trust each other. She knows that I will keep up my end of the bargain; and once the goods are moved from Vladivostok, a messenger will contact her; so, she can know how, when, and where, to receive her payment. We do not cheat or lie to each other. For others to do such a thing to the Three Families Tong would result in...a fatal...consequence. I respect the power and reach of the Tarasovas, the Jardine-Mathesons, and the Yusupovs. Because of that, I would not hold back so much as a single kopeck from you. I see that the boxes are all completely undisturbed; so, I have all good faith that nothing has been removed. We are all acting in *jiāzú chéngxìn*. That is 'familial good faith' in case, perhaps, you are not fully fluent with our Mandarin language and strong cultural customs."

"I have to trust to your good faith intentions and to Alexandra's good business sense. What is my part?"

"Simply to inform your fine crew members that Mr. Hou and the Three Families Tong will assume responsibility for this part of the ship's cargo. You need do nothing more. My messenger will come to your family home on Pekinskaya Street when the business is completed. Until then, rest easy and give my humble regards to your precious wife."

He bowed in a small *wai*, and Boris did likewise. He did not wish to spend any longer than necessary with this supercilious, duplicitous, humblebragger, sycophant whom he trusted about as far as he did the Bengal pirates.

Boris hurried home as rapidly as he could, feeling most uneasy for many and varied reasons. He sorted out his order of priorities and went to see Alexandra first. She was lying uncomfortable in her feather bed munching on fresh fruit and a bowl of fragrant rice.

"How are you this afternoon?" he asked.

"All right I suppose, dear patient Boris. I have a woman's intuition that my bat-in-the cave time is about to come to an end soon."

Boris laughed and made Alexandra laugh for the first time in days, "Surely my dear, you mean 'being in the family way', don't you?"

"Of course, or as my mother, and probably yours would say, 'with child', all such sweet and rather silly terms."

"Why do you think you are near to delivering the new family prince, Alexandra?"

"More frequent and harder belly pains. I can't put my legs together, and they are more swollen than ever. Just like my face. My belly is so big that I am sure I will have ugly stretch marks, and you won't love me anymore. But my water hasn't broken; so, it won't be right away."

Boris was aware of some of the mysterious processes of bringing forth a son having attended to numerous female animals on the Yusupov farms. He supposed the breaking of the waters happened to "grease the skids" as Vlad used to say.

Two days later, Alexander went into frank labor. During one particularly hard contraction, she had Boris feel the baby's head as it pushed against her pubic bone.

"I think it is time to fetch Mama and the midwife. They will know what to do."

Fortunately for her, her mother, aunts, and grandmothers had told her exactly what was going to transpire in great detail, only leaving out the part where some mothers die of exhaustion or hemorrhage.

The midwife, Dominika Rodiovna Golovanova, and the naval physician, Captain Second Rank Vladislav Rostislavevich Fedorov, were brought to the Pekinskaya Street residence by racing troika buggies. Fedorov began immediately to order the necessary large bowls of hot water and piles of towels while Golovanova rounded up the mother, grandmother, and several maids to serve as assistants.

"Prince Boris, and Abram Timurovich, please find a restful place outside the room. I will come to you when the birthing is done."

The two men, so used to giving orders, obeyed meekly.

Then, Captain Fedorov turned his attention to Alexandra and spoke kindly, "How are you, my dear?"

"Hurting like my bottom is going to fall out, Kind Sir," she responded in as surly a fashion as she felt.

"Try to relax. How frequent are your pains now?"

"Less than five minutes apart and getting harder and harder, Doctor."

"Let me examine you, and we can get a good idea of how long it will be; is that all right?"

"Of course…" she groaned and arched her back suppressing a scream. "…anything."

His deft practiced hands and long fingers took less than a minute to know all he needed to know.

"All is as it should be, Sasha," he said in his mellifluous soothing voice, made all the more comforting by using the diminutive for her name as if she were a well-cared for child in good hands. "I think it is time to break your water sac. It will be just a pinprick, then you will feel a great gush of water, which we will collect. You will feel a few minutes of decreased pressure and pain; then I predict, labor will get going rapidly until we have a baby out in a very short time."

"Will it hurt terrible?" Alexandra asked.

Before the doctor's gentle voice could reassure her, Midwife Golovanova announced with all the charm of an Old Testament prophet, "thousands and thousands of women have gone through this since time began. You must be strong. Be a good girl for the doctor. 'Unto the woman he said, I will greatly multiply thy sorrow and thy conception; in sorrow thou shalt bring forth children; and thy desire shall be to thy husband, and he shall rule over thee.' *Genesis 3:16*. That is your duty. No screaming or other nonsense now, young lady."

Captain Federova gave her a withering look but said nothing. He pushed Alexandra's thighs gently apart and found the fully open cervix. He made a four-millimeter cut in the tough translucent covering and out gushed a pail full of thick cloudy fluid. There was a moment of almost complete relief of pressure, and the nearly exhausted girl began to fall asleep.

"No sleeping now, lazy bones. It's time to work. Get ready to push," ordered Golovanova.

"Wait until I tell you, Sasha. Rest for a little bit."

Soon the pains started again, this time more definitive, harder, and more directed towards the portal out of her body.

"Push now," the doctor said, "don't stop until I say so. It is called 'labor' for a reason."

Alexandra's face flushed, and the veins in her neck and forehead bulged. She grunted with the effort.

"Breath, girl; breath. Take a deep breath then start again," the midwife ordered, this time more gently.

The pains increased; the laboring pressure increased; and the exhaustion multiplied until Alexandra thought she would become unconscious.

Doctor Federova pointed at the crowning head of the baby beginning to push through, and Golovanova nodded with a smile.

"Just a few more pushes, and we'll have a baby," Federova said; and Alexandra felt a wave of emotional relief that it was almost over with.

Doctor Federova's fingers manipulated the baby's shoulders; so, there would be no injuries, and gave a gentle steady tug on them. The baby moved quickly down the birth canal but came to a point of tough narrowing at the opening to the outside."

"Scissors, Nurse," he ordered.

She gently slapped them into his palm. He inserted his left index finger under the tight introitus and lifted it away from the baby's glistening slick wet head. He made a small transverse cut on both sides and helped the small head move out followed by the shoulders, chest, belly, and lower extremities. He double clamped the umbilical cord and transected it. Then, he made a very quick motion to lift the baby up and then to bring it done again. The newborn emitted a gusty howl.

"We have a bouncing baby boy, Sasha. Good work!"

Golovanova wrinkled her brow and returned to her usual frown, "It's small," she said critically but softly.

"Ah, my dear midwife, there is a reason for that. We have a surprise."

He said it loud enough for Alexandra to hear.

"What surprise, Doctor? I don't think I like the sound of that," Alexandra responded.

"Oh, dear Sasha; but you will. We have another baby waiting to greet the world. This is a great day!"

Alexandra managed a smile even though she felt like one delivery was enough for today already.

The new baby was a little larger and took some more manipulation to present itself to the world.

"Another beautiful big boy," Federova said happily. "Surely you have found favor in God's eyes."

Alexandra was not quite sure that was true, but she would settle for the gift of the two healthy babies–boys at that–and would ponder the 'favor' part some other time.

"Will you nurse the babies, Dear?" the midwife asked, "it is the best way to make them healthy and happy early in their little lives. Or do you want to have a wet-nurse like those lazy aristocrats like to do and to begin the life of neglecting their little ones right as soon as the poor wee things are born?"

Federova laughed at the midwife's none-too-subtle suggestion about nursing the newborns—an admonition with which he fully concurred.

"What do you recommend, Doctor?" Alexandra asked drowsily.

"Let me show you," he said.

He spread open Alexandra's bodice and put one baby on each side of her chest just below her bulging breasts. The two strong boys began instinctually to crawl over her sweaty slick skin and to root about until their mouths found a ready nipple and began to suck with gusto.

Alexandra felt a sudden gush of pleasure race to her nipples and watched with a satisfied smile as the two boys tried—albeit unsuccessfully—to get milk.

"You aren't ready, yet, my girl," Golovanova told her, "but in a couple of days, you will produce like the best Red Gorbatov cow in the oblast."

Alexandra managed a wan smile and tried to believe that it was compliment.

Doctor Federova shook his head in avuncular acceptance of the rough old midwife's choice of similes; but, noting that his patient did not take offense, he decided not to say anything.

The doctor and the midwife left the babies and the new mother in the gushingly loving care of the house maids and Irina Tarasova while they went out to talk to the two exhausted and anxious men.

"Have a difficult delivery, "Gentlemen?" joked Doctor Federova, which broke the ice.

"Is she all right?" asked Abram.

"Is the baby all right? What kind is it?" asked Boris.

"The babies are doing fine, and they are the human kind."

Boris blushed, "You know what I mean. Boy or girl?"

"Boys."

"More than one?" the two men asked almost in unison.

"Twins," said the ever concrete and pragmatic midwife. "They are going to be breast fed during Alexandra's two-month lying-in period."

Doctor Federova added, "Two months of bed rest is the minimum. We will check her as time passes to see if or when she is ready to get out of bed. Her mother and the maids will care for her and the babies. Both of us are firmly of the belief that those children need their mother and women with whom they are familiar, not a nanny or a hired nurse. The babies need to lie on their mother's chest and lap several times a day. And, it is my studied opinion that you men need to cuddle and play with these two little new rascals. We can teach you how to do it safely, but they like to be handled and massaged and wrestled with. You will get closer to these boys by doing that in the first months of their lives than you will for almost the entire rest of their days. Boris…no relations for six weeks. Remember that.

"Congratulations, Gentlemen. This is an auspicious day."

Another auspicious day came when a Chinese man arrived at the front door a week later and presented Boris with a letter from Hou Eadric.

"To meet me at my home in Millionka, Number 19 Admirala Fokina Street, today, noon. Have ten million surprises for you."

Signed, *Hou Eadric* of the Three Families Tong.

CHAPTER THIRTY-FIVE

'*Qí hǔ nán xià* [When you choose to ride a tiger, it is hard to dismount.]

—Chinese Proverb

"And the day came when the risk to remain tight in a bud was more painful than the risk it took to blossom."

—Anais Nin

Tarasova House, No. 71 Pekinskaya Street, Vladivostok, Far East Russia, June 15, 1879

Irina could not contain herself with the thrill of being a grandmother at such a young age. Even while Alexandra was in labor she planned a baby shower to beat every baby shower ever recorded in the Irkutsk oblast—which she knew was one of those new customs coming their way via Saint Petersburg. After all, she reasoned, there were two babies; and they were the most beautiful little creatures God had ever put upon the earth. No one she expressed that bit of unbiased knowledge to would have ever dreamed of contradicting her. Once again, she invited everybody who was anybody and a great many who were not, to share her joy. Alexandra was too happy to see how much it all pleased her mother to suggest that she had had a small role in the production. There was a mandatory wait—more a superstition, really—that mothers typically do not show their baby to anyone except the boys in the family, the midwife, and other close relatives for forty-eight hours after the baby is born. Husbands and fathers usually had to wait for two nervous days.

Irina investigated everything that might contribute to the reputation of the babies' shower being the greatest ever. Prince Boris learned from a brief telegram from his mother that the tzar had ordered a massive photographic expedition of the entire Russian Empire. The photographer, Sergei Mikhailovich Prokudin-Gorskii, had business connections with the Yusupovs; and Tatiana suggested to Boris that the intrepid explorer/photographer would be interested in obtaining pictures of what the people and the towns of Far East Russia looked like. He was going to be in the Irkutsk oblast during the month of June. Boris wanted very much to get back in his wife's good graces; so, he vowed to get Sergei Mikhailovich to photograph Tarasova House and its occupants and all the guests who came to the party.

Most of the residents of the oblast had seen black and white photographs, and many had framed pictures of themselves on their wedding days hanging in their homes. There were photos of the tzar and his family hanging in official buildings. However, no one had ever seen a color photograph, including Prince Boris. He saw examples of Prokudin-Gorskii's photos and was nothing short of astounded.

He asked the gregarious photographer, "How did you perform such magic? These pictures will create a living history and will be of value for generations to come."

The famous man was not only a marvelous artist and technician of the newest photographic art, but he was also self-effacing and engagingly humble.

He replied to Boris's question, "It is simple, really. I have a wonderful camera which you see here. You can do almost anything if you have enough money, and my patrons certainly do have more than enough. What I learned to do through a lot of trial and error was to take three regular black and white pictures as fast as I can and use red, then green, then blue filters to get the colors I want. That's where the work comes in. I have to mix and recombine the photographs and then project them with filtered very bright lanterns to show true color images."

Boris said, "These colors are better than the real images of the people, the buildings, and the landscapes. I cannot thank you enough for taking pictures of our twins."

The photographs showed two chubby babies in white baptismal gowns with their hands holding rattles and one boy holding a large feather. By a miracle of patience and rapid photo shooting, Prokudin-Gorskii was able to get one perfect picture of both boys sitting still, looking at the camera, and smiling at the same time.

Alexandra was so thrilled with the photographs Boris presented to her, that she threw her arms around his neck and whispered, "I can hardly wait for my lying-in time to be done. It is only five weeks more."

It should have sounded most encouraging, but to Boris it sounded like a life sentence that had to be lived out before he and his wife would be able to be in bed face-to-face. However, things seemed to be going so well that his intention to demand an accounting by Alexandra about her dealings with the Chinese criminal, Hou Eadric, was sliding back further and further into his mind.

The man insinuated himself into Boris and Alexandra's life even on that joyous day. Guests bought gifts for the babies—some mundane like the newest fashion in one-year-old clothing, and some showing more care like the tiny imperial army uniforms created by the seamstresses at the Balagansk Prison. Hou's gift was by far the most interesting and entertaining. He brought forward a fairly large size gleaming white barrel and presented it to Alexandra.

"I understand your boys are lively and are likely to be a handful, Princess. Here is a gift to make you appreciate and enjoy the old saw that boys will be boys. Quick, now, open the top of the barrel," Hou said with a full-face grin that showed his rotten and missing teeth at their worst.

Alexandra tried not to look at his face; so, she pried the top off the barrel. When the lid popped off, she looked in and gave a little shriek followed by a big whole body-laugh. Out jumped two very small white monkeys who celebrated their freedom by running around and jumping on skittish ladies and highly entertained men and boys.

Boris wiped tears from his eyes, and said, "So, boys will be boys; and they will be as full of fun as a barrel full of monkeys!"

A servant carried them away and secured them by a pretty silver chain attached to one foot and to a pole in the mansion room dedicated as a child's play room.

As Boris was directing that activity, Hou took advantage of the moment to say to Alexandra, "I know you have a new voyage coming up, and I have a proposition for you. When you can, come to my place at Number 19 Admirala Fokina Street. It will be worth your while."

With that Hou bowed and melted into the crowd of admirers of the new babies and out into the street. Boris saw him leave and realized that he had not told Alexandra of his trip to Millionka where he obtained paper money in value of ten million American dollars, but in a mix of nine different currencies. The bulk of money had filled the family Phaeton and was difficult to conceal. By special arrangements, he had been able to deposit the money in his and Alexandra's account in the Irkutsk Oblast Bank.

When the guests had left, Boris and Alexandra agreed as they had now for several months to sleep in separate rooms to remove temptations to violate the conditions of the lying-in requirements. Actually–although they never spoke of it openly–both of them had gradually lost the youthful fervor for each other they once had. Boris was more than aware of that and was ashamed that he was beginning to look upon other young women with more interest than he knew was proper.

It was a month before Alexandra felt fully ready to take Hou Eadric up on his offer to go into Millionka to talk business with him. Physically, she was in good health and had been from four weeks postpartum. Initially she had some postpartum depression; but as her body healed, so did her mind. She was ready to return to her husband's bed physically, but the pulsating desire for him which permeated their early months of marriage had gone. She knew it was ridiculous; but at age twenty, she felt like an old married woman for whom girlish lust had settled into a willingness to be a proper but unenthusiastic–maybe even grudging—wife. She was admitting to herself that the excitement of doing international business and having seagoing adventures was more alluring that being a wife. She adored her babies but was beginning to think about arrangements for them to be properly cared for when she went back to sea.

As opposed to her first foray into Millionka when she wanted to have her personal body guard—the massive Don Cossack, Stenka Mazepa—hold onto her arm, Alexandra was not only over her fear of the denizens of Chinatown, but confident that she could hold her own. However, she was not a giddy girl either; so, when she went to Millionka this time, she again had Stenka accompany her.

The length of time spent on polite chit-chat with the tong—or Chinese highbinder—leader was abbreviated; so, they could get down to business. It was difficult to hear each other because of the noise coming from the common room outside Hou's placid office. There was shrill string music of a Chinese fiddle and the squeak and tempestuous outcries of Chinese wind instruments.

"What is that racket?" Alexandra asked.

"Oh, pay no mind, Missy. Just other tongs making sacrifices to gods because they must make war of vengeance against other tongs like the Wah Ching and Joe Boys. Unfortunately, all not so peaceful and business like as the Three Families Benevolent Society."

Alexandra raised one eyebrow but just in her mind. It was none of her business.

Hou put his business proposal to her, "Will need three good ships, one big one for merchandise and two fighter vessels for to protect. Do you have those protect kind of ships, Missy Yusupov?"

"We will have them in another month."

"Good. Plans will take that long. We have goods to transport through Red Flag Fleet territory and then into Honorable British East India waters. Hard to say which is the worst bunch of pirates. Cargo is like the good one you brought back to Shanghai. Am happy to report that the first cargo has been sent on to San Francisco to accommodate the needs of Chinatown there. Seems that the need is eternal and will be source of good business and good joss for long time to come. We will become… how do you round-eyes say?…feelthy rich, no?"

"Yes, if Zhèng Yi and Ching Shih of the Red Flags or Sir Michael Forbisher of the HEIC don't kill us first, or the Chinese or British law enforcement authorities don't capture us and hang us for piracy," Alexandra said, posing the risks succinctly.

"And cannot discount typhoons, or other acts of the gods, Missy. Not say that venture is without risk. Old Chinese proverb which say, *'Yīn yè fèi shí'* [Is foolish to refuse to eat just because of the chance of choking.]' I say, 'Life does not come without risks. Risk of failure is not an argument for not giving good try."

"Good proverb Master Hou, but also recall, *'Qí hŭ nán xià* [When you choose to ride a tiger, it is hard to dismount.]' I needn't tell you that we–like anyone else–must remember that when you take chances you have to live with the consequences. It is difficult to back out."

Silently to herself, she thought of her dealings with Hou Eadric in terms of another Chinese proverb, '*When you sup with the Devil be sure to use a long spoon*.'"

Hou looked directly at Alexandra's eyes and said, "'*Qián pà láng hòu pà hŭ*' [It is a problem to fear wolves ahead and tigers behind.] That is to be obsessed by fears of attack from all sides. Remember, we are not without our spies and our gunships and brave men. It is true '*Qiáng lóng nán yā dì tóu shé*' [that even a dragon finds it difficult to conquer a snake in its hiding place], we have a great knowledge of the area where we are going, and the people who wait for us there. That makes us strong and gives us a definite advantage even against an apparently stronger enemy. I must now ask you the simple and straight question, Missy Alexandra; are you in or out?"

Alexandra paused only a minute before replying laconically, "*Za*."

The potential for great ongoing profit and the guarantee of adventure were too much to pass up. She was 'in'.

Two months later, Alexandra and Boris finalized their plans to take separate commercial voyages. Alexandra would go to Colombo, Ceylon and the Bay of Bengal and make a trade with the Bengali pirates who worked hand-in-glove with that pillar of British Ceylon's high society, Glenleven Armitage.

He dreaded getting any further involved, especially with the drug trade, and most especially with the so-called "ivory" trade. But he had to keep up his end of the company's business, just as Alexandra had to keep up her end by dealing with that cut-throat, Hou Eadric, in transportation of illegal drugs. He longed for the day when the two of them could accumulate enough to retire where the criminals could not find them, with enough money to be comfortable for a lifetime, and where their children could receive an education in safety with decent Christian people—maybe the Bahamas, a place in the West Indies that some of the seafarers had described to him–a paradise run by the British.

Ostensibly, Boris was scheduled to take a voyage to Tokyo, Seoul, Shanghai, Jakarta and back. He would leave with a full cargo and return with a different full cargo. There was nothing unusual about his plans or the cargo on the manifest. The dangers were not significant compared to those Alexandra would likely encounter. According to his ship's manifest, most of his cargo consisted of fine European and British linens, Chinese and Chosŏn silk and porcelains, Japanese *nanbangashi* [southern barbarian confectionery], with candies including those made from Portuguese sugar like *castella, konpeitō, aruheitō, karumera, keiran sōmen, bōro,* and *bisukauto,* precious metals—especially copper and silver—finely crafted steel swords, harquebuses, to be sold at ports along the way, and other products to be obtained in Nagasaki.

Alexandra felt guilty about having engineered the arrangement for her and Boris to have separate voyages, not because she had personal misgiving about shirking her wifely duties; but she did recognize that she was doing to her children what she had always despised and railed against. She convinced herself that it was all for the best; the two little boys would hardly miss her for three months; and then, she would return and give them the childhood they deserved. Maybe by then, the spark that had ignited her passion to marry Boris would return; and normal family life would be her lot. She also felt a measure of guilt because she knew that there was something wrong with involvement in the drug business, even if it was true that the users did so of their own volition; and she and Hou were simply supplying what they wanted and were more than willing to pay for.

Both Alexandra and Boris knew deep down that they were entering a new and more dangerous world, where they were going to beard the lion in his lair—the pirates, the East India thugs, the Bay of Bengal smugglers, and the fury of China seas storms. They were not going to be able tell the other members of the Jardine-Matheson, Tarasova, and Yusupov consortium what they were up to. None of them would approve; so, Alexandra and Boris were on their own.

Preparations were done in parallel for the voyages since the needs were very much the same. They first had to build one and refurbish another combat ready guard ship, heavily armed, and manned by a well-trained and well-provisioned crew of fighters. There were two such ships already in service, and the plan was to have a very large commercial vessel and two guardian ships to travel with them as they sailed to their disparate destinations. The exact details of each other's cargoes were allowed to remain vague to avoid contention between them.

CHAPTER THIRTY-SIX
EVEN MORE TENSE TIMES

Capitalism is the astounding belief that the most wickedest of men will do the most wickedest of things for the greatest good of everyone.

—John Maynard Keynes

On board ships—the *Far East Transporter* and the *Vladivostok Cargo Liner*–July-November, 1879

In truth, Alexandra was trafficking in extremely valuable drugs, and she was going to a place in a country not listed on her manifest as a port of call—Sitka in Southeastern Russian Alaska. Much as he detested himself for doing so, Boris's main cargo on the outgoing limb of his voyage was to be furs, machine parts, European style clothing, iron ore, and long guns to Seoul. In truth, the goods were to be sold in Tokyo for Japanese slave women who would next to be sold as concubines to black African crewmembers and then taken to the west African slave auction centers and traded for black African men, women, and children who were to be taken to the West Indies to be sold into the stiflingly hot, humid, and pestilential jungle plantations. The profits were huge, and the risks small. On the legal documents, he carried, Boris's last ports of call were Lyushunkou District/Port Arthur and Dalian on the tip of Manchuria—a two or three-day sailing trip around the southern tip of Chosŏn from the Yellow Sea and back to Vladivostok on the Sea of Japan. This was planned only as a ruse.

Alexandra met moderate fall storms most of her voyage; but the *Far East Transporter*–after the full refurbishment in Vladivostok–was sturdy and altogether seaworthy. Her two accompanying guard ships frightened away two attacks in the East China Sea, but just as they entered the southern end of the Bay of Bengal through the Strait of Malacca, a force of seven pirate ships swept towards them from the Indian Nikobar Islands.

The sentry standing on the barrel crow's nest platform or the guardian ship, *Archangel*, shouted, "Red sails nor'nor'east at eighty degrees comin' in hard!

The sailors on the *Far East Transporter* caught the sight and informed Alexandra and the ship's lower officers.

Alexandra took the helm and shouted, "General quarters! all hands-on deck! Man all guns! Prepare to repel boarders!"

That included cooks and cabin boys. Every sailor and hand lined up on the main deck saber in hand. The first mate described the incoming force as he got the information from the crow's nest and look-outs on lower spars:

"Seven total red-sailed junks. There's a three masted and a two masted galley, one two masted galley barque, two three masted junks with what looks to be light cannonades, lighter than ours and no match for the security vessels. Aft, there's what they call a pandaren junk and an ibn Nattuta junk. All sails are fully battened, and they are sailing light in the water—probably no cargo, but maybe sixty to as many as a hundred fighters aboard each. Probably gutted out their forty to sixty cabins to make room for the small army of *piraty* [pirates]!"

Alexandra trained her keen eyes on the fastest of the junks and saw that the rowers on the 200-ton fast boats were keeping up a furious pace. Behind them were larger—800-ton vessels—having three decks. The junks moved quickly through the two-three-foot waves and were gaining distance on Alexandra's small fleet.

"Stand in your places, men," she ordered at intervals. "We are better armed, faster, and more nimble than they are. We will take the day. Stand fast!"

Her ships were not only better constructed and better armed, but the drilling in Golden Horn Harbor now paid off. The guarding vessels defied the logic of defensive warfare by turning directly into the flanks of the oncoming junks. It became a question of who would blink first.

The Vladivostok ships were considerably sturdier than the junks, and it appeared to the Bengal pirates that the intention by the commercial ships was to ram them. They broke ranks first and descended into a chaotic scramble to get out of the way of the rapidly advancing European vessels. When the pirate captains were able to see the size of the three Vladivostok ship's guns, they lost their nerve and made a dash to get away from the upcoming fight that they had started.

When her ships were in range, Alexandra ordered the semaphore flags hoisted on the halyards on both the port and starboard yardarms with the company flag first then a simple message in the international code of signals from the remainder: "Fire at will!"

The light guns of the fleeing junks lacked the power to strike any of Alexandra's ships at her carefully chosen distance; so, they fled. Her guns wrought devastating damage to the hulls, masts, and galley sailors and slaves. One junk—the three-masted galley—was too heavy in the water and too light in her gunnery to escape; so, she sunk in a ball of flame leaving her crew to sink or swim in the roiling ocean. Three more were crippled beyond repair and ran up flags signaling surrender. Two junks were boarded by Alexandra's highly trained marines, and the officers and crews surrendered quickly without inflicting injuries on the men from Vladivostok.

Seeing the catastrophic error of the plan to attack the seemingly easy prey presented by the commercial ships, the last combatant—the colorful ibn Nattuta junk—hauled up its surrender flags just before being boarded from both sides by Alexandra's terrifying and screaming marines.

In less than twenty minutes, the battle was over. Alexandra ordered that any of the pirates who willingly surrendered be brought aboard her three ships and loaded onto the ibn Nattuta junk which had been taken over by an able Vladivostok crew. The rest of the ships, what remained of them were put to the torch.

The four ships sailed to the Indian Andaman Islands and made port. There they met the Bengali pirates who worked hand-in-glove with that pillar of British Ceylon's high society, Glenleven Armitage, after sharing prearranged challenge signs ("Who is king?") and countersigns ("Chamaraja Wodeyar IX of the Wodeyar Dynasty"). Alexandra ordered her cargo of legal and illicit Russian goods and the prisoners–who would be valuable slaves–transferred to the one-eyed, one armed pirate captain, who—in return—delivered to Alexandra four chests of mixed national origin gold coins. That payment was a profit four times over the expenses of her investment. She basked in the glow of the shining gold and forgot to think about the odium of being a slave trader.

That mission accomplished, Alexandra ordered her navigator to set a course for Sitka in Southeastern Russian Alaska with one of her cargo holds still filled with drugs to ease the difficulties of Aleuts and dragooned Chinese peasants laboring as slaves in the fur industry.

Boris left the Golden Horn Harbor less than hour after Alexandra's three ships left for Nagasaki; so, he had been informed. His large commercial ship was christened the *Vladivostok Cargo Liner*. His destination was ostensibly Seoul, but actually, Tokyo. There he offloaded the usual cargo of easily marketable furs, walrus ivory, scrimshawed ivory, heavy leather and fur clothing, silk, porcelain, spices, and other luxury goods, boots, leather horse tack, machine parts, European style clothing, iron ore, and long guns.

He delegated the task of loading on the next cargo—kidnapped Japanese women–bound for the city of Cape Coast on the coast of Upper Guinea, one of the major British slave trading centers. He did not want to know about the treatment of the women before they were interned in Tokyo's slave quarters nor about any information about rape and other crimes—including murder–against them while aboard his ship. He was mathematician enough to know that the space set aside for the women was not enough from them to sit, stand, or walk. They would be stacked in like cordwood.

The unlucky ones, usually unattractive country girls, were doomed to lie shackled on the stinking floor for the entire hellish voyage. The moderately lucky ones would be married to black African crewmen and possibly treated relatively decently. The truly lucky ones were those who died.

The voyage was an almost unbearable three-month ordeal for the captors and ships' crews to say nothing of what the slaves—identified on the ship's manifest as 'ivory'–had to endure. Besides the slaves, they loaded precious metals and lacquer including exquisite lacquer dishware from Tokyo. The ship stopped for provisions in the Dutch East Indies, then passed via the Strait of Malacca through the Bay of Bengal and to Colombo, Ceylon for another provisioning stop where they got rid of their Tokyo cargo and took on a ship load of Indian cloth, yams, silks, indigo, pepper, and silver. They picked up fresh loads from the

Spice Islands of pepper, nutmeg, ivory, cinnamon, cardamom, arecanuts, sappanmwood, and rubies from Burma.

The ships followed the old string of pearls route across the Indian Ocean to the east coast of Africa, with stops only for fresh vegetables, local meats of dubious quality, and fresh water. Their next major stop was in the bustling city of Cape Town where the pent-up urges of the sailors were allowed to be vented in the alleys and brothels of the city. Even Boris could not resist. He was one of the lucky ones who was able to escape gonorrhea and syphilis and the terrible treatments that the unlucky ones had to undergo: eating powdered cowhorn, being whacked on the genitals with a cane or a book, applying soothing sandal oil when available, salves and ointments made of herbs, garlic, and hot peppers, strapping lead weights to the waist until the patient regained strength enough to ward off the disease from overactivity of a sexual nature, cauterize sores with a hot iron, applying mercury and *lignum vitae* [holy wood].

The weather was execrable around the cape and up the west coast until they at last made their final landing in the Gold Coast of West Africa. Boris did his business with the slavers in the Cape Coast Castle, one of forty such large commercial forts—or slave castles–built on the verge of the coast. It was one of the main hubs in the trans-Atlantic slave trade. The castles were used to hold slaves before they were loaded onto ships and sold in the Americas, especially the Caribbean. These castles were dubbed the "gates of no return" since they constituted the last stop before crossing the Atlantic Ocean to the Americas.

Hou Eadric had explained some of the complexities of the triangular African to America to Europe international slave trade before Boris left Vladivostok; but it was more than Hou could explain; and more than Boris could assimilate even after spending a week there. He waited in the officers' quarters of the Castle–which were spacious and airy–with beautiful parquet floors and scenic views of the blue waters of Atlantic. He was able to make use of the beautiful little chapel in the castle enclosure for the officers, traders, and their families as they went about their normal day-to-day life completely detached from the unfathomable human suffering they were consciously inflicting on the damned souls below. The negroes were loaded into the stagnant holds of his ships, an image he avoided incorporating into his memory—not altogether successfully. During the entire homeward voyage, he never once ventured to look into the steaming cesspools below decks. He could not avoid watching the daily dumping of bodies over the rails and into the ocean. That he had to put out of his mind actively if he was going to maintain his hold on sanity.

The voyage across the Atlantic to Cuba took forty-three days. On average two slaves died each day and were dropped unceremoniously into the ocean, never to see land since they exited Africa through the 'gates of no return'. The survivors were in wretched condition; and once again, Boris hurried ashore to hobnob with the genteel of Havana society; so, he would not have to see them again. Many of the slaves were sent to fattening farms and given rest; so, they would bring a better price. Others–less fortunate–were whipped to drive them into the roasting humid heat of the sugar cane fields where very few of them lasted more than six months. At least it was a good thing for Boris to see his ship's records no longer indicating 'ivory' aboard.

Because the plantation owners were very anxious to expand their holdings, they had to have slaves; and they needed an ever-increasing supply. It never occurred to anyone in the slave triangle trafficking that taking good care of the negroes would be economically wise because the supply was both cheap and apparently infinite.

The owner of the largest slave auction house, complimented Boris on his delivery of so many black slaves.

He said, "Times will not always be this good for us. You are no doubt aware that in 1807 and 1808, Great Britain and then the U.S. banned the Atlantic slave trade; but we have been able to carry on by smuggling the blacks by barges out to our ships—ships like yours—and bring them here. We have an understanding with our Spanish crown governors to turn a blind eye in return for...certain ...accommodations. So far, our argument has been that having a couple of slaves per farm helps our country's agriculture industry; so, they have not passed any serious laws. However, to those of us with large plantations, it looks like that is going to come to an end. Our colleagues in Asia tell us that they can ship upwards of 100,000 heathen Chinee a year. Since you come from that area of the world, maybe you would like to get in on the fabulous riches this trade provides, my friend."

"I will explore the capabilities and contacts of my company and will send a message to you soon after I get back to Russia," Boris told him.

He cringed at the thought of getting further involved in the 'ivory' trade or what ever the transporting of Chinese peasant slaves was going to be called. Boris decided to make a studied observation of conditions for the slaves on the plantations to convince himself one way or the other if his conscience could withstand more of an assault than what he knew about the maritime slavery conditions. He quietly visited two plantations near the edge of Havana.

The slaves who labored in the fields were started to work at an early age, often working as much as twenty hours a day during harvest and processing times. Other times, he learned, the slaves worked sixteen to twenty hours a day during the times of cultivating and cutting the crops. Throughout the year, no matter how hot and muggy the days were, slaves could be seen hauling wagons, processing sugarcane with poorly maintained and often dangerous machinery. The wretches slept in locked barracoons getting about three and four hours of sleep if their hunger and pain quieted down enough to permit sleep. The barracoons were filthy, stinking, and extremely hot. They lacked ventilation. The standard barracoon had only one window, a barred hole in the brick wall; so, no slave could escape through it.

A moderately drunk overseer–a former Afro-Cuban slave–confided to Boris that many captives died in the rude hut barracoons either from the horrors they experienced on their journeys from Africa or because they caught some deadly European disease like small pox or plague or the endemic island scourge of yellow fever.

On one plantation, Boris saw man whipped into unconsciousness. His back was flayed, then the wounds were covered with layers of tobacco leaves soaked in urine and salt which caused the large powerful man to wake up screaming from the stinging pain. Boris had seen enough. His 'ivory' days were over, but he did not tell the Havana planters that.

As he enjoyed the famous hospitality of the laid-back Cuban planter class, his ship, the *Vladivostok Cargo Liner*, had its filthy holds thoroughly scrubbed by slaves and was loaded with sugar cane, potassium nitrate—called salt peter—a component of gun powder, nickel, iron, and cobalt bearing ore, cement, feldspar, gypsum, lime, limestone, asphalt, bentonite, chromite, zeolite, marble, steel, and sulfuric acid. With the holds straining the strength of the bulk heads and with the ship sitting low in the water, Boris had the navigator set a course for Trinidad off the Venezuelan coast. Boris sailed from Cuba through the Bocas and anchored off the coast of Chaguaramas which lie in the North West peninsula of Trinidad west of Port of Spain. The island country was as exotic as any man on any of the three ships had ever seen. With no apparent prejudice, Spaniards, Africans, free blacks, assorted other people of color, slaves, former slaves, indigenous Americans, mulattos, east Indians, Spaniards, French republican soldiers and nobility, and retired pirates, mingled in a robust haggling commercial society.

There Boris sold the bulk of their load for the burgeoning economy of Venezuela. From there they traveled across the South Atlantic to the Malvina Islands where they had a major rest and provisioning stop in the port of St. Malo in the *Islas Malvinas*, an archipelago in the South Atlantic Ocean. The town connected to Port St. Malo was a flourishing British and Spanish sheep ranching area; and, more importantly, a ship salvage and repair yard. The *Vladivostok Cargo Liner* required some minor carpentry, and Boris and the ship's crew were impressed about the professionalism of the labor force in this extremely isolated set of Atlantic Islands.

The *Vladivostok Cargo Liner*'s holds were partially replenished with sheep skins and dried mutton—at a high price—and some specialized ship building and repair tools which Boris hoped to be able to sell at a handsome profit in Shanghai or Tokyo. From Port St. Malo in the Malvinas they sailed on relatively calm seas around the Cape of Good Hope to the major harbor of Port Elizabeth to prepare for the arduous voyage from the east side of the tip of southern Africa. Near the coast, the waves were high and the winds variable and troublesome. But—with good seamanship—the sturdy three-ship group sailed out into the Indian Ocean.

Their first stop in the Indian Ocean was at Antananarivo, capital city of the huge and primitive French protectorate island of Madagascar. The entire crew took advantage of the pleasant people, climate, and calm of the capital city. This happened to be one of the intermittent periods of peace because of the modernizing influence of Great Britain; through the previous eight decades, a series of Merina monarchs became enthusiastic about the British look which led to the establishment of European-style schools, government institutions, infrastructure, and the introduction of Christianity. By the tireless efforts of the London Missionary Society, Christianity was now entrenched and dominant on the island. The queen had recently declared it to be the state religion. The downside, for Boris—who was beginning to feel pangs of conscience—was that there still remained more than half a million slaves on the island.

Thus refreshed, the Vladivostok crews set sail for the Chagos Archipelago island of Diego Garcia. There was a brief storm lasting two days which poured several feet of water onto the ship, but rather than being a problem, it provided a cleansing for the ship, replenishment of the drinking water, and a respite from the humidity and heat for the next four days. When they sailed to a point where the islands could be seen by the naked eye, they noted that the archipelago consisted of seven atolls and over sixty islands. The largest of them was Diego Garcia.

All the islands were very sparsely populated, and Diego Garcia was the most populous and active of all the islands. It was covered with coconut plantations and was a lush green against the background of the deep blue of the surrounding ocean. They replenished food, water, and coal–for cooking and heating–and took on additional cargo of sugar, live sea cucumbers for sale in Shanghai, coconuts, and dried coconut fiber for cordage. They purchased a small amount of textiles for future sale in the Irkutsk oblast. Boris permitted a two-day visit for the crew after he learned that Great Britain had abolished slavery in 1834.

Diego Garcia had a most diverse and exotic population owing to its rich history. The natives there were Chagossian islanders of mixed African, South Indian, Portuguese, English, French, and Malay descent, and marooned lepers. They lived simple, spartan, lives in their isolated archipelago working in the coconut and sugar plantations, or in the fishing and small textile industries.

From Diego Garcia, the *Vladivostok Cargo Liner* set a course for Colombo for a brief stop for fresh vegetables, then sailed uneventfully across the southern end of the Bay of Bengal, through the Strait of Malacca and into the South China Sea and Pacific Ocean with stops in Manilla in the Philippine Islands, Taiwan, Okinawa in the Japanese Ryukyu Islands, Pusan on the southern tip of the Chosŏn peninsula, and into the Sea of Japan where they hugged the east China coast. A squall—a harbinger of the hard winter to come–greeted them as they neared the entrance into Golden Horn harbor making them wait two extra and frustrating days before they could make berth in Vladivostok. It was the fifteenth of November, 1879

The five-month voyage was a very lucrative venture for Boris and the Tarasova-Yusupov Trading Company. Boris was now the wealthiest he had ever been from his own efforts, which was a good thing for him because he could expect nothing from the Yusupov family except for his remaining trust funds. The voyage was also a turning point in Boris's life because of his brush with the world-wide slave trade. He dreaded the conversation he expected with Alexandra.

Indian Andaman Islands in the Bay of Bengal, on board the *Far East Transporter,* July 30, 1879

Alexandra was flushed with the excitement that came from having made such a major profit on the first leg of her triangular commercial voyage. She and her ships' officers worked diligently for two weeks to prepare the ships for the arduous trans-pacific voyage. All three ships were fitted out with the best equipment money could buy: Ramsden Sextant, Bond Chronometer, Dutch Nautical Charts, James Imray and Son of London blueback North Pacific Nautical Chart, marine chronometer. They now had a traverse board used to approximate the course run by a ship during a watch, a Walker's Harpoon mechanical ship's log to measure distance traveled, Brown's Nautical Almanac which described the positions of a selection of celestial bodies to enable the navigators to use celestial navigation to determine the position of their ship while at sea, a Brown's Almanac which informed the navigator for each whole hour of the year the position on the earth's surface at which the sun, moon, planets and first point of Aries was directly overhead.

She had bargained with Colombo Chinese merchants for a Chip log and sand glass which served to measure the ship's speed through the water, Davis backstaff, dry magnetic compass, *Sciothericum telescopicum* –a sundial invented in the 17th century that used a telescopic sight to determine the time of noon to within 15 seconds. Alexandra had to pay full price for ship's pumps to remove water from leaks, lumber, and carpenters' tools, large rounds of sail cloth, rigging line, pulleys, extra masts, cheek block, hackle, headstays, jiggers, baggy wrinkles, bee-block, cam cleats, cross-blocks, Jacob's ladders, and the hundreds of other small devices which could not be found or made while at sea—because of the omnipotent law of supply-and-demand.

Alexandra gave in to a bit of morbid feminine whimsy by having a brass plate placed on her stateroom clock which was engraved with a *memento mori*: "*Nunc est bibendum* [Eng. now is the time to drink] "*Memores sumus omnes ad mortem*" [Eng. Remember, we all have to die."]

She put the past part of the voyage behind her and first concentrated on navigating back through the Strait of Malacca and into the South China Sea. She ordered her navigator to set a course for Sitka in Southeastern Russian Alaska some 4,000 miles away across the largely uncharted Pacific with one of her cargo holds still filled with drugs to ease the difficulties of Aleuts and dragooned Chinese peasants laboring as slaves in the fur industry—as she liked to tell herself.

CHAPTER THIRTY-SEVEN

UNCHARTED WATERS, UNSURE FUTURE

"My course is set for an uncharted sea."

—Dante Alighieri

We cannot control the wind, but we can direct the sail.

—Mystic Seaport Museum

On board the *Far East Transporter*, mid-Pacific Ocean
July-September, 1879

Alexandra occasionally gave thought to how her husband, Boris, was doing on his voyage for the company. She found herself not thinking of him as often or as seriously as she had before her voyage began. She wrote that off to the hectic busy nature of her commercial enterprise and of her captaincy of an ocean going sailing vessel. A thought nagged at her brain that she should be feeling more companionless at the separation; but, in fact, she was actually feeling more of an estrangement and was not especially troubled by that. Alexandra was more troubled and felt guilty about not keeping her small twin boys more in the front of her mind. Some days, she had difficulty even bringing their faces to mind.

The voyage out into the notoriously wild Pacific Ocean—despite its misguiding name—was more boring than anxiety producing. Her navigator was a professional, and the navigating equipment was working well. The ship was moving swiftly and on course. Their stocks were well-planned, and the bulk of the supplies were untouched. They had used up most of the perishables–those foods that spoiled the quickest. All the citrus fruits—on board to prevent the dreaded scurvy—were totally depleted. The preserved foods were still plentiful; they had dried, salted, smoked, and pickled meat and fish. There were no cans or suitable jars; so, the ship's sailors packed the preserved food in wood barrels or crates. The long-term non-food supplies–water, clothing, extra sail and wood to repair the ship, medicine, weapons for defense, tools, valuables for trade with whatever locals they run into and the guns, rifles, shields, swords, and pistols were in good condition and dry.

Because of the need to replenish their supplies of fresh vegetables and fruits—especially lemons, limes, and oranges–the *Far East Transporter* made its first stop at the island of Taipan which was made up of two separate islands. They made mooring in the capital city of Taikyo on the western island, Pyondu. The natives and the many Englishmen in that section of Taipan were industrious and excellent commercial businessmen. It took less than a day to refill the larders with the fresh food. This time, Alexandra ordered four times as much as she had used on this short first leg.

The sun was unbearably hot when they set sail the following day. One day after that, they encountered the doldrums and the humid hot air gave the men the impression that they were in a bake oven. The ship was becalmed and did not move forward—did not budge a hooter–for the next three days with the crew becoming gradually more disheartened by the day. Then, a minor storm blew up which was more wind than precipitation and that was a blessing, for which the crew gave thanks.

Sixteen days later, tired, bored, but otherwise not much worse for the wear, the *Far East Transporter* sailed briskly into Kulolia, port of Honolulu, Kingdom of Hawai'i, and tied up at the busy wharf by warping in against a fairly stiff wind. The native wharf hand attached a heavy hemp line to an iron stanchion, and the second mate attached a line to a bollard on the deck of the *Far East Transporter* which brought the ship tight up against the quayside. The wharf was studded with cannons pointed seaward.

Kulolia was as busy as the Shanghai Harbor. Tall ships lined the wharf for miles, and an equal number dotted the harbor at anchor. Kulolia—originally Mamala Bay–was the chief port of call for the trans-Pacific sandalwood, fur, and whaling industries. Immigrants on their way to America and to the Kingdom of Hawai'i filled uncomfortable cargo ships having paid exorbitant fees to brokers. They came in waves and by their thousands. 1879 was the start of a mass emigration that—over the next fifty years—would see in excess of twenty-seven million enter America, most to find work, many to escape persecution and poverty; and some who came as businessmen and professionals seeking a better environment to pursue their professions. The ships came into Kulolia both going and coming from the United States with a significant number finding disappointment in the new country and electing to return to the old one.

In addition to the tall sailing ships, the harbor was beginning to fill up with long distance passenger steamers holding thousands of people. For the past thirteen years, the Pacific Mail Steamship Company established a passenger line from Hong Kong to San Francisco to carry American merchants, missionaries, and government officials to Asia and back. The company profited most by transporting poor and ignorant Chinese laborers to and from the United States, many bound for places like Sitka, Alaska where they would live as virtual or actual slaves. The few European and American Caucasians were divided from the Asians by rules related to rank and race.

Alexandra monitored her crew as they disembarked for a two-day rest and recuperation stay in Honolulu. She promised them the best dinner of their lives if they would behave themselves and be sober by five that afternoon. They were all to meet on the lawn of the Iolani Palace. When the officers and crew had all departed, Alexandra took a few minutes to study the fascinating area. The harbor was a forest of masts flying the colors of several dozen nations including more than a few flying the Royal Standard of King Kalākaua with its eight alternating white, red, and black stripes, and its center showing the Hawai'ian coat of arms.

The New England whaling fleet was abundantly evident, since the old whaling towns and their fabulously rich sea captains and merchants used Hawai'i as their Pacific port. There could easily have been fourteen or fifteen whalers in the harbor. In fact, she learned later, the most important commerce flourishing in the kingdom was dependent on American Whalers. Many other American company ships were present in the harbor especially after the California gold rush and subsequent statehood brought Hawai'i and the United States much closer as regular commercial partners with improved communication being carried by the ships moving to and from the kingdom's harbors. The most important part of that commerce for Hawai'ians was that the kingdom exported huge quantities of a variety of goods to California.

She decided that this was a place that would factor greatly in her future shipping business; so, she and her personal body guard, Stenka Mazepa, walked down the gangway and into the teeming throng of humanity moving busily along the wharf. She saw remarkable contrasts: A group of young Honolulu debutantes on Nuuanu Street dressed in immaculate long white dresses; many of the women wore the new San Francisco style modified bustles. They were in juxtaposition to Chinese, Korean, and Japanese coolies, black men and women, and indentured white workers loading sugar onto ships, sweat pouring from their half-naked muscular bodies, and peddlers selling vile looking purple poi from buckets. Alexandra tried some and decided that it tasted as bad as it looked.

She and Stenka moved further into the city, and Alexandra was surprised at how small the city of Honolulu was. Although it was the capital city of the string of seven islands, it was a small town, with no buildings over three stories tall surrounded by sugar and banana plantations. Many of the buildings on the outskirts were little more than mud and thatch huts. There was not a single paved street in the city, and most of the streets were of rutted mud emanating a stench of animal manure.

Alexandra needed to send mail back to her parents in Vladivostok, to Hou Eadric in Millionka, to the taipan in Shanghai, Sir Edwin and Lady were rutted Margaret Appleby, and to her partners in Colombo. She asked a nattily dressed young man where the post office was located, and he directed her to Merchant Street.

"The Kamehameha V Post Office is on the corner, Madam," he said with exaggerated courtesy.

It was easy enough to find their way in the small, city-within-a-city; in Chinatown the street signs were red framed and written in both English and Chinese characters. There were horses everywhere in the city; horses with single riders were the main mode of transportation, especially since walking on the mud and excreta filled ruts of the streets meant ruination to a decent pair of boots. Even the barefoot workers did all they could not to step in the muck and drag the remains into their thatched mud huts—called *hale pili* by the natives. Knowing that she might one day need to do business in Honolulu's Chinatown like she was doing on this commercial visit, Alexandra obtained directions from a woman who spoke pidgin English which took Alexandra several tries to understand.

She and Stenka walked to the border of Chinatown, the Nuuanu Stream. The stream was in its more or less natural state, and no efforts had been made to disguise its function. The stream was the city's sewer system. Rivulets trickled down from better built homes on the hillsides maintaining a steady flow of raw sewage. Outhouses lined the main stream's banks making it effectively the city's principle toilet. They hurried on into the main streets of the Chinese center.

In contrast to the diminutive character of Honolulu city proper, the Chinatown District was a thriving area with an eclectic blend of Southeast Asian cultures including Chinese, Vietnamese, Laotian, Japanese, Thai, Filipino, and Korean peoples as well as Native Hawai'ians, Negroes, and Caucasians. During the 19th century laborers were imported from China to work on sugar plantations in Hawai'i, and many of them became prosperous merchants in Chinatown after their contracts expired.

In 1879, Chinatown was a thriving, hectic commercial district serving its own non-Caucasian population as well as the diverse larger Honolulu community. Because Chinatown was close to the harbor, many newly arriving immigrants from all over the world used the stores and restaurants in the district as gathering places to find friends and relatives, establish contacts, and so where to find jobs, and to make business deals. The businesses in Chinatown had become the second-largest employer of Chinese immigrants after the sugar plantations.

Alexandra asked several Chinese people what their name for Honolulu was–speaking Mandarin–but she could not make herself understood with the predominately Cantonese speaking expatriates from Hong Kong. Eventually she did find an older lady who spoke her language; and she told Alexandra and Stenka that the traditional and still commonly used term as known to the Chinese was *Tánxiāngshān*, which Alexandra was able to translate to "Sandalwood Mountain".

There were the usual opium dens, fireworks sellers, street peddlers and food vendors, but there was not much in the way of valuable items that Alexandra thought would make good commercial products worth transporting. She did buy a few trinkets and toys for her two boys: elaborate gaily colored festival hats, hats in the shape of different kinds of fish, embroidered tiger hats, shuttlecocks, yo-yos, diabolos, parallel jumping ropes, knucklebones, live crickets in small bamboo cages, lacquered boxes, and twin cages for cricket battles. Stenka patiently carried her small treasures back towards the ship.

They took short diversions to see the Kaumakapili Church and a few of the remaining ancient fish farm ponds. They headed towards Waikiki, a disappointingly smelly and marshy place—essentially a lagoon. Five o'clock was fast approaching; so, Alexandra and Stenka hurried towards the Iolani Palace; and Alexandra was pleased that the officers and crew had already assembled on the grounds and looked entirely presentable.

The eyes of the assembled crew turned deferentially towards Alexandra as she walked properly across the expansive lawn. She took her place at the front of the small crowd along with the ships' officers and waited for the arrival of the king and queen.

A spit-and-polish, very obviously pure native Hawai'ian man, handsome, poised, and haughty, marched in his royal livery uniform directly up to Alexandra.

He said, "I am Jonah Kawānanakoa, the king's aide-de-camp. It is my honor to present David La'amea Kamananakapu Mahinulani Naloiaehuokalani Lumialani Kalākaua Kalākaua, *Ali'i o ko Hawai'i Pae 'Aina*—Monarch of the Hawai'ian Islands—and his wife, Esther Kapi'olani Napelakapuokaka'e, Queen Consort of the Kingdom of Hawai'i."

The king and queen were regal in all respects: their sturdy brown frames, perfectly fitting uniforms, badges and sashes of office, and—most important—in their deportment.

"We welcome you to our kingdom, Ladies and Gentlemen and dignitaries," King Kalākaua said.

"And, I also welcome each of you," Queen Kapi'olani said, making it apparent that the king used the European affectation of referring to himself in the plural.

"Please call us King David and Queen Esther," the king said as he and Esther mingled among the assembled crowd.

Queen Esther sought out Alexandra and smiled.

"I am happy to meet a very successful woman, and one who is so young at that. We have been made aware of you and your family and of your exploits as a ships' captain and a leader in the business world. It would appear that times are changing, and we women are beginning to take our rightful places in the world."

Alexandra gave Queen Esther a radiant smile and a short bow.

"I am flattered that you have heard of me. That tells me that you are well read and informed, and that you have an interest in what goes on in the world. The world is coming to you, and you are meeting the visitors on a more than an equal basis."

"Thank you, My Dear, but I have to admit that most of what I learn about the world outside our islands comes from naughty whalers and our new newspapers, the *Sandwich Island Gazette* and the *Journal of Commerce*."

"Then it appears that I will have to obtain copies of those papers to keep myself prepared to do business in such a sophisticated realm."

"And you must return one day as just a tourist. Our tourism industry is beginning to burgeon. In fact, just today, there are three tour steamers in the harbor from America full of vacationers. We will show them a good time."

"Sounds like fun, Queen Esther."

"Indeed. And speaking of enjoyment, it is time for you and your crew to join King David and me in the palace dining room for a genuine Hawai'ian *pā'ina* or *lu'au* feast."

And a feast it was. The food included *he'he poke*—a raw octopus, and soy sauce, sea salt, green onions, and Maui onions salad appetizer; the purple and nearly tasteless taro root paste called "one-finger" *poi*, indicating it's density; *Kalua* pig slow cooked in a pit and covered with banana leaves; *Lomilomi* salmon—fresh tomato, cucumber, red hot chili, and salmon salad which Queen Esther learned about from visiting whalers; *laulau*—slow pit-cooked ono fish wrapped in luau leaves; *opihi alinalina* (yellow foot) shellfish—called "the fish of death" because so many divers were killed trying to harvest the stubbornly limpet-like molluscs from sharp tide pool rooks. It was to be eaten raw out of its shell with sea salt and *limu*—seaweed; and Hawai'ian sweet potato. For dessert, *haupia*—diluted coconut milk, sugar, and salt, was mixed with arrowroot and heated until thickened and smooth, then poured into a rectangular pan and chilled, then cut into small blocks and served on squares of *ti* leaf. Alexandra thought it was very much like *blancmange*, one of her favorite European desserts.

The marvelous food was accompanied by entertainment: lithe dancers, naked above the waist and wearing grass skirts moving with sensuous hip motions, with folkloric dances from Hawaii, New Zealand, and Tahiti; fire dancers and flame swallowers; and music played on ancient Hawai'ian instruments—*keke'eke*, bamboo pipes of varying lengths which was played by holding it vertically and tapping it on the ground, or a *mat kuolokani*—a large ancient timbrel drum; and a *nî ʽau kani*–a harp made of thin coconut midrib called *nîau*. The full stomachs, lilting and soothing music, and a little (perhaps a little too much) *Okolehao*–an ancient Hawaiian alcoholic drink made from *ti* root created a soothing post-prandial lassitude and sedation. English seamen taught eager Hawaiʼian brewers and consumers the art of distillation that changed *Okolehao* into a very strong alcoholic spirit—which produced additional happy somnolence in Alexandra and her crew and great satisfaction on the part of the king and his consort.

CHAPTER THIRTY-EIGHT

MORE EVIDENCE

National Archives of Australia, Victorian Archives Centre, 99 Shiel Street, North Melbourne, Victoria, Australia, February 24, 2014

The missionaries arrived at work Monday morning after a late-night—ten p.m.—party at the Durrell's feeling rather logy. The day seemed long and tedious; so, the elders and sisters felt that they had to keep reminding themselves and each other that they were doing the work of the Lord. After lunch, postprandial lassitude spread like an epidemic among the usually vivacious and Pollyannaish missionaries; and several excused themselves to take naps.

Sister Taylor refused to give in to her bodily inadequacies. She took a quick-step outside in the oppressive heat of the Australian summer, waving her arms, and taking hyperpneic breaths to clear the cobwebs out of her head. As she walked along at a near-trot, her mind cleared—and more importantly—she came up with an idea which caused her to make an about-face and to move at a running walk back into the archives.

She was out of breath and perturbed at herself for being out of shape. She hurried to interrupt her husband, Elder Taylor, from his nap.

"Neal," she said, and shook his shoulder gently.

Neal slowly came out of his dream and looked around dazed for several seconds.

"This better be an emergency, Lisa," he managed out of his fog.

"Not an emergency, Neal, more like a revelation. I think the Spirit has spoken to me about our mysterious Alexandra."

"What did He say?" Neal Taylor asked, seriously now, because one did not question personal revelation in the Church of Jesus Christ of Latter-day Saints.

It was better to listen and learn.

"The thought came into mind as I was walking that I should look into the school files for Irkutsk and maybe even the rest of Siberia to see what we can learn about Alexandra's two boys. Also, I am impressed to look into the 1879 records of the several ports where Alexandra might have stopped on her ship that year. There is nothing about her being involved in any activities where her children were present for that whole year; maybe, she left them to get back to sailing. What do you think?"

"It is a new area, and I think you are on the right track. Let me know what I can do to help."

"I don't think the Holy Spirit would be happy with me if I was selfish. I'll get the other sisters to help. I can't help but think that we are on to something."

The elders were not much interested, but their wives needed something to stimulate themselves; and a breakthrough would do them all wonders; so, they agreed to divide up the work.

Barely a week went by before Sister Clyde discovered the name of a German woman who advertised in the *Vladivostok* newspaper seeking employment. The next week's issue announced that Gertrude Himmelmann had taken a position as nanny and German language tutor for the Yusupov family residing at Tarasova House, No. 71 Pekinskaya Street, Vladivostok. Sister Clyde looked at school records six years and twelve years later in Vladivostok, then Irkutsk and found no record of the boys in the entire oblast. Since 1891 would have had to be the last year of the Yusupov boys' grammar and high school careers, Sister Taylor decided to look further abroad.

"*Why not Novonikolaevsk?*" she reasoned to herself.

Her hunch or, rather, bit of personal revelation, led to finding the names of two boys whose surnames were Yusupov, and only two. They were Nikita and Oral Borisovich, and their superior performances were duly noted in the Novonikolaevsk Military Academy School for Boys.

"Call it serendipity, or coincidence, or dumb luck if you want, Neal; but I know it was a personal revelation; and I feel that we are being helped."

Neal was somewhat more of a pragmatist or scientist in his thinking, not really comfortable with the frequently expressed idea of "knowing" as opposed to "believing"; but he had to admit that this must have been the work of the Holy Spirit; and he was glad to have the help.

Marianne Smith chose to riffle through the ports-of-call records of the Jardine-Matheson-Tarasova and Yusupov commercial activities from 1876 to 1896. It was tedious work, but not particularly difficult because record keeping in Asia, Europe, the Pacific Islands, and the Americas, were quite well preserved and in surprisingly good order. Her work paid off, and she was able to find port calls in Tokyo, Seoul, Shanghai, Colombo, Taipan, Honolulu, San Francisco, and Sitka once in 1879, twice in 1882, and twice in 1885—all identifying Alexandra Tarasova-Yusupov as captain of the *Far East Transporter* and giving clear manifests of her cargoes, including large shipments of raw opium.

She found only one mention of Boris Yusupov as a shipping merchant, that in Shanghai in 1881. Leah Clyde decided—based on that information—to look into records of Balagansk Prison from 1879 forward. Boris was regularly listed as the commandant until 1891 and never thereafter. He seemed to have disappeared, but she found no death notice or obituary.

Good came out of Lisa Taylor's personal revelation: the main thing was that her personal testimony of the Lord and her church became unshakable; and also, the information documented more about the mysterious Alexandra than they had had before. But it also raised more questions and inspired a greater determination to search out other possible sources.

CHAPTER THIRTY-NINE

ON TO SITKA

Midway upon the journey of our life, I found myself within a
forest dark, for the straightforward pathway had been lost.
                                —Dante Alighieri, *The Inferno*

Baranof Castle, American Port of Sitka, Alaska, October, 1879

The three ships in Alexandra's commercial shipping group
landed at the deep draft port adjacent to Vancouver Barracks,
Washington safely after a month-long voyage from Honolulu.
The barracks and its fort were located on the north side of the Columbia
River–about two-thousand yards from the river itself–near its confluence
with Oregon's Willamette River. It took Alexandra and her officers and
crew several minutes to be able to walk steadily on dry land after the
long voyage. A contingent of trappers, Indians, farmers, and stevedores,
waited for them on the dock and gave the seafarers rides to the barracks
where they could sit down to a small breakfast meal and a drink and
talk business.

The trappers and Indians had brought in a huge load of beaver
and sea otter pelts pressed into bales; the farmers had a supply of fresh
vegetables and fruits sufficient for the trip up the coast to the Inside
Passage to Sitka; and the stevedores were ready and waiting to off-load
the *Far East Transporter's* cargo of Hawai'ian and Chinese products,
staples such as coffee, tea, and sugar; wilderness necessities like guns,
ammunition, axes, hatchets, snares and traps, good steel knives; and

useful and decorative items including things such as brightly painted bone buttons, vivid blankets, calico cloth, and mirrors, and to on-load the skins and vegetables. Most of the crew engaged in races to take the kinks out of their legs while the off and on-loading were taking place.

Having gotten that out of their systems, they went on an impromptu and self-guided short tour of the barracks. Since its inception, the army had maintained a guard house on the barracks grounds, now mainly to house the native Chinooks who were forcefully imprisoned there awaiting relocation to less hospitable country than the one they were being forced to leave to make room for the rapid influx of Europeans and Americans moving in to take their land. For hundreds of years before Western explorers arrived, the Chinook Indians had lived along the banks of the "*Wimahl*," or "Big River"—later named by the Europeans, the Columbia.

The issue of relocation was by now largely moot. It was estimated that in the early 1800s, there were nearly twenty-thousand Chinooks in the region. By 1879 when Alexandra arrived, there were barely thirty souls left owing to the white man's predation and diseases. Once the Indians had been effectively removed, Vancouver Barracks and its environs became an attractive destination for early settlers, offering safety, security, and reliable supplies.

The harbor was very busy. Several types of mills—lumber, grist, brick, breweries, and sugar—produced thousands of boxes which were loaded onto commercial vessels for shipments to cities all over the Pacific Rim. The seamen reported that Vancouver had five sawmills, two sash and door factories, a box factory, three brickyards, and the breweries. Plums were dried—then called prunes–and packaged in private plants for shipment to the East via Cape Hoorn into the Atlantic and across the Pacific to islands and Asia.

They encountered a diversity of peoples, but the diversity was largely limited to Caucasians from different parts of the country and Europe. There were many Irish people, who—unlike their reception in the East of the country—were welcomed, worked hard, prospered, and established themselves as valuable members of the community. Not long after arriving the Irish ceased to call themselves "Irish" or "Irish-Americans" and became just, "Americans".

One businessman they met said that "the Irish looked upon past traditions, wounds, hardships—even of the Great Potato famine that brought them to Vancouver–and memories of the 'Old Sod' as irrelevant and in time just 'remote.' Their mobility and transformation from Irish immigrants to Washingtonians also influenced their religious affiliation and identification; many have become Protestants to assimilate or had stopped identifying themselves by religion at all, which had caused so much of "The Troubles" back in the old country," and he added, "I am proud to be an American."

It was apparent that Vancouver was growing rapidly, perhaps too rapidly, since housing was not keeping up with demand. The Irish were known as "go-getters" and had been snatching up land as fast as they could. Despite growing as they did and prospering so well, the Irish were not nearly so populous as the Chinese, Germans, and Scandinavians—all of whom came to Vancouver for the same reasons as the Irish. Apparently, success for a culture in Vancouver was largely based on fertility. A culture of tolerance had grown apace with the diversity of the population moving in. Many of these people were hired by the railroads which were rapidly approaching the coast. Unemployment was unheard of.

Alexandra was impressed with the academy built by the Sisters of Providence for the children of the region, including orphans. It was the largest brick building north of San Francisco. They also founded Saint Joseph's Hospital, a highly respected medical facility. Alexandra felt that her Far Eastern Russia had something to learn from these industrious new Americans.

Georgina, the wife of the barracks commander, General Thomas Anderson, met Alexandra and was impressed with her, especially because of her fluency with several languages and her poised good manners. She invited the captain, officers, and crew, to an impromptu lunch at her home. The general was away on one of many skirmishes with the remaining Indians in the region. The impressive commander's quarters were an Italianate architecture Victorian home built in 1878. Soldiers were obviously used to the general's quarters being the site of many a grand party, even impromptu ones; and they swung into action to produce a fine American meal.

They were served Pike Place Chowder, Spud Fish, salmon on a cedar plank, fresh tomatoes, cucumbers, and celery, huge brown-skinned potatoes smothered in butter, bacon, salt, pepper, and onions, and pitchers of hard cider. Alexandra sent a seaman back to the ship to fetch a two-yard piece of elegant flower design Chinese silk. She gave it to

Georgina as thanks, then conveyed her regrets that her ships had to set sail for Sitka before the late evening low tides stranded them.

Her seamen groaned and griped—as all seamen throughout the ages have done—when it was time to board the ships again. Alexandra and her officers were pleased at the obviously good morale and good health demonstrated by her griping seamen. They set sail at the end of the first dog watch—1800 hours. Four bells rang from the three ships, and the *Far East Transporter* and her security ships wheeled down-stream into the flow of the mighty Columbia to carry them into the pounding surf of the Pacific Ocean.

A week later, Alexander and her ships entered the Alaska Inside Passage en route to Sitka. Along the way they passed a town called Metlakatia; and, for interest, they stopped briefly at Ketchikan, self-styled "Salmon Capitol of the World". The men were more interested in the brothels on Creek Street than they were in seeing the salmon run. Next they made a short run to Wrangell, and, after talking to locals, made a diversionary voyage sail up the Stikine River to see black and brown bears, hundreds of migratory birds, majestic bald and golden eagles, harbor seals, killer whales, humpbacks, and small white beluga whales. They did not stop in Petersburg, because Alexandra was anxious to get to Sitka and get her business over with. She was beginning to feel some pangs of homesickness.

They spent a day and a night in Juneau and took a guided tour by a local resident to see the Juneau Icefield and Mendenhall Glacier. The city was surrounded by great ice capped mountains and dark blue icy waters. The sailors were excited to see Tlingit totem poles which reminded them of the totems so prevalent on Taiwan where they had stopped several times on voyages to the waters east of China. From Ketchikan, they traveled north in the Inside Passage to Gustavus watching the antics of whales, sea lions, and sea otters lying on their backs holding oysters. Evidence of Russian influence was everywhere.

The local Tlingit Indians advised them to turn back south on a calm passage to the west of the better known Inside Passage and on down to the east of the large Chichagof Island in the Alexander Archipelago to its terminus where the passages opened into the icy Pacific. It was a short voyage along the coast through the west (coastal) side of Baranof Island where Sitka [originally known as Novo-Arkhangelsk and Old Sitka in Russian America], was located.

Sitka harbor was a beehive of activity, but there were adequate numbers of mooring sites. Alexandra's *Far East Transporter*, and her security ships–*Igor's Guards*, and the *Lady of Tarasova*—were led by the harbor pilot boat to a wide berth between the U. S. Revenue Marine ship, the *Richard Rush*, and the U.S. Navy's warship, the *USS Jamestown*. As busy and diverse as the Shanghai and Hong Kong harbors and as different from the harbors of Europe as they could be, the ships and boats of the Sitka Harbor were unique. There were: an old Russian steamship, the *Ancon*; large fishing boats built by the boat makers of the Russian American Company decades earlier and still functional and boat builders from Europe and Scandinavia since the Americans annexed Alaska; native trollers, salmon seiners, and longliners serving the Sitka cannery; large heavy canoes made from red cedar trunks; and a boat hand made by Aleuts [also known as the Unangan People], called a *baidarka* [Russian for sea kayak] or Aleutian kayak.

The Aleut/Unangan people—for time immemorial–were surrounded by the violent and treacherous waters of the Northern Pacific and had to develop ways to cope because their sacred lands of choice required water transportation and a hunting vessel. Trees were nonexistent in the Aleutians; so, naturally occurring wood was scarce. The people had to rely on Baranof Island driftwood—in a make-do-or-do-without level of necessity–to create the frameworks of their *baidarkas*–which were then covered with the skins of sea mammals. Unungan women prepared sea lion skins which they sewed onto the frames with bone needles, using a waterproof stitch. Again–bowing to necessity–two types of *baidarkas* evolved, one with a covered deck that was used as a hunting kayak, and another that was open and capable of carrying goods and people from one island to another. The inventive Russians introduced new concepts: a one-hole and three-hole style so light that a young child could easily carry them. *Baidarkas* had prominent ascetic and functional features, including an attention getting bifurcated bow.

Alexandra took time to learn that the very lightweight and maneuverable kayaks were made of seal skin. By long and time-honored tradition, the skins, bone, and sinew, could only be sewn only by Aleut women and stretched tightly over a frame made strictly of drift wood and only constructed by men. *Baidarkas* were treated as living beings by the

Aleuts men; and it was therefore taboo for women to handle them once completed despite the women's role in crafting the skin of the boat.

Men did all the designing of the *baidarka* frames to be light, fast, and flexible, tying together the wooden parts with intricate and spiritual knots braided from tough animal sinew. Unungan women were allowed to sew the skins onto the frames as a token of the womens' contribution. For the Unungan people—men, women, and children–the seagoing kayaks lived as spiritual beings and were essential for their survival.

Russian explorer/traders established Novo-Arkhangelsk, or New Archangel, located on the outer-Baranof Island and the southern half of Chichagof Island in the Alexander Archipelago of the Pacific as their principle commercial hub and as their defensive fort. New Archangel became a prospering and permanent settlement named after Arkhangelsk, the largest city in the region where the leader of the explorers. Lord Alexander Baranov–was born.

In 1808, with Baranov as governor, Sitka was designated the capital of Russian-America in the name of the Russian Empire and Baranoff's Russian-American Company which was formally chartered by Tzar Alexander I. Viewing the Russians as unfair trading partners and interlopers, the Tlingit [known as *Koloshi* by the Russians] established their own fort, on the Chatham Strait side of Peril Strait to enforce a trade embargo with the Russian establishment. That pre-destined a long history of conflict between Russians and native Americans.

From the harbor, Alexandra and the officers and crews of her three ships, hiked all the way to the top of Castle Hill to where Baranoff's Castle perched as the trading emporium and as a menacing symbol of Russian authority until 1867 when the Americans purchased the entirety of Alaska from Russia—which had ruled it for 125 years–in what became known as the best land deal ever completed by an American. The castle—so-called—was only a large two-story, ascetically drab, rectangular brick building with a cupola on top as a nod to its Russianness. It was built in 1836. Alexandra and her captains introduced themselves to the American governor of the island and secured permission to carry on extensive trade on the present voyage and for a promised number of return visits in the future.

The crews headed back to the wharfs to supervise the off-loading of the ship's cargo followed by the on-loading of goods from Sitka and from inland Alaska. The crew off-loaded the boxes of nearly a ton of opium for the native workers, Asian silk and other handicrafts, European men's wool suits, women's formal dresses, calico dresses for the natives, well-fitting shoes, boots, modern winterware beaver hats, Russian fine dress fur coats—considered a luxury even by the capable seamstresses among the Aleuts—and the latest fashions in feathered hats and bonnets. Aleut/Unangan people came in droves from the *kiks ádi's* traditional tribal fishing camp with sea otter, bear, cougar, and beaver skins collected by the natives and carefully supervised by the Russian Alaska Company *promyshlenniks* [fur traders] and boxloads of hand-made native clothing, toys, and statuary—the most valuable of which was walrus ivory and whale bone scrimshaw pieces.

The statues had black writing and pictures as well as being intricately carved—all of which was a match for the finest Chinese ivory carvings sold in Hong Kong and Shanghai. The native crews replenished the ships' larders with fresh fruits and vegetables grown in greenhouses, clean, fresh water from Fish Bay Creek, fresh and dried salmon and halibut, and great slabs of fresh moose meat and dried moose, elk, deer, reindeer, and caribou. On their own initiative, the crew ordered enough of the dried meats to be able to sell them in the ever-enthusiastic Asian markets yearning for new foods to try.

While that work carried on in a professional fashion without her, Alexandra and her captains set about to see the island and its cathedral and businesses. They first visited the Russian Bishop's house which was still in the service of the remaining Russian population. The well-maintained building was constructed of vividly painted spruce wood. The cathedral—in the era of Russian domination—was emblematic of the Russian Orthodox Church authority over a diocese that stretched from California to the Siberian Kamchatka peninsula. It was as colorfully painted as St. Basil's in Red Square in Moscow with a freshly painted blue onion cupola with white stars. The Cathedral of Saint Michael, the Archangel, was the earliest orthodox cathedral built in North America. Its walls were built with logs of native wood with clapboard siding, and multiple domes made of copper with a well-aged green patina and roofs of well-made wood shingles.

The Russians had not realized how much nostalgia they had for their own culture. They entered the cathedral with due solemnity and reverence. Upon seeing the silver plated icon of Our Lady of Kazan–the Sitka Madonna, and festival icon of St. Michael–Alexandra felt an overwhelming urge to return briefly to her religious roots and to worship. The entire setting was conducive to the most spiritual of feelings in the well-educated group of Russians. They marveled and felt great emotion as they took in the royal doors in the center of the *Ikonostasis*—the ornate wall of gold and multi-colored icons and orthodox religious paintings—which separated the nave from the sanctuary. The captain of the security vessel, the *Tarasova Lady,* came from a family of glass makers; and the chandelier captivated him as one of the most treasured of the items in the cathedral. The silk and brocade vestments, handmade bells, the large icon of the *Last Supper* that decorated the tops of the royal doors, the clock in the bell tower, and the large library containing books in the Russian, Tlingit, and Aleut languages were on display and captured the interest and imagination of the well-educated officers—especially Alexandra.

Like other Russian Orthodox churches and cathedrals, this one was distinguished by its intentional impression of verticality and by the bright colors providing a striking contrast with the flat Russian/Alaskan landscape so often covered in snow. This Muscovite Baroque church had the same tiered structure of traditional Russian log churches throughout rural Russian and Alaska. Like those churches, the Cathedral of Michael, the Archangel, was oriented East and West. The main entrance of the building at the West end was dark; and when the faithful entered through that door, they left the dark world sin behind and exited through a glorious golden portion of the cathedral which touched a deep emotion signifying salvation in the hearts of the believers. The main cathedral's striking onion dome was topped by a bright, shining, golden, three-bar orthodox cross.

Two servants of the American governor of Sitka invited the officers to an informal lunch at the castle, which proved to be a very beneficial hour for Alexandra and her ships because she was able to meet with the U.S. naval commander, a generous man. Besides the governor and his wife, and the navy captain and his wife, several of the most prominent citizens—Russian pioneer family descendants who chose to remain when America took possession—were happy to greet the Russians and enthusiastically started up discussions in their native language with the well-spoken Russian merchant sea farers. Alexandra was impressed with the independent qualities and character of the families: the Kashavaroffs, the Kostromitinoffs, the Bolshanins, and the Shutzoffs, all of whom were anxious for news from their former homeland.

The important conversation, however was with Captain Oliver MacTavish, USN. He was charmed by Alexandra, as were most men she met. He had the opportunity to practice his rudimentary Russian with a gently correcting young woman, an attractive one at that.

After the customary pleasantries passed, Alexandra asked Capt. MacTavish, "How dangerous do you think our return passage is likely to be?"

"I understand that you are an able sea captain, Mrs. Yusupov; and in all probability you will be able to navigate back out into the open ocean and find your way back to Vladivostok. My concern for you and for all ships leaving American shores for Asia and East Russia is the presence of so many pirates. I am sure you are well aware of the Red Flag Fleet."

"Unfortunately, all too aware, Capt. MacTavish."

"As capable as you are, I regret to inform you that this is a particularly unsettled time in the Pacific. Pirates now seem to rule the China seas, and the combined American, German, French, Chinese, Japanese, and British, navies are hard put to get control of those nearly lawless seas. It is my very strong recommendation that you allow my fleet of ships to accompany you on your trip home. Frankly, we are itching for a fight; and this may be our chance to save some legal vessels and crews, but also, to strike a blow for the rule of law on the oceans. What do you think?"

"I have always been able to take care of my ships and crews, Captain. What is so different now?"

"Let me show you this week's newspapers in from Shanghai, Hong Kong, Tokyo, and Chosŏn. There is a particularly worrisome article by the taipan of the Jardine-Matheson Company. I understand you are familiar with the company, are you not, Mrs. Yusupov?"

"I am. In fact, I am involved in business dealings with Taipan Sir James Nicolas Sutherland Matheson. Are you acquainted with him?"

"I am, and the navy works closely with him and his company in these matters. So, I think you should take to heart what he has to say and give a studied decision regarding my offer of protection.

He showed her three recent newspapers, less than a month old– *Garakuta chinpō*, from Tokyo, only in Japanese; the *North China Herald*, from Shanghai, only in Chinese; the *Hansŏng Sunbo Newspaper* from Seoul, Korea, only in Hanmun Korean; and the *China Mail* from

Hong Kong, which reported in Mandarin, Cantonese, and English, all prominently featuring the taipan's article. The articles were essentially the same except for minor translational differences.

Office of the Taipan, Jardine-Matheson Company
British Protectorate of Hong Kong
20 October, 1879

This report comes from the combined efforts of the British East India Company, the Jardine-Matheson Company, the Foreign Ministry of France, the Foreign Office of Great Britain, and the office of the First Lord of the Admiralty, London. In brief, it is our collective opinion based on a high degree of assurance, that the waters of the East China Sea, the South China Sea, the Bay of Bengal, the Strait of Malacca, the Sea of Japan, the waters of the Indonesian Archipelago, the Philippine Sea, and the Strait of Singapore, are unsafe for any unprotected travel—personal, commercial, or diplomatic. The governments of the above captioned entities offer their assistance by providing armed escorts and marine soldiers to those who make a proper request. However, be mindful of the extent of the danger from the great hordes of pirates and realize that there will be significant delays. We cannot be responsible for loss of life or property for anyone venturing into these danger plagued waterways unescorted.

Signed:

Sir James Nicolas Sutherland Matheson, 1st Baronet
Tai-pan, Jardine-Matheson & Co.

Alexandra wanted to be able to say that she made any and all voyages on her own and without any kind of interventional help by any man. But she was more of a pragmatist than she was an impetuous and arrogant girl, attributes she recognized as her worst character flaws.

She smiled in spite of her personal misgivings and said, "You win, Captain. Your evidence and arguments are too persuasive. When can we set sail for Vladivostok?"

"I have already sent for a naval force to join us in the Sitka harbor tomorrow. Now that we are in agreement, I can tell you that a British

Expeditionary force will set sail from Manila tomorrow, and the Jardine-Matheson combat security forces will sail into the East China Sea from Shanghai the day after tomorrow. Japan, China, and Korea—what you call Chosŏn–have offered three fighting junks each. I confess that I don't expect much from them, but we fight with the navy we have."

Three days later, the last American ships assembled in Sitka Harbor; and their captains and crews came under the strict maritime command of Captain Oliver MacTavish. Bowing to the superior fire power of the *USS Jamestown*, the greater experience of its navy gunners and marine contingent, and the unquestioned authority granted by the Department of the Navy of the United States, even the civilian combat ready forces were glad to join the flotilla of twelve US naval vessels, and fourteen seasoned hard men in their well-tested ships in fights against the scourge of Asian piracy.

Of the US Navy's seventy-four gun-ships of the line, eighteen, including the large *Washington*, *Independence*, and *Franklin*, were dispatched to the Mediterranean to quell the Barbary Pirate attacks; and sixteen of them remained on service patrols there. Nine of those were in Sitka Harbor and ready for immediate action under Captain MacTavish; and another six arranged to meet the MacTavish force in the South China Sea. Commodore Matthew Perry led the Perry Expedition of four ships to Japan in 1853, and two of the four remained on patrol duty in and around the Sea of Japan. The captains, crew, and marines of those two ships were bored to distraction and were overjoyed to be part of a real fight. Captain MacTavish was comforted to have such a robust armed force, and Alexandra quietly saw the armed force as her own. They set sail the next day.

Luzon Strait, South China Sea, off the outer coast of Taiwan on board the *Far East Transporter*, November 30, 1879

A fleet of forty-two Red Flag Fleet ships left their home base on the tip of Bintan Island, Indonesia, passed through the Malacca and Singapore Straits and into the heavily traveled major shipping lane stretching from the westernmost corner of Malaysia and into the South China Sea. They traveled under cover of darkness undetected, aided by a dense storm cloud. They could not resist and dispatched one pirate junk to capture an overloaded coal ship sailing between Singapore and Pontianak, a port on the western coast of the large Indonesian island of Borneo. The *Pini 5* recognized the hopelessness of their situation and ran up flags of surrender. Fifty Malay men wearing torn shirts of chain-mail and carrying razor sharp machetes, their faces bronzed by dirt and sun, boarded the ship, took everything of value off the ship, including personal belongings of the officers and crew. They screamed at the hapless people on board the ship, smashed the rescue boats, set fire to the ship and escaped quickly enough to rejoin the forty-two other pirate ships. They saw this as good joss; it would be easy pickings from here on out, just as it always was.

The heavily armed US Navy flotilla with the *Far East Transporter* safe in the center of the security and combat ships, moved more swiftly now than in the past several days when they fought their way through a prolonged tropical storm which kicked up heavy seas and drenched the ships until they could not make forward progress. This morning, however, the weather was clearing.

The third mate was drowsy, having just been awakened to serve as the mate of the morning watch. It was shortly after 0430, and he was waiting for the two bells to sound indicating that it was 0500. It was They had successfully sailed from Sitka—only accessible by sea, and then only with the sturdiest of ocean-going vessels–through Alaska's Inside Passage into the open ocean and were four days. It was going to be a clear day; the day-peep light was light enough to see a few hundred yards out across the mirror calm sea. He looked at a dark shape off the port bow well to the southwest. Was it a new storm beginning to close in?

He could not draw a conclusion; so, he called out, "Vessels, ho."

On second thought he called, "Two bells, and all's well."

He was still uneasy about the call of "all's well". Had he been looking at the other secure ships in the flotilla surrounding his? There was something there. What was it? It was getting a little lighter. His senses were now fully awake and alert. He was now sure that it was not a something but a host of things…almost certainly ships…maybe four hundred yards distant. A rogue lightening flash lit up the things for less than half a second but enough to show a field of bright red.

His pulse quickened; his blood pressure went high enough to start a headache. He knew the rest of the crew–to say nothing of the seasoned naval sailors and marines–would give him a tongue lashing that he would not live down for weeks if he got everyone up on a false alarm. He dithered; then, he made up his mind. Better to be scorned as a fool than to be the man who could have saved all his mates and failed because of anxiety.

He clanged the alarm bells and shouted, "Ships ho. Red sails. Looka Chinee pirates!"

The *Far East Transporter* came alive like a kicked ant hill. Within minutes, the men on her three ships were in their fighting positions but keeping a low enough profile to prevent the pirates from realizing the magnitude of their readiness. Through her new hand-held nautical night vision telescope—28 inches long closed and 34 inches extended—which was long, heavy, and rather cumbersome, but had excellent optics. She was able to see the red junk sails plowing towards her. The end holding the objective lens was 82mm– 3.25mm–to yield such clear images. She was able to identify the bow of the well-known Chinese junk *Ning-Po*, which was infamous for its success as a smuggler in the Yellow Sea. In a few minutes she was able to count forty—more or less—red sails thus erasing any hope that she was about to encounter friends. Her body guard, Stenka, looked through the telescope a few minutes later when day was beginning to break and confirmed the ominous findings.

Her security ships and Captain MacTavish's naval fleet appeared to her aided eye to be in full readiness—all hands-on-deck, and all positions manned. It was a waiting game now. The large *USS* ships, the *Jamestown*, *Washington*, *Independence*, and *Franklin*, moved into position four abreast to present the most menacing visage possible to the attackers. The *Far East Transporter*, *Igor's Guards*, and the *Lady of Tarasova*, gathered together immediately behind the naval vessels with all guns primed and ready for the fight. The other ships under MacTavish's command drew up alongside the protected commercial vessels, including two of Commodore Perry's four Black Ships–the paddle-wheeled steam frigate *Mississippi* and the *Susquehanna*, a side-wheel steam frigate—and fourteen of the smaller ships from the Mediterranean formed a rear guard.

The Red Sail pirate fleet suddenly began to spread out into four groups of ten, each group sailing determinedly towards one of the larger USS ships. They were apparently unaware of the size of the armaments and the skills of the gunners and the marine fighters because they came head on–all sails unfurled–and began firing a cannonade from one hundred yards out, all of which missed by more than twenty feet. Presuming that the pirates were testing for distance, he ordered his ship's semaphores to signal "Spread Out".

The sudden change of course by the American ships caused considerable anxiety in the Red Flag Fleet. The captains knew that something was afoot, but their strict training to follow orders and not to improvise held them to an increasingly poor choice in the battle. Finally, Zheng Shi came to a conclusion and had flags hoisted to regroup the junks in her small fleet. Now able to see the massive armaments arrayed against her, Zheng sent word to two of her junks to turn about and head to the pirate island of Talicud in the Sulu Sea off the coast of Mindanao to fetch reinforcements.

MacTavish ordered his ship captains to hold their fire until they were less than seventy-five yards from the leading junks of the pirate force. He knew that that was the absolute range limit for the pirates, but within easy range of his more modern artillery.

The navigator nodded his head to Capt. MacTavish that they were passing closer than seventy-five yards. MacTavish sent up semaphores to order one half of the guns of all forward ships to direct a fusillade at the six most forward junks of the pirate force.

CHAPTER FORTY

*Pursue one great decisive aim with force and determination...
in strategy everything is very simple, but not on that account
very easy.*

—Karl von Clausewitz, *The Art of War, Book III*

Decisive Battle of the South China Sea

Northwest of the Luzon Strait, South China Sea, and northeast of the coast of Taiwan on board the *Far East Transporter,* November 30, 1879

The excitement and tension aboard the naval and combat ready commercial ships was palpable and fixated the attention of every hand on the ship from the captain to the cook's dish scrubber. With the enemy within plain sight, Capt. MacTavish ordered the marine drummer to sound "Battle Stations!" and every member of the crew rushed to his or—in the case of Alexandra, her—assigned places. To the inexperienced eye, it would have appeared to be chaos; but, in fact, it was an organized rush of disciplined activity. The ships' usually noncombatant hands swiftly moved every item on the decks not needed for battle belowdecks, put out the galley fire; furniture in the captain's cabins was moved belowdecks to make as much room as possible for the gun crews; and a detail of men climbed to all the ship's fighting tops to make emergency repairs to battle-damaged rigging as the occasion might arise. Below decks, the surgeon and his mates laid out their bandages and instruments and made ready to care for the wounded. In a controlled frenzy, sand was scattered along the decks for better footing; tubs were filled with water for drinking and firefighting; and the big guns were given a rapid final inspection.

On the spar deck and gun deck, the gunners and marines set themselves to getting her armament ready for immediate use. Each of the gun-deck long-barreled cast iron 24-pounders had its own crew. Eighteen immense short-barreled 32-pounder carronades were behind broadside ports, and three bow-chaser guns were carried on the forecastle—all manned by highly disciplined and experienced crews thoroughly familiar with their particular gun. The spar-deck battery included chase guns as well as the-32pounders.

Different types of ammunition having selective purposes were available in the gunnery batteries: the guns had flint firing locks with a double-headed cock holding two flints and could be quickly reversed if one flint became worn or lost. The 24-pounder deck cannons were nine and one-half feet long from breech to muzzle, weighed three tons along with its carriage, and had a hefty 5.8 inch bore. The barrel was the finest made in the world–a black-powder smoothbore firing only round iron shot.

The gun carriage was controlled by an arrangement of lines and tackle. Ammunition was mounted on an iron rack, a hold over from the old Royal Navy ships of the line. The rack was called a brass monkey. Brass was preferred to iron because iron tended to shrink in the cold and all the cannon balls to come loose and to scatter onto the deck. Sailors' definition of very severe cold was "cold enough to freeze the balls of a brass monkey".

Other types of ammunition were assigned to other cannons: Dismantling shot–several different types of special shot used to tear up an opponent's sails and rigging, including bar shot—two ball halves connected by an iron bar, chain shot, an iron ring to which several lengths of chain were fastened, star shot in which the sections of chain opened up, star-fashion, in flight, scatter shot which consisted of two round shot connected by a short chain; grape and canister scatter shot–large and small–to be used at close range against an enemy's crew.

The near frantic hurry was nonetheless orderly. Each gun had its crew and its stores of necessary artillery gear to be able to fire and to keep firing: barrel, carriage, rammer, breech, quoin, sponge, muzzle, truck, linstock with slowmatch, vent, train, train tackle, side tackle, water bucket, trunnion, powder box, cascabel knob, breeching, and handspike.

Gun crews checked the loads in their massive weapons and waited in silence for the action to begin.

The ships' captains gave the order: "Attention on deck. Ready the guns."

The gun crews unfastened the lashings holding their guns secure at sea. Gun carriages were not fixed to the deck; if one should break loose in a seaway, the consequences could be dangerous to the ship and fatal to the men who had to bring the massive rolling weight under control. Almost nothing was worse on a ship than a loose cannon, and eventually the term came to be applied to a person who was erratic, unprepared, and unable to think before acting.

Each man in a gun division had a specific task. Upon the captain's orders, the crew removed the covers that kept dampness out of the bore and took their various necessary implements from their racks. Firing locks were opened and lengths of slow match-cord soaked in an inflammable solution were ignited starting a slow burn; match-cords were put in safe places along the gun deck for use in case a lock should fail. Below the frigate's waterline, the gunner and his assistants opened the forward and after magazines and rushed to break out sausage-shaped flannel powder cartridges for the guns and carronades. Other men took their assigned stations along the lower decks to pass cartridges up to the gun crews.

Many US and Royal Navy captains drilled their men in firing at longer ranges and taught accuracy and coordination of fire. Capt. MacTavish took the opposite view. He ordered close quarters firing and relied on short-range rapid fire, believing it to be the principal test of a well-trained gun crew. The captain's order to commence firing was passed by megaphone to the division officers, who then directed their guns. The captains' order, given when his ship moved broadside and close enough to attack the long hull of the enemy ship, was, "Fire as she bears!"

The fully ready team moved into quick action. The gun was already in its recoil position for loading; and the man to the left kept a strain on the train tackle to hold the ponderous weapon in place while the man at the muzzle rammed the load home. The man at the breech pierced the powder cartridge with a priming wire before inserting the priming tube–in his left hand he held a linstock, a wooden staff holding a piece of burning slowmatch. The gunnery team nodded that the gun was ready to fire then the two side tackles were used to run it out. In rapid succession, the gun powder bag was dropped down the barrel; the priming wire pierced the powder bag to make sure that the flame of the primer would ignite the powder charge; and the lighted match-cord touched to the powder. The gun captain pulled the lanyard to trip the firing lock.

Suddenly, hell broke loose with acrid smoke, the tang of gun powder, and an explosion at close range that deafened the gunners even though they tried to cover their ears. The moistened sponge extinguished sparks in the bore after firing. The worm cleaned unburned fragments of cloth powder bags from the bore. The handspike helped to move the gun carriage and to raise the gun breech; so, the wedge-shaped quoin could be moved to adjust the gun's elevation. The tompion kept the bore dry while the gun was not in use.

The tremendous concussive force required to send a cannon shot on its way at many hundreds of feet-per-second made the gun jump back on its carriage with great force in accordance to the scientific dictum that for every action there is a reaction. In the crowded space of the deck of the ship, this reaction had to be controlled. The gun's recoil was partially absorbed by combinations of strong springs, hydraulic cylinders, and powerful men holding ropes to bring it safely to a stop. One sailor died when the safety equipment failed, and the multi-ton gun shot back across into the man standing by the opposite side railing.

As the firing commenced, each captain took his station on the quarterdeck, from which he could direct the helmsman and order the handling of guns and sails. The marine detachment took their positions with loaded muskets, some on deck and others in the fighting tops. It was their time to wait until the din and smoke of the cannonade cleared enough to assess the situation. Other than the man killed by the loose cannon, there were no casualties on the US flotilla. The pirate ships which received the brunt of the US attack suffered battering, penetrating and splintering of their hulls and decks; shattering and dismounting their cannons; mangling and destroying the rigging; cutting to pieces and blowing the masts into the disturbed ocean; piercing and tearing the sails rendering them useless; and severely wounding and killing the majority of the ship's companies. Six of the pirates' ships were out of commission, and two sank unceremoniously into the fathomless deep.

Thus severely wounded, the Red Flag Fleet fell into disarray with every ship and every man for himself. The US ships pulled to within boarding distance of those vessels still afloat and fired guns loaded with grapeshot and canister sweeping the enemy's decks like a giant shotgun with devastating effects on the already shell-shocked survivors. To finish, every ship which could manage a direct hit fired "hot shot"–iron round shot, heated bright red in the US ship's galley stove for use against any flammable target. The sizzling balls found their marks and embedded themselves into the wood of a bulwark, a ship's cabin or storage unit, or a ship's hull, igniting fires which could not be extinguished for lack of water, buckets, or men to do the work. Several junks blew into smithereens when the ignition occurred in powder storage holds.

Capt. MacTavish and Capt. Alexandra Yusupov had not come to score a gentleman's victory nor to cause a battle defeat which would discourage future incursions into public sea lanes. They had come to kill, to destroy the Red Flag Fleet and every pirate they could find thereby preventing any chance of retaliation.

The thundering guns of eleven ships pulverized all six pirate junks and sunk four more in less than two minutes from the order to "Fire as she bears!" Two minutes after that, American marines and enraged local Alaskan fishermen attached grappling hooks to the remaining junks in the second rank of boats, dropped boarding planks from deck to deck, and began a slaughter of the outmanned and outgunned pirates. The decision was made to take no prisoners, and the pirates who survived the initial mano-a-mano attack saw no salvation but to leap into the sea. Most them were sucked under as they swam into close proximity to their junks, and the junks were purposefully sunk by the US naval officers and gunners.

Zheng Shi ordered a full and scattered retreat of the remaining junks, but no one except the men next to her heard the order. She escaped in a life boat and was rowed to a rear echelon ship. She commanded the captain to relinquish his authority. She ordered the remaining pirates to hoist all sails and to leave for the fortified villages on the southern coast of Mindanao and Basilan and on the islands of Balangingi and Tunkil in the southern Philippines under the protection of her fellow pirates–the Balangingi and Iranum Samal–and the Sultan of Sulu. The Sulu/Celebes Seas were historically the most dangerous backwaters in the world, and November, 1879 was no exception.

Capt. MacTavish and his officers, and Alexandra and her armed commercial fleet were all well aware of the dangers of these pirate infested waters and the massive marine army still viable among the islands. It might have been prudent to retreat to the safety of Shanghai, Hong Kong, or Tokyo; however, the US navy captain also knew that as soon as the pirate commander reached her safe haven, an armada of nearly 1800 pirate junks loaded with upwards of 50,000 or even more fanatical and drug crazed fighters would come to punish and destroy his small fighting force. He gave a quick set of orders:

"Three of our ships stay behind to destroy the rest of the junks and to kill all of the pirates here. The rest of us will pursue the fleeing junks and take them out. It is possible that we will be able to hit the harbors of those fortified islands before the full armada can get underway. We are going to try, because this may be the only chance to destroy this nest of vipers we will ever have. Stand to your guns. You are the US Navy; and you will prevail!"

No marine or sailor who ever heard that command, "Stand to your guns" took it lightly or thought of it as a chance to take part in glory. Nothing required more courage that to walk a plank from his safe ship or swing on a rope to a ship wallowing in the roiling sea and then meeting face-to-face at arm's reach with man after man intent on taking his life or grievously wounding him and leaving him to the tender mercies of the amputation-happy ship's surgeons. Even the bravest and most hardened of men cringed at the thought having the ammunition of his flintlock pistol run out and of being slashed or stabbed by a dirty saber, cutlass— the vicious back–slashing sword, scimitar, or pike, or having to find himself where it was kill-or-be-killed with bare hands and feet. There would be no prisoners; no quarter asked, and none given. Many men became deeply religious that evening.

CHAPTER FORTY-ONE

WAR WITH THE SULU
SEA PIRATES

The art of war teaches us to rely not on the likelihood of the
enemy's not coming, but on our own readiness to receive him;
not on the chance of his not attacking, but rather on the fact that
we have made our position unassailable.

—Sun Tzu, *The Art of War*

**On board the *Far East Transporter*, off the southern coast of
Mindanao, Basilan, Balangingi, and Tunkil in the southern
Philippines, December 14, 1879**

Red Flag Fleet Admiral Zheng Shi Sao could see the advancing
American combat fleet drawing ever closer each day. She
computed the distance to the fortified cities of her fellow pirates—
the Balangingi and Iranum Samal—and the Sultan of Sulu as she did twice
every day. She wanted desperately to believe that she could reach there
before the enemy ships drew close enough for a battle at sea. However, she
was the ultimate pragmatist and recognized the objective truth: her slow
junk would be two days away from safety when the Yankees caught up
with her. She had four beat-up junks and fifty men left—nothing against
a whole navy. She might have another six or maybe even twelve junks if
she could stall, but she was not at all confident that the white-eyed [blind]

gweilo [European white person] captain was easily fooled. She was equally certain that he could not be bought off.

Oliver MacTavish was racing against the clock. If the remainders of the Red Flag Fleet ahead of him could make it to their safe port, he would have to tuck his tail beneath his legs and head for Shanghai and ignominy.

"Full sails, full speed ahead," he shouted.

The officers and sailors—who had been standing about nervously awaiting the skipper's decision—flew into action. All sails were unfurled; all guns were manned; all hands were on deck. The American flotilla raced towards the Red Flag Fleet junks and what they knew might be the next sally in an all-out war. Every man and woman in the fleet believed in the cause and were ready to kill or be killed.

Alexandra had a mixture of emotions—exhilaration and excitement, anxiety and fear, wonder and awe, perplexity and conundrum. She maintained an inscrutable and brave face lest she convey any anxiety she was feeling to her men, many of whom were novices when it came to battle. The *Far East Transporter* took its place at the center of the rapidly moving USS contingent and strove to keep up. Capts. MacTavish and Tarasova-Yusupov followed their progress relative to the Red Flag Fleet through their telescopes and could tell that they were gaining on the pirates at a rapid pace.

Standing at the helm of her junk, Zheng Shi Sao could tell with her unaided eye that the hated round-eyes—*nǐ èr dàyé de* [damn on his second uncle] were gaining; and, furthermore by her reckoning, they would be upon her before she could get her island-based fighters into their junks and able to lend her assistance. She maneuvered her junk to where she was leading the fleeing pack planning to let them bear the brunt of the initial attack and, hopefully, to allow her to escape in the chaos.

Capt. MacTavish did not buy into Zheng's plan. Instead of engaging the rear guard, he swept quickly around them and moved into position directly in front of Zheng's junk. He had no difficulty recognizing her standing at the helm. Her flamboyant garb was the stuff of legend in Asian seas. She made no attempt to be obscure or self-effacing. Zheng wore a mid-calf length scarlet silk dress with an open bodice which showed the large dragoon tattoo on her neck. Her face was rather plain, and she had some graying beginning to show in the hair that peaked out from beneath her brocade cap. The sheath-like dress was not deceiving: she had double cross bandoliers of ammunition for her pair of flintlock pistols, a wide belt that served to protect her belly and to grant ready access to her ever-present long dirk and a barong from the Sulu Archipelago, a highly sharpened multi-curvilinear Javanese Kris sword, and six death star throwing devices. Her feet and lower legs were protected by knee-high heavy black books folded over at the top.

MacTavish and Zheng's eyes locked in defiance and challenge.

"Prepare to be boarded," MacTavish commanded through a foghorn.

"*Lǎolao!* [Never]; You surrender and be spared," the Chinese pirate answered in response.

At MacTavish's order, the *USS Jamestown*, fired a single cannon shot which gravely damaged the after deck of the junk. Zheng knew that she could not sustain another.

"Approach under white flag, Captain," she said, less defiant now.

In the few moments that it took for MacTavish to send his second-mate and five marines to the junk in a lifeboat, Zheng slipped overboard on her port side, opposite to where the *Jamestown* was standing in the water.

Unfortunately for Zheng, the watch officer of the *USS Atlanta*, sitting just behind and to the portside of the junk saw her escape attempt. He sent two fast boats after her and subdued her without a fight.

While Zheng was being taken into custody, the marine contingent from the *Jamestown* boarded the junk without a fight. The pirates had been ordered by Zheng to fight to the death to give their admiral a chance to live to fight another day, but they were not suicidal. While they had never given a ship's company compassion and had inflicted brutal wounds, beheadings, tortures, rape, and enslavement, they expected better treatment from the Christian Americans.

MacTavish had Zheng brought to his sloop-of-war.

Once aboard, he offered her a steaming mug of chai which she gratefully accepted.

"Greetings, Admiral Zheng Shi Sao," he said in a surprisingly polite manner which threw her off guard.

"Good afternoon," Zheng responded in her stilted and imperfect English.

"Would you prefer that we converse in Chinese, Madam?" he offered.

"Jess prease. Best I talk in Cantonese."

"Let us sit and talk about pleasant things until I can get my interpreter who is on another ship."

The two leaders and his first and second mates sat down on comfortable cushioned chairs in MacTavish's state room. If it was his intention to impress her with the futility of further resistance, he was successful. The *Jamestown* and the remaining ships of his flotilla were in motion, racing, in fact towards the southwest.

Alexandra Tarasova-Yusupov was brought alongside in a fast boat, and she was helped up the Jacob's ladder and onto the main deck. The sailors saluted her and escorted her to the stateroom.

"Captain," she said, "you sent for me, Sir?"

"I did, Captain. I trust you had an exciting ride."

"Most bracing, Sir," she said with a broad smile feeling lucky to be in one piece.

"I presume you recognize Admiral Zheng Shi Sao, Captain?"

"I have seen paintings…and wanted posters."

At this Zheng laughed and gave a small bow.

"I asked you here to translate. I am in hopes that you speak Cantonese."

"Fluently, Sir."

"*Neih hou*, Madam," Alexandra said in Zheng's native language, taking care to enunciate the tonal qualities to distinguish between Cantonese and Mandarin.

They are both tonal languages but have different tones giving different meanings to the same sound. Mandarin has four tones per sound, while Cantonese has from six to as many as nine tones per sound. The two languages have different vowels and consonants; and for the most part, the differences are such that Cantonese people cannot understand Mandarin speakers and vice versa.

That broke the ice, and soon the two women—who came from opposite ends of the earth culturally—were carrying on a vigorous conversation in the language common only in Guangzhou Province–where it originated–and Hong Kong. It is the lingua franca in the southern provinces of Guangdong and Guangxi, including Hong Kong and Macau. MacTavish wisely did not interrupt the flow of what was indecipherable even as human speech to him. He waited until there was a lull before he asked Alexandra,

"Please tell me the gist of your conversation. I want only one thing from it. She must agree to send a letter in her special code, ordering her pirates to stay in their fortified port cities and to accept a parlay with us in the harbor. We must avoid a major fight at all costs; she doesn't need to know that, of course."

Alexandra related the conversation in generalities. They spoke of their childhoods, cultures, and life's experiences. Then, Zheng confessed her fear that this was the end for her. She had defeated the Europeans, the British, and the Chinese—who had been reduced to using fishing boats as their navy after their encounters with her. However, she was tired. She feared that she would eventually be taken to hang in Hong Kong because the round-eyes from America had very convincingly trapped her. She was ready to capitulate but had several conditions she wanted to extract from the handsome navy officer."

Both MacTavish and Alexandra laughed at that.

"Now, I think it is time for you to translate; so, I can be certain that the message is received accurately, and her response is what I want to hear. This is delicate, Alexandra, our careers–maybe even our very lives– ride on what we can get her to say and do."

"I'm ready."

She signaled to Zheng that they should resume talking and that it was now time for her to translate for the pirate admiral and Captain MacTavish.

Each question and each answer were laboriously asked and answered from Cantonese to English and back.

Q-"We are hurrying towards Ciudad de Isabela and the Zamboanga Peninsula to put a halt to piracy and slavery in the Sulu/Celebes region. We wish to accomplish that without bloodshed. We offer you amnesty if you make that happen, Zheng."

A-"But what can such a humble one as me do that would help? I am your prisoner."

Q-"You can write a set of orders in your language and in your handwriting to have your people stay in their homes, turn in their weapons, and wait for us. We will grant them amnesty as well."

A-"That is generous of you, Kind Sir. I will do as you ask."

A quill pen and parchment were brought to Zheng.

"I regret that the letter must be written in both of the main Sulu languages—Tausug and Yakan. Most people throughout the archipelago speak Tausug, but on Basilan Island where we are going, most speak only their old Yakan. Also, I must apologize once more, Kind Sir. The letter must be in our own special pirate code or else they will believe it is a trick."

MacTavish asked Alexandra, "Do you speak Tausug and Yakan?"

"Sorry, no. I cannot speak or read either."

"Then we must trust Zheng; is that what you say?"

"Not quite, Oliver. We can find one of the local hands who speaks and reads one or the other of those languages."

"Zheng, you start writing. Alexandra, take the first mate and find the interpreter. Be quick about it. We are less than a day out of *Fuerte Isabel Segunda*. Time is of the essence."

Zheng had finished a two-page letter for the chieftains of her fortified islands by the time Alexandra and Lieutenant Forsyth returned with the member of the galley crew from this work station.

MacTavish handed the missive to the cook who read it with assiduous care.

"What does it say, Man?" Capt. MacTavish asked brusquely.

"Oh, Good Sir, Missy Zheng says that she gives order to all pirate persons to lay down their arms and to stay off junks. They to sit in homes and wait for kind American navy persons to come and give them… freedom…not sure of the word."

Zheng said, "Is amnesty."

"Ah, so. After that they will no longer be pirates or sellers of persons, and they can go about their lives as Philippine citizens with full rights. No have to be punished, ever."

He raised his eyes first to Zheng, who gave a slight nod, then to Capt. MacTavish and Alexandra.

"Is good," pronounced Zheng and smiled at the cook.

"I guess we will have to trust you Zheng. Remember, things will go badly for you if this is a lie."

"I fear you too much to lie. I swear on the life of the Virgin Mother."

A fast boat was dispatched to *Fuerte Isabel Segunda* with the important orders, and the *USS Jamestown* and the *Far East Transporter* and the flotilla raced on taking advantage of fair seas and a brisk wind at their backs. In the several hours left before they reached the Isabel Segunda harbor, Alexandra had the member of the galley crew write down the gist of the letter that was sent to the best of his recollection. This is the message sent by Zheng:

Good captains and friends:

Tell this to all our people in all our cities in all our islands. All is lost for the Red Flag Fleet and for your humble servant Zheng Shi Sao. Have been taken prisoner by the American Navy who makes demands and gives promises. Demands are that you bring all of your weapons: dirks, *kampilians*, scimitars, barongs, your bamboo spears with the iron spearhead, your swivel guns, and all else, and pile them on the wharf. Do not go onto your ships. Go to your houses; stay inside; and do not come out until the American officers say you do that. Failure to obey will result in loss of heads, lands, homes, families. Obey me.

Signed,

Zheng Shi Sao,

Zheng Shi Sao,

Admiral Red Flag Fleet

Two days later the American warships and commercial vessels weighed anchor in the bay of Fort Isabel Secunda. Seeing no one in the city or near the stone fort, MacTavish dispatched a heavily armed contingent of marines on three lifeboats. They were in the city for two hours before returning with a disappointing message; there was not a single human being in the town, nor was there a single boat of any kind.

MacTavish and Alexandra were furious.

MacTavish ordered the master-at-arms to place both the member of the galley crew and Zheng Shi Sao in irons and stand them under the yardarm of the mainsail.

A heavy hemp rope was slung over the yard and looped over and through a heavy pulley. "Prepare a collar," MacTavish commanded two ordinary seamen who quickly and expertly applied tallow to the rope's end and wound thirteen loops to make a proper hangman's knot.

Fully aware of the number thirteen as the world's most well-recognized unlucky number, the man and woman in shackles gulped, paled, and stared at their shoes.

Alexandra lifted the Bangsa Moro cook's chin to force him to look her directly in the eyes.

"What did Zheng Shi's letter really say?"

The master-at-arms put the noose around the man's neck and shifted it to the side so that his head was forced into an angle with his neck. The two hefty sailors on the other end of the rope pulled it taut, and it forced the terrified islander to stand on his tip toes.

"Are you deaf?" she asked and nodded to the sailors who inched the noose slightly higher.

"No, no, Missy. I hear you. Can't talk. Choking."

"Are you ready to write down what the letter said…NOW!"

He nodded his head as vigorously as he could.

"Lower him."

MacTavish looked directly at Zheng and said with quiet malice, "Pay close attention, Pirate. Look and learn."

Alexandra removed the noose and sat the trembling cook down at a table conveniently available a few feet away. She handed him a pen, ink, and two sheets of paper.

"Write," she said. "If you write a lie, you will get your neck stretched. Then you will never marry, have children, or have any ancestors to light joss sticks for you. Understand?"

"Yes, yes, Missy. No lies. Had to lie first time because afraid of the dragon lady. Must protect me from her when I tell the real truth."

Zheng gave him a dagger stare, but he ignored her and penned a note in pidgin English that he hoped would save his life. He knew that Zheng was going to die minutes from then which reduced his level of fear

> Good captains and friends:
> Tell this to all our people in all our cities in all our islands. All is lost for the Red Flag Fleet and for your humble servant Zheng Shi Sao if you do not make good plans to disappear. Have been taken prisoner by the American Navy who makes demands and gives promises. Demands are that you bring all of your weapons: dirks, *kampilians*, scimitars, barongs, your bamboo spears with the iron spearhead, your swivel guns, and all else, and pile them on the wharf. Do not go onto your ships. Go to your houses; stay inside; and do not come out until the American officers say you do that. I say, go fast to south end of Mindanao and hide in hills above Fort of Sepac. Know that I will find a way to trick the round eyes. Failure to obey me will result in loss of heads, lands, homes, families. Obey me now.
> Signed,
> *Zheng Shi Sao,*
> Zheng Shi Sao,
> Admiral Red Flag Fleet

"Is this the truth, Muhummad ibn Kabungsuwan?" Alexandra asked the cringing cook.

"Yes, Missy. All truth. Madam Zheng say she cut my throat and privates if I not tell you lie about first letter. So solly. Many times solly, Missy. Tell truth now."

He began to cry, the most demeaning thing a Moro man could do in his entire life. That act alone convinced MacTavish and Alexandra that he had been scared straight.

MacTavish looked directly into Zheng Shi Sao's cruel opaque eyes and said softly, "Why should we not stretch your neck? Maybe your only choice is to ask me to have the executioners break your neck fast. My inclination is to go slow and watch your eyes bulge for a few minutes while you die. What say you, Madam Liar?"

"Not like to be insulted. Not want to have war with America or American navy. Wanted only to have people to hide and save their skins. Ready to do all to make piracy go away."

"And slavery?" asked Alexandra.

"And that important part of our economy go away, too. Time of fighting should stop, I say."

"Prove it," MacTavish said. "I ask you again why should I not hang you, Madam Pirate?"

"Take rope off. We talk. I can and will make both bad things go away. You guarantee Zheng that she can live like normal Chinee, keep her money, not be hunted by government peoples; and Zheng will go around and convince pirate peoples that it is not longer possible to live safe selling peoples and pirating ships. Will take monies from China, Brits, and American round-eyes. I not want more than £100,000 for me."

"How can we possibly trust you?"

"Will go around to my towns and talk to my people while you listen. Gold haired girl can come. Will only speak English and Mandarin; so, she not find it difficult."

Alexandra knew she and Oliver MacTavish had to find a way for Zheng to save face; so, she said courteously, "Perhaps, Admiral Zheng, we have misunderstood what you have said, and all is well. Perhaps we misheard your utterances and thought good was evil, and black was white."

"Yes, Missy with the golden hair. You say right. Now we can work together as friends. Is there a word for such misunderstandings?"

"We do have a word for them, it is mondegreens."

"Never heard it before. Is good word. I will try remember it."

Reluctantly, MacTavish had his men dismantle the gallows even though he had never intended to hang either of the miscreants in reality.

Alexandra took Oliver aside and asked, "What is your plan if she fails to deliver a peaceful solution?"

MacTavish took no time to answer, "Fire and steel, shock and awe."

He had a very serious look on his face. The fight would be blood and suffering and would likely end in a lethal defeat for his fleet.

He hoped his bluff had worked and committed the next four weeks to traveling with Zheng and ibn Kabungsuwan to make it so. The entire fleet traveled around the south Sulu/Celebes sea area and stopped in every pirate port they could manage in the time allotted to the project. It was dangerous, but to everyone's great surprise—even Zheng's—it was successful. They gave the same presentation in Fort Isabel Secunda, Basilan, Jolo—the great slave market–Tawitawi, Banguinqui, Sulu, Talipao, and finally they completed the mission in Maimbung at the Sulu Sultan's Daru Jambangan—Palace of Flowers.

The sultan put it best: "It is time for this history "written in blood and tears and nourished in pain and suffering" as the Spanish say, to end. Throughout my archipelago, no more shall we keep slaves for the dirty Dutch slavers taking peoples to the Dutch East Indies. No more shall use our junks, Iranun garays armed with a lantaka at the bow, Moro paraws, or wooden galleys, to attack ships. No more shall we have to hide and to fear the governments and the navies. No more shall we have starvation without doing slavery and pirating. No more shall traders and government vessels fear our menace."

"Agreed. Sultan, you guarantee that Zheng and her pirates go to their homes and stay there; and we will guarantee that the governments will not come hunting for them or you. We will pay a sum of money to assist you and your people to resume decent lives without committing crimes," Capt. MacTavish promised on behalf of America for whom he might have been able to speak and on behalf of China, Portugal, all of Europe, and India for whom he had no authority to speak.

It was not necessary that the sultan or Zheng know that part, and it was a bluff he hoped would bear fruit. As time passed, it was amazing even to the bluffing Americans and the war-weary Chinese, Japanese, and the pirates that the bluff had worked.

Ultimately, Alexandra learned much later that Zheng left her profession as a pirate, murderer, and slaver and returned to her old profession of prostitution. She was given a stipend by the government of Hong Kong to build a casino next to her brothel where she prospered doing legitimate work. She married her son–adopted son–had two children with him, and died of old age in her bed in the brothel. She never entirely outgrew the gruesome reputation she deserved among the Cantonese people. Two generations and more remembered when her Red Flag Fleet established a harsh despotic pseudo-government over many coastal villages in the province. She imposed levies and taxes on the struggling settlements. She and her pirates robbed many innocent and defenseless towns, markets, and villages, from Macau to Canton. No one forgot the rape of one village where they beheaded 80 men and abducted all their women and children and held them for ransom until they were sold in slavery. But even that memory dimmed over time and the change of generations.

The sultan was better than his word. He convinced the competing pirate organization—the Cantonese Pirate Coalition operated by pirate chieftain Wu Shi'er and the Muslim *Badjao* [Sea Gypsies] to see the wisdom of following Zheng's example. The bulk of the Sulu/Celebes pirates had grown tired of being afraid and of fighting for everything. They settled near the former Maranao pirates' lairs. Slavery died out when the old slaving forts and towns were destroyed by Chinese soldiers. The Balinguingui pirates became farmers. The forts of Marawi and Sepac served the army for a time and then were allowed to deteriorate into ruins.

The base of the Sulu Sea economy changed from wholesale slavery and piracy to become predominantly agricultural with farming and fishing as the main sources of livelihood. The islands' fertile soils and moderate and humid climate was ideal for growing a variety of crops: abaca–a type of banana from which a tough and useful fiber is produced–coconuts, edible bananas, coffee, oranges, and lanzones—a tree fruit which the islanders learned to change from sour to sweet–as well as exotic fruits, durian and purple mangosteen–the health producing fruit of the evergreen tree of the same name.

The Sulu Sea is one of the richest fishing grounds in the world. Fishing led to the discovery of pearls resulting in the Zamboanga Province developing a highly successful pearl industry on Marungas Island. With the opening of trade with foreign countries, the Sulu people began to make products of value including using the backs of sea turtles being polished and made into a trays and combs. Because they no longer had to depend on the risky life of piracy, the people learned how to build beautiful and useful boats and woven fiber mats. In time, the people became industrious enough and good enough businessmen to succeed at coffee growing and processing and created a large export fruit plantation system. They learned fruit preservation and shipped the preserves all around the world.

Absent piracy and the distasteful and dangerous slavery trafficking business, the gifted craftsmen and women—and even children—delved back into their roots and began to develop businesses making handicrafts with Islamic, Filipino, Indonesian, Malaysian, and Oriental products. These included boats, knives, swords, hatchets, and spears; bronze and brassware, hand woven indigenous cloth; embroidered textiles; beautiful and intricate shell craft including valuable jewelry, the long thought to be lost art of traditional house carvings; and carved wooden grave markers which became popular all around the world during the late nineteenth century.

Six weeks after concluding negotiations with the Sulu sultan, Alexandra and her weary shipmates and employees made their way back to the Golden Horn Bay of Vladivostok. It was the dead of winter and freezing to the point that it would not be long before the bay froze over to the point that only the sturdiest of ice-breakers could penetrate the barrier to the far eastern Russian port city. Communication was inadequate; so, her arrival went unannounced. She and her crew battened the hatches and locked the storage holds containing so much valuable booty and commercial items before they left their ships at the wharf to go to the hotels or their homes until the light snow and sleet turned a blizzard, and the blizzard to heavy drifted snow. Hauling the cargo to the company's holding sheds could wait until it was calm enough for people to work without freezing to death.

When Alexandra arrived back at the No. 71 Pekinskaya Street Tarasova House, Boris was spending the week in Balagansk taking care of his prison duties. It was an incongruous situation. He worked fairly hard to bring the neglected infrastructure back to an acceptable level of safety and security at an imperial army pay level that was not a hundredth of what he could glean from one voyage as a partner in the Matheson-Tarasova-Yusupov, et. al. enterprises. He knew it would be the height of folly to step away from his position, thereby leaving him open to criticism in the ranks and at the mercy of the Okhrana whenever another crisis swirled around the tzar and his family or the army. He got little satisfaction out of doling out punishment to men and women who were not far different from himself and terms of their tzarist and Okhrana defined crimes. However, he did so by swallowing his pride and his honor because to do otherwise would bring his house of cards existence tumbling down. Already there were tidbits of news indicating unrest throughout the empire and threats against the tzar and his family.

After four days of resting in warm quarters, Alexandra, her ships' crews, and the small army of Tarasova Fur Company workers—including her parents—cleared a pathway through the heavy deep snow to the *Far East Transporter* and its burgeoning holds. They brought with them every dray animal, cart, and troika, to move the precious goods to the Tarasova sheds. Abram and Irina were astounded at their daughter's success—a treasure trove which would net them the equivalent of a king's ransom, enough for them all to retire to a life of leisure. They offloaded bales of the best decorated silk in all of the Orient, Chinese toys, animal pelts enough to fill one of their fur sheds to its maximum, gold and silver coins in chests that took four men to carry, handmade artifacts of surpassing beauty and value from far-flung ports as diverse as India and the Bay of Bengal to Chŏson and Alaska.

There was a dray wagon sized load of bearer bonds and promissory notes and more: exotic crops like mangosteen from the Sulu Sea, knives and swords of the highest quality taken as booty from Sulu Sea pirates in exchange for their freedom, precious gem jewelry expropriated from Zheng Shi Sao, and Buddhist Nephite Jade statuary by the wagon load obtained through fair trade which was worth double its weight in gold in Europe and the rich cities of the East and those in the rapidly expanding richness of American markets.

One shed was filled with coconuts, sugar, hemp, coffee, tea, and spices from the islands. There were one hundred drums of *Okolehao*, the Hawai'ian alcoholic beverage. They filled half a shed with finely broken up best-quality hard anthracite coal.

"Well done, my brilliant daughter," Abram Timurovich told her. "More important than all of that is the family, My Dear. When do you see Boris Nikolaiovich, and your little sons, Nikita and Oral Borisovich?"

Alexandra blushed scarlet. She had almost forgotten her twins' names.

CHAPTER FORTY-TWO

MILITARY TRANSFERS

I left my home in NanTze, Taiwan, to serve as a full-time missionary in northern California in 2005... The missionary work was difficult, and people often yelled at us. We had few investigators. It seemed to me that the work was not going anywhere... I was convinced I would be transferred... I also knew that my Heavenly Father knew my thoughts and frustration. He understood my weakness, and He sent His servant to reassure me... Throughout the next five weeks, my companion and I witnessed many miracles as we exercised enough faith to work hard.

—Lena Hsin-Yao Cho, *The Church of Jesus Christ of Latter-day Saints, On-Line, June 2015*

Storms don't last forever.

—Pastor T.D. Jakes, *Everything Love, the Good Vibe*

National Archives of Australia, Victorian Archives Centre, 99 Shiel Street, North Melbourne, Victoria, Australia, February 28, 2014

Elder and Sister Smith finished their mission and flew home in early February with mixed emotions—thrill in anticipation of seeing their nine grandchildren again, nostalgic sadness at leaving their mission friends, and a hint of frustration at not having succeeded in unraveling the mystery of Alexandra Tarasova-Yusupov to their satisfaction. The day they left was one of the exchange days which took place every eight weeks. Their replacements–Elder Cecil and Sister MaryAnne Cheevers from Heber City, Utah–arrived the same day turning it into something of a chaos with no significant time for emotional upsets. Most of the afternoon was spent in getting the Cheevers settled into the apartment which would be their home away from home for the next eighteen months. As they helped the Cheevers unpack, the other missionaries explained their private little quest to learn all that could be learn about the woman they now referred to as, "The Mysterious Alexandra Tarasova-Yusupov, or sometimes they added the patronymic making it Alexandra Abramovena Tarasova-Yusupov.

The Cheevers were glad that they would have some kind of a project outside their archival work, which frankly, to Elder Cheevers, sounded deadly dull—one of his worst nightmares, that of being bored for long periods of time. His doctor had diagnosed him with adult attention deficit disorder, but he sloughed that idea off by saying he had "ants in his pants" and had always craved activity over sitting around.

The Taylors had only two months to go, and watching Nephi and Marianne Smith leave and the Cheevers arrive made them feel a little uneasy about their mission work; should they feel guilty about considering themselves short-timers, or should they lose themselves in the work of the Lord…and the work of ferreting out tidbits of information about Alexandra. They decided on the latter.

Thus reoriented to the work by the following morning, Lisa Taylor followed up on what they had been learning about Boris Yusupov. There was no real history—at least, no narrative; but Lisa was determined to find out more about his apparent transfers. She and Neal took turns delving into the records of Balagansk Prison and of the town. Lisa hit on the idea of checking postal records and had her first success in the afternoon.

"Look, Elder Taylor…"

He said, "Lisa, you can use my Christian name when we are alone; it is not a sin, you know. I don't even think it breaks the mission rules."

"All right, Neal, where was I…Oh, yes, I found something that may be useful about our young husband, Boris. The Balagansk postal service kept mail drop-offs separated by sections of town and by institutions. There were dozens and dozens of posts to the prison over the years. So many that I just narrowed my search down to the years from 1879 when we know for sure that Boris was receiving documents of his work at the prison to 1895, which was the last record we have found of him in Balagansk, or in Vladivostok, or the Irkutsk oblast for that matter. He seems to have disappeared about then.

"So, I went into the Balagansk Prison Archives which were surprisingly complete. I looked through them real carefully to find anything mentioning Boris, no matter how trivial. Twice in 1880 and again twice in 1881 it was recorded that…and I quote 'Maj. Gen. Yusupov, Commandant of Balagansk Penitentiary personally applied the punishments ordered by the general staff.' Usually, the documents did not specify what the punishment was; but in one of the 1881 documents the prisoners for whom the punishment was ordered was a group of one hundred new arrivals. They came to Balagansk in July of that year, and each one of them was to have twenty-five lashes by the knout. The orders separated common criminals—the minority—from the political prisoners—anyone who had offended the tzar or the royal family in any way. None of them were to have a simple leather strap or cane applied. The common criminals were to have their backs lashed by a cat-o'nine-tails. I looked that up. It was a whip made with nine knotted cords or thongs of rawhide attached to a handle.

"The Russian knout—reserved for the political prisoners–consisted of several dried and hardened thongs made of rawhide interwoven with wire—the wires at Balagansk were specified as being hooked and sharpened so that they tore the victims' flesh—was even more painful and deadly. A particularly painful, though not so deadly, type of flogging was the bastinado which was reserved for women, children, and the elderly which involved blows delivered to the soles of the feet with a light rod, knotted cord, or lash. With the exception of the bastinado, flogging was formerly executed with great brutality. Failure to exert enough vigor would result in the man doing the whipping—in this instance, Gen. Yusupov—to receive half the same whipping. The backs of the condemned were frequently torn into strips, and salt was poured into the wounds to increase the pain. In each of the four instances, it was tersely described that 'the commandant carried out the sentences with efficiency'."

"Did you say that punishment was in July of 1881, Sister Taylor?" asked Elder Cheevers.

"Yes."

"I think I know why. I just googled it on my Blackberry. The tzar was assassinated in March of that year by some crazies, and the imperial army and the secret police—whatever they were called back then—went on a rampage. They sent all sorts of poor souls to places all over Siberia, many to the far north where they were expected to die of exposure. It makes sense that Boris Yusupov was ordered to make examples out of the ones sent to his prison."

"I'm sure you're right. Makes one glad to be and American," his wife said, "and the idea that we're living in the most evil of times just means that people who say that kind of thing don't know or don't remember history."

"I wonder what he felt about all of that," Sister Durrell said.

"Gives one the chills," Sister Clyde said.

"I did find a couple of other documents naming Gen. Yusupov." Sister Taylor said when she was able to regain the floor. "They were similar. The first one came from the general staff of the imperial army ordering the general to travel to Port Arthur to participate in putting down the rebellion there. The second just ordered him to go to Novonikolaevsk. It was unclear who gave that order or why."

"That one was in 1895, isn't that right?" Elder Cheevers asked.

"Any idea what was going on in the capital of Siberia at that time, Elder Cheevers?" asked Elder Durrell.

"No clue. I'll have to google it tonight after work."

"Speaking of work, maybe we ought to give a little thought to getting some done; so, this day doesn't seem to have been a complete waste by the Brethren or the Victoria Provincial Council," said Sister Durrell, as if either the church or the provincial entity would ever really know or care if they had a little diversion one day out of eighteen months.

CHAPTER FORTY-THREE

CHRISTMAS, 1881

I truly believe that if we keep telling the Christmas story, singing the Christmas songs, and living the Christmas spirit, we can bring joy and happiness and peace to this world.

—Norman Vincent Peale, *Gooseberry Patch, Christmas Classics Cookbook*

Tarasova House, No. 71 Pekinskaya Street, Vladivostok, Far Eastern Russia, December 24, 1881

Christmas festivities were moving along at a fever pitch. The decorations were nearly finished, and the kitchen staff had the food preparations well in hand. Irina wanted this year to be something very special because—for the first time in four years—the entire family was there to enjoy the best day of the year. Alexandra's brothers brothers, Veniamin and Valéry, had timed their return from commercial voyages to be able to have the rare pleasure of joining the whole family—which included the servants.

Alexandra had not seen Boris since they each left on their commercial voyages nor the two toddlers, Nikita and Oral, who were now over three-years-old. Since her return to Vladivostok, she had spent as much time as possible re-bonding with the children, who were now mischievous rascals who loved nothing more than to hide from her or to run away from her when it was most inconvenient. She became deeply attached once more and was as happy as she had ever been in her life.

Boris was due home from leave the day before European Christmas—by the Gregorian calendar. She was excited enough having the whole family back together that she asked Abram and Irina to allow them all to have two celebrations—European Christmas on December 25, and on January 7, by the old Julien calendar. Traditional old Russians loved having the Russian holidays on the old calendar; so, her parents acquiesced with alacrity—anything for a party this year. Because four-fifths of the country's population were Orthodox believers, and because Catholic, Protestant, and Orthodox, holidays were very close together on the calendar, New Year's and Christmas—the second most important Orthodox holiday after Easter—were celebrated by almost all of the populace.

Abram had a beautiful *Ded Moroz* [Grandfather Frost] costume made to surprise his family and the children of their close friends on the twenty-fourth when Irina had planned her usual overly exuberant party. To fetch Boris home from the docks in Vladivostok, he rode the troika in costume with the family's three handsome white horses abreast pulling the sled. A three-year-old daughter of the family cook rode with him, dressed as *Ded Moroz's* granddaughter, *Snegurochka*, holding an evergreen tree on the seat beside her. They had been sent word that the *Diana*—one of three Pallada class cruisers of the Imperial Russian Navy—would arrive two days late because she had to wait for an ice breaker to clear the way through Golden Horn Bay. She was accompanied by one of the other Pallada class cruisers, the *Aurora*. The little girl was beside herself with anticipation when the *Diana* finally made port on the twenty-fourth.

General mayor Prince Boris Nikolaiovich Yusupov emerged from the quarter deck and walked down the gangplank.

"That's him," whispered Abram to the little girl.

She screamed for joy with all of the enthusiasm a precocious three-year-old girl could muster, "*Dyadya* [Uncle] Boris!, Uncle Boris!, Uncle Boris!, over here. See *Ded Moroz.* I'm *Snegukrochka.* Look over here!"

He was trying to look the sober part of the conquering hero returning home from the wars; but the little girl's outcries were infectious; so, he laughed until he cried tears of joy as he marched up to her and the great symbol of Christmas and the New Year, *Ded Moroz.*

"What is your name, Sweetheart?" he asked.

The little girl suddenly became shy, looked at her feet, and stammered, "Oh, Uncle...I...I...I am...Ivanka...Ivanka Igorovich Skevar."

"You look lovely, Ivanka. Who is this old man with you? Is he Father Frost?"

He was afraid she was going to cry; so, he swept her up in his arms, kissed both cheeks and hugged her tightly. From that moment on, little Ivanka treated the tall important man as her uncle; and Boris was glad to have another child in the family.

Her courage returned, and she answered his question, "No, silly. He is the *Otets Sem'i* [Father of the Family—Patriarch]."

Boris rewarded her with a big smile and a little laugh, which she shared.

Abram—Father Frost—gave his son-in-law a great bear hug and a mug of hot tea.

"Welcome home, my boy. Welcome back. We worried about you. Once you settle in and spend some time with Alexandra and the boys, you must tell us all about it."

"I am very glad to be home and to be with family again. I will tell the whole family about the Russo-Chinese war when we are sitting by the big fire and sipping hot chocolate."

Ivanka snuggled between the two large men, and the troika sped across the smooth ice road to No. 71 Pekinskaya Street and home. It was not so out of the ordinary that the Tarasovas let down the barriers of class and caste to welcome Ivanka, her family, and the less elevated people in Vladivostok to their celebrations. Even the population of Saint Petersburg–the capital of the Russian Empire–consisted of social strata nested within themselves like Indian castes except for a very few times each year—mainly Christmas, New Years, and Easter–that the traditions of their lives—whatever their social strata: aristocracy, high society, factory workers, servants, students, paupers, even Germans, converged to make them united as joyous Russians.

The three travelers hopped out of the troika and raced each other to the front door. The two men somehow could not work up enough speed to catch Ivanka, and she won the race which pleased her immensely. She ran into her mother's arms and told her all about her day in staccato syllables embellished with repeated large dollops of creative whimsy.

When her cyclonic entry soliloquy finally faded away, Alexandra threw her arms around him and enveloped his body with her warmth. They unabashedly kissed, and Boris had to carry his portfolio in front of his waist for a few moments.

Blushing brightly, Alexandra changed the subject that was now on both of their minds.

She said, "Time to meet your boys, Boris. They're going to be a little shy to begin with, but they will warm up in a few minutes and won't leave you any peace."

Alexandra took Nikita's hand to present him to his often-absent father. Before she could take hold of Oral's small hand, the precocious Ivanka grabbed hold of it and marched along with Alexandra to be part of the formal ceremony.

She blurted, "Oral and Nikita, this is our *Dyadya* Boris! He is home from the war!"

Alexandra made the gentle correction clarifying the relationships, "This is your *Papa*, boys, and Ivanka's *Dyadya*."

The family all laughed as Boris hugged his three-year-old sons who spoke in their own twin language to assure each other that all was well. Even the gathered servants joined in the merriment occasioned by little Ivanka's temerity and the twins' unintelligible foreign world gibberish.

Veniamin and Valéry waited their turn and together encircled their brother-in-law with a robust Russian bear hug. Irina demurely stepped up to Boris to kiss his cheeks three times. He gave her such a strong familial smile that she opened her arms, and he hugged her and lifted her off her feet.

She blushed and gave him a theatrical "naughty boy" look, and announced that, "Dinner is served. Cook and I hope you are very hungry."

Veniamin, Valéry, Nikita, Oral, and Alexandra, possessively took Boris's hands and arms to escort him to the dining room. Ivanka could not find an arm or hand; so, she wrapped her arms around one of his long muscular legs, causing Cook no end of embarrassment. Boris hobbled in an exaggerated limp, and everyone good-naturedly accepted that it was all part of the joy of having Boris home again and of the Christmas and New Year's season.

The servants had been busy doing the necessary preparations for the Christmas meal: In Russia, on this Christmas Eve, the men of the family built a fire in their house yard and roasted a pig–or a sheep in some areas–on a long wooden spit. The whole roasted pig or sheep–called *pečenica*–was a traditional part of Christmas dinner. People who raised their own swine dedicated one for the *pečenica* a month or two before and feed it with better fodder. It is traditionally killed on *Tucindan*–the day before

Christmas Eve–by hitting on the head with a lump of salt. Its throat was then cut, the blood being collected and mixed with fodder. Feeding cattle with this mixture was believed to make them thrive. Slaughtering and butchering the animals required every male to participate while the women did the cutting and preparing of the lard bacon, sausages; and Cook and her loyal staff prepared the other traditional specialties. Cook, Irina, and Alexandra, chose just the perfect meats for their delicious cabbage rolls, and steaks, and saved the grease for baking cookies.

Like the rest of the welcome home, the traditional Christmas Eve meal—the Holy Supper–at Tarasova House was a great success: Before the feast, the long table was covered with a white cloth to hide the grains of wheat which were placed under the white table cloth to signify a rich harvest, garlic to ward off evil spirits, and a bit of sugar as a wish for a sweet life. The table was set with an extra place for the spirits of family members that had passed on as an added plea to bring good crops. Straw was scattered around the table by the family's and the servants' children, as a reminder of Jesus' birth in the manger.

Atop the hand-embroidered white cloth, decorations included a caricature ostrich sitting on eggs–its body made from a coconut, its neck from a banana, its head from a small fresh winter apple with holes or berries for eyes, and its beak made from an almond. Like most Russians with any means at all for a festive meal, the Tarasovas had a partridge and a traditional greasy goose.

The Tarasovas had no objection to being eclectic and generally accepted local traditions as their own. The rural Russians in the oblast celebrated St. Basil's Day on the seventh of January (by the Julien calendar). Basil was the Bishop of Caesarea—and tradition held that he was the patron saint of pigs. Accordingly, on the traditional new year, the locals and the Tarasovas ate suckling pig. No one made a comment that they were amalgamating the two holidays for their own blowout feast.

In keeping with fond Russian Orthodox traditions, the Tarasova's "Holy Supper" consisted of twelve dishes, each one in honor of one of the twelve apostles of Jesu; but in reality, there were far more than the twelve traditional dishes. When Russians celebrate Christmas, Russian Orthodox Christmas customs take center stage while other borrowed traditions from Eastern Orthodoxy find their somewhat less prominent place. Principal dishes on the Christmas table in old Russia included a variety of pork–roasted whole pig, stuffed pig's head, roasted meat chunks, finely sliced pork cooked in pots with semi-traditional porridge, jellied pork *kholodets* [meat aspic dish]. Christmas dinner in the Far East also included many other meats: goose with apples, sour cream hare, venison, lamb, whole fish, and whole baked chicken. The large quantities of meats on the festive table was testament to the oversized features of the Russian oven—designed for preparation of large portions to accommodate the other Russian tradition: large families.

No Russian feast–especially those at Christmas and *Paschka* [Easter, and the word for Jesus himself]—could be successful without sweets, especially a dizzying assortment of pies: both closed and open style *pirogi* [meat hand pies]–*vatrushkas* [Sweet Russian farmer's cheese buns with berries], *coulibiacs* [a *pirog* filled with salmon or sturgeon, rice or buckwheat, and hard-boiled eggs], *kurnik* [or tzar *pirog*, a dome-shaped savory pie filled with chicken or turkey].

In addition to the assortment of pies, Cook made boats of *pilaf* in which rice was cooked in a seasoned broth. The Tarasova variety had a golden-brown color by first sautéing it lightly in oil before the addition of broth. Cook Skevar prepared cooked onions and other vegetables, a mix of spices, and in the various pies, some had pork or beef meat; some had fish, vegetables, pasta, or dried fruit. Cook Skevar made— with loving care—*saeki* [their favorite: hangover stew from Chosŏn. The dish was a spicy and steaming stew made from beef broth with cabbage, bean sprouts, radish chunks, and chunks of congealed ox blood eaten for the purpose of starting up the sluggish brains of hungover drinkers in the morning], *shangi* [a hot Szechuan paste and hot ginger paste from Mumbai, India], *kalachi* [assorted foods from Kalachi, India including Chicken Peshawari *Karhai* and Ghaffar-Chicken *Malai Boti*], cooked casseroles, and *blini* [a Russian pancake traditionally made from buckwheat flour and served with sour cream, quark, butter, caviar and an assortment of other garnishes].

Pie fillings were as many and as diverse as the cooks' imaginations could dream: including herbal, vegetable, fruit, mushrooms, meat, fish, cheese, and mixtures. Very sweet dishes served on the Tarasova Russian Christmas table included berries, fruit, candy, cakes, angel wing cookies [*Angel wings* are a round Polish traditional sweet crisp pastry made out of dough that has been shaped into wings], biscuits and honey, and *česnica* [a sweet bread with a traditional silver coin inside]. The person who found the coin in his or her bread received a special blessing for the new year to come. The Tarasova House rules and rituals decreed that the dough be prepared with the strong water. When ready, the silver coin and small objects made of cornel wood—carved to represent chickens, oxen, cows, swine, horses, bees and one or two butterflies—were inserted into the dough.

Beverages included drinking broths and sweet soups, *sbiten* [*honey* and *sbiten'* spices, red wine, and juices' flavor were boiled down separately and then these two parts were combined and re-boiled], *kissel* [a Russian fruit drink], hot chocolate, hard cider, local and foreign wines, and an assortment of beers. With the close proximity to Manchuria, the Far East Russians had developed a strong liking for green and black Chinese tea and the traditional *Kutia* made from cooked wheat, honey, poppy seeds, raisins and walnuts. *Kutia* was more a Christmas porridge than a broth or beverage, with the seeds included as a symbol of hope for the year ahead.

The table remained covered; and no one was allowed to peek, until Father Gregor arrived and gave his blessing, then a prayer and blessing. Abram, as head of the family, greeted each person present with the traditional Christmas greeting of "Christ is born!" to which they all responded, "Glorify Him!" The bread was then torn by hand by each guest at the table and shared with all present. Then Father Gregor lighted candles in honor of Jesus—as Light of the World—and then uncovered the magnificent feast table.

The guests paused for a moment to take in the grandeur of the table while Father Gregor lit a candle, blessed the family and house, and recited the Lord's Prayer. After that, the family members kissed each other on the cheek saying: "The peace of God among us, Christ is Born." Several religious toasts with the family's best wines were made, and the family and guests dove in without further ceremony or further thoughts of proper decorum.

Exhausted, lethargic from postprandial lassitude, and more than a little drunk, the family retired to their separate rooms for a well-earned sleep, or in the case of Boris and Alexandra, not until after another athletic match was consummated. The servants cleared the table and cleaned the room, then had their own feast from the more than ample leftovers. They all took large bags full of the marvelous food home to their own families—thereby providing all Tarasova House with a Christmas feast fit for kings.

The Christmas day meal itself centered on roast pig, with side dishes including sausage, roast potatoes, nut strudel. *baklava, kourabiethes, melomakarona,* and other traditional pastries which were baked on Christmas Eve [*khetum*] to be ready for the actual day. *Christopsomo* [bread baked on Christmas Day–literally "Christ's bread"] was a decorative traditional delicacy. A cross was formed on the top of the bread and at the end of each bar of the cross, a walnut was placed. In most Orthodox countries, pork is the traditional roast meat as well as lamb. Families around some parts of the Orthodox world gather for a lighter Christmas Eve dinner which generally consists of rice, fish, *nevik*–a vegetable dish of green chard and chick peas–and yogurt/wheat soup. Dessert in those countries usually includes dried fruits, and nuts, including rojik, which consists of whole shelled walnuts threaded on a string and encased in grape jelly, *bastukh*. This lighter menu is designed to ease the stomach off the week-long fast and prepare it for the rather more substantial Christmas Day dinner. Tarasova House, like the Yusupovs and the Romanovs, observed a much more elaborate and grand fare for both meals.

After the Christmas dinner, the children of the family and of the servants' families brought presents of fruits, nuts, and candles to older relatives. Grandfather Abram made the sign of the cross on the little ones' foreheads, in order for them to be healthy. The men of the family then served *božićni kolač*–a round loaf with a *Christogram* impressed with a wooden seal on its upper surface. The women prepared for each male member of the family a round loaf called *ratarica*, suitably sized for the male recipient–the biggest one for the head, and the smallest one for the youngest boy. Theoretically, the men baked a *pletenica*–a loaf shaped like a three-strand braid–for each female member. In reality, the cooks made the *pletenicas,* lest disappointment and rancor prevail.

Cook's sister, Magda, took Ivanka by the hand early in the morning Christmas Day to the stream to collect water in a bucket. Magda dropped an ear of maize and a bunch of basil brought from home into the water and took it back home to her family. That water collected on early Christmas morning is called the strong water and is believed to possess a special beneficial power. Each member of the family washed his or her face with it, drank a glass before breakfast; and the infants of the family were bathed in it. On her way back home, Magda, by tradition, picked several cornel twigs, with which children were lightly struck that morning to strengthen their health and to remind them to avoid sin.

Later in the afternoon, a group of boys [the *vertepaši*] from Saint Sophia's Cathedral dressed in variegated costumes and went from house to house in Vladivostok carrying a *vertep* [lit. a "cave"–a litter constructed as a wooden model of a house or a church with two dolls inside]. One doll represented the *Theotokos* [Mother of God]; and the other–laid in a model of a manger–represented the Christ Child. The *vertepaši* boys sang Christmas songs, and recited poems praising the birth of Christ. For reasons lost to antiquity, the *vertepaši* fenced with each other with wooden swords in front of houses.

The *vertepaši* greeted each member of the household with "Christ is born!", and the residents responded with "Truly, He is born!" Tradition required that during the Twelve Days of Christmas everyone greet and respond the same way to every person encountered.

A Tarasova tradition coming from the fact that so many family members missed many Christmases was that each of those members must tell an exciting tale about the adventures away from home. Abram and Irina asked Boris to go first.

He gathered everyone around him in a circle and began to weave his tale.

"Many of you have not heard of the war our country has been fighting in Manchuria. That is a part of China, not at all far from Vladivostok, to the south and west. The origins of the conflict go back to 1840 when the very weak state of Qing, China lost a major battle. Then several other European empires took slices of the China because the Qings were too weak to counter them. Our Russian troops walked into Outer Manchuria–including Sakhalin Island–under a treaty with the Qing which said that the victorious Russians could claim as much land as a man can walk around in a day. Finally, a formal border was drawn in the Treaty of Aigun in 1858 and in the Peking Convention in 1860. That is when Vladivostok became a Russian city for the first time.

"I received orders to travel to Lüshun in March, 1880 to lead the Russian expeditionary force against the Manchu Eight Banners, local Manchurian nationalists, and Han Chinese who wanted to drive the Russians from our rightful lands there. It was my secret responsibility to take back the lands of Greater Manchuria from China and to reestablish our control over the coasts, ports, and the tribute world we established by the 1860 treaty. I was assigned to Port Arthur, a fort used by the Chinese as a naval base to guard the entrance to Bao Hai, or the Gulf of Chihli. We found the Port Arthur fortifications and preparations to be ridiculously poor to begin with. The Chinese soldiers and naval personnel lacked any semblance of military bearing; their dress was unkempt and dirty; and they wandered about the place with little in the way of direction. They were not professional soldiers; and we easily defeated them. They retreated to Mukden in far north eastern Manchuria—closer to Vladivostok than to Port Arthur. It took us until early December to clear the way for the coming battle in Mukden.

"The insurgent Manchus, local foreigners from all over the world, and the Honghuzi warriors proved to be much more effective than the Han Chinese we had encountered in the region of south Liaodong Peninsula where the coastal facilities and Port Arthur were coming under proper Russian control. Winter was fierce and terrible—so much so, that all military activity on both sides was put on hold. My staff and I were holed up in a deep trench covered with barbed wire and surrounded by a mine field. We were freezing. It was lonely and drab. We were wet all of the time. Men were getting sick. Then one of the men remembered that it was Christmas. He began singing, *The Forest Raised a Christmas Tree.* Since only human voices are allowed to carry the music or to give voice to the lyrics, it was a great touch of home, because the man—a mere corporal—had such a fine voice. He was joined by our chaplain, Father Ignatius; and soon, all of us were singing songs like, *God Eternal, Christ Is Born Today*, and *Good Eve to You.* Even the air seemed warmer. I slept well that night with dreams of Alexandra, the boys, and home. It was the first good sleep I had known in four months.

"A rapid thaw turned the entire Mukden area into a spring thaw mud field. We made progress then. The Chinese bandits, the *Honghuzi* demons, and the scoundrels from everywhere finally surrendered. We rounded them up, tied them together, and drove them into the river to drown. That was a lesson to all who opposed us and the mighty Russian empire.

"Those of us who had been in the thickest of the battles were granted leave for a month, and that is how I came to be able to share Christmas with all of you this year."

The family and servants gazed at Boris with unfeigned admiration; he was their unadulterated hero. Alexandra could not look directly at him. She was aghast at the description of his treatment of the vanquished

Chinese enemies. She tried not to show it; but Boris, ever perceptive, took notice.

"Our story is not nearly so heroic or so grim," said Veniamin and Valéry. "We spent an interesting Christmas in the colonies—Alaska—in 1878. We imported Chinese silks and metal goods and exported back to Vladivostok thousands of gorgeous furs. The weather was very bad; so, we had to stay in a little town called Nanwalek where we spent Christmas Eve and Day. The native people—the Sugpiaq–celebrated by singing hymns of Orthodox Christmas at the Saint Sergius and Herman church in Nanwalek. There were only about 300 people of Alutiiq and Sugpiaq descent plus our sixty native Russians. We all sang in Slavonic—the same liturgical language used by the Orthodox Church in Russia and Eastern Europe. It's a remnant of the fur trade era and Russian colonial times which are vanishing since the tzar sold Alaska to the Americans.

"The Christmas Eve services were just like ours here in Vladivostok; but afterwards, we did something very different–called starring–which represents the journeys of the three wise men who came to see the baby Jesus. It is a kind of Slavic caroling where the people follow a star shaped wooden frame with the icon of the nativity. People follow the star from house to house and sing carols at each home. The singing starts in front of an icon on a shelf beside the family Christmas tree. The visitors receive special food treats at each house and tell each other, 'Happy day to you, Father Frost'."

"Nanwalek used to be known as English Bay. Father Abram and Mother Irina, you probably remember Nanwalek by its Russian trading post name—Alexandrovski–during the fur trade of a hundred years ago. Once the Americans took over the territory, the people changed the community name back to the original Native name of Nanwalek, meaning "place by a lagoon." Papa, to remind you, Nanwalek is situated along Cook Inlet at the southern tip of the Kenai Peninsula. The religious evening of starring started at the chief's house where the Subdeacon Ephim Moonin said a prayer. The chief told the story of the nativity. It was like home to us. We were glad to see that the old stories are preserved in Alaska just like they are here in Russia. And, it makes you want to help the needy, again, just like here in Vladivostok.

Valéry continued, "The first houses visited are the ones having newborn babies and elders. The old ones keep the Sugt'stun language alive. The elders try to teach the children their old native language by having them substitute Sugt'stun for Slavonic part of the time. Many of the Sugpiaq people worry that the children and grandchildren will lose their language, their culture, and their religions; they will get lost and become wandering lost souls."

"Sounds wonderful," said Irina. "Now, it's your turn Alexandra, my wayward daughter," and smiled affectionately.

"All right, everyone. I was gone four Christmases ago, before the twins came along. That was…let's see…1878, the same as when Veniamin and Valéry were in Alaska working with the Russian Fur Company. I was in northern Chosŏn, a city called Sinuiju, located on the northwest coast, right by Dandong across the Chinese border.

"We were driven there by a bad storm and because we needed resupplying. It was a couple of days before Christmas Eve; and we had three choices: we could stay on board the ship and celebrate traditional Orthodox Christmas; we could go into Sinuiju and have a Chosŏn Christmas; or we could cross the border and share a Chinese Christmas with the Christians there. We had a vote and chose to stay in Chosŏn.

"The mayor of the city was most gracious and invited us to the town center building to enjoy the festivities as his guests and more like family coming home for the holidays. We met there and then went to the home of the local Protestant minister, Horace Underwood, and his wife. We are used to having strong drink; so, we were surprised when they served us only punch, tea, coffee, and lemonade. Apparently, those early American missionaries in Chosŏn were supporters of what they call the temperance movement—the anti-alcohol social wave--which they said was beginning to sweep their country. Their house was decorated with evergreen sprigs, a small spruce tree with candles and bows on it, and areas with crucifixes, colored glass balls, and small wrapped presents. There were three fireplaces with crackling fires which were most welcome because it was very cold.

"After drinking the nonalcoholic drinks, everyone was given a small cake with a cross on it, then we were given small gifts of useful items, like combs, toothbrushes, hair ribbons, and small flutes. I was given a pair of silk slippers. All the gifts were presented by the host using both hands in the Chosŏn way. Children were given a few Chosŏn *sangpyungtongbo* and *mu* coins and some charms for the New Year.

"The mayor introduced entertainers who gave musical performances and recited poetry. Traditional drums. Then we all said, '*Sung Tang Chuk*

Ha' which means Merry Christmas in English. We did not learn the translation into Russian. Towards evening, we had a meal of *Bulgogi*—barbecued beef, sweet potato noodles, and their favorite kimchi. For dessert we had a Christmas rice cake decorated with fresh fruits, *baesuk*—steamed pears—walnuts wrapped in persimmons, and red bean paste. The meal was what they called a 'pot-luck' with all the Christian townspeople bringing one part of the meal. Many of the poorer people brought only some good Chosŏn sweets to share.

Then, there was a knock on the door, and in walked a Father Christmas or Grandfather Frost kind of character, called Santa Kullusu or Santa Haraboji by some. He was dressed in an evergreen suit and traditional robes. He wore a traditional old *gat*—a flat topped hat from the previous dynasty. Some nonChristian people came, and we saw an interesting mix of old Buddhist, Confucionist, and Shamanist traditions which blended perfectly well with the Christian practices. The outside customs included prayers for a good harvest, lots of different foods, and firecrackers. Everyone seemed to tolerate and even enjoy the diverse customs.

Because many people had to travel long distances to get to Sinuiju, the people combined *Seol*—lunar New Year's Day celebrations—with the Christmas ones and served *tteokguk*, a rice flake soup. Everyone had to take some to signify being one year older. The beautiful children performed the *Sebae* ceremony—New Year's Bow to their elders. These traditions were much older than Christianity, which was not seen in Chosŏn until the sixteen-hundreds. Our hosts told us that we would also be celebrating the seasonal festival, the *Daeboreum*—or greater full moon tradition. We all ate a special food called *ogokbap*—a dish made with five grains and served with a mix of cooked vegetables.

"Then we played children's games until we were so tired we could hardly stand up. The mayor provided carts, wagons, and rickshaws, to get us back to the ship. We toasted each other with *Makgeolli*, the mayor gave us. It was strange looking—kind of grey, and lightly sparkling rice wine. It was a little bit thick with a strange mixed set of flavors–slightly sweet, tangy, bitter, and acidic all at once. I'll say this: after all that sweet punch at the Underwoods' house, the *Makgeolli* was welcome; and I slept like the dead the rest of the night."

When the story telling time was over at Tarasova House, everyone bade everyone else a good night, a Merry Christmas, and a Happy New

Year. Alexandra and Boris were more enlivened and excited than tired from the full day, and they once again pledged their undying love to each other and to the family. They retired to bed but did not sleep until nearly dawn. More athletics.

CHAPTER FORTY-FOUR
THE GROWING SCHISM

"It sounds plausible enough tonight but wait until tomorrow.
Wait for the common sense of the morning."
—Count Leo Tolstoy, *Anna Karenina*

"When we two parted / In silence and tears, / Half broken-
hearted / To sever for years, / Pale grew thy cheek and cold, /
Colder thy kiss; / Truly that hour foretold / Sorrow to this."
—George Lord Byron, *When We Two Parted*

Balagansk Prison Infirmary, Balagansk, Irkutsk Oblast, Far Eastern Russia, February 28, 1882

Alexandra missed talking to and sleeping with her dashing husband now that he was required to be at his official work place in Balagansk. She knew that he had received a preemptory set of orders to return forthwith to the prison to attend to the reception of newly arriving convicts. He was equally as reluctant to go as she was to have him go; but–unknown to her–his reasons were not quite the same as hers. He was glum and grouchy when she asked him if he could stay with her for a few more days, and that was quite unlike him. He would not elaborate when she pressed him for more information.

She decided to surprise him by taking the two boys in the Tarasova troika over the frozen road to Balagansk to see him at work and to arrange for the family to stay for a few days at the only building in Balagansk that could remotely pass for a hotel—the newly constructed log rectangle ostentatiously called, The Balagansk Inn. Boris had not written or sent messages for the last ten days; so, Alexandra found it no problem to keep the secret of her surprise visit from her husband.

Alexandra settled her baggage into the storage room of the inn, saw to it that the three horses were given grain and put out to a good pasture, ordered the troika sled to be placed in the carriage house, then gathered up her boys, Oral and Nikita, and slipped and slid over the icy roads to the penitentiary compound.

At the gate, she told the guard, "I am Alexandra Tarasova-Yusupov. My boys and I have come to see the commandant, General Mayor Prince Boris, please."

Without hesitation, the young private gave a crisp salute, swung open the gates, and said, "Yes, Madame, he is attending to duties at the rear of the main building. It would be better for you to check-in at the reception desk before seeking him out."

Alexandra had no intention of having anything or anyone spoil her surprise; so, she replied with her signature fluorescent smile, "Of course, Sir. Just as you require."

He never got past her smile and believed her completely. He returned to his soul numbing job of guarding the gate where nothing had happened in all his twelve months of assignment to Balagansk Prison. His main worry was frost bite–and well he should–because a few of his comrades lost toes to the cold over the winter.

Without looking back, she hurried her boys along the south wall of the main building, where she hoped the warmer route to the rear would be found. The boys complained, and her feet were losing feeling to the cold. She wished fervently that she had worn her good foul weather gear and had obeyed the orders she gave Oral and Nikita to wear earmuffs, heavy woolen gloves, and extra socks, in their thick-soled boots.

The two boys were cold and hanging back, too tired to move as quickly as their mother. She rounded the southeast corner of the main prison building and saw a sight unfolding that stopped her in her tracks. She ordered her two small boys to halt and to stay put.

On the frozen gravel pad in front of the prison's parade ground bleacher seating stand, she saw a dozen upright poles planted in the ground in three precisely even rows of four. Hanging from a point near the top of each pole was a heavy chain about four inches long which was attached to a sturdy iron ring. To the rings, heavy leather straps secured men's wrists at a height where they had to stand tip-toed to support themselves. They were stripped to the waist despite the freezing weather. The backs of three men were decorated with eighteen criss-crossed bleeding stripes. Standing behind the fourth man on the row, holding a rawhide whip was her husband, Boris. Alexandra thought she was going to faint. A brutish Cossack stood beside Boris holding a bucket of water. He counted as Boris wielded the whip—eighteen times for each man.

Some of the men cried out in pain, especially when the Cossack splashed what had to be salt water which stung and kept the wound edges from closing-up to relieve some of the acute pain. Oral and Nikita's faces were ashen as they began to realize what was going on in the area they could not see. Alexandra pushed the boys back and prepared to retreat, but her attention was riveted on her husband. How could he be doing this? Why was he doing this barbaric thing? She studied Boris's face intently as he lashed the backs of the men with machine like efficiency. His gaze never wandered from the back of the man he was whipping. His jaws were clenched, whether in concentration, or in revulsion, or as a consequence of his exertions. He switched whipping hands from right to left fairly frequently, obviously related to fatigue, or weakening, or from lack of enthusiasm for his enterprise.

The man he was lashing at the present moment sagged and hung by the wrists, obviously unconscious. He was old, thin, and sickly in appearance. The Cossack kicked his thigh hard enough to arouse the old fellow, then the Cossack jerked him to his feet. Boris resumed lashing. Inadvertently, Alexandra cried out. Boris turned at the sound, and their eyes locked for a brief, poignant, haunting, moment. Alexandra turned her back on Boris and scooped up her twins. She ran to the front of the prison building where she placed them on the ground and took their hands and ran as fast to the gate as the little boys could go.

Without a word, the private watching the gate saluted, opened the gates, and watched dispassionately as the three gentlepersons moved away over the frozen and snow-covered ground towards the area of the Balagansk Post Office and the Inn. Moving like a Fury, Alexandra ordered that the troika be brought to the front of the Inn and the horses hitched to the sleigh. She ordered two chambermaids to pack hers and her boys' things into their bags without any folding or other time-consuming niceties. She over-paid the inn keeper and over-tipped the help. Without looking back, she and her sons trotted as fast as it was safe for the horses to go away from Balagansk and the images pounding in her mind and that would be a source of nightmares for the rest of her life.

Once he saw his wife looking on as he whipped those whom he believed to be innocent men and saw the look of horror and dismay in her eyes and on her face, Boris continued his labor at a much quicker pace. Occasionally, the Cossack had to remind him that he had shorted a prisoner by one stripe, or occasionally even two. His eyes were red, his teeth were bared in anger befitting a wild beast; and his brain pressed his entire body into getting the task done as expeditiously as possible. It took another hour, even at his accelerated rate, to finish the odious task.

His wife's look had condemned him. He was a demon, an ogre. He was beyond redemption or forgiveness in his own home or certainly in the hereafter. When he was done, he abruptly marched away and found his bed. There he piled on blankets, pulled them over his head, and began to cry—the agonized weeping of man who knew he was damned. His anguish equaled anything the burning flames of hell or the torment of whips or scorpion stings, or infestation by burrowing worms could produce. The pain was in his soul. He was still whimpering in exhaustion when he finally fell asleep.

Balagansk Prison Infirmary, Balagansk, Irkutsk Oblast, Far Eastern Russia, March 7, 1882

Boris completed everything he could find that needed to be done at the prison over the course of five days. On the sixth–which happened to be the Sabbath–he took a deep breath and went to the infirmary where he knew that the majority of the recent internees who had been flogged would be recuperating.

He asked for Duke Michael Vaughnovich Uskin and was told by a thoroughly uninterested orderly that the old man had died the day he was brought into the infirmary. Boris had to turn away; so, the hardened old soldier would not see the tears that sprang hot and salty into his eyes.

"Misha, Misha, you cannot be dead," he moaned to himself. *"My old friend and comrade-in-arms, Misha, what have I done?"*

Learning of his old friend Misha's having died at his—Boris Yusopov's—hands was unbearable and cast a deep pall over the rest of his grim visit to the infirmary. It took two hours to make his apology to each and every man he had whipped.

The gist of what he said—with deep feeling and gravitas—was, "My friend, my fellow Russian, I am terribly sorry for what I did to you, for the whipping. I know that you are innocent of *any* crime, much less the one for which you were sent to prison here and to be beaten. I understand your anger and your anguish as good Russians. I, too, am a good Russian who was sent here for no crime. My only reason for being here and for having to hurt you, was because I knew three of the conspirators who attempted but failed to assassinate the tzar. As I read your charges, I understand that you are here for having had the misfortune to be an associate in one way or another of the criminals who actually did kill our tzar.

"I will do all I can to lighten your burdens during your stay in Balagansk. Soon…fairly soon…you will be released from your incarceration and pardoned of your so-called crimes and will be able to live in Far Eastern Russia unmolested. You know that you will never be allowed to return to the Rodina, because you know why the Okhrana behaved so abominably. The Department for Protecting the Public Security and Order—"the guard department"–had you sent here, and you know that it was a monumental injustice. I repeat, my brothers, that I am heartily and forever sorry."

Tarasova House, No. 71 Pekinskaya Street, Vladivostok, Far Eastern Russia, March 4, 1882

Freezing March winds howled down out of the canyons and off the ice bound lake surfaces as Boris drove his three horses to their limits to get home before dinner was served at Tarasova House on this the coldest day on record. The family was seated at the great table but had not yet been served when Boris burst through the two fourteen feet tall entryway doors. He was disappointed when he saw that there was no empty seat by Alexandra. He was distraught when he saw her look away from him intentionally. He took the seat kept empty in memory of the ancestors, thereby eliciting looks of frank disapproval from everyone in the family. He had done the equivalent of dropping his cigar into the punch bowl as the tzar was about to be served. He knew all of that, and he did not care. All he thought about was his wife—his icicle of a wife, at the moment—

sitting in her chair with her father on her right, and Abram's elderly aunt on her left. He had to talk to her this evening, or all was lost.

The meal was excellent, as usual. The conversation was stilted and empty, the stuff of empty cocktail party prattle. Although the fireplaces kept the room snugly warm, there was a chill in the room. Though this was a gathering of family, it felt to everyone there that it was a meeting after a funeral of a hated great-grandfather that was about to descend into internecine strife with an unyielding squabble over expected inheritances.

Finally, Boris could not tolerate the pretenses of civility, and he would not permit a continuation of him being frozen out from his wife and family. He spoke first.

"Abram and Irina, it is time for Alexandra and I to have a serious talk. I ask that you do us the courtesy of allowing that conversation to be held in private and now. I know you have heard things about me and my work. However, you do not know the whole thing. After tonight, I hope that will all be cleared up."

He turned towards Alexandra.

She had an expressionless face, as devoid of caring and emotion as if it had been carved from alabaster.

"I have no desire to talk to you, Boris. Now or ever. It is time for you to go, find a new place to live, find new relationships among your aristocratic friends."

"We must have a real understanding, Alexandra. Silence is the same as ignorance, and almost equal to lies. Do me this one–perhaps one last– courtesy of hearing me out; and I will listen to what you have to say without interrupting you."

"If I agree, will you agree never to trouble me again?"

"If–after I have had my say–you do not want to have anything to do with me, I will absent myself entirely and without rancor."

"All right. We can go into the withdrawing room and have this talk. I want my father and mother to be right outside of the door so that they can come if I call."

"Are you actually afraid that I might or that I *could* do you physical harm, my dear little wife? That is the most unkindest cut of all."

"Oh, cease the drama, Boris. I am no Julius Caesar."

"And I am no Brutus, Alexandra. And this is no Shakespearian drama, nor is our conversation on the level of a mass stabbing. It is a misunderstanding between husband and wife."

"Then, let us repair to the withdrawing room and get it over with," she said gritting her teeth and rising from her chair in such a way as to put the greatest possible distance between her and Boris.

Five minutes later, they sat facing each other on chairs situated ten feet away at Alexandra's insistence. The gulf was such that they might as well have been separated by an ocean.

"I request the opportunity to go first, and to have the courtesy of you hearing me out until I have finished. After that, you may say whatever you wish; and I will respect your privilege," Boris politely requested all the while fighting back his sorrow and his anger.

"Go then."

Her face was a marble statue of pure hate and implacable disgust.

"What you saw is not as simple as you think, Alexandra..." he began.

She rolled her eyes.

"Please hear me out," he repeated.

She nodded her head.

"I was a general mayor, a decorated hero, an aristocrat in the best of standing with the tzar and his family. His brother is—or probably, was—my godfather. I had the attention of the general staff of the imperial Russian army with every likelihood that I would be promoted shortly to general lieutenant and find my place on the general staff. The future was bright; I was a prince, scion of the wealthiest and most influential family in all the Russias."

Alexandra had not heard this before, and her face registered her growing curiosity.

"Then a series of unfortunate incidents occurred to ruin all of that, not of my doing except the very first one, which I could never have imagined would bring me down...it was so innocent.

"I will be brief, because the story has so little to it. My only fault was to make a boyish error. While I was in the general staff academy, I chose to share an apartment with some people I should not have. They were Alexander Soloviev, Andrei Zhelyabov, and Alexander's girl-friend, Sophia Perovskaya, all of whom were flirting with the philosophies of Mikhail Bakunin and his Land and Liberty reformers party. I was peripherally interested...curious, really...but I did not subscribe to any of their theories, and most certainly not to any of their subsequent actions.

"I presume you have heard of these people, Alexandra?"

"Who hasn't?" she snapped, but without the rancor that she displayed earlier in the conversation.

"Yes, well, I could never have imagined the trouble they would bring to me, to the tzar, and to the empire. Let me give a little summary: In October, 1879, the Land and Liberty group split into two factions with a majority of members–who favored a policy of active terrorism—going on to establish a violent organization, the infamous *Narodnaya Volya* [People's Will]. Those maniacs decided to assassinate Alexander. The next month, my presumed great friends, Andrei Zhelyabov and Sophia Perovskaya hatched a plot to use nitroglycerine to destroy the Tzar Train. However, the volunteer terrorist made a fool's mistake and destroyed another train instead. The People's Will's next plot was an attempt to blow up the Kamenny Bridge in St. Petersburg as the tzar was passing over it. They were bumblers from the beginning; so, that attempt was also a failure.

"Because Alexander II and the Russian government dragged its feet about writing a new constitution, the People's Will made plans for still another assassination attempt on the tzar's life. It will be of no surprise to you that the plotters were: Sophia Perovskaya, Andrei Zhelyabov, Gesia Gelfman, Nikolai Sablin, Ignatei Grinevitski, Nikolai Kibalchich, Nikolai Rysakov and Timofei Mikhailov. My only association was with Sophia and Andrei of that deadly group and that very minimal and temporary.

"At any rate, on February 17, 1880, one of their associates— Khalturin—built a crude bomb in the basement of the building under the dining-room where Alexander was scheduled to eat. The bomb was scheduled to explode at exactly six-thirty in the evening. This time, their planning and execution were almost perfect. The bomb exploded precisely when they wanted it to. The People's Will were certain the tzar would be in the middle of his meal with the bomb went off. Unfortunately for them, but fortunately for Alexander; his main guest, Prince Alexander of Battenburg, arrived late; and dinner was delayed. When the bomb exploded, the dining-room itself was empty; and Alexander was unharmed. However, he was enraged because sixty-seven people were killed or badly wounded by the explosion.

"In his fury, Alexander gave the Okhrana carte blanche to find and to destroy all of the plotters and their associates. Perhaps, Alexandra, you can see where this is leading. By early February, 1881, the Okhrana discovered that the People's Will had developed another plot led by

Andrei Zhelyabov to kill Alexander. The secret police foiled the plot, and Zhelyabov was arrested but refused to provide any information on the conspiracy. He brashly told the police that nothing they could do would save the life of the tzar.

"On March first, 1881, the tzar traveled by carriage from Michaelovsky Palace to the Winter Palace in St. Petersburg. An armed Cossack sat with the coach-driver and another six Cossacks followed on horseback. Behind them came a group of police officers in sledges. It was deemed a fairly serious set of security precautions. However, all along the route he was surveilled by members of the People's Will. Near the Catherine Canal, Sophia Perovskaya gave the signal to Nikolai Rysakov and Timofei Mikhailov to throw their bombs at the tzar's carriage. The bombs missed the carriage and instead landed amongst the Cossacks. The tzar was unhurt but unwisely insisted on getting out of the carriage to check the condition of the injured men. While he was standing with the wounded Cossacks, another terrorist–Ignatei Grinevitski–threw the bomb he had been saving for just that opportune moment. Tzar Alexander II was killed instantly and the explosion was so great that saboteur Grinevitski also died from the bomb blast.

"This is what became of the surviving conspirators: Nikolai Sablin committed suicide before he could be arrested, Gesia Gelfman died in prison, and my so-called friends, Sophia Perovskaya, Andrei Zhelyabov, Nikolai Kibalchich, Nikolai Rysakov, and Timofei Mikhailov, were hanged on the third of April, 1881. You might ask, what has this to do with you, and more, what has it to do with what you saw at Balagansk Prison a week ago, Alexandra? On the surface, you might ignore the cause and effect involved. But my associates and I did not have the luxury of escaping attention of the Okhrana.

"The government issued an edict condemning everyone who had had any association with the monsters in the People's Will Party or with any of the plotters individually. The commandant of the General Staff Academy realized that if the Okhrana caught up with me, my life would be forfeit, no matter all my service, high born birth, family influence, or great wealth. He told me as a friend and ordered me as a superior to leave at once for the Far East. He saw to it that I be placed in a position befitting my rank. Just before I left, his final words to me were, 'This is not over. The Okhrana will hunt you and make every effort to find some flaw or mistake on your part. I will see to it that you are given orders from time to time that will be found favorable to you by the general staff, and the government. Have no communication with your family, or they will fall under your same condemnation.'"

He paused and took a drink of bottled sparkling Evian water–the French curative elixir won in conflict from Switzerland–to soothe his scratchy dry throat, then continued, "So, each time a group of political prisoners was delivered to Balagansk, I was required to demonstrate that they were being treated as criminals. This last group of one hundred came with specific orders: I was to whip each person—young or old, male or female, healthy or sick—with eighteen strips with a single strap rawhide whip. I was given the right to use a cat-o-nine-tails if I thought the prisoner deserved harsher punishment. I did as little as I could and still escape a negative report being sent back to Moscow by a spy, and I never resorted to the cat. My orders included a personal threat. If I was weak in carrying out the punishment, I would take the prisoner's place hanging from the stake. With the possibility of facing twenty-four separate beatings, I knew I would never survive. That brings me to what you saw."

There was a long pause after Boris said his piece.

Then, Alexandra quietly asked, "Is that all you have to say, Boris?"

"Not quite, Alexandra. I want you to understand and to accept me back as your husband in every sense of the word."

"I presume it is my turn now, Boris. Try as I might, I cannot forgive what you have done or what you stand for—the cruel tsarist government and all its wicked servants. I was going to demand a divorce before I heard what you had to say, but your information has given me a chance to rethink my position. The church forbids divorce, and I and my children would suffer if I made the effort. I will continue our marriage in name only. You must find new quarters, new friends, and a new life. Because our business matters are contracts set in stone, I cannot force you out of the family business or from the business with Jardine-Matheson Company. But, you and I will not work together, sleep together, eat together, or make new business contracts together, for as long as we both live."

Her face was livid, and her brow was sweating from her passion. Boris recognized the finality of her statement, and his attitude changed to the opposite of his previous placating requests. His face turned to stone—the face of the implacable warrior about to lay waste to Ottoman Turks. She would live to rue this day.

He took a breath and said simply and calmly, "Alexandra Abramovna Tarasova-Yusupova, you will regret this decision of yours for the rest of your days. Never forget that I am a Yusupov and that I have enormous resources at my command. Pray as much as you want, I will reappear in your life."

CHAPTER FORTY-FIVE

THE FINAL BREAK AND
NEW LIVES

In three words I can sum up everything I've learned about life:
It goes on.

—Robert Frost

The hardest thing to learn in life is which bridge to cross and
which bridge to burn.

—David Russell

Tarasova House, No. 71 Pekinskaya Street, Vladivostok, Far Eastern Russia, October 28, 1882, Midnight

The straw that broke the camel's back for Boris came in the form of orders from General Staff Headquarters on October the 27th. He was ordered to board the Imperial Navy Ship *The Potemkin* for transportation back to Port Arthur two days hence to assume the position of post commander and director of military operations in Manchuria. This was to be for the duration of hostilities, and he was directed to bring his entire family with him to occupy permanent quarters on the naval base. He had only two days to determine what the rest of his life was going to look and feel like. He had long since ceased even to have thoughts about reuniting with his stubborn and unforgiving wife. His previous passionate love for her had turned to ashes and evolved into an equally passionate hatred. Boris had promised to cause Alexandra to rue

311

the day she threw him away. No one did that to a Yusupov. Now, his goal was to inflict a hurt that would not heal.

It was approaching midnight when Boris and two of his sergeants major approached Tarasova House. The first—and most important obstacle—to getting into the mansion was to get control of Abram's borzois [lit. fast]. He had a generally affectionate relationship with the Russian wolf hounds—very much like greyhounds–which were ferociously protective of the house and its occupants whom they knew by smell. He had prepared in advance. The three men cleared the back fence and cautiously approached the rear entrance to Tarasova House. There were no human guards; neither Abram nor Irina considered that necessary in those times of peace and plenty.

Twenty yards before the men reached the rear entrance, Boris heard the borzois tearing towards them, and knew that the thin, powerful, and fleet of foot animals would be upon them in a matter of seconds. The two sleek creatures reached the three men hell bent on tearing them to pieces. Boris held out thick steaks–dripping with fresh blood–one for each dog. Before taking the steak, both dogs rushed up to Boris and took his hand gently in their mouths, thus conveying smell and taste of one of the people who belonged in the house. They devoured the steaks, ripping and tearing the meat apart and swallowing large chunks whole. Boris had laced the beef steaks with small pellets of opium and soaked them in tincture of chloral hydrate. In a few minutes, both dogs were drowsy and stumbled about aimlessly. Shortly, they lay down on the hard ground fast asleep, a condition Boris had been assured with persist for hours. He only required minutes. There was a soft snoring coming from the dogs and a steady susurrous whispering of the white birches in the gentle breeze. Otherwise there was silence.

The three men surreptitiously made their way through the unlocked servants' entrance and into the dimly lit lower floor hallway. Like their opinion that armed guards were unnecessary, the lord and lady of the house—like all of their neighbors—were conspicuously lackadaisical about other simple security measures like locking doors. The intruders removed their boots and padded on the shining parquet and stone floors in their heavy stocking feet. Boris knew the way to his sons Nikita and Orals' bedroom so well that he could have made it there in pitch dark. He had his sergeants major move slowly and as silently as humanly possible past the governess's bed chamber next door to the twins' nursery.

The soldiers were relieved to hear nothing but the soft puffing breaths of little boys who were fast asleep. Boris and one of the sergeants major picked up the boys gently and cuddled them in their strong arms. The three men and their precious cargo slipped back out the way they had come in and exited the rear door without making a sound or disturbing the sleeping household. The dogs remained where they had dropped from the sleeping potions they had eaten–alive, but dead to the world in slumber.

Neither child awakened as the three kidnappers lifted them over the back fence of Tarasova House and into Boris's droshky. He held them on his lap while one of his men drove to the wharf. The other took the gig in which they had ridden from Balagansk back to the prison. Sergeant Major Ustrefski helped Boris and the two children onto *The Potemkin* along with the copious—perhaps excessive–personal possessions the general mayor had brought along for his prolonged stay in Lyushunkou District/Port Arthur and Dalian City on the tip of Liaodong Peninsula of Manchuria–for all intents and purposes–a planetary distance away from Alexandra and the Tarasovas in Vladivostok. His important assignment was a state secret and would not be divulged by anyone who knew about it, and that was a precious few anywhere and no one in Vladivostok or the Irkutsk oblast. There were no written records in the oblast.

CHAPTER FORTY-SIX

PARTING OF THE WAYS

"The next best thing to being wise oneself is to live in a circle of those who are."

—C.S. Lewis

There is a destiny that makes us brothers. None goes his way alone. All that is sent into the lives of others comes back into our own.

—Edwin Markham

National Archives of Australia, Victorian Archives Centre, 99 Shiel Street, North Melbourne, Victoria, Australia, August 25, 2014

Over the past three months, three missionary couples had bade farewell to their brothers and sisters in the gospel leaving only Elder LaRen and Sister Katherine Durrell remaining from the original five couples who had worked with personal fervor on the mysterious Alexandra Tarasova-Yusupov project. The new couples arrived in the mission district in Melbourne one couple at a time over four months making the Durrells the most senior couple of the senior couples. It was up to the Durrells to get the Wrights, the Nicholsons, the Smedleys, and the Gablers, to buy into the project without having them argue that it was breaking mission rules to spend the Lord's time on frivolous personal enterprises.

The newbies were lukewarm at best towards the zealous search for information on the one person—Alexandra—at the possible expense of the hundreds of thousands of others for whom they were tasked to provide digital copies of their vital statistics and documentary records. The breakthrough came when Elder Peter Wright and his wife, Nedra, found a surprising record related to Boris Yusupov's military career. The finding dredged up as many questions as it did answers and provided nothing about Alexandra by itself.

Elder Wright presented his finding at lunch during a very cold wintery day in August.

"I found something that might pertain to our subjects of research," he said. "It is about a general named Yusupov and two other soldiers who were engaged in fighting in Novonikolaevsk—what was the name they called Novosibirsk in those days–during the Bolshevik revolution. Incidentally, I learned that "Bolshevik" means majority while "Menshevik" means minority in Russian parlance. Anyhoo, I digress. I got almost everything I learned from a famous old Russian history *The History of the Imperial Army*, by General Field Marshall, Ivor Strabiskinov. Let me begin by telling you a bit about the fighting in Siberia during that dreadful time. First of all, I am an avid amateur student of military history, and I can tell you that this was one of the most confusing and bloody revolutionary wars in all of history. It would take me three months to explain or to try to explain what went on. All I will do, today is to set the stage for the few mentions I found of our Boris Yusupov—or just Yusupov.

"You recall that the Bolshevik Revolution led by Lenin, Trotsky, and Stalin was in full swing late in 1917. There were many differing factions in the fighting on both sides. Yusupov was on the side of the White Army which consisted of sometimes allied but a loose confederation of forces united only by their anti-communist sympathies. These forces included such disparate interests as landowners, republicans, conservatives, *bourgeoise* [middle-class citizens], reactionaries, pro-monarchists, liberals, army generals, non-Bolshevik socialists who still had grievances and democratic reformists voluntarily united only in their opposition to Bolshevik rule and even some Western Allies, especially the British.

They espoused monarchism, capitalism, and several different forms of socialism, with variable amounts of democratic and antidemocratic policies. Early on, the White Army did fairly well despite lacking strong support of the peasant populace, aggravated by forcible conscriptions, terror, and harsh autocratic policies.

"The White's military forces led by General Yudenich, Admiral Kolchak, and General Denikin, controlled significant parts of the former Russian Empire for most of the war. From January to November 1919, the White armies' advances from the south (under Gen. Denikin), the east (under Adm. Kolchak) and the northwest (under Gen. Yudenich) were successful, forcing the Red Army and its allies back on all three fronts. Gen. Lieutenant Yusupov was first mentioned as a leader of a Novonikolaevsk brigade known for its ferocity in driving back fanatical Reds. By June of 1920, however, the Red Army was able to halt Kolchak's advance assisted by a Black Army offensive against White supply lines."

"Black Army?" asked Elder Jack Perry Nicholson. "Never heard of them."

"That's too far afield for this discussion. Let me get together with you later this week, or you can Google it."

Elder Wright continued, "Gen. Yusupov was mentioned in the history as having lost several battles and having had to retreat. The interesting thing there is that the official reports list two more Yusupovs as having acquitted themselves well—first names Nikita and Oral, former students of the Novonikolaevsk Military Academy School for Boys. By the end of July, the Whites had extended their gains westwards. Shortly before the fall of Yekaterinburg on 17 July 1918, the former tzar and his family were murdered by the Ural Soviet to prevent them falling into the hands of the Whites.

"That was so dreadful," Sister Francis Nicolson exclaimed.

"Like everything else in that awful conflict," Elder Wright said.

He continued, "In Omsk the Russian Provisional Government quickly came under the influence–then the dominance–of its new War Minister, Rear-Admiral Kolchak. On November 18, a coup d'état established Kolchak as dictator. The members of the Directory were arrested, and Kolchak was proclaimed the Supreme Ruler of Russia. General Lieutenant Prince Boris Nikolaivich Yusupov was mentioned once as being second-in-command.

"During the summer, Bolshevik power in Siberia was eliminated; and it appeared that the Whites were going to gain full power and to reestablish the power of the tzars with Gen. Yusupov occupying an important position in the new government. The British occupied Murmansk and–alongside the Americans–seized Arkhangelsk; but things did not go well for Kolchak—and I presume for Yusupov–in Siberia. To make a long story short, Kolchak was defeated and retreated in Siberia; the Allies pulled their troops out of the cities before the winter trapped them in the port. The remaining White forces under Yevgenii Miller evacuated the region in February 1920, and the remains of the White forces commanded by Wrangel were beaten in Crimea and evacuated, thereby heralding the end of the White Army.

"After an abortive offensive at Chelyabinsk, the White armies withdrew beyond the Tobol River. A White offensive was launched against the Tobol front; however, in October the Reds counterattacked, and thus began the uninterrupted retreat of the Whites to the east. I am now getting to the last mention of the Yusupovs in the military history of Russia.

In Siberia, Adm. Kolchak's army disintegrated. He gave up command after the loss of Omsk and designated Gen. Grigory Semyonov as the new leader of the White Army in Siberia. Not long after that Kolchak was arrested as he traveled towards Irkutsk without the protection of the army and turned over to the socialist Political Center in Irkutsk. Six days later this regime was replaced by a Bolshevik-dominated Military-Revolutionary Committee.

On February six and seven, Adm Kolchak and his prime minister, Victor Pepelyaev, were shot; and holes were chopped in the deep ice of the frozen Angara River. The two men, and possibly several others, were dropped into the frigid, rapid flowing stream just before the arrival of the White Army in the area. Yusupov was mentioned as having been arrested along with his admiral; and, after that, there is no further official record of him having survived."

"Well, thanks for that bit of grim news, Elder Wright," said Sister Margaret Smedley ruefully.

He laughed, "Don't mention it, Sister Smedley."

It was Monday–P-day–and all the missionaries were ready for another trip down town, as the Gablers called it. They were ticking off the list of sites to visit in their tour books, and this brought them to their starting point, the incredible Melbourne Aquarium with its transparent tunnels where it seemed as if they would be able to pet one of the great animals from the deep. It was a gorgeous day, and they basked in the moderate sun on the Melbourne Observation Deck on the fifty-fifth floor of Melbourne's tallest building—the Eureka Building Skydeck, where they dared each other to walk the vertiginous plank for a belly-tightening experience of a lifetime.

They went back to the archives for a picnic and a nap. Peter and Nedra Wright, Goeffrey and Margaret Smedley, and Glen and Marilyn Gabler cleaned up after lunch; and the faithful troop of missionaries went back to the important didactic work of digitizing records for Victoria Province and Australia for a self-imposed evening shift.

BOOK TWO

CHAPTER FORTY-SEVEN

ARRIVAL IN MELBOURNE

I think Melbourne is by far and away the most interesting place in Australia, and if I ever wrote a novel or crime novel of any kind, I had to set it here.

-Peter Temple

The Hotel Windsor, Spring Street on Bourke Hill, Victoria Province, Melbourne, Australia, December 12, 1884

Australia—a large island–is also the world's smallest continent. It lies southeast of Asia between the Pacific and Indian oceans; its diverse landscapes and climates are home to a wide variety of plants and animals. The continent is generally warm and dry all year round, with no extreme cold and little frost. Average annual rainfall is 17 inches [42 centimeters], much less than the mean for all the countries of the world of 26 inches [66 centimeters]. As a result, insufficient rainfall can and frequently does cause droughts that threaten to destroy crops and to impact the lives of Aussies severely. The country's limited rainfall can also cause problems with water quality and availability. Because Australia produces most of its own food, a water shortage for plants and animals can cause agricultural production to suffer. It takes a hardy soul to be an Aussie.

Alexandra arrived in Sandridge Port, Melbourne on a delightful summer day—December 12, 1884—after a very pleasant but anxious steamship voyage on the Cunard steamship, *The Great Britain*, from

Bristol. The pleasure was being able to luxuriate in a splendid, middle outside, stateroom; and the anxiety was occasioned by her necessarily hasty departure from Vladivostok, which was enduring one of the worst winters in Far East Russian history. She waited on the departure deck as the gang plank was lowered. She was in no hurry because she wanted to see that all her baggage—which was very considerable—made it to the wharf. Most of the first-class passengers disembarked as she watched. She had five forty-inch metal stateroom trunks with key-lock clasps and reinforcing leather straps, four heavy leatherette suitcases for her dresses and hats, and a dozen two-part portmanteaus, grips, and valises—all waterproofed to withstand the sea spray of steamship travel. A small army of hired hands carried the luggage from the first-class compartment and loaded them onto three four-horse vans. Alexandra left *The Great Britain* and entered a shining black barouche for her ride to the aptly named "Grand Hotel".

Her arrival warranted considerable attention, even a newspaper article with a photograph. Observers commented on her regal bearing, her form-fitting salmon-colored big-bustled Victorian Petrova gown showing a bit too much décolletage for local tastes. Her striking knee-length hair—the color of platinum–was swept up into a chignon ornamented by jewel crusted tortoise shell combs. She wore sensible medium heeled, high-button, shoes made of salmon-colored kid leather. For all that finery, her most striking features were her porcelain-perfect white face and her Aphrodite figure. Other than to give instruction to the luggage handlers and the barouche driver, she did not speak to anyone.

Once she was ensconced in her five-room apartment, she summoned the business manager to get his advice on beginning her business ventures in Melbourne.

"Mister…?" she paused.

"O'Dwyer, M'am, at your service." he responded.

"Mr. O'Dwyer, I will be in your hotel for a month or so. During that time, I wish to acquire a suitable business building and to buy or to commence construction on a new house. I will need the services of an attorney, an accountant, a real estate agent, and a banker. I presumed that you would possess that kind of information. Am I correct?"

"With all modesty, Ma'am, you have found the correct hotel and the right man to fulfill you needs. I expect it will take me no more than three days to assemble appropriate candidates for each of the positions you expect to fill. You can interview the candidates in the hotel's business conference room. Before you see them, I will have a brief dossier prepared for you to study. Will that be satisfactory?"

"More than satisfactory. I appreciate your service and will not demean it or you by offering a tip or gratuity. Rather, I will pay you for your services and your counsel on a regular basis. Will that be acceptable to you?"

"Oh, Ma'am, my services come with the hotel stay. I expect nothing further."

"Mr. O'Dwyer, I have found in doing business, that the best service comes as a part of regular compensation. I will ask a considerable amount from you, and I would be uncomfortable if I were feel that I was taking advantage."

He shrugged, smiled, and reached out to shake her hand.

"Business associates, then, Mr. O'Dwyer," Alexandra said and gave him a robust handshake quite unlike the effete and dainty grasp he might had expected from a delicate Victorian young lady.

A small nod by Alexandra sufficed to indicate that their business was concluded. O'Dwyer returned a small courtly bow and exited the room. As soon as he was gone, Alexandra used the conference room telephone to call her old friend, bodyguard, and now business associate, the Don Cossack, Stenka Mazepa. It was necessary to call through the hotel's switchboard.

Stenka answered, "*Zdravstvuyte.*"

The operator said, "Please, Sir. Is there an English speaker in the home?"

Stenka said, "*Da*, I am English speaker. Vhat is vanted?"

The operator said to Alexandra, "The number you are calling has been answered. You will be speaking to a man with a heavy accent."

Alexandra said into the phone, "*Privet moy drug.*"

Stenka replied in English, "And hello to you, my friend."

"I am here now. I just got off the boat."

"To stay?"

"This will be home now."

"I am glad you haf come, Alexandra. I haf been lonely for home ant friends," the old man said.

"I understand the feeling, Stenka. I trust the money has been enough."

"Indeed, zo. In a moment I vill tell you some good newses about money; but first I vont to know if der iss any newses about the poys, Nikita ant Oral."

"Still nothing, Stenka. My parents and I have searched everywhere in the oblast, wrote to all our friends and family everyplace, even contacted Boris's family—who were not very pleased to hear from me. I tried to get information about Boris's military assignment. The general staff secretaries brushed me away; *ob"yavleniye"* ['classified'] they said everytime. So... nothing for three years since Boris took them that terrible night."

"I efen tried a few Europeans I know; and, no surprise, I learnet nothingk."

"So, there is nothing more I can do. I left the reward offer in place, but no takers for the whole time. Better I get on with life here. In Vladivostok, there is nothing but sorrow and frustration. You said you had some good news, Stenka. I could use some just now."

"Ah, ja. Remember you sent money ant a letter for me to gif an old family friend of your father's?"

"I remember...Stefan Petrokowsky. He lives here, right?"

"He does. Health is not zo goot now but is rich man. Zo am I. That was back in seventy-eight ven you wrote. Was ven the golt poom was getting started. Petrokowsky hat a good site for golt—couple streams, and some successful dry panningk in the hillsides nearpy. Ve collected some ant had it analyzed py an independent assayer fella. Vas very goot both for placer ant open cast mining. Lot off vork, lots off money. Sold our claim after four years. You remember?"

"Of course, I do. You made a fortune and banked it."

"Is right. Better to say ve did. Equal shares ass agreet. Put it in Commercial Pank off Australia—biggest in Victoria–last year. Maybe zo much as twenty million Aussie dollars."

"Did you buy land like we talked about; so, we would not just let the money waste away in banks?"

"I dit, even though old Petrokowsky didn't tink vas goot idea. Lant vas cheap and getting cheaper all the time. Lot of the miners ver goingk belly up, and ve got der lant. Ve now haf somethingk like coupla thousand hectares off prime acreage. I hafto say, Alexandra, ve would be richer if ve had invested in golt miningk."

"I understand the thinking, Stenka; but I have been following the economy here and have been learning about international banking. Maybe you don't know it, but Barings Bank in London is slowly going under; and they are hinting at filing for bankruptcy as early as this year. Most European and American economists think the gold boom everywhere and especially in Melbourne is about over and that we are going to see a huge bust. It will be good to have real things, like real estate and physical gold. Change comes hard, my old friend; but we need to get our money out of banks and into real estate and gold and hold on until the bust clears itself. That way we can save ourselves and then be able to become very wealthy again. I have done a lot of studying, and I am sure of this. You can do anything you want with your own money, but as the major shareholder, I am going to make the changes with *our* money."

"I, too, haf pen hearingk zuch rumors, Alexandra. I vill go wit you. Old Petrokowsky will take his money and buy lant for more golt mining."

"His privilege and his risk, Stenka. We shall see what happens."

After a good rest and a hearty Aussie *brekkie*–a Bushman's breakfast: thick bacon, pork sausages, fried potatoes, onions, and mushrooms, *shakshuka* [classic Middle Eastern dish of eggs, softly cooked vegetables and bircher muesli]–the next morning, Alexandra had another talk with O'Dwyer about Melbourne's business future. What she learned was shocking in its stark reality.

"You know, Alexandra, when you first looked into investing in Melbourne a few years ago, this place was incredibly successful."

"It was going through a boom," she agreed.

"The gold boom, and then the land boom. The gold boom is pretty much over, although many old timers are not willing to admit it. The land boom is crazy right now; but it cannot last, in my opinion. The signs all point to another five years—ten at the most—before the bottom falls out."

"What signs?"

"We changed from a small town to a small city to a rapidly growing city to a city growing faster than the infrastructure and the treasury could support. Early in the boom, the city was beautiful. It became known all over as "Marvelous Melbourne", and that it was. At its zenith, the gold boom brought incredible progress and very real problems that needed to be solved. Sudden wealth transformed this small port town into a frantic world center in a matter of months. The wharves were constantly jammed with shipping, cargo and migrants disembarking. A huge engineering project was undertaken to make the port more efficient and safer. Society turned upside down. Gold diggers, carpenters, and stevedores literally threw money away. They drank champagne from buckets and sloshed it on the muddy roads. Low-life Irish maids and ladies of the night paraded around in fancy coaches and cabriolets dressed in silks and diamonds.

"When the gold boom started to decline, the miners left for better pickings. The city's tax base declined slowly at first then very rapidly. The infrastructure with such crucial things as sewage service failed. Sewage now runs in the streets. Can't drink the water or even wash your clothes in it.

"The city fathers made a serious and bold decision to save the city. The remainder of the treasury was poured into constructing fine and attractive buildings some even twelve stories high: banks, government offices, civic buildings—the Customs House, Post Office, Treasury House, Parliament, and post office buildings. The government's apparent confidence inspired the building of churches, coffee palaces, and hotels, all built by out-of-work miners. Architects and construction companies prospered beyond anyone's imagination. Towers, spires, domes, and turrets reached towards the sky. A magnificent huge telescope was built here.

"It became a popular pastime for the citizens to visit Melbourne Observatory at night to observe the planets, moon and stars, through with the Great Melbourne Telescope. Living conditions improved. The tax base improved, but it was a house of cards. Much of the city smelled so bad you could not stand to go there. Instead of being "Marvelous Melbourne" it has gotten to be known by almost everyone here as "Smellbourne".

"No one seems to see that we are in a land boom now, and that it is a bubble that will burst. My recommendation, Alexandra, is to use your money to buy property throughout Australia and to hold onto it. Property values will climb again after the coming fall. You will use the classical 'buy low and sell high' plan if you exercise courage and patience, and you will succeed beyond your wildest imaginations here in Australia."

Alexandra was sobered by everything she had heard. She knew that she was currently rich enough to weather the Australian economic storm which was beginning to spread throughout the civilized world. She spent that afternoon divesting herself of stocks, bonds, and cash, and changing into gold bullion and precious gems, warehouses full of invaluable Chinese and Japanese silks, and bales and bales of cotton and woolen fabrics. Then came the major occupation of the next three days in Melbourne.

She began buying up good but undervalued property in Sydney, Canberra, and Perth. She retired early, exhausted by her frenzied buying and selling and the stress and anxiety of each decision. She would be either a pauper or a princess by the time all this boom, bust, and boom again played out.

The next day was Melbourne's turn. It was a nice day; so, she took a landau to Stenka's house. Together they took a cook's tour of the city. They started at the Wharf where there was moderate activity, but not as frenetic as she had supposed a working day should have been. Carts, drays, vans, and wagons were being used for carrying goods; but as a sign of the lessening times, they were also being used to carry people–those of the lower orders; but still, the conveyances were better suited for animals. This appeared to be a harbinger of difficult times to come.

In the past, large ships like *The Great Britain* were unable to navigate the curving and rather narrow and shallow Yarra River. Cargo destined for Melbourne in that era had to be unloaded at Hobsons Bay and transferred by rail or by cargo lighter to warehouses concentrated around King Street, an expensive and inefficient process. During the late seventies, the colonial government determined to find a solution that would make Melbourne an important international port of call.

The solution was bold, even drastic. The marine architect hired by the province decided to change the course of the river by cutting a canal south of the original course of the river which shorted the river's course and made it considerably more convenient. In 1884–when Alexandra landed in Melbourne–ships were able to sail as far up the river as Queensbridge and to take advantage of a turning basin which was created. In the years leading up to 1880, when Melbourne was "Marvelous Melbourne", new arrivals—thousands every day–chased a single dream—gold—and cared very little about how the city looked. Alexandra was reminded of the attitude prevailing in Asia when she was involved in active trading. There everything revolved around the three Gs—God, Glory, and Gold. The similarity was disturbing.

Lodging houses and hotels–mostly of flimsy construction and temporary character–were packed to bursting point, many charging by the hour. Makeshift houses of iron, lumber, and canvas sprang up on the city's edge with strictly pragmatic and utilitarian values—no ascetic concerns. After 1880, the town's gentry began an effort to make the city presentable and important, beyond its being a center for gold prospectors. Now, Alexandra and Stenka were looking upon urban rot approaching collapse. Stenka was used to the sight, but Alexandra was shocked. The only building that looked like it did in the marvelous era was the first Melbourne International Exhibition building, built in 1880.

"Looks to me like there's a profit to be made here, Stenka," she said.

CHAPTER FORTY-EIGHT

SUCCESS IN MELBOURNE

Nothing can take the place of persistence. Talent will not. Nothing is so common as the unsuccessful men with talent. Genius will not; unrewarded genius is almost a proverb. Education will not; the world is full of educated derelicts. Persistence and determination alone are omnipotent. Press on has solved and always will solve the problems of the human race.
—George Romney, *Give Yourself to Something Great,*
Baccalaureate Address, University of Utah, June 5, 1960

Number 8, Chapel Street, Victoria Colony, Melbourne, Australia, November 19, 1889

Melbourne was becoming one of the largest cities—as judged by geographical area—in the world, in no small part due to the efforts of Alexandra Abramovich Tarasova-Yusupov, who—at the youthful age of twenty-eight, and unmarried at that—was becoming one of the grande dames of the city and a notable, even as far away as Sydney. Alexandra had dropped the patronymic from her name and avoided discussion of her Russian background. She and Stenka had poured millions of dollars into real estate over the past five years. Old streets were being repaired and cleaned; old neighborhoods were beginning to see new buildings; these made to last. For the past year, she and Stenka had concentrated their energy in the South Yarra and Prahran neighborhoods to create a post suburb where she could live in luxury and security. Paved streets, sewers, electricity, and police officers were now a regular part of the neighborhood; and other neighborhoods were beginning to follow suit.

Their investments were slowly beginning to reap rewards. Many Australians recognized the need to save Melbourne and decided to invest in businesses, buildings, and to make their homes in previously neglected and decaying parts of the city in order to attract other investors; and, more importantly more solid citizens.

Alexandra's house—at Number 8, Chapel Street, near Greville Street in Prahran—was a handsome Edwardian mansion; and Stenka's was located around the corner at Number 10 Grenville Street. Twelve new homes had either been completed or were in various stages of construction in the neighborhood around Alexandra and Stenka. It appeared that the two Russian émigrés had the Midas Touch, and investors studied their purchases—even their scouting movements through the areas of Melbourne that were beginning to rise again—to make their own land buys. This resulted in a self-fulfilling prophecy for Alexandra and Stenka.

So much so, that Alexandra happened on a pair of plans to guarantee their affluence for as far ahead as they could foresee. With Stenka, she started the Greater Melbourne Realty and Land Company to help prospective buyers and sellers to meet, and to grease the skids to hasten closures. She started the Greater Melbourne City Improvement Association patterned after similar organizations in London, New York, and Paris. Her concept was different from the others in that it was a bottom-up rather than a top-down plan.

Her ambitions were not altogether altruistic although many slum conditions were improved and the lot of the impoverished in Melbourne's poor neighborhoods were improved. Slums were sites of poor land values, and Alexandra and Stenka bought them at pennies on the dollar. The sellers were then free to leave and pursue gold prospecting in the burgeoning gold-mining centers of Ballarat and Bendigo, which was their original desire. The buyers were willing and even eager to buy up land and to make it part of a thriving Melbourne in the making. The Greater Melbourne Realty and Land Company was more than eager to help both sides of all transactions–for a fair realtor's fee.

By spring of 1889 The Greater Melbourne Realty and Land Company had land and buildings spread out over the central metropolis located on the large natural bay of Port Phillip along with expansions into the arid prairies beyond stretching out to the Dandenong and Macedon mountain ranges, Mornington Peninsula, and Yarra Valley. Stenka had learned an old ditty from British sailors which seemed to describe the capitalistic policy of their enterprise and sang it quietly every time they made a particularly lucrative transaction:

Top of Form
Bottom of Form

My father makes counterfeit money
My mother makes synthetic gin
My sister sells kisses to sailors
And oh how the money rolls in
Chorus
Rolls in, rolls in, oh, how the money rolls in, rolls in
Rolls in, rolls in, oh, how the money rolls in

My brother's a slum missionary
Out savin' young lassies from sin
For a shilling, he'll save you a redhead
And oh, how the money rolls in
Chorus

Grandma's a boardin' house keeper
She takes pretty workin' girls in
She hangs a red light in the window
And oh, how the money rolls in
Chorus

Stenka became ill with tuberculosis in May and was unable to participate in their day-to-day business activities. That meant that Alexandra now had to handle all the major and minor details of getting a tramway started. In the spring, the tram extended only from Swanston Street to Chapel Street; and getting funding for her planned throughway to the wharf area was becoming ever more difficult because the financiers found it difficult to lend large sums to a woman with no man backing her up. Alexandra had to make less than fully fair deals with the patrimony of Melbourne and of Australia as a whole in order to complete funding.

Although she felt like she had quartered some of her integrity to get the funding, the tramway was a reality by the end of November.

The Greater Melbourne Realty and Land Company participated in the establishment of a hydraulic facility in 1887 which manufactured elevators; the result of that fundamental local success—was the construction of high-rise buildings comparable to those seen in New York City, London, and Berlin. The company's most ambitious project—which required obtaining funding from almost every bank in Australia and not a few in America and England—was to improve the railway system to a safe and reliable transportation network that rivaled the one in Switzerland. Plans were made for a grand opening celebration for the Melbourne Tramway system to coincide with the city's Christmas celebration. Nearly every major thoroughfare within the Melbourne Center area was now interconnected.

Alexandra loved her new home, in part because she had created it herself; and it was neither a Tarasova nor a Yusupov construction. Each time she arrived at that thought, her mind drifted back to what she had lost. Her husband had betrayed her in the most bestial way by stealing away her two children. Neither the man nor the boys had been located in more than eight years of searching. She had lost half of her working capital because Boris had taken his portion of the accounts' assets when he absconded. He was technically owed that much of the money legally; but ethically, it were an abomination in Alexandra's mind—another betrayal. The betrayal was made all the worse because—under Russian law—she could not even obtain a divorce after years of legal wrangling. Alexandra resolved never to trust a man again.

She would control her life, and, certainly, her assets so long as she lived. She had managers, accountants, and attorneys, to ensure against another predation. Alexandra had used up so much of her time searching for the boys that Jardine-Matheson severed relations with her. Her parents maintained their good relations with the giant maritime corporation, and their wealth accumulated rapidly over the years since Boris had left. That had led to acrimony between her and Abram and Irina until she decided to make a break with them and to emigrate to Australia. After three years, she no longer corresponded with them. She stopped using her Russian patronymic and also the inclusion of the Tarasova portion of her surname which added an exclamation point of finality to her Russian life.

Before the evening of the tramway celebration, Alexandra visited Stenka, concerned that he would not be around much longer. She loved the old man and genuinely valued his wisdom. He had some studied wisdom to share with her that night.

After an exchange of their usual pleasantries and sharing aperitifs, Stenka became serious and asked for Alexandra's full attention.

"My tear, I vill tire qvickly, ant I have sometingk to tell you. Ve haf zeen a golt boom ant a crash and lately a lant boom. Both ver expected. Now, you must expect another crash. Land prices haf gone crazy. Ve, ant a few others have mate fortunes. But, my tear, dis cannot last. I predict a crash before the turn off the century. Promise me that you vill get out of lant, buildingks, ant loaning money to speculators. You are rich. You can become poor. Get out or you vill end up like Henry Frenchman and H.H. Walsh up in the Plenty Ranges, Louis John Michel and his friends at Anderson's Creek, the Brentanis in Collins Street, the Forresters, the gold and silver smiths, the Clinches, and the Hobarts to name a few."

His voice faltered. He coughed up a little blood.

"Get out off the biznesss now," was the last thing he could manage.

Stenka died a week later.

The day after the tramway celebration, Alexandra arranged for a Russian Orthodox funeral in the humble little home in Collingwood that served as a chapel. No priest was available, but subdeacon Ivan Ioannis Dionisii came all the way from Sydney to officiate. He was the grandson and namesake of Father Dionissi, the Russian Orthodox chaplain who conducted the first orthodox service in Russia in 1820.

Alexandra spoke as the only friend of Stenka's after Dionisii completed the formal ceremonies.

"Stenka Mazepa was a Don Cossack, a very brave fighter, a man of courage in all aspects of his life. He served me as a guardian and protector during my girlhood and several times came close to making the supreme sacrifice for me. He was loyal to a fault to my mother and father, and that level of loyalty was the pattern of his life. He was among the faithful Russian Orthodox from his childhood on and should be kept in your memory here in Melbourne as such forever. He and I were business partners at the time of his death, and it is my pleasure to announce that he will leave a sum sufficient to build a real chapel for your community. It is too bad that he could not live long enough to see its completion."

There were a few white lies in that short eulogy, but Alexandra was certain it would have been to Stenka's liking. He possessed all those good attributes; he was a lifelong proud Cossack and a warrior; and he was orthodox to his core and to the end. He–of course–never heard of the chapel he was going to bequeath and which would become the Mazepa Orthodox Religious Center in time. Alexandra did not begrudge a kopek of the generous contribution.

What was important to her was Stenka's last advice, and Alexandra heeded it assiduously. The day after his simple funeral, she began to dismantle her companies, business associations, and to liquidate all her holdings. That process took three full years while the Melbourne economy began to unravel at the seams. The land crash was worse than the preceding gold rush crash. By the end of 1889, the land boom and fully run its course. Alexandra sold as fast as she could, sometimes at bargain prices. The economically embattled city watched falling asset prices, shrinking commodity prices, diminished use of transportation systems with resultant falling prices and profits, severely increased pressure on borrowers resulting in mounting defaults.

The defaults undermined the stability of Melbourne's and then all of Australia's lending institutions. Widespread failures were evident early among the land banks and building societies beginning in 1891 and that frightened trading bank depositors. In 1892, the unthinkable happened–the suspension and then liquidation the Mercantile Bank of Australia followed a few months later in 1893 of the Federal Bank of Australia. What destroyed the banks was their interdependent linkage with the building societies—many brought into being by Alexandra and her company.

The "Great Crash" was in full swing.

The population of Australia suffered increasing anxiety about the safety of the other twenty-two banks in the country. Melbourne was hit first and worst. Bank shares carried additional liability, and many of the demands for payment were triggered by suspension heaping misery on top of loss. The fall gained an inexorable momentum as bank shareholders—most Australians–began dumping stock as fast as they could before depositors could begin to look for safer investments. By the late 1880s, the boom had run its full course to the end.

Falling asset prices–compounded by shrinking commodity prices– increased pressure on borrowers; and they defaulted by the hundreds, thereby further undermining the stability of lending institutions all over the country. The domino effect led to widespread failures particularly among the land banks and building societies which intensified fears of trading among rank and file investors and depositors, builders, and bankers to say nothing of the panic at the highest levels of government. Victoria premier, James Munro, pleaded for sanity.

By 1892, the Mercantile Bank of Australia—where Alexandra had once kept the bulk of her deposits—filed for suspension then liquidation of its assets. In January of 1893, the prestigious Federal Bank of Australia failed—an unthinkable catastrophe before the fall. Both banks were unfortunately too closely linked to building societies Alexandra and Stenka had so vigorously promoted. Alexandra had saved herself by not communicating her qualms about the over-inflated land and construction industries until she extricated herself. She salved her conscience by whispering the age-old saw that "business is business". Even average middle-class Aussies developed seriously heightened anxiety about the safety of the other twenty-two banks fueled by newspaper reports telling of personal and business failures and suicides. Many bank shares carried additional liability for both banks and shareholders.

The bank share security measures were triggered by bank suspensions and further wounded investors. Bank shareholders began dumping stock long before depositors began to look for safety elsewhere as Alexandra had done, but it was a case of "too little, too late." Big banks and heavy investors were left holding the bag in the end; "business was business".

Compounding those losses came the loss of new deposits which led to dangerous promises such as making guarantees with gold coin and making notes fully convertible to gold coin. That resulted in irretrievable losses and bank failures around the country. The *coup de grâce* for Melbourne came when the Commercial Bank of Australia–the largest bank in the colony and the center of the land and building speculation boom—shut its doors in April. By six weeks later thirty banks were gone.

CHAPTER FORTY-NINE
SALVATION IN SYDNEY

[All the ancient wisdom] tells us that work is necessary to us, as much a part of our condition as mortality; that good work is our salvation and our joy; that shoddy or dishonest or self-serving work is our curse and our doom. We have tried to escape the sweat and sorrow promised in Genesis—only to find that, in order to do so, we must forswear love and excellence, health and joy.

—Wendell Berry, *The Unsettling of America,*
The Art of the Commonplace:
The Agrarian Essays. The Unsettling of America, p.44

Number 8, Chapel Street, Sydney, British Colony of New South Wales, Australia, December 1, 1895

From 1860 onwards, Sydney evolved a stable political environment and economy which persisted relatively successfully through the financially tumultuous nineties despite both the gold boom, the land boom, and two subsequent bust eras. Alexandra Yusupov—as she now fashioned herself to escape some of her creditors and a public that held her and Stenka Mazepa responsible for the land bust—found a safe-haven in the burgeoning city months before the collapse of land speculation and supportive banks and other lending institutions hit Melbourne so disastrously. She lost money; but in the instances where she could not sell properties at a profit or even for what she had originally paid, she was at least able to hold on to the land and buildings for long enough to outwait the crash–at least she hoped.

As soon as Alexandra arrived in Sydney, her first project was to buy land in the heart of the city and to build a fine home. Unlike her early experience in Melbourne, her progress was stymied by the antiquarian structure of the law which required that a man—almost always a husband–be responsible for all major family expenditures. A woman was barred from purchasing and owning property herself unless she was a widow whose husband had purchased the property originally. Similarly, her efforts to do business as a realtor or to purchase and sell land for profit met a stone wall placed in front of her by men.

"There, there, my dear," was the phrase Alexandra loathed the most in all the English language.

Alexandra was not one to give up easily. She looked about for solutions to her problem of having too much money and no way to make use of it for profit; and she did not have a home. She was forced—for the time being—to take up residence in one of Sydney's better hotels, the Australia Hotel located in Castlereagh Street. It was not as if she would be living in anything even approaching deprivation or squalor. The hotel described itself as "the best-known hotel in all of Australia", as "the premier hotel in Sydney", and later more grandiosely, "*The* Hotel of the Commonwealth." All of that was true, if a little overinflated.

A major benefit of living in the hotel is that it was situated along one of Sydney's most important thoroughfares in the bustling city center, granting access to all–or almost all–of the city's and the country's movers and shakers in politics, finance, and business; it provided a wide and useful variety of services—for a fee. Alexandra loved the fact that it was next door to the Theatre Royal where such luminaries as Sarah Bernhardt appeared. The drawbacks included: it was too expensive; her quarters were too small to permit her to have an adequate office; and—most important to Alexandra—she could neither own it nor control it.

Harking back to her previous business experience, she took a trip to Chinatown. The community was located in the south of the business district near Darling Harbor within walking distance from her hotel. A few discrete inquiries led her to a five-story–typically Chinese–office building on the corner of George and Hay Streets. Her facility with both major languages—Mandarin and Cantonese—granted her friendly access to local businessmen and women who suggested she meet the main "fixer" in Chinatown. She followed the bilingual street signs to the building, climbed the stairs to the fifth floor, and knocked politely on the door bearing a small brass plaque, "Wáng & Dau".

After a few minutes wait, the door was opened; and Alexandra met a handsome middle-aged woman who reached out her hand to offer a western handshake.

"Good morning," the woman said in softly accented English, "I am Wáng Caihong."

Remembering that the name Wáng was the most common surname in northern China, Alexandra smiled, shook Caihong's hand and said, in English, "And my name is Alexandra. I am originally from Vladivostok, near Manchuria. Are you comfortable in English, or would you prefer Mandarin? I am fluent."

Caihong blushed and bowed.

"I am not quite as fluent in English; so, my native tongue would be better, if it pleases you, kind lady. And my father, the venerable Wáng Wen Sheng, is more inclined to be helpful to persons who speak our northern dialect."

Alexandra changed to Mandarin, "Your name is beautiful, Caihong—a rainbow in the sky—if I remember correctly. And your father is surely aptly named for his being a literate person and is also highly successful."

Again, Caihong blushed, "You are too kind. Please enter our humble home and place of business. May I tell honorable father the nature of your business with him?"

"Please do. I seek his wise advice on doing business in Sydney. Since I am only a worthless female and unmarried, I have found it difficult even to buy myself a proper home."

"It is the same for Chinese people," Caihong said, "honorable father will understand. I am sure he can be of help. If you could sit here at the table and have some chai while I speak to him…?"

"My pleasure, Caihong. Please convey my gratitude for being invited into your pleasant home and for the honor of being able to consult his wisdom."

The tea was hot and fragrant. The room was decorated in a variation on a theme of red from the Harbin carpets, to the watercolors on the walls, to the molded ceilings decorated with a brightly painted orange-red dragon motif. She heard the distinct shuffling of slippered feet; and, remembering her etiquette, she quickly removed her shoes and stockings and placed them neatly on the chair next to her.

An elderly wraith of a man stepped silently into the room accompanied by his daughter.

She said, "Missy Yusupov, I have the honor to present my venerable father, Wáng Wen Sheng, mandarin of the court of her majesty the empress."

Alexandra got up from her chair, bowed very low, and with a sober face filled with genuine awe, said, "Mandarin Wáng, I, a mere woman not of your court, bow humbly with full respect. I am aware of your great accomplishments, not least of which is that you passed the *jinshi* exams with the highest scores in the 2,000 year history of the tests. I know that I stand before a great master of knowledge of the Confucian classics, a remarkable example for us all."

She bowed even lower and held her reverential position until Mandarin Wáng bade her, "Lift your head, daughter. You do yourself and your family very well with the courtesy you show. You have come a considerable and tiring way to speak with me. Please let us sit and reason together."

As custom dictated, Caihong assumed a head-down kneeling position behind and to the left of her father. He sat on a low raised platform covered with patterned red silk pillows directly in front of Alexandra. She maintained silence and sat stiffly in her red silk chair until the elderly master of the Qing Chinese dynasty civil service spoke. Alexandra knew him to be a *juren* [gentleman and judge of upper-gentry status]. It would be a dreadful *faux pas*—nearly tantamount to an act of *lèse-majesté*–for any woman to speak before directed by the mandarin.

Mandarin Wáng wore a bright blue colored silk brocade coat indicative of a civil servant of the highest rank and black trousers. The coat was embroidered in black with dragons and his family crest along the sides and a mandarin square [rank badge]—a large embroidered square badge sewn onto the surcoat embroidered with detailed, colorful bird insignias indicating the rank of the official wearing it; in the case of Wáng–a mandarin of the first degree–there were beautiful cranes with wide spread wings in the front and golden pheasants on back. On his head, he wore another symbol of his rank, a *Qing Guanmao* [consisting of a black hat of woven rattan with a button on the top since it was summer]. Because the family was coming to dinner for a reunion that evening, the mandarin's button was made into an ornamental finial, almost as if the family expected the empress to attend. Red silk tassels extended down from the finial to cover Wáng's hat; and a large peacock feather with three "eyes" was attached to the back of the hat, showing that the privilege of wearing it had been granted by the empress herself.

Up close, he was very small, tired looking, and very old with deeply etched yellowing skin. He had a wispy goatee and a long scanty white mustache that appeared to be unmanageable. His face was lined with years, decision making, suffering, and cares. But for all of that, his eyes were alert, intelligent, and dominating. His irises were so dark that he did not appear to have pupils. Despite his obvious age and wrinkles, the man maintained an aura of self-possession and control belying his infirmities of age which transmitted the appearance of a strong man—despite his diminutive size—and one to be reckoned with.

Mandarin Wáng nodded his head slightly and began to speak in a high squeaky voice that required Alexandra and Caihong to lean forward and strain to hear him.

"Missy Yusupov, I have known of your coming to Australia for some time and of your courage and industrious nature both in Melbourne and now in Sydney. You have been wise in protecting yourself against the wolves at the door; and it is my understanding that you have placed your money and treasure in safe, but temporary places. Is that the correct understanding, my dear?"

"Yes, Mandarin, it is; and that is the reason I have come to consult with you and to receive wisdom not available among the Caucasians."

He laughed–a small short chortle–more like a cough than a laugh.

"The *bái mù* [stupid, white-eyed, lit. blind] round-eyes seem not to be able to control themselves when they get money. They seem not to know about family or putting away something for the bad days ahead. Knowing nothing, they are unfit to give financial advice. Can you accept advice and help from a person not of your race, Missy Yusupov?"

"I certainly can, Mandarin. It is an honor for me that you would even consider consulting and a lifelong debt of friendship if you can find a way to save me from the growing financial disaster here in Australia."

"I am tired now, my dear. I will rest, or—as you Europeans say—I'll sleep on it."

Alexandra walked back to the Grand with a lightness in her step, having had a figurative weight lifted from her shoulders. Although she had just met the venerable Chinese mandarin, she instinctively trusted him. He would help her; it would be a long-term assistance; and her debt would be considerable, but fair. He had spoken to her as if she were a daughter or a favored niece, and she intended to reciprocate. Leaving Chinatown, she passed a flower market called *Tiāntǐ huā* [Celestial Flowers] and stopped in to make a purchase. She found ten different paintings of bouquets of flowers offered by the proprietrix which Chinese people love and find a measure of nostalgia attached.

"Madam Lee," she said, speaking Mandarin and smiling, "Would you be so kind as to send one of each of these bouquets—the best you have–to Miss Caihong Wáng. Her address is…"

"Kind lady, everyone in Chinatown knows the address of the mandarin and his daughter. If I might be so bold, this gesture could be…how do you say?…misinterpreted coming from a…*Wàiguó rén* [foreigner]…if you will forgive me for using such a word…It is more appropriately the gift of a family member."

"Thank you, Madam Lee, you are most perceptive and kind to inform me of the etiquette of this custom. However, rest comfortably that I consider myself to be a favored member of Mandarin Wáng's family, and he and Caihong hold me in similar regard. Please do your best to send a pleasing token of my familial caring for them once each week for the next three months."

Madam Lee gave Alexandra a very brief quizzical look, then shook her head and attended to business. How could a round-eye understand?

Alexandra realized she was making a very calculated risk and might well be over-stepping, but she wanted more than anything else at the moment to make a deep connection with the mandarin and the Wáng family tong. She crossed her fingers as she made the full payment. It never occurred to her that she would be cheated or short-changed by Madam Lee. It simply was not done.

The following morning, a porter knocked on her hotel room door.

"Yes?" Alexandra asked.

"There is a Chinese man in the front lobby who says he has a message for you. I can send him on his way, if you wish."

"No thank you, James," she said reading his nameplate. "Here is a little something for your trouble and effort."

She gave him a generous tip—in gold, since paper money was suspect during this period.

There was no problem picking out the messenger. He was the only foreign or non-Caucasian person in the entire lobby.

She stopped in front of him and carefully avoided smiling—considered rude in a first meeting or anytime with strangers. He gave her a small polite bow and proffered a small cream-colored envelope with Chinese lettering.

She thanked him and opened the envelope to see what the letter said and to determine if a reply was necessary.

> Office of the Mandarin,
> Chinatown, Sydney, Australia
> 10 December, 1895
> Alexandra Yusupov:
> Estimable Miss Yusupov. My father directs me to inform you that he has made successful inquiries on your behalf. Three days from this day, please meet with the mandarin in his place of business at the noon hour. Other interested and significant persons will attend. The favor of a reply is requested.
>
> Humbly submitted,
Wáng Caihong

Alexandra's reply was simple and direct:

> 10 December, 1895
> Venerable Mandarin Wáng Wen Sheng:
> Dear *Zūnjìng de shūshu* [Honorable Uncle]: I will be honored to meet with you. Thank you for your service.
>
> Your humble niece,
Yusupov Alexandra

CHAPTER FIFTY
FAMILY IN SYDNEY

"I don't know half of you half as well

as I should like; and I like less than half

of you half as well as you deserve."
—J.R.R. Tolkien, *The Fellowship of the Ring*

"All happy families are alike; each unhappy family is unhappy in its own way."

—Leo Tolstoy, *Anna Karenina*

"Happiness is having a large, loving, caring, close-knit family in another city."

—George Burns

Office of the Mandarin, 2289 George Street, Chinatown, Sydney, British Colony of New South Wales, Common-wealth of Australia, December 13, 1895

To avoid any possibility of being late for her meeting with Wáng Wen Sheng, Alexandra arranged for carriage by a Hansom Cab. She purposely dressed very modestly, making certain that she chose a dress which did not expose her chest in the least. She chose a simple print high-necked dress which did not hug her curves, had bell-like sleeves, and had black lace frothing at the hem of the dress. Her shoes were low heeled and lace-up—semi-boots. Alexandra thought they were grotesque, style-wise; but she knew she had to keep uppermost in her mind what mattered to the influential mandarin.

She arrived precisely on time at 2289 George Street and climbed the stairs five stories to the mandarin's office. Caihong showed her in with more warmth than she had shown on Alexandra's previous visit.

"Best greetings...may I say 'sister'? And welcome back."

Alexandra's bow was precisely equal to Caihong's, and she said, "Many thanks, Sister. I am in your debt for what you have done to influence your father, the mandarin, in my behalf."

This time Caihong took Alexandra directly to Wáng Wen Sheng's office. He was dressed in a black western suit, white shirt and tie, and his almost knee length white hair was combed out all the way. She cast a questioning glance at Caihong, who whispered,

"It is our custom that the man never cuts his hair after age ten."

The mandarin concluded his conversation with the two other men in his office before turning to Alexandra.

"My dear Alexandra, it is so good of you to come again on such short notice. I wish to introduce you to two of my seafaring friends. Liu Chang and Zhang Jiao-long, this is my daughter, Alexandra Yusupov. Alexandra, it is my pleasure to have you meet Liu Chang and Zhang Jiao-long, who are business friends and members of the Wáng Family Tong. They direct the ocean business from here to Hong-Kong and the other cities of Australasia. I believe you good friends and family can be of help to one another."

Mr. Liu was dressed in rough but clean sailors' clothing, appropriate for the business at hand, Alexandra thought. He appeared to be the more forward of the two visitors despite his smaller stature. He had a moon shaped Han face, thick lips, and bad teeth—a common look one saw on the streets of Chinatown. To Alexandra, it was as if a complicated deal had been consummated, and all that was left was for her to learn what her role was to be.

She bowed, placed her two hands in front of her chest and bowed, "It is a great pleasure to meet you, gentlemen. May I ask, what is your family relationship to the mandarin?"

"Of course," Chang replied with a barely suppressed laugh, "we are cousins."

Alexandra laughed heartily, and the three men all joined her. It was a standard Chinese joke that anyone less close than a sibling, spouse, or parent was a cousin by default. She was pleased that they laughed. Men seldom laugh with anyone but well-trusted family members. She took it as good joss and a positive harbinger of things to come.

The mandarin said to Alexandra, "We have done some research on you, Daughter. You are known as an able sailor, an excellent fighter and leader of men. You had your captain's papers when you were still a girl. You have done successful business with the East India Company and with Jardine-Matheson. It is said that you are on friendly terms with the taipan. For that reason, I and these friends of mine believe we can do business with each other which will bring profit to all and will benefit our family tong."

"I would be most privileged to be considered part of the Wáng Family Tong. I look forward to proving myself. I also seek to put my money in safe places and to earn profit from my investments. I trust that I can work with you to benefit each of us."

She was now less the demure younger sister and more the business woman who would not settle for disrespect. She approached the subject adroitly and with a degree of circumlocution, but she was determined to be treated with respect and to make a profit equal to her efforts, just as was expected by every man in the room.

"You do yourself credit by your candor," the mandarin said. "We agree to the principles you describe. It is time for us to become specific. Mr. Zhang is best acquainted with maritime business. He will present the proposal."

Mr. Zhang was tall for a Chinese, and his dress was the most western of the three men in the room. He had adopted the western custom of shaving his face and keeping his dark hair short and neatly combed. He had on a suit that would be stylish in New York, London, Shanghai, or Tokyo. It was gray with faint pin stripes and no cuffs, a very new—even avant-guard look—which made him stand out in a group. He had wide set eyes, a large nose, and a cleft dimple in his chin. He appeared to be rich and wise, a good appearance to have among Chinese men.

"We propose," he said, "that you invest your money to buy two of our ships. Both are sturdy cargo vessels well tried at sea. The ownership will be registered in Hong Kong, where there is no law against the ownership of property by women. Perhaps you remember the famous lady pirate Zheng Shi?"

"I have had dealings with her personally."

"So, we hear. We learned of your exploits from a handsome American navy officer by the name of Captain Oliver MacTavish."

Alexandra's eyes lit up when Oliver's name was mentioned. It embarrassed her that the observant Chinese men did not fail to register the emotional nuance.

"Sadly, you cannot make the ownership here in Australia. We can make the purchase for you, do the work of getting the documents in order, and find reliable crews—all in Hong Kong. I hardly need tell you that we have men of Wáng Family Tong who will serve as officers. We guarantee their character and competence. You will put up the initial funds in full. After that, we will share the profits and costs on a sixty-five to thirty-five percent basis favoring us, because we shall do the majority of the work."

Alexandra waited for a few moments with bowed head.

"Sixty to forty favoring me, because I will be taking the most risk."

The men looked soberly at each other. None of them had ever haggled with a woman, especially not with a formidable one like this young Russian woman. Thoughts flashed through each of the men's minds during this disconcerting confrontation: Zhang's thought harked back to Confucian writings, "*The Book of Articles and Words Explanation tells us that the meaning of woman comes from the word 'submission'. Does she not know her place?*"

Mr. Liu considered Alexandra's proposal to be impertinent, "*The father is the god in the eyes of the son, so is the husband in the eyes of the wife*". *Has no one taught her?* Mandarin *Wáng* fretted in his mind, "*perhaps I have been hasty in being so generous to this round-eye girl. She seems not to have had drummed into her head the moral code for women—the 'Three Obediences and Four Virtues'. On the other hand, I must admit to myself that if she cannot negotiate with strength with we men who favor her, can we expect her to prevail in the open market?*"

Wáng Caihong struggled to keep her thoughts and feelings from showing on her face or in her mannerisms. "*I care for her as a sister, but Alexandra appears to be going down a road that leads away from tradition and may cause ill will in the family if she does not soon see the error of her ways. If she is to be accepted even as a visitor, she must outwardly show the three obediences; she must indicate that she can comply with the time-honored traditional role of women—"Be obedient to your father before marriage, your husband after marriage, and your son when the husband dies." That takes time in a well-run family, and she has been reared by barbarians. She continues this haggling at her peril."*

Alexandra sat placidly with her hands in her lap. It was for the men to make the next move in this nuanced emotional chess game. Much was at stake.

Zhang blinked first, "Perhaps as a demonstration of our good family will, we could offer an arrangement of fifty:fifty. That seems more than fair, does it not, lovely lady?"

Alexandra pondered briefly, "when I first met with you I felt a strong duty to myself as a mere woman to hold out for sixty or even sixty-five percent because it is my true belief that my life's work and savings are under threat in these difficult times. I have been to sea, and I have been in combat at sea. I know first-hand the risks. But...I also know the value of family and of long-time relationships which even out the profits and losses and the apparent greater compromises made by one side or another."

The mandarin thought, *"she is weakening and will go for Zhang's fifty-fifty. I had thought she would hold out longer."*

"I will settle here and now for fifty-five for me and forty-five for you gentlemen because you and I both know that is more than fair. I am sure you would feel guilt and loss of face if you looked into the mirror and saw a man who bullied his weak and defenseless sister. Consider that my family members; it is my final offer."

Caihong's face was tranquil and expressionless. She kept her eyes down as a good woman should do, but the steel in her spine was evident to each of the three hardened businessmen and the daughter of the mandarin who had sat through innumerable such negotiations over the decades since her girlhood. In the back reaches of her mind, she secretly rooted for Alexandra, but also feared that contention might be the result.

The mandarin, Zhang, and Liu looked to each other. None of them gave a positive or a negative nod. On a day of such things, Mandarin Wáng broke tradition and shocked everyone in the room by asking his faithful and wise daughter what she thought.

Caihong's heart skipped a beat...then another. She gathered her courage. She had never been asked to give her opinion except in very private business meetings with her esteemed father. She struggled to find the right words.

"Venerable Father, Lady, and Gentlemen, we are living in a changing time. Girls go to school. Unmarried women work without supervision by a man from the family. Married women go so far as to obtain professional degrees to become doctors, solicitors, and business owners. It is not so great a stretch in these unusual times to accept that a very intelligent and capable young woman could succeed in a man's world. I believe the time has come to test the hypothesis. Give Alexandra what she wants and let her prove herself. I would wager that it will be profitable not only for her but for the tong in the days to come."

She bowed low and let her hair fall forward to hide her face. She worked to control her breathing.

The three men looked soberly at one another, then, as with one accord, they stood up from their chairs and walked to where Alexandra was sitting. She stood and waited expectantly. The mandarin gave a small quick bow and extended his right hand. Alexandra took it and gave it a firm squeeze and a shake. Then she placed her left hand over her right. The formal ceremony of agreement was repeated with the two other men and with Caihong.

"Done," said Mandarin Wáng.

Three weeks later, the three men called on Alexandra at the Grand Hotel. They all climbed into Mr. Zhang's modern large Berlin carriage and drove through the crowded streets to the harbor. Alexandra helped Mandarin Wáng out of the large four wheeled carriage.

"Mind your head, Esteemed Father," she urged him with filial gentleness as he alighted; so, he would not catch his head on the frame of the hood.

"You are worse than a nagging wife, Dear New Daughter," he said and both of them smiled broadly at each other.

The four business and family tong members walked slowly up the gang plank and onto the first steam commercial vessel owned by the new association, *The Sydney Cargo Express*. For the record, the tong was the owner; the mandarin the CEO; Alexandra, Liu Chang; and Zhang Jiao-long vice-presidents and Wáng Caihong the secretary. The ship–like the nearly identical vessel owned by the tong–*The Wáng Family Tong Transfer Vessel* was listed with the Hong Kong ship registration system. There were no nationality requirements for officers and crew who serve on Hong Kong registered ships, and nearly every civilized nation in the world accepted the registry. Ownership, registry, and certification of officers did not discriminate against national origin, ethnicity, gender, or religion. Alexandra was legally listed as the captain of the *Sydney Cargo Express* and Messrs Liu and Zhang were listed as co-captains of *The Wáng Family Tong Transfer Vessel.*

Alexandra beamed with pleasure as she set foot on *The Express*—the ship she owned and captained as a matter of public record. That fact gave her the most security of any financial transaction she had entered into in the past five years. The group's tour was the picture of efficiency. Alexandra demonstrated her command of sailing every step of the way. The Chinese crew in their crisp white uniforms and queues shampooed and oiled stood at rigid attention to meet their new captain. The teak decks were polished to mirror brightness; the ship's sails were fully unfurled and were obviously bright new canvass; and the officers and crew bowed as Alexandra reviewed them. To the surprise of everyone, she walked to the rear of the gathered crew, pointed at the youngest man on the back row and directed him to step forward.

He was almost trembling with anxiety.

"What is your name, Sailor?" she asked crisply but gently.

"Chou Yu-en," he answered.

She handed him a short coil of hemp rope, "Yu-en, please tie a bowline on a bight for me," she ordered.

He fumbled for a minute or two but finally accomplished the task. She took back the rope, untied the rope's knot, then tied another bowline on a bight in seven seconds—so quickly that the observers could not separate the movements of her nimble fingers. She then tied a reef knot and an anchor bend with the same remarkable facility.

"You did well, Yu-en. You have been well-schooled by your seniors. Continue to practice and seek to teach others to become excellent sailors as you strive to be."

He bowed low, an expression of wonder on his face. There was no doubt about the skill and knowledge of the round-eye woman, and she won the respect of the entire crew.

CHAPTER FIFTY-ONE

AN AUSTRALIAN MARRIAGE

Marriage is like a walk in the park—Jurassic Park

—Anonymous

"A good marriage is one where each partner secretly suspects they got the better deal."

—Anonymous

National Archives of Australia, Victorian Archives Centre, 99 Shiel Street, North Melbourne, Victoria, Australia, November 22, 2014

It seemed to Sister Durrell that she and the other service missionaries had been doing more playing and partying than doing their duties to the Lord and the people of Victoria lately. She thought she was the worst of the bunch because she had been spending so much—too much—time trying to find out all there was to know about the mysterious Alexandra Tarasova-Yusupov. Admittedly, what she had found was significant; she was able add an additional name to Alexandra—Bradshaw. She and Sister Wright almost simultaneously found a record in the archives of a marriage. There was no license or evidence that there was anything of a celebration. The newspapers were all silent. Anyway, their mystery girl was married to Kyle Dewit Herman Bradshaw on June 2nd, 1898. This was recorded in the Records of Proceedings of the Victoria Courts.

The two sister missionaries reported their discovery to the rest of their co-workers: "We have the date- June 2nd, 1898, the place-the Victoria Court House, and the names of the couple–Kyle Dewit Herman Bradshaw and Alexandra Tarasova-Yusupov. We could not find another thing about the marriage, but we are going to look for any issue."

"Sounds like bodily fluids," said Elder Gabler, the group's unofficial joker.

"Oh, silly. That means progeny," said Sister Gabler, always trying to cover for any gaffes committed by her dry-wit joking husband.

"Oh," he said innocently.

It was P-day, and it had to be a brief one because of the evening's plans. The group of sturdy seniors marched to their next walking tour site—the Parliament Gardens and a guided visit to the State Houses of Parliament that they had missed on their first try. One of the church members had offered to show them things they had missed on their previous walks. The first stop with her was into the Royal Arcade to see the statues of Gog and Magog that toll once an hour by the side of Guant's Clock. It was fun–a bit of whimsy–otherwise not prominent in their careful lives. They saw things they missed at St. Patrick's Cathedral, including the statue of Irish patriot Daniel O'Connell standing in the courtyard to honor all the Irish who were so numerous among Australia's early immigrants. They ended their brief tour with a relaxing on-your-own-walk-around in Southgate development with its upscale atmosphere so reminiscent of downtown Salt Lake City or the embarcadero area of San Francisco.

That evening was a farewell party for the Durrells and the Smedleys at the Conservatory Restaurant. The Durrells had completed their eighteen months, and the Smedley's had to return to the states for health reasons. The mood was convivial, something of a bitter-sweet note with a couple going back after a successful mission, a couple returning for serious medical tests, and the remainder left behind not even certain that replacements would be sent. Katherine was anxious that the effort to solve the growing mysteries of Alexandra would simply wither on the vine for lack of encouraging little successes and declining interest.

CHAPTER FIFTY-TWO

FINANCIAL SECURITY

I'm focusing on me. I'm focusing on my family's security, my family's financial security, so that's all I can do.

—Conor McGregor

I need nothing from my companion. No money, no financial security, no emotional support, nothing. All I want is the freedom to be myself.

—Kangana Ranaut

Offices of Jardine, Matheson & Co., 20 Pedder Street, at the corner of Des Voeux Road Central, Hong Kong, China, November 18, 1899

Although historians were not likely to make much out of the meeting that Alexandra was about to attend in the Jardine, Matheson offices that day, it was going to represent a sea change for the peoples of the south and east China coastal cities. Business in the region would never be the same. The meeting was to be held in the strictest of secrecy among men and women for whom business privacy and secrecy was an existential way of life. In the future, Alexandra would never make reference to the Meeting; but the change in the way she did business was enough to cause people who knew her to presume that something dramatic had occurred making this, her last commercial voyage.

Simply seeing the people attending the meeting would alert intelligent observers that something was afoot. No one outside the secretive cabal could have fathomed the reasons why these dedicated enemies and cutthroat competitors were about to meet in collegial harmony. Besides Alexandra Tarasova-Yusupov, Mandarin Wáng Wen Sheng, and Wáng Caihong, his daughter of the Wáng Family Tong, others included Hou Eadric of the criminal enterprise Three Families Tong, Harvey M. Dent of Dent & Co., Patrick Queensbury, representative of the East India Company, Walter David Russell, chief executive of Russell & Co., Wǔ Guóyíng of the Ewo Hong, a Qing dynasty business conglomerate [co-hong] established in Canton—which served as the quasi-Qing government representative, Abram Tarasova representing the Tarasova-Yusupov Co., and Taipan James Matheson of the Jardine-Matheson Co.

The meeting was held with the utmost decorum—no mention of the pet names they had for one another: "Bent" Dent, Jardine, "the Iron-Headed Old Rat" (a name he was proud of since it was Empress Dowager Cixi's descriptor for him), which carried over to the current taipan, James Matheson, "Opium" Russell for Walter David Russell, "Viking Princess" for Alexandra, and "The Hair Man" for her father. There was too much at stake to give minor offense that could rise to divisive retaliation among the thin-skinned group of ego-maniacal introverts and narcissists.

By mutual consent, Patrick Queensbury spoke first. His British East India Company controlled fully half of China's foreign trade—land and sea—mostly owing to his fleet of fast and elegant tea clippers and his dominance of the tea trade.

"Ladies and gentlemen, competitors, opponents, I speak for myself and for the East India Company officially. I hardly need to tell you that we face serious competition, and–more than that–real opposition. The competition comes in the form of trading companies sprouting up like weeds everywhere and all the time. The opposition is almost upon us. Most of you are aware that ships and traders are already here in Hong Kong and Shanghai to break our monopoly–the Canton system—mainly the East India monopoly. We know of the Netherlands, Denmark, Imperial Russia, the upstart United States of America, and free-trader groups from Great Britain itself. The Chinese oppose us on several grounds; they consider it to be in their best interests to trade with many countries and interests; and they steadfastly oppose our opium trade. They have gone so far as to say that opium is a poison for the user and for China itself. Furthermore, they have established the co-hong combination of Chinese commercial companies which receives preferences, even over most preferred nations such as Great Britain.

"The governing board of the British East India Company has studied the situation with great care and at considerable depth. The conclusions reached include that Queen Victoria's government is adamant about opening up commerce here; it is lukewarm at best about the opium trade; and they have already sent a Royal Navy Fleet on its way under the command of Admiral Sir William Heartcliff-Weatherby. The crown now favors Chinese hongs, Hudson's Bay Company, thirteen factories not under our control, Japan, Korea, and Germany; and they are all determined to break our monopoly.

"We meet here today to determine what we must do. Speaking for the British East India Company, we must form our own co-hong and work together; or this time next year, none of our businesses will be still functioning. Let us hear from each of you. What will you do? Will you join our new venture? Will you join the co-hongs of the Chinese or the organizations of the British? Will you try and go it alone? Or will you sell out your holdings to the new co-hong?"

The taipan spoke next with his usual brevity and brusqueness.

"You all know how much I hate the East India Company. Why wuld Aye even think 'o joinin' with those scoundrels? It's simple; Jardine-Matheson will unite with Patrick Queensbury and the accursed East India because it's the only way to survive. 'Tis the worst of options except for all the rest. Aye am hopin' it'll be temporary."

Mandarin Wáng, "Opium" Russell, Yury Golocrispin for the Empire of Russia, and "Bent" Dent, all gave brief statements agreeing that they would join the co-hong in order to survive. Alexandra stated simply that she would not enter into the compact; Hou Eadric similarly refused—in his case because he knew that the rest of the partners would vote against him joining because of his infamous reputation as a criminal; and Wŭ Guóyíng of the Ewo Hong politely declined because his government would not allow his co-hong to do so.

A month later, the new co-hong was in place, still dominated by the British East India and Jardine-Matheson as a close second. The *London Times* reported that the Chinese Merchant Fleet had been sold to Russell and Company for three million dollars. Russell brought the fleet under the banner of the new co-hong for four million U.S. dollars in order to stave off bankruptcy because of it's three-million-dollar indebtedness. Once again, Alexandra made the decision that saved her and the Wáng Family Tong from financial disaster. The co-hong eventually failed because the separate members could not get along. The British East India and Jardine-Matheson Companies survived and went their own ways. Great Britain herself suffered a serious deflation because it had been forced to go back to a gold standard and had an enormous trade deficit.

Mandarin Wáng allowed Alexandra to sell her fleet—now twelve steamers—back to the family tong for a small profit. He believed in the new co-hong, but she was adamant that it was in her best interests to leave the co-hong and, moreover, the shipping business. She privately believed that the shipping business was in for serious decline because of the excess number of companies now involved. It turned out that she was correct. The capricious Chinese empress vetoed further access to the Chinese market causing the crash. Alexandra turned her sell-out into other investments which made millions, and the other attendees at the meeting eventually lost millions. Hou Eadric was hanged from the gates of Hong Kong city a year later for his crimes associated with the financial manipulations of the Empress's funds.

CHAPTER FIFTY-THREE

APPROACHING A NEW WORLD, A NEW LIFE

Life is a series of natural and spontaneous changes. Don't resist them–that only creates sorrow. Let reality be reality. Let things flow naturally forward in whatever way they like.

—Lao Tzu

"Stepping onto a brand-new path is difficult, but not more difficult than remaining in a situation, which is not nurturing to the whole woman."

—Maya Angelou

Number 8, Chapel Street, Victoria Colony, Melbourne, Australia, January 23, 1896

Because of the success in divesting herself of her shipping interests in a period of maritime business chaos and falling profits, Alexandra kept one of the steamships as a personal yacht—an unlikely bit of vanity for her—and re-christened it, *The Alexandra*, with no apology or hypocrisy of false modesty. There was still the nagging problem of being unable to buy or sell anything in Australia without a husband. Telling the truth about her marriage to Prince Boris Yusupov would put the kibosh on any further effort to marry successfully in Australia. She had long ago determined not to do anything so foolish; so, she began plotting a way to marry, to remain independent, and to avoid any complications of a new relationship all at the same time—a conundrum with no easy solution in sight.

No one came courting, and no one was expected. When something finally did transpire, Alexandra put it down to serendipity. Her house on Chapel Street in Melbourne had fallen into a fair measure of seediness since she had not been able to keep up with the maintenance, repairs, and the need for additions while living in Sydney. Correcting the bit of unsightliness in the middle of the block in Melbourne became her vocation and her avocation during the preceding six months.

Alexandra met the foreman for her project at a job fair in the city. He was minding an exhibit for one of the large development construction companies and was singing *The Bastard from the Bush*, a distinctly bawdy ballad not fit for polite society. Alexandra began to laugh and realized it had been a long time since she had done so. He took a glancing look at her and continued his impromptu performance as if he was completely unaware of his audience by singing *Go the Shears, The Old Bullock Dray,* and *Euabalong Ball*. Finally, as a tribute to his virtuoso impromptu performance, she laughed so hard she had to sit down.

When she regained control, "Hello, she said.

"G'day," he responded.

"Tell me, please–besides doing opera–do you do repairs, remodeling, or other rather small projects?"

"Well, M'am, it's not grand opera—just Australian ditties; and no, M'am, I only work on large developments. You are not likely to find someone looking for a small kind of a job, what with the boom in housing these days."

She looked disappointed.

"Thank you for your time, Sir." She said, "I wish you well in your pursuits."

"Pardon me; where are my manners? My name is Kyle Dewit Herman Bradshaw."

"Pleased to meet you, Sir. I am Alexandra Yusupov."

"Thank you. I think you are the only person who has even bothered to speak to me today. Truth be known, I am a builder looking for work; and this idleness is nearly driving me out of my mind. I'm no bludger. I tell you, I'm right fair dinkum. Can you tell me about your project?"

"First, are you as good a builder as you are an operatic divo?"

"Better," he said, "and I can prove it."

"References?"

"Better than that. Give me half an afternoon; and I'll take you to see my work; it will be living proof."

"You have piqued my interest. Not a bludger, not on the dole; and you look reasonably presentable. When will you be available?"

"Not to be impertinent; M'am, but I have a question of my own. Do you have the money for a bang-up job?"

"I do."

"What man owns the property?"

"It is owned by the Wáng Family Tong of which I am a ranking member."

"Well, aren't you one with surprises, Mrs. Yusupov? I would have bet the farm—but maybe not quite the house yet—that you were Irish or Scottish. I never would have guessed that you were a Chinee."

"You would have lost the bet on my ethnicity. We all have our secrets, Mr. Bradshaw."

"Please call me Kyle."

"All right, Kyle. Let's get down to a little business; all right with you? And, I'm Alexandra Yusupov."

For the next three-quarters of an hour they traded information and developed an early and tenuous level of trust. She relented and asked him to call her Alexandra. They agreed to meet the following day at Alexandra's property on Chapel Street.

The day began early.

"Let's have a Captain Cook," Kyle said.

She nodded in agreement that they needed to have a look, as much as she dreaded having anyone look at her run-down property.

Kyle picked up Alexandra in his "vintage"—as he described it, but "seedy" as Alexandra viewed it—forty-year-old curricle. It was a two-wheel open carriage fashionable and popular with the young sporty set of that now bygone era. The two horses were beautiful matching bays, sleek and eager. They first drove to No. 8 Chapel Street and stopped in front of Alexandra's house. In the stark light of the cloudless morning, she was instantly aware that the place was dilapidated and in need of more than repair or even serious renovation. Kyle was gentleman enough not to say anything right off. They took a tour of the grounds which were strewn with trash and garbage, the leavings of hobos who had taken the place over several years ago during the bust. The backyard's vegetation was entirely weeds and stood almost six feet high. Lean-to board huts lay in shambles or had fallen over with the winds of winter. Alexandra felt like she might cry.

The tour of the house itself was worse. Inside and out, mold had infested the walls and decorations. There was termite damage in the supports and joists above the concrete foundation, and parts of the floor and ceilings had caved in. There were several areas where the transients had started fires using Alexandra's expensive furniture as kindling, and destroying parts of walls, floors, and ceilings in addition. Rats–dead and alive–were the only long-term occupants. The fixtures of the kitchen and the fireplaces had been torn away by vandals, and would-be artists had painted crude, vividly colored, drawings on the walls and in the stairwells, most of which were anatomically accurate pornography. Kyle quickly escorted Alexandra away from the sordid gallery and the decrepit interior.

"Say it, Kyle," Alexandra said somberly.

"The truth?"

"As bluntly as necessary."

"It's a dog's breakfast. There is nothing salvageable about it. The house is uninhabitable and unfixable. The city building code would never grant a certificate of occupancy no matter how much we—I mean, you—put into it. The raw property is worth more that the house and the property as they now stand. Sorry to say it, Alexandra. You would be better off to tear it down; plow up the ground; and start again from scratch. I know a little something about this town. The neighborhood is no longer the best and might not even be really safe for a fine lady like yourself. Maybe it would be best to get another plot of land and start over again."

He looked at Alexandra with sympathy.

She said, "Another victim of the gold and land busts. I've seen plenty of them. However, my friend, I have another option."

Alexandra had purchased a Collins Street property during the hey-day of "Marvelous Melbourne"–the gold boom era–as the site of her future permanent home. She now had the resources to make that happen. Kyle D.H. Bradshaw was a long-time resident of Melbourne and seasoned builder during the booms and busts of Melbourne's turbulent history; so, he was suitably impressed with the location.

He expressed that impression by citing the old saw that the three most important things in real estate are, "location, location, and location. And, this, Alexandra, is a location!"

Collins street was laid out in 1837 in Mornington Peninsula–south of Melbourne proper–and became the city's main street soon thereafter. At the western end of the street was Batman's Hill, named for the Tasmanian adventurer and grazier–a person who rears or fattens cattle or sheep for market—named John Batman. In 1896, when Alexandra and Kyle were planning to build, it was still a major street in center of Melbourne, even more important than it was in the early nineteenth century. Alexandra's property—two city blocks on Collins Street beginning from the intersection with Elizabeth Street in fashionable East Melbourne–had never had a building on it, unlike the rest of eastern Collins Street which was becoming known for its grand Victorian home architecture. The eastern end of Collins Street was known locally as the 'Paris End' due to its slavish copying of French architecture and the affectations of the inhabitants.

"I know a construction company that would buy your Chapel Street property, Alexandra. Would you like me to contact them?" Kyle asked.

"I guess I will have a big loss selling the place now and in its present condition."

"I'm afraid so—maybe fifty percent off what it cost you to build it."

Alexandra shook her head, then said, "Go ahead, Kyle. Give it your best try."

"I will. I still have contacts and am owed a few favors. I'll see if I can call in a marker or two. No worries, mate, she'll be right."

"That would be helpful, and I would be grateful."

"What are mates for?" he asked, making a presumption.

She responded, "Indeed, I think it is accurate that we are becoming friends. I have a pattern of being a good friend, and I seldom am on the receiving end. It will take some getting used to, Kyle."

He gave her a toothsome smile and patted her back, the first time he had touched her. She smiled back and patted his hand as he withdrew it.

They spent the afternoon looking at other properties, none of which were the least bit enticing. It was evening before they decided to call it a day.

Kyle said, "Well, Boss Lady, I think we know which property we want to build on. Think we should apply for a building permit tomorrow?"

"I do. I am too tired to think anymore today."

"And, I'm hungry," Kyle said, "Would you be my guest for dinner at the Middle Park Hotel in Port Phillip? They've got pretty good tucker there."

Alexandra hesitated a moment. She scanned his face and decided that this was a business dinner, or, at worst, a gesture of friendship.

"*How bad could that be?*" she thought.

"All right. I'm famished. If you would be so kind as to take me back to the hotel; so, I can freshen up. I won't take but a minute."

"Take all the time you want. I have a change of clothes in the back of the carriage. I will pop into the hotel's dressing room and wash up a bit and change into fancier clothes."

They were both somewhat excited and anxious. Was this a date, or just having a meal with a new friend at the end of a long day? Alexandra was not sure what to wear, whether to offer to pay—as in a Dutch treat—or what obligations she might be incurring. She realized that–despite her years in Australia–she was not sure of where she fitted in or about what passed for etiquette in this strange country. She decided that Kyle Bradshaw was a nice enough man, and an honest one. She would just be forthright and ask him what was appropriate in the place the Aussies called "down under".

True to her promise, Alexandra dressed in a simple evening dress and no jewelry and hurried down the large curving hotel staircase. Kyle was waiting, and he was dressed in a long-sleeve patterned shirt, no tie, and a pair of clean khaki slacks. He had slicked back his thick unruly brown hair which still glistened with water. His face was strong and bore lines of too much time in the sun. Unlike many of the Australians she had encountered–especially men–his broad smile revealed a full set of big white teeth. He was clean shaven, an improvement over his appearance during the day. He had a large square jaw with a striking butt chin–which–along with his strong hazel eyes, were his most striking features.

Kyle helped her into the curricle; and they drove across town to Canterbury Road in Middle Park, Port Phillip. He stopped in front of the attractive Middle Park Hotel and had a valet park the carriage and feed the horses. He took her arm, and they walked into the hotel and met the maître d who escorted them to their seats in the grand dining room.

The head waiter was at Kyle's side as soon as the maître d left them, "My name is Gerard," he said, "would you care for an appetizer?"

Kyle looked at Alexandra with a question. She shook her head.

"No thanks," Kyle said. "May we just have the dinner menu, Mate?"

"Of course, Sir. May I recommend the WH barramundi?"

"Sounds great to me," said Alexandra.

"Yes, let's have it. Is it still the best fish in Australia? Better than the John Dory? I mean the fish and not the gossip?" asked Kyle not sure that Gerard knew Aussie talk sufficiently well.

"Indeed, it is. Are you hungry tonight?"

"I certainly am," said Alexandra.

Kyle liked that. She was no shrinking violet, more of an Aussie girl than he had expected.

"Me, too. What do you suggest, Mate?"

"A side of tuna tartar. It goes well with the mashed potatoes and mixed vegetables."

"Bring it on."

"Some wine?"

"You choose. That all right with you, Alexandra?"

She nodded.

"I think you would like our local shiraz-based sparkly from the old Auldana winery in the Adelaide foothills, I'll bring a chilled bottle."

"I'm thirsty, too," Alexandra said quietly to Kyle. "The wine or local champagne sounds like fun, don't you think?"

While they waited, Alexandra decided to get out a question that had been bothering her.

"Kyle, should we share the costs? I imagine this will be pretty expensive."

He started to speak but damped down a sharp reply deciding that she was just trying to treat him as an equal—one of those inbred Australian customs.

"No," he said, "let me play the gentleman this once."

Enough said. She nodded and smiled at him, acknowledging his place as the man. He appreciated that and smiled back to let her know that he understood her interest in equality and all that Aussie stuff.

The basic rules of Australian social etiquette do not relate to which spoon to use or how a fork should be held. It was considered arrogant to be identified as the one who should be served first. From the beginning in a country whose main first white inhabitants were convicts, most of Australia's rules related to expressing equality. Australians wanted to be treated as equal irrespective of their social, racial, or financial background. Otherwise, almost everything else was acceptable and that appealed to Alexandra after her upbringing in stuffy Russian society.

The tuna tartare came first as an appetizer, and the two hungry mates wolfed it down and quaffed their first goblets of the local bubbly. Alexandra had eaten barramundi before, but this was the best in her experience. She was hungry and all but licked her plate which made Kyle laugh out loud.

She said, "Well, Mate, you handle those big mitts for hands pretty well for a carpenter."

He laughed and came back with a rejoinder, "And you, wee matey, seem to be able to drink a pub crawler under the table. Pretty good for a Chinee."

They both laughed somewhat conspiratorially. She had passed the standard test of Australian society.

"Alexandra you are a good old girl. You give as good as you get when you take the piss."

"*Takin' the piss*" is a quintessentially Australian phrase applied to making a usually crude joke about someone at the table or an ethnic group. For example, had her Russian friends been present, they might have asked her, "Why ever would you want to marry such a low-life bugger?" when that man was present. Of course, the friends wouldn't actually mean that he was a low life bugger. On the contrary, they would just be trying to say that they think he is a good bloke.

Alexandra felt herself to be glowing, just a little. Whether it was the wine, the heat of the room, or her excitement over being asked out to a dinner with a strikingly handsome and fetching man, she was unsure. She muttered to herself that she was acting like a girl. And she rather liked the idea.

For dessert they shared a large New Zealand Pavlova made with a meringue shell, whipped cream, and fruit—one of New Zealand's national desserts. Kyle also ordered a dessert wine for them to share.

"What is your suggestion for a dessert wine?" he asked Gerard, the head waiter.

"Are you feeling adventurous, Mate?" Gerard responded and gave a fulsome smile to Alexandra.

This was getting to be more fun than she could remember for a long time

"We have a delicious sweet little something which is made from grapes infected with what is called 'noble rot' a grape grown in the

Riverina Vineyard in New South Wales. It is like a sauterne from France. Ours is called De Bortoli Noble One Botrytis Semillon."

"That's a mouthful, Mate," said Kyle, who had probably already had one too many.

"Are you game?" asked Gerard.

"Aye, Matey, I think we are. All right with me and my sheila."

Alexandra nodded agreeably.

They finished off the bottle, and Alexandra was certain that she had had more than she should have. She still had her wits about her, though. She prepared herself for a possible test to come. Kyle was more than a little drunk and would believe that her defenses were down. She determined to put an end to any advances that might be coming her way that night, even though she was not altogether certain that she wouldn't welcome them. It had been a long time. A very long time.

She need not have concerned herself. Kyle–though unsteady and tipsy–was a perfect gentleman. He drove home at a sensible speed; fortunately, the horses were not impaired; and they maintained a straight route back to The Hotel Windsor on Spring Street without the slightest incident. Kyle pushed himself out of the curricle and struggled to walk around the carriage to the other side to help his new mate out, like a gentleman should. The ruts in the road, and the severe distance around the entire coach proved to be too much; and he faltered half way around and had to lean on the side of the carriage.

Alexandra tried not to laugh at his slapstick performance, but it was too much for her; and she laughed until tears rolled down her face. Kyle looked at her forlornly, but could not help himself; so, he sat on the road and laughed until his belly hurt. Alexandra walked herself up to the lobby and arranged for one of the valets to drive the poor man home.

That night she slept like a proverbial log and awakened the next morning with a nasty hangover headache. She ordered a beer as 'the hair of the dog that bit you' to lessen the effects of her night of indiscretion. She took a long shower, rubbed her skin to a definite pink with a rough Turkish towel, and made a game effort to get down a solid breakfast. It was still early enough for her to make a try at a bit of self-analysis.

She sat in the lobby with an hour to go before Kyle came to escort her to the real estate office. She made an effort to read *The Argus* newspaper but found the combination of double vision and inability to concentrate too much for her efforts to glean any news. She was able to ponder what she seemed to be getting herself into. She liked Kyle but admitted that she did not really know him or that much about him. She resolved to remedy that starting that very day. She knew she was harboring serious secrets, and she thought about the possibility of informing this man of her past if they became serious. She quickly dropped that idea. Her most important thought was about how she would convey to him what she wanted out of a marriage—a status she had to have in order to prosper in Australia—and how he might take it. She would eventually be proposing a highly unusual marriage arrangement if their relationship got that far.

For the time being, she decided just to roll with it and have some fun, something lacking in her experience the last several years.

CHAPTER FIFTY-FIVE

ANOTHER MARRIAGE?

Bigamy is having one wife too many. Monogamy is the same.
—Oscar Fingal O'Flahertie Wills Wilde

Bigamy is the only crime in America where two rites make a wrong.

—Bob Hope

National Archives of Australia, Victorian Archives Centre, 99 Shiel Street, North Melbourne, Victoria State, Australia, November 8, 2015

Newcomers to the Mission–Elder Samuel and Ethyl Breckinridge from Toronto–were avid genealogists on their own time, working for Ancestry.com as professionals before being called on a mission for the church. They were a perfect fit—everything good that everyone said about Canadians–their affability, calm temperament, slow to anger, eager to please, good education, conservative devotion to their church, and an avid curiosity about the world around them. Someone told them about the research project to find out all that could be found regarding a mysterious woman called Alexandra Tarasova-Yusupov. They never watched television and were not particularly keen readers; so, they settled right in to the search.

Ethyl had learned that Alexandra had been married, although there were no certain records of a marriage yet documented that she could find. She laboriously scoured the New South Wales and Victoria provincial marriage records with the presumption that she must have married sometime in her late teens or early twenties as most girls did in the nineteenth century. She knew Alexandra's birthdate: 5 April, 1861 in Balagansk, Far Eastern Russia. She did the math and began to search records in Victoria from 1875 to 1896 when she would have been thirty-five years old. Nothing. She looked in Irkutsk oblast in Russia during the same years. Nothing. She was about to give up; but she decided that their Alexandra may have been something of a nonconformist; so, she searched later years; and finally–in the records for 1899–she found a verifiable document. Verifiable because the missionaries already had a request for probate filed by a man stating that he was Alexandra's husband, Kyle Dewit Herman Bradshaw, in 1931.

The marriage date listed in the probate request for Bradshaw and Alexandra Yusupov was 4 September, 1900. The missionaries knew that this was one of the major milestones in her life, but it also brought up certain questions uncomfortable to the pious family-oriented Mormon missionaries: Did she ever get a divorce from her first husband? She had children by the first husband. What became of them? The missionaries dedicated themselves to finding the answers to those questions—or else they would have to conclude that their sweet Alexandra was a bigamist. That was unacceptable.

The records experts were tired missionaries by afternoon on this P-day. They were determined to wake back up with their weekly walking tour through Melbourne. Their planning took them on a bus to East Melbourne to see the step back into the Victorian era with its enclave of Victorian homes, neat inviting streets, pubs, B&Bs, Darling Square, and for a stop at the graceful bluestone mansion of the Anglican Archbishop of Melbourne. They wanted to try to learn something about one of Australia's mysterious sporting obsessions, cricket. They visited the MCG [Melbourne Cricket Ground] and were given a tutorial on the game in the library of the museum. They were all more confused about cricket when they came out than when they entered the building. They were pretty much lost after the first statement by the librarian, "Cricket is a bat and ball game." Terms such as runs, innings, bowl and field, bowler delivering the ball, hitting the stumps, dislodging the ball, leg before wicket, Twenty20 (twenty overs), to say nothing of the labyrinthine Laws of Cricket would have to be fodder for study some other day.

Elder Glen Gabler said, "I guess I'm just not smart enough to play cricket."

This said by an M.D., PhD.

CHAPTER FIFTY-SIX

AUSTRALIAN ADVENTURE

"You are forgiven for your happiness and your successes successes only if you generously consent to share them."
—Albert Camus

The honest prenuptial agreement: I'll do everything for you; you'll become too demanding, fulfilling none of my needs. I'll leave and blame you.
—Cathy Thorne

Number 1-8, Collins Street, Victoria Colony, Melbourne, January 3, 1898

Alexandra described her successful year in Australia—1897—in a rare letter to her parents in Vladivostok as being the most successful financially and socially in her recent memory. She completed her new house with the able efforts of her construction foreman Kyle DH Bradshaw. She opened up her usually very closed personal life to Abram and Irina to let them know that she and Mr. Bradshaw were "seeing each other". In fact, they had been a popular and well-known couple in Melbourne circles for nearly a year.

She knew her father would be pleased to know that she had no debt associated with the construction and that her finances were sufficiently in the black to allow her to purchase a small race horse farm on the outskirts of the city, a share in the city's opera company and its theater, its first telephone exchange and partnered with John Jones in the Sydney to Melbourne Stagecoach Line which was partially subsidized by the government of New South Wales. Unable to maintain her Australian façade of humility, she admitted to having purchased the latest and finest Cobb & Co. Brougham—the handsome four-wheel iteration–as her everyday vehicle. It was shiny black with gold trim, and a chauffeur kept it in mint condition. She noted parenthetically that she had six servants and a matched pair of the best black Friesian light but powerful draft horses from the Netherlands. Her closing remark was an expression of hope that everything was going well for them and would they write back to her at their earliest convenience.

She never received a reply—not that she expected one given the dubious reputation of the Australian postal system and the even more questionable transoceanic delivery system. It also occurred to her that her parents had written her off entirely–as had her husband, and apparently, her children, by Boris. She wasted very little time feeling sorry for herself; it was the way of the world and the pressing needs they were experiencing in a precarious part of the world.

The rather casual nature of her relationship had to change if Kyle was to be the useful man Alexandra needed for her ambitious business ventures. Alexandra was determined to be the one governing the nature of her connectiveness with this man. She listed her basic requirements in order of priority as: Kyle's usefulness as a man to serve as the titular head of the family in order to conduct business; her ability to obtain a contractual arrangement which allowed her to use her significant fortune to her own advantage but under Kyle's name—as annoying as that would be at best; his appropriateness as a social partner; and last, his contribution as a...de facto husband in the physical realm of things. She—like her Victorian sisters around the civilized world–could not bring herself even to think of descriptions relating to the bedroom. Finally, she knew she had to have this conversation with Kyle soon and frankly before the courtship period began to wane.

Alexandra arranged for two meetings with Kyle—the first, a formal business meeting complete with lawyers, and the second, an informal social—even romantic—"assignation" in the form of a rather lavish and private picnic.

Kyle provided the segue for the business meeting.

"Alexandra," he said, "we are in business together on a loose—too loose—basis. It is apparent that you are the financial partner, and I provide the day-to-day work of making things happen. You and I get along well. I appreciate that you don't treat me like a hired hand or a servant, but we are not yet actually partners. Don't you think we should make some sort of contract?"

"Thanks for bringing that up, Kyle. I have given the subject quite a bit of thought. I trust you to keep my confidences, and I am going to share one with you now that should probably lead us to make a formal business contract as you suggest. You know that I have money, but I am sure you are not aware of how much. I also know that you are aware of how difficult it is for a woman to function in a business world—a man's world, which I hate. I have some very definite ideas about how my wealth and your expertise can be joined in a mutually beneficial business partnership. I would like us to meet with the lawyers at McInerny, Martin, and Neal, Solicitors and Barristers who have handled some of my important matters. Would that suit you?"

"I guess we're going to be partners; so, let's be businesslike. But, Alexandra, I don't know about you; but it's more than that for me. You might not like to hear it, but I've fallen for you. I can be just a construction bloke if that's what you want, but I'd rather you'd be my sheila."

"I want that, too, Kyle; but it's more complicated. We need to work out some things for the long term. Will you do that for me?"

"Anything."

"Then I want to do something for you. Not to be businesslike exactly, but I want to be serious about our relationship. The feelings part; so, I have arranged for us to have a picnic—just the two of us. I'd rather do that after the business contract meeting, all right?"

"Not to repeat myself, but 'anything.'"

Two days later, Alexandra and Kyle sat in the comfortable offices of McInerny, Martin, and Neal, Solicitors and Barristers. It was apparent that the firm was successful: the furniture was very comfortable and obviously expensive. The hardwood floors were polished to a gleam and partially covered with hand knotted Asian or African carpets; Alexandra guessed that they were from Morocco because of the signature pattern of the wooden windows of a harem. The receptionist's desk was beautiful and obviously French. The receptionist was a stiff, middle-aged, fleshy, no-nonsense, matron who told them that they would be admitted to Mr. Martin's office in a few minutes. She offered them Evian water and frog cakes shipped to Melbourne from Balfour's Bakery in Adelaide.

Quentin Martin invited them into his office which was a monument to clutter. If there was a filing system, neither Alexandra nor Kyle could decipher it. The man himself was the opposite—small, fussily neat, and dressed in a Henry Pool & Co. of Saville Row Regency suit, vest, custom white fine Egyptian cotton shirt, bark colored herring bone spats, and wing-tip shoes. His attempt at sporting a dapper Victorian gentleman's mustache and beard failed for want of thick enough facial hair. The beadiness of his eyes was unfortunately accentuated by the presence of pince-nez glasses pinched onto his oversized nose.

"Welcome, Mrs. Yusupov, your business reputation precedes you. I am not familiar with Mr…Bradshaw. I am Quentin Martin solicitor-at-law at your service, Sir."

"For the present, Mr. Martin, we would appreciate it if you would address your conversation to Mrs. Yusupov. We seek advice on how to avoid the awkwardness and inconvenience of the bias in the law towards females," responded Kyle.

"Then, Mrs. Yusupov, why don't you tell me what is on your mind. First of all, would you prefer to speak to me alone?"

"Everything to be discussed in this room today involves both of us, Mr. Martin. We will both be present throughout."

"Then–by all means–let us commence, Madam."

"I will be brief. Mr. Bradshaw and I are considering marriage. As awkward as it is to talk about, there is a considerable disparity between our financial holdings, with mine being the larger. Australian commercial law discriminates against women and makes it difficult if not impossible for women to enter into business transactions without doing so behind a man as titular head of a family. I have every intention of doing business: buying and selling, building, striking legal contracts for investments, and the like. We are not crusaders. The law will be changed one day but not before I am too old to benefit, I fear."

"Well and unfortunately stated, Mrs. Yusupov."

"Yes…so we wish to marry and to conduct married and family life like anyone else, except for certain financial activities. We ask you to tell us how to have me invest my money in my projects under the umbrella of Mr. Bradshaw as my husband. I wish to be able to make day-to-day decisions such as land purchase, hiring and firing, and determining the course to be taken in my businesses. So that you will not think me selfish and unfeeling about my husband-to-be's interests, we wish to set aside a portion of our mutual assets for Mr. Bradshaw to control for his own business enterprises, and a third account for our mutual living and pleasure."

"Mr. Bradshaw, does this concept of Mrs. Yusupov's meet with your approval?"

"Thank you for asking. Currently, the lady is very wealthy on her own. After we are married, I am sure that our mutual business interests will also be mutually profitable. I am a patient man. We can enjoy each other's company and enjoy an affluent lifestyle for a long-married life. So, yes, I am in agreement. I have to ask Mrs. Yusupov: this is a bit sudden. Are you sure that you want to marry me?"

"Of course, I do, silly. It has been as obvious as the nose on your face for months now. Today is just the business day, and tomorrow we will see to the proposal and the romance," she said with a self-assured laugh.

He responded with a large grin.

Mr. Martin was thoughtful and waited three or four minutes to digest what he had just learned and to think about how to handle his clients' problem.

"I must say this is rather unusual, despite the general issue for women… for families, in the nation. Our laws are more than a little backward, as you know. The solution is not really so difficult, however. First of all, we are not about to launch a referendum on an entrenched policy; even if we should win, it would take years and years. Secondly, we will have to draft what is called in the law, a "prenuptial agreement". Are either of you familiar with the legal concept?"

"I'm not," said Alexandra.

"I have heard of it, but isn't it usually a protection for marital partners so that the rich husband can't be fleeced by his younger and attractive wife; and the wife can't be booted out of the marriage with all of its mutual benefits without her receiving some money or land, that sort of thing?"

"That's it in a nutshell, Mr. Bradshaw. I can draw that up. In order for the document to be helpful rather than hurtful, both of you should be involved in every line and paragraph of the agreement. With that agreement, and with the further agreement that Mrs. Yusupov—then Mrs. Bradshaw—can use your name to do business without tedious meddling by other parties, including the government, making life inconvenient. Shall I begin to draft the documents?"

"Yes," Alexandra and Kyle replied at the same time.

As they walked back to their carriage, Kyle asked Alexandra bluntly, "Do you intend to treat me as a man, and not a kind of a shill, Alexandra? I need to know that. We can enjoy your money, but I am not a gold digger who would trade his manhood for a...mess of pottage, as the Bible put it."

"I knew this would be very awkward. But you must understand that I was treated very poorly by my late husband in Russia. I have felt very vulnerable ever since whenever I even thought about the possibility of marrying again."

"I understand. I do love you, Alexandra; and I am determined to make our relationship work."

"Well, Kyle, you haven't even proposed yet."

"I rather thought your speech to Mr. Martin presumed that."

"You don't know much about girls, apparently, Mr. Bradshaw. I am down deep a romantic. I expect a beautiful proposal, maybe even tomorrow. You know, flowers, down-on-one knee, hands imploring, a pledge of undying troth...all of that. The money is an incidental."

"Well, my dear, I will have to get my gumption up and prepare for a romantic day to end all days."

CHAPTER FIFTY-SEVEN

TOP OF THE WORLD

"The money you make is a symbol of the value you create."
—Idowu Koyenikan, *Wealth for All:*
Living a Life of Success at the Edge of your Ability

Boredom always precedes a period of great creativity.
—Robert M. Pirsig

Number 1-8, Collins Street, Victoria State, Melbourne, Commonwealth of Australia, March 30, 1912

The years…the decades…passed with alarming speed Alexandra mused, as she took inventory of herself in the foyer gilt framed mirror. She had been married to Kyle for nearly twelve years. It seemed impossible for her to admit that her second wedding was three children, twenty-five major investment successes, and a wonderful experience of traveling the globe that had taken place in that seemingly brief span. The years had not been particularly unkind to her. She was rich by anyone's calculation. Her husband was still strong, handsome and virile—still a "catch". He had been perfectly decent to her and the children—honest, affable, kind, and funny. In any other ordinary family, he would have been considered a good provider. In fact, they lived on what he brought in; and they lived an affluent life.

Alexandra, however, had accumulated enough of a fortune to be considered a millionaire, i.e., she netted more than a $ million dollars

(AUD) a year and had stable conservative investments with relatively easy liquidity of nearly one hundred million dollars in Sydney and Melbourne alone. She was–by experience–not trusting of banks or even of Australia itself enough to keep her money centralized in any single country or type of investment.

Her accountancy firm—Wilson, Bishop, & Henderson–estimated her total net worth as nearly $ five hundred million AUD or $ three hundred seventy-five million USD. She had seen the handwriting on the wall when the debate began on establishing a national Australian currency. She divested all her provincial and private bank notes in exchange for the new Australian dollars as soon as the *Australian Notes Act of 1910* was passed, and the new ten-shilling notes came off the press and completed her transference when the new security notes were printed. Her safety consciousness prompted her to spread out her investments to China, Russia, Germany, Argentina, Canada, and France. The types of investments ran from currency exchanges, stock and bond holdings, raw real estate and gold and silver bullion hedges against future economic downturns, real estate ownership in housing developments, hotels, factories, clothing businesses, and mining and minerals.

Her fifty-one-year-old reflection in the full-length mirror was no less satisfying, the half-century mark notwithstanding. She had a trim, still rather voluptuous, form; clear—largely unwrinkled—white skin; a full head of long lustrous natural blond hair; she was not a bluehair yet. She cut a fine figure in the latest fashion. She could still turn a wandering eye towards her "well-turned ankles". She had never strayed and never intended to. Kyle had admitted to having had one brief fling for which she forgave him, and their marriage seemed to be rock solid.

Her three children: Irina, age eleven; Kyle, Jr., age nine; and Margaret, age six, were healthy, rambunctious, and bright. Kyle and Irina were off to Trinity Grammar School–an independent, Anglican, day and boarding school for boys–in Sydney and Wynona Boarding School for Girls in North Sydney respectively where they had survived homesickness and excelled scholastically and in athletics as their proud parents knew they would.

Her only cause for being less than happy all the time was that she had no idea where her two sons and her former—and technically still legally–husband, Boris, were and whether or not they had escaped the frequent battles involving her general mayor husband and the twins he had stolen from her. If she dwelt too long on such thoughts, she would become depressed; and she could not afford to do that. With all the positive things about her life, she would be an ingrate if she did not thank God for what she had. She determined not to blame God or herself for the empty holes in her life. It was a source of frustrating discomfiture to her that she had to lie to her husband–to deny her bigamy–and not to show her feelings of being in mourning when birthdays and holidays came around.

For all the triumphs, worries, elaborate planning of her activities, and the enjoyment of her considerable fortune, Alexandra felt as if something was missing in her life to give her a sense of true fulfillment. She did not know what prompted such feelings nor did she have an idea of how to resolve them. She had decided that this was silly and something she simply had to live with or to forget somehow.

One of Kyle's more endearing qualities was that he did not treat her like a spoiled rich girl, a grand lady, or anything more than the world's best wife—which was the honest way he saw her. His teasing was a form of affection, a way of saying that he treasured and loved her.

When she dolled up for an evening out, and did her face just so, he would give her a back-hand compliment like, " I guess you won't have to double bag your face tonight" or even suggest that she only needed to be a one-bagger—which was the equivalent of being 'coyote ugly' and that she would need to hide her face in public to avoid embarrassing her family or frightening puppies and little children.

He never ceased to surprise her with his depth and breadth of knowledge of Aussie slang—"sline". Alexandra was always his 'sheila', but sometimes his 'small heifer', an allusion to her voluptuous figure— which he loved dearly and lusted for regularly but gave her a moment of pause to be sure it had not been a real insult. That was true even when he joked about her having been eating watermelons when she was pregnant with the three children. He would raise an eyebrow and question her about her past activity, "or were you just overeating watermelons?" Frequently, when she could not quite fathom what some strange Aussie bit of slanguage meant, he would chide her with a disdainful look for being "from away", meaning that she was born, bred, and lived away, and was not quite a true Aussie yet. All of those mild insults were common parlance among friends in Australia and all the more common between affectionate spouses and close friends.

Alexandra took up hobbies. She loved her flowers, and when she covered her hands, her farmer's pants, and flanno with dirt, Kyle would come out with his now well scripted litany.

"G'day, Sheila, nice pair a daks and the black and blue flanno yer wearin'. Pick 'em up new?"

After giving him an Aussie salute to brush away some flies, "Nice of you to notice, Kyle," was her usual rejoinder.

"Got to hand it to ya, Sheila. Makes you look poor but honest—nothin' of a bludger, you. Who could ask for more than that?"

Rejoinder: a shrug.

"Crikey, Alexandra, you've been doin' a bit o' hard yakka. How 'bout I scramble us up some nice brekkie?"

"Oh sure, my grand chef husband, thinking of something like a choccy biccy and some of that left-over dog's eye are we?"

"It hurts me to think that all I care about in the way o' gourmet food is a crusty chocolate biscuit and meat pie which is–after all–our national food."

He said it with theatrical down-turned sad eyes as he always did.

"All right you lazy blighter, I'll clean up and get us some brekkie. Actually, I have some fresh John Dory straight from Sydney Bay. That and some fried mashers, and a cold one; and you should be fit as a fiddle."

"Blimey, wench, fish again?!" would be his last attempt at a serious insult, all the more pathetic because they had not had good fish for over a month.

"I'll do the clean-up. That'd be a fair crack o' the whip, wouldn't it?"

During breakfast, it was their custom to tell each other their plans for the day, and at supper they told each other what they had actually done; Kyle's rendition was usually fairly fanciful.

"Have the neighbor's ankle biters been in our apple trees again, Luv?"

"No, I had Mrs. Thompson and her three children over for a spot o' tea yesterday afternoon, and they were cleaned up and well behaved. Tell the truth, I do love kiddies and miss ours lots during the school year."

"Me too," Kyle said wistfully, "it was better when I was young. Went to the local public school and had a lotta time for fishin'. Those were good times, and I turned out all right without a fancy private school. You weren't here in those days. The way it worked was that there were two Melbourne systems: the Denominational School Board (DSB) for the churches and the National Board which was funded by Parliament—

which had to be voted in every year, making schooling and teaching an unsure kind of thing. The National Board managed non-sectarian schools which provided combined reading, writing, arithmetic and separate but required religious instruction. I went to the Melbourne Grammar School, which was open only to boys, of course."

She gave him a lifted eyebrow which was a comment on his statement about having gotten a decent education and also about him having turned out all right.

"At least, I think so," he said.

"Tell the truth, I am trying to figure out what to do with myself today. The lawyers, business advisors and the CPAs are tired of seeing me. I've worn out my welcome. I think I'll just shlep around, maybe try and find a new hobby. I'm about done with my planting, and I think the flowers are going to look great, if I don't say so myself."

"You've a green thumb, you do, Lassie. I can't successfully plant a handful of nettles, perennials, or woody weeds."

"I guess you'll have to leave that part of the farm work to me, Hubby."

He shook his head to indicate, "Guess so."

"What's on your plate today, Kyle?"

"I'm gonna go out to the suburbs and check on some down market properties—be a stickybeak–maybe offer them half the askin'. See what shakes out, eh?"

"Good on ya," she said, glad that he would be out of her hair for most of the day.

She always enjoyed their back-and-forth bantering. With him gone, and no children to take care of, Alexandra took half an hour to decide on what she was going to occupy herself for the day. She thought about crocheting, knitting, macramé, making pottery, writing letters, having a little shopping spree; bubkis came to mind; and nothing captured her interest enough to get into an activity.

It was sunny; so she took a little snooze on the chaise longue on the back lawn.

No sooner had she gotten to sleep than a young man's voice interrupted with, "Catchin' a few flies, are ya?"

She worked to wake up and to see who was rude enough to awaken her from such a nice and time killing slumber. There were two young men wearing black suits with long coats, white shirts, and dark, narrow ties standing there, hands folded behind their backs. Unusually for men so young, each of them wore a black bowler hat. It was hot, and they were sweaty; so, their Sunday dress seemed well out of place, especially in comparison to the Australian boys Alexandra knew living around her. The speaker had a distinct Aussie accent and was obviously facile with the slang. The other young man was younger and shyer; the Aussie was obviously the senior of the two in authority.

"Are you lot both from down-under here, boys?"

They had a look of innocence about them; so, she held back the accusation that they were being rude to come into her back yard to surprise her.

Instead, she said, "You must be about something pretty important to be all gussied up in your Sunday-go-to-meeting clothes on a Tuesday. You morticians, maybe?"

Both young men laughed heartily and tipped their hats.

"No, M'am, we're ministers of the gospel…missionaries of the Mormon church. You ever heard of it?"

"Can't say I have. Where's your church?"

There was an awkward pause.

The Aussie spoke quietly, "Well, actually, there is only one in all of Australia at the moment. It's in Woolloongabba, up near Brisbane. We have our regular Sunday meetings here in the basement hall of the Duke of Wellington Hotel on the corner of Flinders and Russell Streets. Maybe you are familiar with it."

"I am aware that it is probably the oldest hotel in Victoria, and not in the best of condition."

"You're right, M'am. But we have to make do or do without for the time being," said the other missionary.

"Boys, my name is Alexandra Bradshaw. What are your names, if I may?"

"Aye am Elder Phillip, M'am," said the Aussie.

"And I am Elder Young. I'm from Utah."

"That's in America, right?"

"Yes, M'am."

Alexandra paused for a moment until a little something she had heard came to mind. She was too curious not to mention it, even if it would come across as rude and gossipy—a regular John Dory.

"Ah, yes," she said, "so how many wives do each of you have?"

She was not even sure that her memory was serving her correctly or that this was the American church that did have polygamy.

"None, M'am. We're too young. Our church does teach the true form of marriage or 'eternal marriage' as we know it which is plural-marriage. Marriage is very sacred and takes place in our temples if we are worthy," Elder Young said.

Elder Phillip continued with an answer that Alexandra had not even asked because he knew that the polygamy was open to misinterpretation by the gentiles.

"Mrs. Bradshaw, we should clear up something once and for all about our peculiar institution. Gentiles—non-Mormons—charge us with motives of lust when we Mormon missionaries travel abroad or to the eastern United States. Our enemies accuse us of recruiting young women for our Utah harems. That wicked concept is commonplace even in Australia, I'm afraid. Let me assure that such an idea could not be further from truth."

"Hmmh, interesting," was all Alexandra said. "Another question comes to mind. Do you both have the same first name?"

"No, 'elder' is the priesthood office we hold. Male missionaries all have to be ordained elders to be able to preach the gospel in the name of the church."

"I'm getting forgetful. What did you say the name of your church is?"

"We're commonly known as 'Mormons' but that is not the real name of our church. It is the Church of Jesus Christ of Latter-day Saints. We are often referred to as the LDS church for short."

"Well, the whole thing is a mouthful. I'll stick with 'LDS'. I told you my name is Alexandra, and I want to know your first names. You do have first names, don't you, or is everything strange about you and your church?"

"While we're on our missions for two and a half years, we are known as elders rather than by boy's names which would detract from our sacred effort."

"So, it would be a bit too informal for you to call me 'Alexandra'? What do you think you have to call me…just Mrs. Bradshaw?"

CHAPTER FIFTY-EIGHT
Strange New Interests

"The work of our missionaries is a magnificent expression of the Lord's redeeming love."
> —Elder (Apostle) D. Todd Christofferson

"More of you young men and women will catch this wave as you strive to be worthy of mission calls. You see this as a wave of truth and righteousness. You see your opportunity to be on the crest of that wave."
> —President Russell M. Nelson, *Catch the Wave*

Basement Bar of the *Duke of Wellington Hotel* on the corner of Flinders and Russell Streets, Melbourne, Victoria State, Commonwealth of Australia, March 30, 1912

The Mormon boys would rather have talked about their religion, but it was difficult to curb the flow of the strong minded lady; so, they answered what she asked, "No, M'am. Because we feel a bond with our brothers and sisters all over the world, and we are all children of God, we would like to call you Sister Bradshaw."

Alexandra thought about it for a moment. It sounded formal, a bit archaic, and quite unusual by Australian standards. The more she thought about it, the more she came to like it; the prefix was rather warm, she thought.

"All right, Sister Bradshaw it is."

"Would you like to more about our religion...Sister Bradshaw?"

"I would. Tell me honestly how many LDS people are there here?"

"Can't say for sure. Maybe ten, maybe less. There are more during months when American tourists come to Australia."

"Then, how many in Australia?"

"Not to be vague intentionally, Sister; but I would say something like five hundred to five-fifty. See, what happens is that many converts to the church leave for our place in America in keeping with the Prophet's revelation about the migration to Zion."

"This gets stranger the longer we talk. It's fascinating, I must say. Now, tell me about this Zion place; and why new converts have to go there; and do they all have to practice polygamy? Oh, and one more question. I remember someone from England once telling me that Mormons have horns. Is that right?"

Both elders broke into uncontrollable laughter.

"Nope. Have a Captain Cook, Sister Bradshaw. Look at our foreheads. That's a bit of nonsense put out by our enemies," said Elder Phillip.

She had thought the young man overly stiff, but he did laugh at the preposterous idea that Mormons had horns. The laughter did assuage a minute feeling she had had about the sect.

Alexandra downed the last of her cold Melbourne bitter, and said, "Boys, let's be serious. I don't have all day. Why don't you tell me all about your church?"

Elder Young took the lead at this point.

"We couldn't tell you all about our church in a month or even two. We have thirty-six introductory lessons about the church, and we would like to teach you at the rate of one-a-week–or maybe even two–if you are really interested. First, let me answer a couple of the questions you posed: Elder Phillip and I were called to the Australasian Mission which covers a pretty huge territory, and we will be hard pressed ever to get to a fraction of it. We'll do our level best. You had some questions about why we ask members to move to our homeland in the western United States.

The doctrine of the gathering comes from our prophet in order to build up our strength and to develop an educated and strong people. The gathering principle has made the church unique in colonial Australia as the missionaries have been recruiting converts to help build Zion in North America and has led to something of an emigration out of the Australian colonies. Mind that, this has been occurring during a period when the general tide of immigration has been flowing *into* the country. That is an important reason why the number of Australian convert members is now so extremely small. Britain has seen a lesser effect; so, the membership is growing rapidly there.

"I am the grandson of one of our prophets. Maybe you have heard of him? Brigham Young?"

"I have. He is the one who led you Mormons to the west when they were being murdered by bigots in the east, and he is the famous polygamist, right?"

"Right," said Elder Phillip. "And I am some sort of great, great, great grandson of Admiral Arthur Phillip. You know your history. He was a Royal Navy officer and became the first Governor of New South Wales. He founded the British penal colony that later became Sydney."

"How interesting. I never met a descendent of one of the very early pioneers."

"To continue," said Elder Young, "Until about the last eight or ten years, the question of whether the gathering weakened the branches of the Australasian or any other mission around the world was not meaningful to the leaders—the Brethren—or the general membership of the church. The Brethren never had any intention of establishing permanent units of the church outside Zion, especially not overseas, before the beginning of this century, except perhaps in Polynesia to serve the Lamanites."

"Lamanites?" Alexandra interrupted.

"*Book of Mormon* people," Elder Phillip answered.

"*Book of Mormon* people?" Alexandra asked, getting perplexed.

"Does anyone else hear an echo?" Elder Phillip asked.

Everyone laughed.

"So, Rome was not built in a day; and we have thirty-six lessons to share with you. All will become clear," said the American elder.

"When can we come by and give you the first lesson, Sister Bradshaw?"

"Tomorrow morning. My husband will be gone, and we will have privacy and quiet."

"Do you think he would like to hear our Gospel message, Sister?"

"I doubt it. He always says he avoids going into a church house for fear of causing lightening strikes."

"Before we leave, would it be all right for us to have a word of prayer, Sister Bradshaw?" offered Elder Young.

"I suppose so."

"Who would you like to offer the prayer, Sister?"

"Certainly not me," said Alexandra who had never given any kind of prayer out loud except in response to the priest's petition in the litany during her Russian Orthodox Christmas or Easter services. "Why don't you do it, Elder Phillip?"

"My pleasure."

Alexandra heard the first prayer in her life that was simple and directed to "Father in Heaven" and without any kind of memorized or scripted prose or poetry or intercessor. It was rather refreshing and heightened her interest. She asked herself honestly, was she interested in the new religion? or was she just attracted to the handsome, clean-cut, well-dressed young preachers?

"*Time will tell*," she thought to herself.

The first lesson was about a young American boy—age fourteen—who was being hounded by multiple churches—none of which Alexandra had ever heard of except the Methodists whom she met in China—and decided to pray to God for guidance after reading the Bible. The outcome was like nothing Alexandra had ever heard about except in the miracles of the Bible. The boy had a vision or some sort of incredible experience: he saw and talked to God, the Father, and Jesus Christ, His Son. Alexandra was intrigued but extremely dubious since that went against everything she had ever understood from the scriptures. She was—like all the people around her and from her past—certain that the age of miracles or of God's appearance to a man was passed. The only one she could recall offhand from her Bible reading was when Moses saw God's finger.

She asked the elders what heaven was like for the Mormons. That was cause for further consternation.

"In heaven, we will become resurrected in time and live with our Father and Mother in Heaven and with our families from earth. We call it 'the plan of salvation'. It will be busy and happy."

There was an unmistakable question mark on Alexandra's face.

"What concerns you, Sister?" asked Elder Young.

"I have not digested the idea that your boy prophet, Mr. Smith, saw God and Jesus. Now, you tell me something I never heard preached from any pulpit. We have flesh and bone bodies after we are dead? We live with our families like regular people?"

"Simply put, yes," said Elder Phillip.

"What does your church teach, Sister?"

"All my life I learned that we are spirits or maybe angels; but real bodies? married life? children? real work? Sounds like nothing I ever heard."

"Sister Yusupov, what do you...*you* personally believe?"

"I haven't ever really given it much thought; but now that I do, I can't imagine heaven without my husband, my parents, my children, my brothers. I think everybody believes that deep down."

"Would you believe me if I told you that none of the Christian churches teach that, nor do the Jews, or the Muslims, or the Buddhists. Only the Church of Jesus Christ of Latter-day Saints. And that is because the Prophet Joseph received a revelation from God about it. It was part of the truth that he brought forth in the 1830s. The church started with only six members in 1830 but has grown to 393,000 by 1910."

"1830...Such a short time ago and such a lot of growth. I have always been sure that there were no more miracles or visitations. This is discombobulating, boys, really too strange for me to take in all at once."

"That's why we have thirty-six lessons. You will have plenty of time to absorb it and to become converted. When you do, you will want to be baptized."

"I was baptized when I was a baby; so, I won't be needing that again."

"We'll have a lesson that, too. Be patient."

"We will be by your house on the Sabbath tomorrow at nine in the morning to take you to church with us. Is that okay with you?" asked Elder Young.

"What does 'okay' mean? Apparently, it's good. Is that some kind of strange American word?

"You're right about the meaning, and we say it all the time. It just covers the idea of all is right or correct and is such a good word that we are beginning to hear it in all our travels. Funny how something catches on. The word became popular in America about 1840, when supporters of the Democratic political party used it as the nickname for their candidate for the presidency who came from an area called Kinderhook in New York. He was "Old Kinderhook". It got shortened to "OK" which caught on for Martin Van Buren who got reelected and then became a kind of household word for everything or any particular thing that was good or at least, all right."

"I never heard that before, Elder," said Elder Phillip. "I never thought of 'OK' having an origin; it has just always been there."

"My pleasure, Companion. That's why you came on a mission; to learn more about the world from a learned American."

He said it with a wry smile, and the two young men had a good laugh. Alexandra liked the relaxed and confident manner they demonstrated but was not at all sure about their doctrine—*pretty strange stuff*, she thought.

Basement Bar of the *Duke of Wellington Hotel*

The two Mormon elders picked up Alexandra at nine in their borrowed surrey and drove her to the old hotel where their Sunday meeting was to be held. The upper floors were typical Victorian—dark woods, winding stair case, Persian carpets on hardwood floors, stone fireplace mantles, and uniformed hotel personnel. Descending into the basement area was a different story. The lights grew dimmer; the carpets more threadbare; and the smell of old beer, whiskey, cigar smoke, and urine becoming stronger with every step further down. She had to take out her perfumed handkerchief to withstand the stench of the basement barroom itself.

"Sorry, Sister Bradshaw. We'll have this place in decent shape by ten."

Four older couples arrived shortly thereafter and pitched in to assist the elders in the clean-up. First, they swept up the debris, and one older lady carried a burlap trash bag up the stairs to get rid of it. Then, they sloshed the floor with foaming Pretty Kitty— "the New Australian Solution of the Domestic Problem—cleans everything but clothes"–soapy water from a wringer bucket and used four large rag mops to scour the ground-in filth. The soap had a pine smell and improved the ambience of the room immensely as soon as the mopping started. They sloshed clear water on the floor four times to clear it of soap scum, wiped down the bar, set the bar chairs into a classroom arrangement, and pronounced the room ready for the Lord to enter.

"Better," Alexandra commented which brought smiles to the members and the missionaries' faces.

Elder Phillip conducted the meeting. He started by acknowledging the presence of the new investigator, Alexandra Bradshaw, and then announced several items of what he called "branch" business, including a pot luck supper on Wednesday, and a house repair effort for the following Saturday on the widow Benson's home. He recited the agenda for the meeting: invocation by Sister Owens, opening hymn—*Israel, Israel, God is Calling*, then a "sacrament" hymn—"*I Stand All Amazed*". Next, performance of the passing of the sacrament [eucharist] by the priesthood members–one elderly man and the two young missionaries–to be followed by a musical number–fiddle solo by one of the older men—an investigator like Alexandra. Next, was another hymn–*We Thank Thee O God for a Prophet*–and then the bearing of testimonies–a term which Alexandra did not quite understand. None of the hymns were the least familiar to the Alexandra, the investigator; and finally Elder Phillip announced the benediction by Elder Young. Although it was a formal prayer to close the religious meeting, it was given with the same simple friend-to-friend sort of communication except for the use of prayer language with thee, thy, and thine used whenever referring to the deity.

The body of the meeting was unlike anything Alexandra had ever heard of—a sort of ad hoc, from-the-heart, set of mini-sermons or sharing of experiences of the hard things of life experienced by the simple people of the congregation. There was no priest or preacher, just common people. Every person in the very small gathering "bore" his or her testimony. The common threads were that they "knew that the Church was true"; they knew that "Joseph Smith—a man they had never seen—was a prophet just like Peter, James, and John, were prophets"; they knew that a man named "Joseph Fielding Smith, Sr.—a man who was the nephew of the other Joseph Smith, the founder, lived in Salt Lake City, Utah in America, the current president of the church—was also a prophet of God"; and several recited recent miracles in their lives—including miraculous healings, findings of things lost, promptings that removed them from danger, and insights into what they or their children must decide when they were presented with conundrums.

It was so different that it was bewildering, disturbing, fascinating, and inspiring. She had to look up polygamy in the *1911 Encyclopaedia Brittanica* to be sure what the Mormon institution was about. She learned that what everyone—including the Mormons–called polygamy was technically inexact. The encyclopaedia described polygamy as the practice of having more than one spouse. What the Mormons practiced was polygyny—men having more than one wife. Alexandra had never even heard of polyandry—the practice of women having more than one husband. It was only practiced in such strange places as India, Tibet, parts of China, and Africa. She decided that she had to learn more about those Mormons and their "polygyny" before she got any further into the process of possibly joining the church.

CHAPTER FIFTY-EIGHT

AUSTRALIAN CHILDREN

The best way to find yourself is to lose yourself in the service of others.

—Mahatma Gandhi

Service to others is the rent you pay for your room here on earth.

—Muhammad Ali

National Archives of Australia, Victorian Archives Centre, 99 Shiel Street, North Melbourne, Victoria State, Australia, November 30, 2015

The senior missionaries hit a dry time in their search for information on their pet project, the life and adventures of Alexandra Abramovna Tarasova-Yusupov Bradshaw in contradistinction to their rapid and efficient gains in converting the hand written mundane life documents of the citizenry of Victoria Colony/State to easily found digitalized information. They often spoke of what life must have been like for their interesting project person, whether she ever learned of their LDS church, what her relationship with her new husband and her children was like, and what the woman thought, dreamed, worried, or hoped about.

During the previous several months, only one new document turned up—the official applications to the University of Melbourne of the three Bradshaw children when they turned seventeen: Irina in

1918, Kyle in 1920, and Margaret in 1923. No other records of their scholastic achievements or even if they finished college were available. Marriage certificates were found for Irina who married an attorney, Donald Wadsworth Tufts, in 1923, and Kyle, who married Miranda Rebecca O'Toole, in 1929. Apparently, Margaret remained a spinster. No other documents could be found for Alexandra's children or any of their issue.

Australia, Victoria, and Melbourne have a rich educational heritage. There are seven Melbourne-based universities, fifty-one different campuses in the state, with thirty-four of them in Greater Melbourne. The University of Melbourne was founded in 1853, the first university in Victoria; and it is the second oldest in Australia. Fortunately for education in Victoria, the inauguration of the university was made possible by the wealth resulting from Victoria's gold rush and paid for prior to the great gold and land busts. It's main campus was located in Parkville, a close suburb just north of the Melbourne central business district. Several other campuses were later located across Victoria. Fortunately for Melbourne and the State of Victoria, the decision to create a first-class university resulted in it being a civilizing influence during the hectic years of "Marvelous Melbourne" and the doldrums of the bust when poverty and crime were rampant enough to change the city's nickname to "Smellbourne". One of its most significant accomplishments was to begin the admission of women in 1881.

The senior missionaries' quest for further information seemed likely to end with this set of findings. Her husband, Kyle Dewit Herman Bradshaw, filed for probate in 1931, presuming that she died in 1921, although there was no documentary evidence of that presumed event ever found by the probate court or the zealous missionaries.

CHAPTER FIFTY-NINE

FINANCIAL CONFLICTS

**Sometimes I have so many financial conflicts
of interest that I can't even keep them straight.**
—Michael Arrington

Green is not a financial issue; it is a heart issue.
—Andy Stanley

Number 1-8, Collins Street, Victoria State, Melbourne, Commonwealth of Australia, April 4, 1912

Alexandra pondered what she had seen, heard, and learned about the Mormon church and what it meant for her and her life. It was nothing like her religious upbringing, except that the Russian Orthodox and the Mormon Church were both Christian. The meager meeting place in the basement of the Duke of Wellington Hotel with its stench of urine, beer, and cigar smoke, and its lack of gold or crucifixes compared poorly with the grand chapels ["the arks of salvation"] of the Orthodox Church. The education of the lay priesthood of the Mormons compared unfavorably with the highly educated Orthodox priests and their long history. The roll of women and the institution of plural marriage was troublesome, to say the least; but, the comparison of the role of women came out in favor of the Mormons even with polygamy.

She was interested enough–Alexandra admitted to herself–to have accelerated the rate at which she was meeting with the young missionaries and receiving their lessons. In a little over a week, she had been given the first four lessons: The Joseph Smith story, the Book of Mormon, the Plan of Salvation, and the Restoration of the Priesthood. It all made common sense and was enticing if she could get over the unpleasant room that passed for a chapel. There were thirty-two more lessons to go…what more could there be to this new and very different American religion? More to the point, was she going to make a major life's change and follow this modern-day prophet in America? What would her friends, her family, and her old Russian priests think? What would they all advise her to do?

Kyle was patient up to a point. He had already given in to her obsession with making money at the expense of her family. That was the real reason why she demanded that the children be sent away to boarding schools. Now, she was tinkering with this new religion being sold to her by a couple of young boys. Everyone he talked to referred to the Mormon church as a cult. Her concentration on it was beginning to concern him and had him asking himself if that church would inveigle her to run away to America and to leave him.

He looked into his and Alexandra's financial holdings in detail. The two shared one major account which could be accessed by either of them up to one-half of the total value. After that, both partners—spouses–had to sign to remove any more money. He had two accounts from which only he could withdraw funds—the total value of liquid funds was $220 million AUD. Alexandra had four accounts that he could identify with a total value in liquid funds was $700 million AUD, making her one of the richest women in the world. They shared one real estate account holding deeds valued at $200 million AUD, but that was subject to the fluctuations of the real estate market and the demand for the properties. Each of them had another account holding a mix of gold bullion, real estate deeds, stocks and bonds, which were held in two separate safety deposit boxes for each of them. Only the named owner could access those boxes. The value of his was about $100 million AUD total, and hers was almost $300 million. They had two life insurance policies with each other as owner and as beneficiary in the amount of $2 million AUD. None of the accounts had had any significant funds withdrawn in the recent past, and none of them had had withdrawals of which he was unaware. His concerns about Alexandra running off to America to be part of the westward migration of the Mormons seemed to be unfounded, and he relaxed his guard partially.

Kyle began to think that his attitude towards Alexandra's flirtation with the Mormon church and her obsession with money was at least in part responsible for what he saw as a growing rift between them. He knew that his and Alexandra's relationship was complicated, more than other couples, he believed. He was determined to keep them together and set out that very evening to begin mending fences.

"How about havin' a night out at the flicks, Luv?" he asked during dinner.

Alexandra was surprised at the attention to her that his question suggested and thought it was a good thing.

"What's playing, Kyle?"

"There's an interesting new kind of flicker going at the Pacific Cinema at Bulahdelah, New South Wales called *Moora Neya,* or *The Message of the Spear.* It tells about the abos. I heard it's pretty interesting."

"We're not supposed to call them that. Now they're Indigenous Australians. And, yes, I'd like to see it. Anything so long as it's not *The Story of the Kelly Gang.* I've seen that at least a dozen times."

"We're supposed to get some films in from America, but none of them are around here yet. I checked."

"So, we're off to the countryside for a small-town entertainment fare. Sounds like fun," Alexandra said and flashed her husband her man-reducing smile.

"*That's a good start,*" he said to himself.

Three days of travel on mostly dirt roads brought them to Bukahdelah. The name of the town derives from the language of the Worimi Aborigines who occupied the area before white settlement began. It means 'meeting place of two rivers'. In Buklahdelah, they discovered that the film would not be shown at the quaint little theater until seven in the evening which left them three hours to kill. They did a little mooching around the lake area which was pretty. Then, they asked at the local bank where a good restaurant could be found in the village.

"G'day folks. Yer in luck," said the bored teller, "there's a pretty up-side little place behind the church. Can't miss it. Ye can git bumps and grinds or snags anytime. Tradies all swear by it—that's a good recommendation right there."

"Is the restaurant on the big end of town?" Kyle asked with a joking smile.

"Bettern a ham sandwich," the elderly officious little man answered, meaning that it was better than a poke in the eye with a sharp stick or a dog's breakfast.

Taking note of the doubt on Alexandra's face, the teller gave a small shrug and a smile and said to her, "No worries, mate, she'll be right. It's called the Buklahdelah Fine Eatery. Yu'll like it."

Alexandra was hungry enough to settle for the eggs and coffee and the sausages the teller said were always available.

The restaurant was nicer than either Alexandra or Kyle expected; not exactly "the big end of town" but recently painted and clean. The signs had been made professionally, and the tables and chairs looked new. They asked for menus and were pleasantly surprised to see a well designed and printed bill of fare and that there was a fairly large selection of appetizers and entrees.

The waitress–also the owner and cook–gave them a few minutes then returned asked "What would yous like?"

Alexandra was undecided; so, she said, "Get his order first, please."

Kyle ordered breaded veal with fresh vegetables and mashers with a Castlemaine Ale.

The waitress wrote down his order.

"And fer you, M'am?"

"I'd like to have the fried chicken, some veggies, brown bread, and a Cab Sav."

The waitress wrote down her order, then paused for a moment to study what she had written.

"Sorry, Sir," she told Kyle. "Cook says we're outta veal."

"All right, I'll have the chicken, too."

Another pause.

"Mustta slipped ma mind. The shipment of chicken isn't gonna get here till tomorrow."

"How about the meat loaf?" he asked.

"I'll settle for a plate of your special John Dory. Is it good?" Alexandra tried.

"Yeah, its good…when we have it."

"Let me guess, you don't have it today?"

"'Fraid that's right, Ma'm.

"So...I'll have the meat loaf, too and lots of ketchup. And I still want a bottle of Cab Sav."

"Uh, I'll have to check on the meatloaf...be back in a jiffy."

She was gone for nearly five minutes. Kyle was holding back laughter.

"What's funny, Kyle? I'm hungry."

"Me too. I'll bet you a twoonie that it's ixnay on the meatloaf as well as the rest. You on?"

"No, I think you are going to win that bet."

Sure enough, the waitress returned with a negative expression on her tired face.

"Sorry, Mates. Outta meat loaf and Cab Sav, too."

Kyle could not hold back any longer. He started to laugh, a belly jarring guffaw.

"So, what do you suggest, Mate?" he asked the waitress.

"Why'nt yous have the bumps and grinds and the snags. They're real good. Aye also recommend our apple pie for dessert. I'll bring yous a coupla bottles a Victoria Aitken's bitters to wash it all down."

"Is the pie ala mode?" asked Kyle.

"Nope. Ice cream won't git here 'til next week."

Now, Alexandra began to laugh. So hard that tears streamed down her face. After such a good laugh, she could enjoy sunnyside up eggs, coffee, pie, and bitter beer. She decided that she was not really in the mood for chicken, meatloaf, fish, Cabernet Sauvignon, or ice cream anyway.

The Pacific Cinema in Buklahdelah was fairly delapidated and could have used a new coat of whitewash. It had a flat storefront façade with a single door. Behind the rectangular face of the building was a long box of a building covered with corrugated tin originally brightly colored with paint. In 1911 it was more gray than white and was pockmarked with areas where paint had peeled and fallen to the weed strewn ground. It was definitely not the 'big-end' of town or architecture.

Moora Neya, or the Message of the Spear was set in territory familiar to Kyle from his youthful travels. The area of the aboriginal station was in Brewarrina just west of the Darling River, and that brought back memories of his cowboy days as did the action involving the aborigines in their full war paint—authentic as he recalled it. The movie–like all of the silent movies of its time–was stiff and jerky with action flitting on and off the silver screen. The plot was worse even than those seen in the amateur playhouses around Victoria.

A handsome, well-mannered, gentleman named Harry fell in love with the remote station owner's daughter. He was dressed in white clothes, including an exceptionally clean white western hat. The heroine was a remake of Pearl Pureheart–virginal, sweet, and beautiful. The oil-can-Harry-model villain was the station overseer who was cruel to the innocent aborigines who strove to please the overseer and to protect the delicate heroine. The evil-doer made crude advances towards the heroine but failed to succeed because Harry appeared on the scene and beat the evil incarnate anti-hero to a nerveless pulp.

When he came to, the evil overseer attempted to get some of the local Worimi Aborigines to kill Harry with a promise of a paltry sum of money and some liquor. One of the indigenous aborigines—faithful and true to the kind station master and the lovely and kind heroine—refused and alerted the guards in the station building by writing a message on his spear. Harry was just about to slough his mortal coil when the area's rough but honest stockmen raced to his rescue as the wicked aborigines corrupted by the overseer began to perform the "Death Dance" around the fallen hero. The stockmen managed to kill the overseer, to drive off the aborigines, and to save Harry. At the end of the flick, Harry and the heroine were reunited as the scene faded to dark as the pleasant evening drew over the happy throng.

The movie was made in early 1911 with a total of forty-one scenes and was written for the silver screen by one man because of budget issues. It was not entirely certain that the movie would ever get made because of labor issues. The big end of town moviemakers were told they could hire aborigines as extras for two cents a day. They balked and would not budge on the day that filming was supposed to begin. After a strenuous labor negotiation, a compromise was achieved in which the aborigines would work industriously for four cents a day and a tobacco stick at the end of each working day.

"How'd you like the flick?" Kyle asked as they made their way back to their hotel.

Alexandra struggled to maintain a soda-cracker expression on her face before answering.

"Interesting," she said.

A small hint of a naughty smile curled the corners of her lips.

"Out with it," Kyle said. "I thought it was pretty exciting, didn't you?"

She could not hold back and started to laugh hard enough to bring tears to her eyes and to make her face flush.

"Kyle, I know you went way out of your way to woo and to entertain me; but I have to tell you that I think that movie was just about the silliest production I ever saw. I've seen better Chinese operas. The story had perfectly good people pitted against perfectly bad people, and the ending was as predictable as drought in the outback. The movie made my eyes jump around. It was flickering and jerking until I could not keep watching. I will make a firm prophecy. Movies are never going to make it in the entertainment world. It was a waste of ten cents a piece for us to go, except that I—at least—got a good laugh out of it."

Kyle gave out a heavy sigh.

"You are a hard one to please. You were not thrilled by the epicurean dinner we had or by the exquisite surroundings, china, and cutlery. You turned up your nose at the fine evening's entertainment. Next, I expect to hear complaints about our world class hotel."

They both laughed, slapped their thighs, and hooted, especially when the visual image of their fourth-class accommodations came to mind. None of that bothered Kyle since the comedy of the evening was prologue to a marvelous night in the seedy hotel with the lumpy bed. Both Kyle and Alexandra harbored thoughts that the getaway trip might produce another Bradshaw baby.

When they arrived back in Melbourne, it was a scene of serious and violent turmoil. What had been a battle of words and threats when they left had grown into an ugly strike. H.V. McKay, owner of the Sunshine Harvester Works in Melbourne, took upon himself a crusade to crush the long strike that had begun in 1911 and was still creating the worst of divisions of Melbourne society. The strike came about because of McKay's attempts to circumvent the Harvester Judgment by the courts. There were riots under way in the streets of Melbourne when the Bradshaws drove back into the city. It had now achieved the dubious distinction of being the longest strike in Victoria's history. Bitter as that strike was, the seaman's strike was worse and even more bitter and violent. Kyle and Alexandra determined to get involved; unfortunately, on opposite sides.

CHAPTER SIXTY
IDEOLOGICAL CONFLICTS

I don't accept ideologies that are not a product of consensus.
I don't have an ideology, but I do have a sense of what's right
and what's wrong.

—Ruben Blades

Number 1-8, Collins Street, Victoria State, Melbourne, Commonwealth of Australia, May 2, 1912

Alexandra and Kyle discussed the labor strife as if it was an abstract concept which did not touch them in the beginning. The bitter arguments, and rallies, and the violent struggles on the waterfront and in the streets surrounding the Harvester factory were becoming increasingly acerbic and more amaroidal as the days wore on. The three-month seamen's strike brought shipping around Australia to a standstill. Hundreds of Melbourne workers were stood down, and coal and food supplies dwindled. Riots and bombings were becoming commonplace. The Arbitration Court was created to minimise industrial disputes, but the number and degree of vitriol from strikes continued unabated through the year.

Although Kyle was ostensibly a hard-hearted capitalist, his struggles and the memories of the pain of being unfairly treated as a young workman colored his every thought about the industrial strife. Alexandra was at her core an aristocrat and could not be shaken from her belief that the good which came to the lower classes and to the working man emanated from the profits garnered by large businesses and farms which employed huge numbers of people. Kyle saw no value to a class system. Alexandra saw no future for a lawless and classless society. Kyle fretted over and set out to spend his money to help the impoverished workers and their families. Alexandra felt threatened by his actions which made no sense. She made her support for the men and their families who were locked in a struggle to preserve the economy, and indeed, civilization. She was determined to keep the way of life she knew strong against the inroads of the great unwashed. Kyle became evermore vitriolic about the need for a populist government that would overturn the unchristian, corrupt, quagmire which held the majority of the citizenry in thrall.

Their differences in background, in religion, in gender, in life's experience, and in what their marriage meant to each of them had not been of any significance to them before the hard reality of the industrial strife in Melbourne raised its ugly visage. Now, it appeared; ideology was everything. Alexandra had been told long ago that the three reasons for couples to divorce centered around sex, religion, and money, in that order. Now, the ideological issues were becoming so intense that partisan politics and the attendant ideologies were factoring in an increasing number of failed engagements—the parents could not accept a fiancé who was not in agreement with their brand of politics—and of divorces with each party to the divorce choosing family politics over the union of the spouses.

Despite the delightful rapprochement they achieved during their recent mini-honeymoon in Buklahdelah, the maelstrom that they encountered in Melbourne's city streets and in the parlors, pubs, libraries, and party gatherings led to implacable arguments and irreconcilable differences. In a matter of days, it became nearly impossible for the couple to have a conversation about the price of bread or the beauty of a flower without the discussion becoming politicized and emotionally charged with negative electricity. By the third day, Alexandra and Kyle found excuses not to sit down to meals together because that was where their conversations usually took place. By the end of the week, they arranged to sleep in separate bedrooms by nonverbal mutual agreement.

They were entering into a "Y" in their lives, with the directions of their interests, enthusiasms, and activities diverging steadily away from each other; something neither of them would have wanted or even imagined a fortnight ago was now the definition of their relationship and their now separate existences.

A day after the Bradshaws separated from each other to sleep in separate bed rooms, a strike breaker was killed by men who had been out on strike for three months outside the Sunshine Harvester Works. Melbourne riot police came in force and bludgeoned their way from the back of the throng of battling strikers and scabs. Fifteen men and women ended up in hospital; the strike leaders and several of the most violent strikers and an equal number of scabs were part of the hospitalized enemies.

Alexandra saddled her bay mare, Waltzing Matilda, and rode as fast as she could to the Harvester Works in time to see the last of the violence by man on man and man on property. Like every Melbourner, Alexandra knew that the Sunshine Harvester Works' problems with labor started as long ago as 1907 when workers started a protracted industrial dispute with legal battles and intermittent strikes. H.V. McKay–the owner and manager–locked horns with the several unions which represented the workers at the Sunshine factories. The unions based their complaints on claims for higher wages and better working conditions. McKay–on the other hand–took a different tack. He argued that he should continue to receive import protection.

Eventually the case was heard before Judge H. B. Higgins at the Commonwealth Court of Conciliation and Arbitration in Melbourne. Judge Higgins heard evidence from employees and their wives regarding conditions at the factory and costs for supporting their families and sympathized with them. In what came to be known as the Harvester Judgment, he required McKay to pay his employees a wage that guaranteed them a standard of living which was reasonable for "a human being in a civilized community", regardless of his—Hugh McKay's–capacity to pay. McKay successfully appealed that judgment.

McKay continued to pay pauper's wages, and the cries and complaints of the workers and their families fell on deaf ears. Alexandra knew all this; but she was appalled by what she saw, even though the wounded and one dead man had been taken away before she arrived. The level of carnage inflicted on the factory buildings and a few small homes owned by managers tore at her heart strings and eclipsed all the cries from the poverty-stricken workers. She knew Hugh Victor McKay and his wife, Sarah Irene, and knew that they had slaved their entire lives to build his fine buildings, to make excellent agriculture machinery, and to provide secure employment for over three thousand men and women. She looked over wreckage: smoldering framework of the factory, mangled reapers and binders, Albion mowers, Globe hayrakes, Climax ensilage cutters, pneumatic silo fillers, McKay's grain pickling machine, Braybrook strippers, Sun grain and fertilizer drills, and hundreds more strewn about as if a giant child had destroyed the farm implements—his toys—in a moment of childish rage.

She rushed to the McKay's home to offer help. Sarah was weeping as if she had lost a child. Alexandra threw her arms around the distraught woman and attempted to comfort her.

"There, there, Dear," she cooed, "no worries; she'll be all right."

"She'll never be all right! We've lost everything…everything…to those ingrates, those heathen curs."

"I'm telling you, Sarah, there'll be a better day. Just you wait. You and Hugh will build it all up again."

"I don't see how. We'll be in the poor house before the year's out, Alexandra."

Alexandra held Sarah's head on her lap until she fell asleep, then she gently lifted her Sarah's head, placed a pillow under it and left her to a much-needed sleep.

Hugh stepped quietly behind Alexandra and tapped her gently on the shoulder.

"That was very kind of you, my dear," he said. "And I am gladdened to know that I have at least one friend. It was above and beyond for you to travel all this way just to see us in our time of calamity."

"I could not have stayed away, Hugh. I am angry and deeply saddened over your loss. It is so monstrous."

"You can scarce imagine, Alessandra. I have an old photo in my chest of the original Sunshine harvester standing outside our blacksmith building—hut, really—in Drummartin. That was by the family home at the time. Sarah and me were young and just getting started then. I invented and got a patent for the first stripper harvester, and I hired a few lads to help me put it together. It was clear back in 1884. We worked ourselves half to death to build our company, to employ workers and to feed and house them. And this is how they repay me."

"It is unfathomable, Hugh. Those ingrates apparently don't remember the black nineties when anyone could consider himself lucky to have any job or a roof or his family's heads or enough food to keep body and soul together. You saved their ungrateful skins, man. You don't deserve any of this."

Hugh looked as if he might begin to cry; so, Alexandra looked away to spare him. It broke her heart.

"Think I'll catch a few winks. I'm tuckered. I hate to think about having to get up tomorrow morning and going to the works to see what, if anything, can be salvaged. God bless you dear. Take a little time this afternoon to go visit Howard and Matilda Smith, Huddart and Elizabeth Parker, and McIlwraith and Mary Margaret McEacharn. They're hurting almost as much as we are, lass. Do 'em good to see you on their side."

Alexandra's dander was up, and her sympathies were aroused to near fever pitch. She spent the rest of the day visiting and consoling the shipping magnates of Melbourne.

The beginning of the strife between the dock workers and the owners was an action against the Associated Northern Collieries [coal mining establishments], launched by the Attorney-General of Victoria against all of the colliery members of Associated Northern Collieries and the shipping companies–Adelaide Steamship, Howard Smith, Huddart Parker and McIlwraith McEacharn and the Union Steam Ship Company of New Zealand, the Melbourne Steamship Company, and James Patterson and Company–in 1910. The prosecution lasted almost eighty days until mid-December 1911. The corporate and individual defendants challenged every aspect of the prosecution, including denials of membership of the Coal Vend—their working organization–despite making and receiving payments. Judge Isaacs found that each of the defendants separately and all collectively were engaged in a combination with intent to restrain inter-state trade and commerce in Newcastle coal to the detriment of the public, which was the primary issue in the court's mind.

The defendants appealed to the High Court, primarily on the basis that the *Australian Industries Preservation Act* required proof of intent not just to increase prices, but to cause detriment to the public. The High Court—composed of Crown Justice Griffith, and Justices Barton and O'Connor in September, 1912 said that the intent of the original and legal agreement between the ship owners and the colliery owners— one and the same–was to *prevent* unlimited and ruinous competition and to fix the "hewing rate" paid to miners. The public was not just the consumers of coal, but so were the mining companies and the workers alike. Raising the price paid for coal as the companies wanted was determined to benefit the general public of Newcastle. It followed that the intent of members of the Coal Vend was to protect the prosperity of the Newcastle and Maitland Districts. There was no proof that the public suffered a detriment; there was no evidence of intent to cause any such a detriment. The Attorney-General unsuccessfully appealed to the Privy Council.

The stevedores, other dock workers, ships' hands, and coal miners, were infuriated at what they considered a manifestly unfair decision and proof that the "big-end" of town would always win in the crooked courts. They saw their only recourse to be violence, and a strike broke out more or less spontaneously which devolved into riots, destruction of property, massive financial costs, and bitterness that persisted as long as any of them lived and as long as there were unions in Australia.

Alexandra studied the court cases; and to her, it was as plain as the nose on her face that the rule of law came down on the side of the owners; and that was that. Her sympathies—as in the Harvester case—were strongly on the side of the hard-pressed owners. She first visited Howard and Matilda Smith, owners of Adelaide Steamship who had befriended her during the "smelbourne" era when she was afraid she might go under.

She knocked on the door of the Smith mansion and was admitted by the butler whom she knew well from previous visits. She asked to see Matilda.

When she saw the ashen faced middle-aged woman, it seemed that Matilda's hair had grown grey just in the past year.

"Oh, my dear, how dreadful it must be for you. Our whole class of people are under attack, and you and Howard are bearing the brunt for us all."

She hugged the slight lady who began to cry.

"You are too kind, Alexandra. You have come in our time of need. Thank you. I don't know what we will do. This dreadful strike is likely to go on forever, I'm afraid."

"Oh, Matilda, nothing is forever. This will pass. In fact, I think the judgments of the high court make it perfectly reasonable for you and the rest of the colliers and ship owners to hire non-union workers with the blessing and protection of the constabulary."

"Do you really, Alexandra? That would be such a ray of hope. The cause of right and of the law on our side. I hardly dare hope. You are so smart. I am sure you are right in the long run. I must cling to that thought. Thank you, Dear, for coming."

By tea time, Alexandra had conveyed her positive message individually to the Parkers, and the McEaharns. By the time she talked to Mcllwraith McEacharn, she had formulated a plan for a way for her to help the struggling owners.

"I want to do more that just talk the good hope to you and the rest of the owners—my people—Mcllwraith. For the remainder of the strike and the terrible financial losses you are suffering, I will contribute $50,000 a month towards your needs against the rabble."

"Ordinarily, I would not consider accepting such a gift, but rather, consider it a loan. Times have deteriorated to such a degree that I am forced to accept your generosity, Alexandra. My fellow owners and our wives will be forever grateful to you. We will overcome this trial and will get back on our feet again. We will then be in a position to be of benefit to you should the need ever arise."

Alexandra could not visit the officials of Union Steam Ship Company of New Zealand, the Melbourne Steamship Company, and James Patterson and Company, because they were located outside Australia, but Mcllwraith assured her that he would let them know of her generosity.

They shook hands solemnly. Alexandra returned home tired but satisfied that she was on the side of the angels and had made a genuine contribution to her class.

CHAPTER SIXTY-ONE

INTRANSIGENT POSITIONS OF ALEXANDRA AND KYLE AND THE CONSEQUENCES

"We love being mentally strong, but we hate situations that allow us to put our mental strength to good use."
—Mokokoma Mokhonoana

...she felt an irresistible longing to begin life with him over again so that they could say what they had left unsaid and do everything right that they had done badly in the past. But she had to give in to the intransigence of death.
—Gabriel Jose Garcia Marquez,
Love in the Time of Cholera

Melba Hall, University of Melbourne, Victoria State, Melbourne, Commonwealth of Australia, November 12, 1912

It was Alexandra's nature and practice to keep her business and personal life private, and she seldom confided in anyone about them. The nearest she came to candor was with her husbands, Boris and Kyle. Now, Boris was nowhere to be found; and Kyle was at best her opponent; and, at worst, her enemy. Certainly, he no longer had access to her innermost thoughts, feelings, and plans. So, with that in mind, she arranged a meeting with her three children at the University—a place where prying eyes and ears would not be privy to their conversations.

Music studies at the University of Melbourne began in 1891 just before the great recession; and by 1912, it was recognized that the university had to have proper facilities. Victoria lacked funds and interest in spending its sparse treasury on frivolities such as a center for art, despite the fact that building of a concert hall was part of the initial plans. Dame Nellie Melba found this neglect unacceptable and took matters into her own capable hands. She presented a concert to raise funds in a memorable and amazingly successful evening. The program Dame Melba presented, featured herself as the principle soloist, the Victorian Professional Orchestra, and the Melbourne Repertory Theatre Company. The concert raised the princely sum of 1000£. The new hall was—of course–appropriately named "Melba Hall". The beautiful and highly useful building provided for classes on a wide-range of subjects: music aesthetics, music history, performance, style and interpretation, and provided the university and the city and province an acoustically well-designed venue for orchestral rehearsals, recitals, performances, and examinations.

Alexandra's interest in coming to Melba Hall was not for any of those reasons. She needed a relatively quick, convenient, and private place to talk business with her three children. None of them would be known or recognized because Alexandra had only toured the campus one time several years ago, and the three children were still in boarding prep schools.

"We're so happy to see you, Mother. This is a special occasion for all of us. You and Father have been so busy with all your business ventures and politicking, and we have been so absorbed in our school work that we haven't been able to have a decent conversation for months," said Irina, the eldest at twelve, as she gave Alexandra an emotional bear hug.

Of the children, she was the only one who looked like her mother while the other two favored their father.

"As you asked, we have just the place for our talk," said Kyle. "My music teacher, Professor Stiglitz, arranged for us to use study room 111A from noon until one."

Kyle was two years younger than Irina and was the family prodigy. He would probably start university the same year as Irina if he continued to progress at the same rate. Margaret had just turned eleven and was so excited to see Alexandra that she could not talk. Instead she cried and poured out her homesickness and longing in a fervent and prolonged embrace.

The family sat around a round discussion table in room 111A. The wife and daughter of the Melba Hall director brought in a platter of small cakes and pies, as she did every day for the students with whom she had bonded almost as if the young people were family members.

"Thank you very much, Mrs. Adams. These look delicious."

"Really taint nothin'," she responded. "More like a tschoske, and I'm just an old cooko," she said and blushed.

"Nothing of the sort. They are genuinely beautiful and delicious—nothing that's not genuine or schlocky. You are permitted to be proud of your work and to be able to take a 'thanks' or two."

"Yes, M'am, and I thankee. I consider it a privlige to see these beautiful and talented young sheilas and blokes doin' such hard yakka ta get ahead. I like to do a little fer 'em."

When they were again alone, the four Bradshaw family members reminisced and laughed, told jokes, shared gossip, and gave their opinions about current affairs. When there were only ten minutes left before they had to vacate the room, Alexandra turned serious and got down to her business.

"I have an important purpose for coming here to see you three today. What I am about to tell you has to stay among just the four of us until I am not available to give explanations, agreed?"

"Not even Father?"

"Not even him. In case something should happen to me…"

"What? Is something wrong. Are you sick? Are you in some sort of danger? We're still your tackies; we deserve to know," said Irina.

"Nothing like that and nothing to worry about. Just being prudent. Now, back to where I was going. You know that your mother is a very wealthy woman—not something I want noised around, right?"

The three children nodded.

"I want you to be provided for well if the time comes that I can no longer provide; and I pray that day will never come. Or if hard times come, and you need a cushion to protect you from financial downturns. You are too young to remember the great recession—the "smellbourne" days–but it is possible that such a time may repeat itself. You can never tell about these things. So…what I am going to do is to set aside a large sum of money in a trust with people I trust. When you turn twenty-one you become the sole owner of your one-third of the money. You can do with it what you want, but I advise you to seek the counsel of the people to whom I have entrusted the money about using your share wisely."

Each of the children pondered her declaration for a few moments, then precocious Kyle asked—with the guilelessness of youth—"how much money, Mother?"

Alexandra was not sure whether or not to give them that information. She had given the matter considerable thought.

Finally, she said with complete candor, "250 million dollars each."

Kyle made her laugh when he asked, "Aussie or American dollars?"

"Aussie. And don't be greedy. I have an envelope for each of you containing instructions about who to see and when to make the effort to arrange transfer of the funds. You may be surprised when you read the information; but let me assure you that I consider these people my family; and I trust them with my wealth and my life. You should, too."

After the conversation, they went to the Victoria Hotel on Little Collins Street. By prior arrangement with the restaurant, the chef prepared meat pie made with rare roasted kangaroo spiced with fennel and sweet grass, a dish which was becoming less and less popular in the country but was delicious served in the traditional fashion by the traditional chef and accompanied by baby beets. They finished up with good English Grey tea and Chocolate Indulgence.

"I'm choc a bloc," said Kyle.

"We're all full, Son," said Alexandra. "Remember this meal and this day."

Alexandra kissed them all goodbye and told them to be good and to be the best students possible. She told them she hoped to see them soon, something she had to manage her facial expression as she said it. Then she was away to Sydney.

Alexandra had a single-minded purpose in Sydney; and as soon as she got off the train, she hired a Hansom Cab to take her to a five-story, typically Chinese, office building on the corner of George and Hay Streets, with which she was thoroughly familiar. It had the feeling of home and family to her. The familial feeling was more than a fleeting sense, of course. She climbed to the fifth floor. She knocked on the familiar door bearing the small brass plaque reading, "Wáng & Dau". As Alexandra had hoped and expected, the door was opened by Wáng Caihong. Caihong's face broke into a delighted smile.

"How happy it is to see you, my Dear Sister," she said.

Alexandra responded, "How wonderful it is to see you once again, dear 'rainbow in the sky'," and the two women embraced as long separated sisters.

"I presume this is not just a social call, Dear Sister," Caihong said, getting to the point quickly as she always did.

"No. I am very happy to see you as a sister and friend and the mandarin as a father; but I do have serious business to discuss with you and your father, if that would please you."

"He has had a boring day. You realize that he is most aged now and cannot get out. He decries his loss of independence and usefulness. It will do him good to be of service."

Mandarin Wáng Wen Sheng and head of the Wáng Family Tong had heard Alexandra's voice and was enthusiastic to see her.

Alexandra bowed low, and Wáng gave a small nod. He had aged significantly since she had last seen him; she reckoned that he was over a hundred by now. They chatted briefly about old times, about her ventures with the family in the shipping business, and about the encounters with pirates. Alexandra could see that he was getting tired; so, she edged the conversation to why she had come to Sydney.

"Blessed Father, I have not forgotten that I am a member of the Wáng Family Tong. As I recall, you are still managing some investments for me."

"Yes, Dear Daughter. Have you come for a reckoning? Caihong, fetch my abacus if you would."

"No Father, I come as a daughter with an important request."

"Anything for one of my family."

"As you know—because you have spies everywhere, she chuckled—I have become quite wealthy. I have a problem to solve in another place, and I want to set aside funds for my three children, Irina, Kyle, and Margaret. I ask of you to arrange for my funds to be placed in a secure institution with the opportunity for my money to make money. I ask that the children be able to receive the money when they become of age twenty-one. Most importantly, Dear Father, I ask that you exert your influence to see that they are protected both financially and physically. You are well aware that we live in difficult times."

"It will be done as you wish. I am on the board of both the Bank of New South Wales, and of a *yinhang* [a silver institution] as we call banks–the Commercial Bank of China. Due to weaknesses of traditional

Chinese law regarding money, our Chinese financial institutions have focused almost entirely on commercial banking based on close familial and personal relationships, and their working capital is primarily based on the float from short-term money transfers rather than long-term demand deposits. In my middle age, I saw the need for more modern English type banking; so, I worked my way onto the governing body of the government bank. Because of that, I can conduct business in secret as I do in the Sydney bank, and I can also arrange for you–as a member of my family and of the Wáng Family Tong—to be able to have a secret account with a long-term demand account. Would that suit you, my dear?"

"Perfectly; and, as always, I am in your debt. Although we are family, I wish to do things the correct Chinese way. I wish to structure the arrangements in such a way that the Wáng Family Tong can receive ten percent of the profits of the account as payment for its management and to do so in perpetuity. Would you find that acceptable, Mandarin?"

"You are a good daughter, Alexandra, and have a good business head. When things are done for no profit, they are usually not worth the cost, as the old proverb goes. Since I am getting on in years, and my eyesight is so poor, would it please you to have our Caihong handle all the complexities of the arrangement?"

"Perfectly, Dear Father. I trust her with my wealth and with my life, and she can trust me to the same great degree. We must not over tire you, now. Caihong and I will get the work done. I thank you and wish you a thousand years."

In less than an hour, the documents were completed. Caihong was experienced, skilled, and industrious. Alexandra's requirements were precise and fairly simple: The account was to be a secret known only the the necessary tong members, Alexandra, and her children. Accounting was to be made biannually or on demand with information going to Alexandra and Caihong who would determine who else should receive the information. Each child, upon achieving his or her majority should receive $250 million AUS plus accrued profits. Advice from the financial master of the family tong should be offered to the young Bradshaws and an invitation to become part of the Wáng Family Tong if they wish, but none of that was mandatory from either side.

Alexandra left Caihong with a power-of-attorney to withdraw $750 million AUS from her Sydney accounts over the course of the next two years—the delay was suggested by Caihong to prevent unwanted attention to a transfer of such large sums in a short time. She took another Hansom Cab back to the huge Central Railway Station, located at the southern end of the central business district. She was back at Number 1-8, Collins Street in Melbourne before midnight.

Erskin Place, Melbourne, Victoria Province, Commonwealth of Australia, October 23 to November 11, 1912

Kyle Bradshaw's diversion from his wife led to his immersion in the plight of striking workers and the plight of the poor in Melbourne. His growing animosity towards the big end of town, the swells, the unfeeling government officials was fueled by a visit to Erskin Place with the head of the Dock Workers Union, Henry Clapham. Kyle had been like most reasonably affluent and educated Australians; he had looked away or walked on the other side of the street when approached by ragged beggars. He never did business or had any other reason to visit places like Erskin Place, a notorious slum. He and Henry had become fairly good mates during the dock strikes that had just been settled with a pittance of a wage increase and fantasy improvement in work conditions, as always. The strikers had been essentially starved into submission and pummeled by the government.

By all Kyle had read or imagined, Erskin Place was beyond his ken. Ideally, a city's housing should provide safe, orderly, secure, comfortable shelter if not actual luxury so that families can live reasonably healthy, productive lives. In the big end of town where Kyle and his wife lived the buildings were made with modern housing stock. They provided decent heating and cooling, had few major structural problems, and a minimum of problems with damp and mold. By contrast, Kyle noted in Erskin Place, bad housing made it much more likely for family members to get sick and to stay sick. He became determined to do something to improve the lot of slum dwellers.

CHAPTER SIXTY-TWO
MISSIONS' END

Although the angels rejoice over the testimony you bore as a missionary, continuing your post-mission journey toward your *life's mission* can involve unexpected challenges.
—Wendy Ulrich and Dave Ulrich, *lds.org*

National Archives of Australia, Victorian Archives Centre, 99 Shiel Street, North Melbourne, Victoria State, Australia, December 26 (Boxing Day), 2015

It was a great day in Melbourne and all the rest of Australia—boxing day—and for the LDS senior missionaries. It was happily comparable to Christmas Day in the states, and the overpowering desire to share gifts made the last two weeks a special joy. There were special parties and joyful get togethers among the people who had become fast friends during their eighteen-month missions. It was not lost on any of them that in three days there would be no one left in the national archives who knew or cared about the hobby-project of researching the life of a woman named Alexandra Tarasova-Yusupov Bradshaw. It was not even really clear if she ever actually used the name of Bradshaw. Alexandra was apparently a secretive woman. When she left her husband, children, and presumably, Australia, sometime in the early 1915 to 1920 period, it was as if she had walked into another dimension.

Elder Bradley, the most recent missionary to arrive from the states and his wife were not able to complete their mission—not because of any fault or infirmity on their parts, but because the church—in its wisdom and through revelation—had decided to have only Australian citizens do the archival work. That would give them enhanced commitment to both the work and to the church. He put the conundrum of working on the pet project succinctly for all of them.

He quoted Winston Churchill—taking a few liberties: "'Alexandra is an enigma wrapped in a riddle,' and I fear that she will be our mystery woman until we all reach the celestial kingdom."

The oldest and longest serving missionary of the group, a retired dentist named Elder Worthy, said, "Pride goeth before a fall; speak for yourself."

CHAPTER SIXTY-THREE

THE AUSTRALIAN RIFT OF THE EARLY 1900s

> "It sounds plausible enough tonight but wait until tomorrow.
> Wait for the common sense of the morning."
> —*The Time Machine*, H.G. Wells, 1895

Erskin Place, Melbourne, Victoria State, Commonwealth of Australia, October 23 to November 11, 1912

Kyle and Henry trudged through the forlorn streets of Erskin Place in North Melbourne taking care where they planted their shoes since the streets were muddy and served as the sewer system for the slum. Children and emaciated dogs played in the mud without a care. Smoke billowed from the chimneys of the nearby factories making Kyle's throat raw and his eyes to sting. Trams and horse-drawn carts moved helter-skelter through the rutted roads and alleys. The housing stock was of strikingly poor quality. Most of the dwellings had small—on average under 50 square meters– living space with separate living quarters, wash house, and privy. Those living quarters had no real bathrooms or facilities for sewerage. Bathing involved hauling buckets of heavily polluted water, often up several flights of stairs for a washrag once-over.

Bathing was a luxury that required too much time and effort to accomplish with any frequency. In fact, the popularity of June as the month for weddings came about because for many slum dwellers the yearly bath took place near the end of May; so bodily odor was still under some control by June. The same water had to be used for drinking and cooking. Survival required straining the water through cheese cloth followed by prolonged boiling of the water and a good memory. Babies were bathed in the grey water left over from clothes washing.

Erskin Place—like other slums throughout Australia—provided only a squalid existence with all houses facing back-yards or railways. The ramshackle housing, with leaky roofs and holes in the walls was the norm and not the exception; and the streets were woefully over-crowded and posed real risks to people's health just as did the poisoned air and the appallingly filthy streets. Many streets were no more than narrow winding lanes lined with tiny weatherboard and brick houses—many of which had long since converted to boarding houses–that dated as far back as the 1850s. Horses rushing down such lanes were a danger to oblivious children. Erskin Place–like other housing areas for the poor—was homogeneous and unchanging. The denizens of such places were locked into a never-ending cycle of poverty, producing too many children for the family's income, and crime.

Disease was rampant and serious. Treatable diseases, fractures, and head trauma more often than not went untreated because the poor had insufficient means to afford to see a doctor or to go to a hospital. They suffered lasting disabilities and premature death from problems that the rich could either avoid or could receive preventative and curative care.

Hank said, "Do you realize that as recently as 1901, an epidemic of bubonic plague struck here and killed several dozen people, most of them children and the elderly. There was not a single case seen in any family outside this fetid slum."

"I never heard of that. I guess not much news gets out about these places," Kyle commented. "I guess no one really cares."

Hank nodded. Kyle was being rapidly converted to the cause of the poor without Hank even half trying.

"Kyle, I want to take you to the home of one of my men from the dock. It will be the final way to convince you that something needs to be done. The more people like you that come in here, the louder will be the voices being raised to the government. You are a builder, a developer. Did you know that inner city developers have no obligation to contribute anything to essential public infrastructure; so, no kind of community facilities like sewer plants or affordable housing ever becomes obligatory?"

"I didn't know that either, Mate. It's a bloomin' shame, and I guess that's why bupkis gets done."

"We're here," Hank said. "This here's my boy, Fred Shine's place. It don't look like much outside, but wait 'til ya have a Captain Cook at the inside."

Hank knocked on the door of the shanty; and after what seemed to be an especially long wait, the door opened. A young man opened the door a crack, and, seeing who it was, let the two men in. Kyle had his first Captain Cook [look] at the inside of a shanty scarcely fit for keeping pigs.

"Hank, good to see ya. Come in. Sorry there ain't no place ta set and its kinda a dog's breakfast in here—hard ta get good help these days."

"And a g'day to yous," Hank said, taking note that there was another man and two grimy tackers present in the room.

Fred was right, there was no furniture; literally no place 'ta set'. Kyle and Hank stood and looked around. Kyle was glad he did not have to sit down; he was afraid he might catch something. The tiny hovel was built with three walls of corrugated iron, and an open side facing the back alley which was covered by a tattered sheet of canvas. The roof was made of old thatch with worn-out clothes stuffed into the holes. Kyle could hear the scurrying of little feet running about in the dirty thatch. There was only one room, and it was tiny. A baby cart was hanging from a rafter because there was no space on the floor. The single source of heat was a fireplace which held a three-inch thick layer of old soot and ash and gave out no heat. Two little children played with mud balls on the dirty bare floor; the room served as kitchen, bedroom, living room, and store room. There was barely space enough to stand.

An older man whom Hank seemed to know was leaning against one of the walls holding cards in his right hand and a bottle of cheap Rutherglen Muscat red wine in the left. Evidently Kyle and Hank had disturbed Fred and his friend from their fascinating game of Swedish Rummy.

"How's it hangin', Mikey?" Hank asked the red-faced bruce bloke with a gin blossom nose.

"None too bad, Hank. You foine?"

"Can't complain."

"Any news on when there'll be work? asked Mikey with a slur in his speech.

"Any time now, I'm told," Hank said although he knew no more than Mikey did about it.

"So, we'll be keepin' on the dole for a while longer. Down-market blokes the like of us never do git a fair suck off the sauce bottle. Ain't right, but it ain't never gonna change, neither."

"Ya got that right, Mikey."

Having finished the scintillating conversation with the two drunks and taking in the depressing scene long enough, Kyle and Hank left.

"Known those bruces long, Hank?" Kyle asked.

"Too long. They're both bludgers and are second or third generation dole grabbers. The strike could notta come at a worse time for blokes like them. They never seem to rise. A man can sorta understand what the big end 'o town means when they say that all of us down at this end are worthless as a billabong fulla spit. You saw 'em today. I never seen either of 'em when they weren't legless as any other drunk layin' around in one the ditches in any of the slums."

Kyle nodded, but the visit to Erskin Place produced serious food for thought for him. They stopped for a pint at one of the gin joints on the wharf before heading home. The docks were only recently coming back to life after the damages done during the strike. It was only a little less dismal that Erskin Place.

After supper, Kyle sat down to write a serious letter to Alexandra—a last try to get her to accept the dreadful inequality extant in Australia and to join him in his planned efforts to lessen the suffering in the slums and among the menial laboring families. It was heartfelt and imploring. He had a bit of hope that working together in a good cause might help heal the growing rift between them.

> November 12, 1912
> Dear Alexandra,
>
> I have missed you sorely. I want things to get back to the way they were when we took our little honeymoon trip up to Bulahdelah. You have to admit that we've had some good old times. I think we can be fair dinkum again if we give it a try.
>
> There is something I want to ask you. Please take a little walkabout with me to see one of the slums and conditions at dockside. They are terrible and getting worse all the time. I know you are woman with a big heart, and you will want to help before more people die of disease, starvation, and crime. We have enough to help, and we should. Please, just one walkabout. Everything I read says that poor-quality

housing makes the already poor blokes even worse off. The slums are crowded with struggling young people, people with disabilities and sicknesses that get worse without proper care and education, renters, foreigners, and indigenous people. All of those try to get along with wretchedly low incomes, and can't get full-time employment, if any.

There is a massive separation between rich and poor, both classes leading completely separate lives from each other. Might as well be from different foreign countries. Where your house is located shows your social status. The rich live at the top of the hill where we do. It very rarely ever floods; we're away from the dirty air and filthy streets that come from factories' smoke. The poor live down at the bottom of the hill in the slums; just as soon as they seem to be getting a bit ahead, they get flooded. All the time they are surrounded by bad air, infectious diseases, and their streets and homes down there at the bottom end of the market are horribly unsanitary, unsafe; and the houses are too little for people to live decently because of the crowding. You have to see what most of the houses are like: for those living in them. Houses—if you can call them that—are just prefabricated iron boxes that were shipped from Asia. They freeze in the winter and roast in the summer. Women and children live miserably and die too young.

Imagine not having enough money; so, you have to rent and to live in those cans. You got no skills, no education; so, you can't make enough to pay the rent; and you are out on the street; and nobody cares a hapenny's worth. We have a house ten times the size of the average in the slums. We have separate bedrooms for the adults and children. The kitchen is inside, and we have specialty rooms like a laundry, sitting rooms, game room, and an inside bathroom. Lots of those poor blighters just use the ditches and the streets as their bathrooms. We even have a nice clean garden. We have a much lower chance of catching diseases and also far better medical care if we do.

Alexandra, we can't change it all; but we can do something. We must do something. It will haunt me to the grave if we don't. I love you. Please love me and come back to me; so, we can work together on this.

Love,
Kyle

There was never any reply, written or verbal.

Melbourne Magistrates' Court, Corner of Russell and Latrobe Streets, Trial Division Building, Commonwealth of Australia, January 24, 1913

The case of Mikey Dixon v. State of Victoria, Commonwealth of Australia
Date: 24 January 1913

Presiding Magistrate, Hon. Isaac Douglass-Winthrop

Barristers: For Mikey Dixon, Plaintiff-Christopher Bernard, QC. For the State of Victoria et.al., Defendant-Larimer Devin Cullimore, QC.

Nature of the Cause: Plaintiff alleges that the Defendant [State of Victoria, City of Melbourne, Port Authority of Melbourne, and Departments of Sanitation and Security] failed to carry out their fiduciary duties for the citizens of several impoverished neighborhoods by not providing proper zoning, policing, sewage management, clean and safe culinary water, failure to maintain order, failure to provide education for the children of the neighborhoods in question, and protection from flooding and spread of infectious diseases.

Witnesses for the Plaintiff: Kyle Dewit Herman Bradshaw, Builder and Notable Citizen, Henry "Hank" Clapham, Elected Leader of the Dock Workers Union, Fred Shine, Citizen of Erskin Place Neighborhood, Melbourne, Mikey Dixon, Dock Worker and Citizen of Erskin Place Neighborhood, Mrs. Ruth Prescott Housekeeper, Citizen of North Melbourne, housewife and mother of ten, Augustus Byron Moore, President of the Australian Labor Party.

Witnesses for the Defendants: Hon. Quentin Overton McBride, State Senator representing Melbourne in the senate, Lord Mayor Thomas James Davey, City of Melbourne, Constable Mervin "Merv" Fenwick, law enforcement officer, Erskin Place Neighborhood, Mrs. Alexandra Tarasova-Yusupov Bradshaw, Notable Citizen of Melbourne, housewife, business woman, and mother of three, H.V. McKay, Notable citizen and Owner of the Sunshine Harvester Works in Melbourne, Augustus Byron Parker, Notable Citizen and President of the Associated Northern Collieries, McIlwraith McEacharn, Notable Citizen and President of the Adelaide Steamship Company.

Judgment of the court:

Slums are a manifestation of the two main challenges facing human settlements in general and development in Victoria State and Melbourne City specifically: rapid urbanization and the urbanization of poverty. The court stipulates that slum areas have the highest concentrations of poor people and the worst shelter and physical environmental conditions. The issue of the case of Mikey Dixon v. State of Victoria, Commonwealth of Australia, 24 January, 1913 is the question of what person(s) or what social entity(s) should be held responsible for the causation of the poverty and therefore to be responsible for repair of the problem. The plantiffs insist that the rich, reputable employers, the state, and the city, are responsible either individually or collectively.

The first question is–of course–whether an actual problem exists or is inner city poverty more a perception on the part of activists who view life through the prism of their own social, economic, religious, and ethnic perspectives. Seldom admitted by such people is the positive side of so-called slum life. Studies done by British and Australian institutions of higher learning correctly point out that slums are the first stopping point for immigrants. Inner city concentrations of newly arrived people provide the lowest cost and, in fact, the only affordable housing that will enable the immigrants to save for their eventual absorption into greater urban society peopled by such as the defendants in this action. As the place of residence for low-income employees, slums keep the social and economic institutions of the city—including Melbourne—functioning in a variety of different and effective ways.

The majority of slum dwellers in developing country cities such as Melbourne and Sydney earn their living from informal sector activities located either within or outside slum areas, and many informal entrepreneurs operating from slums have clienteles extending to the rest of the city. Most slum dwellers are people struggling to make an honest living, within the context of extensive urban poverty and formal unemployment. Slums are also places in which the vibrant mixing of different cultures frequently results in new forms of artistic expression. Out of unhealthy, crowded, and often dangerous environments can emerge cultural movements and levels of solidarity unknown in the suburbs of the rich. A fact often overlooked is that slum dwellers have developed economically rational and innovative shelter solutions for themselves, however inadequate or inappropriate the solutions may seem to people in the higher strata.

It must be accepted as a given—unfortunately–that poverty is the underlying and most important causation of the existence of slums and the slow progress towards the goal of adequate shelter for all. The important studies from the University of Melbourne have demonstrated beyond reasonable doubt that provision of improved housing and related services through slum upgrading or even physical eradication of slums will—by themselves—fail to solve the slum problem at issue in this case. Solutions based on this premise have failed to address the main underlying causes of slums, of which poverty is the most significant.

Urban stratification has multiple dimensions: economic, political, cultural, social, ethnic and—as demonstrated in Mikey, et. al.–spatial. These stratifications find expression in various status markers. For example, people in different strata will often dress differently and they may use different vocabulary or pronunciation. There will also often be differences in what and how much they possess, the type and amount of food they consume, and their living environments. By tradition, status also prescribes certain behaviors and 'manners'. Segregation by ethnic groups, which, in turn, have been associated with specific occupations, occurred widely in preindustrial cities. Ethnic quarters tended to be self-sufficient, physically and socially separated from the rest of the city. Often, they have their own unique social structure, including political leaders and schools. So, one of the questions prompted by this case is "should slums and slum life be eradicated and permanently changed?"

Ideally, housing provides us with the secure, comfortable shelter that people and their families need to live healthy, productive lives. In general, we have a modern housing stock with good heating and cooling, few major structural problems and few problems with damp and mold. By contrast, bad housing makes it much more likely you will get sick and stay sick once ill. The Reserve Bank governor acknowledged young Australians need their parents' help to buy a home in Sydney.

The answers to the questions posed constitute the findings—the judgment—of this court. Nowhere in Australian law are inner city developers found to be under obligation to provide or even contribute to essential public infrastructure, such as affordable housing and community facilities, based on density bonus systems anymore than they must provide special services for the affluent to enable their children to receive advanced educational degrees. Reputable employers have been required to provide livable minimal wages for workers and their families, and no more.

Any action by this court to impair free action of union and employer boards, city, county, and national governments and would deprive such entities of any value under the law or in the eyes of ordinary citizens of Australia. The law prevents this magistrate from doing so. Therefore, I find in favor of the defendants.

Since the legislative bodies and, therefore, the courts, have not seen it prudent or lawful to enact such reforms as demanded by the plaintiffs, this court makes the following suggestions to citizens with an interest in making changes for the people living in Australia's slums:

1. Seek legislation to require governmental entities to mandate slum conditions reforms and to provide funding to do so.
2. Provide mandatory education for all Australians to enable them better to participate in their own welfare.
3. Unite labor organizations, syndicates of employers, benefactors, and governmental institutions to study conditions and to provide realistic solutions which can be implemented.
4. Urge governments to raise taxes on the public and on businesses if such is required to effect the changes above.

A benefit of establishing such requirements along with designation of what persons and what organizations are responsible will–of necessity–lead to accountability. Failure to establish such changes will necessarily cause blame to fall on the shoulders of agitators such as the present plaintiffs without excuse.

Signed,
Isaac Douglass-Winthrop
Hon. Isaac Douglass-Winthrop,
Presiding Magistrate, Melbourne Magistrates' Court

Alexandra waited for the reading of the magistrate court judgment before doing anything of importance regarding her life with Kyle and, indeed in Australia. Having been fully vindicated—so far as she was concerned—by Judge Douglass-Winthrop's finding, she considered that much of her problem with Kyle was a dichotomy of classes. In short, she was right; and he was wrong; and never the twain shall meet, as Kipling stated in his classic poem. She could no longer be content to live in a marital arrangement so completely mismatched. It was time—posthumous–for her to rectify the situation.

Kyle was conveniently away on business—another one of his hair-brained money-making schemes. He and a partner were exploring Milford Sound on the South Island of New Zealand determine the prospects for making their fortune in the fur seal business. Alexandra recognized it as an excuse to stay away from her. Therefore, the timing was right.

She had the servants pack twelve new stateroom trunks with her best dresses and other high-quality items she would need for an extended stay. She also filled four steamer trunks with sturdy outdoor clothing and equipage, including the new eye protectors called Foster-Grant sun glasses from America. She planned and replanned each item she was going to take and forced herself to define a purpose that would make it worth her while to keep it with her. Satisfied with her efforts, she set about to manage her accounts.

She sought out her creditors and paid off every one of them, including the very small debts. When that was completed, she took a Hansom Cab to the Victoria branch of the Commonwealth Bank and the Queensland Government Savings Bank where she removed all her money and had it transferred to her account held by Wáng Wen Sheng, head of the Wáng Family Tong.

"How is such an account managed, Madam?" the concerned bank assistant asked.

"It is held in the Commercial Bank of China—one of the institutions the Chinese refer to as a *yinhang* or silver institution. Here is the account number and the names of the signatories. They are Wáng Wen Sheng, his daughter, Caihong, and me. Can you make a wire transfer of the funds?"

"Of course. We use Western Union. Will that be satisfactory?"

"Completely. The funds will be held under the name of Wáng Caihong as I require complete anonymity."

"I beg your pardon, Mrs. Bradshaw, but do you have that much trust in a Chinese person?"

"I have complete trust. It is a family matter."

The assistant manager could not resist raising one eyebrow to give the patron a dubious look. It was ignored; so, the employee decided that it was not any of her business and quickly completed the process.

The process–and even the conversation—was almost identical in the Queensland Government Savings Bank. Alexandra had to admit to herself that it was rather discomfiting to be a person with no money in a city where she had lived for so long. She hurried from the bank to catch her train to Sydney. She was escorted aboard the Victorian Railways Premier Train and to her first-class compartment by an obsequious under-conductor named Franklin. She tipped him two dollars, and he looked at her as if she had just guaranteed his children's educations.

The ride was smooth and comfortable except for a mandatory transfer of trains in Albury owing to the break-of-guage in the tracks. She had to walk down a long island platform to the new train on an old-style narrow guage track with Franklin carrying her en-suite luggage. He nearly swooned when she gave him another two dollars—more than five days pay—as a tip. It amused her to see him bow and scrape and to have a chance to imagine giving herself a secret pat on the back for her ability to be so generous, another of the perquisites of her class. The trip to Sydney was without incident and entirely comfortable—even luxurious. She was served two fine meals in her stateroom. Attendants in starched white coats attendants served from silver dome covered platters onto lace-edged linen table clothes with matching napkins bearing the train's monogramed logo. The eight utensils were silver, and the three glassware offerings were an exotic assortment of Imperial Dragon, Hindu

Ganesha, and Tropical Elephant goblets imported for exclusive use by the railroad.

High tea included buttered bread with thinly sliced cucumber, Egg Mayonnaise, thin slices of medium rare roast beef, an assortment of cheese, tuna, and tinned salmon with a slice of Polish sweet pickle, and an English scone. Alexandra chose a well-aged Chardonnay from the Australian wine offerings and crème brulee for dessert. Dinner was more that she could eat: Beef Wellington, small portions of roast lamb and mutton with side servings of horse radish and Hollandaise sauces, cold mixed frutos del mar salad, an assortment of fresh vegetables, and choccy biccy and Italian gelato assortment for dessert.

CHAPTER SIXTY-FOUR
HOOROO TO AUSTRALIA

Here's to champagne, the drink divine,
That makes us forget our troubles;
It's made a dollar's worth of wine,
And three dollars' worth of bubbles.

*—The Up-to-date Bartenders' Guide: a Valuable Ready Reference
Guide to the Art of Mixing Drinks, Containing All the Standard
And Popular Drinks, With a Choice Selection of Appropriate
Toasts* (1913)

—Toast from Harry Montague

First Class Area, Port Jackson, Sydney, State of New South Wales, Commonwealth of Australia, January 28, 1913

Mormon missionaries, Elder Phillip and Elder Young, hitched a ride with a farmer from his farm in the suburbs to Port Jackson, where he would off-load pigs for shipment to New Zealand. The two overly dressed young men brushed straw from their black suits and walked a mile and a half along the quay towards the First-Class Area where they had agreed to meet with Mrs. Bradshaw before she left on a voyage.

"Any idea where she's off to, Elder Young?" asked the Aussie who was the senior companion of the pair.

"Not really. I gathered it is for a long time, though."

"I got the idea that it was maybe five hundred K south of Woop Woop. Maybe even Utah to join the saints for all I know?"

"Could be, but I doubt it. She would have been one of our baptisms if that was her intention, don't you think, Elder?"

"Probably right."

"What time are we supposed to meet her?" Elder Young asked since he left all issues of time to his Australian companion who both acknowledged was the more reliable of the two.

"No later than half past one. Crikey, we're gonna be late if we don't get more of a move on. *Av-a-go-yer-mug*; we'll never make it if you don't get those Shanks's ponies movin' a little faster. It's not all that hard to move your legs more often and to make your steps farther apart. Let's get a sweat up. We go flat chat, and we'll be finished in half the time."

"I must have been here a long time, Compie; I think I'm getting to understand your Aussie language," said Elder Young refusing to take umbrage at his companion's criticism.

"Not quite, Mate," Elder Phillip said, "You hafta keep in mind that Australia is the lucky country. First thing is it is not 'Ausssie'. We are '*Auzzzies*'. Get the difference in pronunciation?"

"Ah, yes. Thanks. I hadn't paid attention before."

"No offense meant."

"None taken."

"Did I tell ya that you've really gone and got yourself all tarted up? And that I take a liken' to yer new bag a fruit?" asked Elder Phillip.

"Suit cost me half of my monthly ration from home; the shirt, tie, and shoes set me back another fifteen percent. I should look like someone from the big part of town just for the cost of it all. That's the truth."

"Bloody oath it is. It's gotta be yer best bib and tucker." said Elder Phillip, his face having lost its usual jesting look.

They came to the First-Class Area sign and hesitated for a moment before Elder Phillip nodded for them to go in.

"We got as much right to be here as any of those swells," he said to justify their choice.

"Right-O," Elder Young said, and pointed at the most elegant woman in the entire reserved area. "That has to be our Sheila."

"It'd be a grand disappointment if it isn't," Elder Phillip said, "but I want to ask somebody to be sure."

He approached a burly wharfie and asked, "G'day, Mate. Do you happen to know if that fine lady there leanin' on her brolly is the important Mrs. Bradshaw?"

"Aye do, and she is."

As brash as ever, he led Elder Young over to where Mrs. Bradshaw stood looking over the harbor and city.

Elder Phillip could tell that she was paying them no mind.

"She's away with the pixies," he said to Elder Young.

"We gotta get our chinwag goin' sometime, and now is as good a time as ever."

"Ow-yar-goin, Sister Bradshaw?"

Alexandra was mildly startled.

"I'm fine. I was just gathering a little wool, I guess. I'm glad you two could make it to see me off for places unknown. And you on time and everything."

"Must be a mighty fine place you're headed, Sister Bradshaw. You are dressed up fit to kill, if you don't mind me saying so," Elder Young said to her.

"I'm hoping so, and it is nice of you to notice."

Elder Phillip broke in, "Well we wouldn't have presumed that you got those duds from Vinnies."

Alexandra laughed, partly at her self. She would not be caught dead in a St. Vincent De Paul's charity store.

"Like yer frilly brolly, Sister. Looks like the Ridgie didge straight from Paris."

"I like it, too, if I don't say so myself. It might even rain," she said with a small laugh. "No worries mate. She'll be apples!"

"We'd like to give you a little spiritual lesson, Sister, if you think you have time. Maybe you will get to meet some more elders wherever you're goin. Who knows what might come of that?"

"Let's find some shade."

Elder Phillip found a good spot where bales of aboriginal calico cloth stood high enough to block the sun's rays.

"I've got a real possie spot here in the shade," said the irrepressible, Elder Phillip.

"I think you've found the bonzer spot."

They ate as the missionaries took turns giving the next two lessons in the *Introduction to the Church of Jesus Christ of Latter-day* Saints pamphlet. Elder Phillips had read the lesson several times before coming to meet the prospective new member, and he had all but memorized it; so, he could recite the new ideas as rapidly and fluently as possible. The lesson was on baptism, especially on the fallacy of baptizing infants before they could sin. He paused for questions. There were none; so, Elder Young gave lesson five—the most difficult of the lessons—about the first principles and ordinances of the gospel. It was easy for him since he had been required to read about them, memorize them, and preach on them in Primary–the Sunday school for children–since as far back as he could remember.

They closed with a short folksy prayer, then Elder Young asked if Alexandra was going far away or for a long time.

"Will you be yonks, Sister Bradshaw?"

"Not sure; come see; come saw. Maybe weeks, maybe years."

"I hope not unless you are on your way to Utah."

"You can never be sure what is going to happen, Elder. I just can't say."

"Are you travelin' with anyone else, Sister?"

"No, I'll be alone."

"That's pretty hard," Elder Smith said... "I mean to be Pat Malone way out there."

Elder Phillip wanted to lighten things up; so, he said, "No worries mate. She'll be apples!" and gave Alexandra a warm Aussie smile.

"Good onya," said Elder Young, trying out his shaky grasp of Australian strine.

The first boarding call came; and Alexandra said, "Sorry, brothers. Looks like I'll have to get going."

Both boys quickly reached for the small gifts they had brought for their prospective new member, lest she forget them and the church.

"We have little somethings for your trip, Sister Bradshaw."

Elder Phillip handed her a small bouquet of Wattles, Australia's national flower.

Elder Young gave her a book of Australia's first stamps, printed in 1913 for the first time. Alexandra was charmed by the gesture and by the stamps themselves—they featured a kangaroo standing on a map of Australia. And—so she could not forget the source—the stamps were inscribed in bold letters, "AUSTRALIA POSTAGE". The two young men handed Alexandra a book called *The Songs of a Sentimental Bloke* by CJ Dennis and a nice leather-bound *Book of Mormon*; so, she could not forget the religion. They signed the books with both of their names... their full names and addresses.

She shed a tear and quickly wiped it away to prevent losing courage or showing more emotion than she ought. She gave each elder a brush kiss on the cheek and laughed when the puritanical young men blushed.

She turned to leave, and Elder Phillip gave her one parting bit of advice, "Remember to pray every day, Sister, and Bob's yer uncle."

Alexandra laughed at the young man's impertinent and quintessentially Australian enthusiasm as she walked into the passengers-only Circular Quay Overseas Passenger Terminal—officially, the Sydney Cove Passenger Terminal—and saw a large formally dressed coterie of dignitaries waiting to send her off, much to her chagrin. She had hoped to go in style, but eschewed fanfare since it had the potential to alert her husband of her departure. She was met by the crème de la crème of Sydney society: Frederic John Napier Thesiger, 1st Viscount Chelmsford, GCSI, GCMG, GCIE, GBE, PC, Governor of New South Wales, Thomas Denman 3rd Baron Denman, Governor-General of Australia, and James McGowen, outgoing Premier of New South Wales, and their wives.

White-coated railway waiters served French 75 champagne cocktails accented with an assortment of different citrus accents, choice Augustora and Peychaud bitters, a dash of Curacao, and sugar. Pretty girls in pinafore dresses with the railroad logo on the left breast served creamy chicken liver pâté on fresh Parisian toast, pork rillettes–a rustic pâté made from meat poached in its own fat, then shredded, and stored in some of that fat–pickled dried apricots, and clothbound cheddar gougères.

The greetings and discussions of matters both light civilities and weighty policy issues were cordial and complimentary to the departing demi-queen. Alexandra–for all of her attempts at modesty—loved every second and syllable of the festive departure gathering.

Her wit ingratiated the ladies.

"I have a question," Lady Thesiger said to Alexandra.

"The answer is, 'money'," replied Alexandra resulting in a robust round of laughter from the upper-crust women who were unused to even slightly irreverent answers.

Finally taking her leave with promises on all sides to keep in touch, Alexandra climbed the gangplank escorted by the ship's activities director and onto the Anchor Line oceanliner, the SS Cameronia, and taken to the First-Class Area Passenger Outwards and Customs Lounge.

The ship was a twin propeller triple-expansion 1700 passenger ocean liner steam-ship owned by the Glasgow-based Anchor Line and built by D. and W. Henderson and Company at Glasgow in 1911 to sail under the United Kingdom flag with every amenity and safety feature extant at the time to persuade and please the affluent traveler. The large—11,000 GRT–liner was 515 feet in length, 62.25 feet across at the beam was capable of a maximum speed of 19 knots. The powerful ship's propulsion was provided by a twin propeller, triple-expansion, 15,600 IHP steam engine. It was one of the largest, fastest, and most luxurious ships afloat.

Seated in a soft leather covered office chair in front of a round table with a large checkerboard designed top made of an assortment of precisely cut hardwoods polished to a high gleam, Alexandra was given her ship's passage and customs documents to fill out and sign. Most of the documents were routine, listing ports of embarkation and debarkation, reason for travel—vacation—race, religion, name of spouse, and Australian residence information. A more difficult portion of the custom's requirements was to complete a dictation test in one of the recognized European languages. Colored race or illiteracy were disqualifying factors to prohibit exit or entry of undesirables, including the colored races, Muslims, Hindus, Athiests, those with contagious diseases or criminal records, or who were considered to be morally weak, those who were unable to support themselves, and those believed to have occupations that would take away jobs from members of the United Kingdom or the United States. An immigration officer read a fifty-word passage in English which Alexandra was required to write out in a legible hand with a minimum of mistakes. She passed without a problem.

The great ship edged out from the wharf area and passed North Head–the important northern edge of the seaward entrance to Port Jackson–which played a major role in the cultural and military life of the colony of New South Wales, following the arrival of the First Fleet in 1788 and in the business and social life of Alexandra and her Chinese family. The 'Heads', signified arrival and departure at Port Jackson and Australia since 1788. For Alexandra, it was a moment of final hooroo from Australia and her life there.

BOOK THREE

CHAPTER SIXTY-FIVE

CHURCH HISTORY

"Inspiration is discovered in the fact that each part, as it was
revealed, dovetailed perfectly with what had come before. There
was no need for eliminating, changing, or adjusting any part to
make it fit."

—Prophet Joseph Fielding Smith,
Doctrines of Salvation, 1954, v. 1, p. 170

The apostle Paul, the foremost defender of spiritual religion,
never ceased trying to get the Jews to give up their confidence in
outward works and rituals, and to lead them to spiritual realities.
Yet I feel that the great majority of Christians have fallen back
again into that sickness.

—Desiderius Erasmus Roterodamus,
The Dagger of the Christian Soldier, 4th and 5th Rules

Conference Center, Church of Jesus Christ of Latter-day Saints, 60 West North
Temple, Salt Lake City, Utah, USA, March 26 through April 3, 2016

The senior missionaries who served in the Australia Victoria
Archives digitalization project scheduled to meet in Elder and
Sister Durrells' room in the Joseph Smith Building [formerly,
the Hotel Utah] during the April biannual conference of the LDS church
in Salt Lake City on Saturday evening after the Priesthood Session. The
get-together started at nine-thirty p.m. with lemonade and cookies
purchased from the famous Lion House Pantry Café—a tradition for

groups of returned senior missionaries. The house was originally built in 1856 by Brigham Young, second President of The Church of Jesus Christ of Latter-day Saints, to accommodate his large polygynous family of fifty-six children from sixteen of his fifty-five wives, and their many adopted, foster, and step-children.

As most of such occasions are, this was a joyful one except for the untimely death of one of their number–Nephi Smith—who passed through the veil separating mortal and immortal life in an untimely way three months previously. Since all of them believed whole-heartedly in an eternal life hereafter, and that Nephi—a thoroughly good man, a true saint—was with his loving Heavenly Father and those of his ancestors who had passed on, none of them were seriously sorrowful, not even his loving wife, Marianne.

Glen Gabler, the latest self-appointed court jester for the missionary group burst into the room after everyone else had taken their places at the family-style tables.

He shouted, "Aussie! Aussie! Aussie!, and rest of the missionaries responded appropriately with "Oi! Oi! Oi!" feeling a bit sheepish in the crowded café.

They needn't have felt the least bit inappropriate as evidenced by the enthusiastic clapping by their co-religionists throughout the large basement eating facility.

Because he had made such an outburst to announce his arrival, Glen was unanimously elected to offer the blessing on the food. After dinner, Katherine Durrell–the de facto leader of the group's search for history of the mysterious Alexandra Tarasova-Yusupov—was given the floor.

"Sorry that I haven't got anything dramatic to share tonight, but I do have something that Elder Durrell and I discovered in our research in the The Family History Library."

The library is a major genealogical research facility located at 35 North West Temple, in downtown Salt Lake City close to Temple Square and the Conference Building. The library is open to the public free of charge as an act of generosity for all the world and is operated by FamilySearch, the genealogical arm of The Church of Jesus Christ of Latter-day Saints.

The idea that something—anything—new had been discovered piqued the interest of the former missionaries.

"What we found was something none of us would ever have imagined. *Sister* Bradshaw, as she was known then, met several times with a pair of Australasian missionaries, Elder J. Hales Young and Elder Samuel Randolph Phillip. Elder Young was on of the great greats of President Brigham Young, and Elder Phillip was one of the great, great greats of Admiral Arthur Phillip–the Royal Navy officer who became the first Governor of New South Wales. He founded the British penal colony that later became Sydney.

"Both of those missionaries have passed on, unfortunately; but Elder Durrell and I were able to find their journals from their incredible missions back in the early 1900s. They described attending church with Mrs. Bradshaw in the basement bar of the *Duke of Wellington Hotel* on March 30, 1912. They even called her Sister Bradshaw, but still there is not record we could discover of her having ever been baptized into the church. For your interest, the mission was organized in 1851 as the Australian Mission then in 1854 was changed to the Australasian Mission, then it was again renamed the Australian Mission again in 1898 when the New Zealand Mission was added. Charles Henry Hyde was the mission president during the period when Alexandra was in Australia. There were only something like 450 members in the whole country and maybe something like ten or eleven in all of Melbourne during that time.

"The last known record of Sister Bradshaw—or Tarasova-Yusupov— as we know her–came from a short article in the general Melbourne newspaper, *The Argus*, on January 28, 1913. Here is a digital copy of the society section, *Comings and Goings*, on page eleven:"

> 'A happy throng gathered at the First-Class section of the grand ocean liner, the *SS Cameronia*. Among the dignitaries at the gay send-off festivities were Frederic John Napier Thesiger, 1st Viscount Chelmsford, Governor of New South Wales, Thomas Denman 3rd Baron Denman, Governor-General of Australia, and James McGowen, outgoing Premier of New South Wales, and their wives, and Alexandra Bradshaw of this city, reputed to be one of the–if not the–richest women in the world. We wish all of them a save voyage whereever the winds and waves take them.'

"This little article did not even indicate the destination of the voyage."

"Have you had a chance to check possible ports of call to see if a ship's passenger list might give us a clue as to where she landed?" asked Sister Nedra Wright.

"Nary a one," answered Sister Katherine Durrell. "Glen and Marilyn Gabler pitched in to help. They are their stake's genealogy experts and are very imaginative when it comes to finding locations, ships', trains', and bus, information. Together, we searched all the major European and Asian ports, Russian ports—with special emphasis on Vladivostok. No Bradshaw."

"Any luck with the names, Tarasova or Yusupov?" asked Peter Wright.

"Nothing, zip, nada, zero, *nichego*."

"I hate to think it, but maybe we are defeated," observed Sister Louise Nicholson.

"As the Lord wills," said Goeffrey Smedley, currently the patriarch in northern Utah.

CHAPTER SIXTY-SIX

THE WAY HOME

All that is gold does not glitter. Not all those who wander are lost.
—J.R.R. Tolkien,

The Fellowship of the Ring

We travel, some of us forever, to seek other states, other lives, other souls.
—Anaïs Nin, *The Diary of Anaïs Nin*, Vol. 7: 1966-1974

On board the *SS Cameronia*, from Sydney to Shanghai, from January 28 to March 12, 1913

Alexandra went out of her way to maintain anonymity, even if the other passengers might consider her to be haughty and unapproachable. She spent most of her time with a gentleman escort offered by the shipping company; so, she would not be lonely or unhappy. His name was David C. Nelson, a retired architect from London, who was enjoying a pleasant retirement sailing around the world for free. Alexandra did not ask for his personal information, and he did not offer any particulars; nor did she, which suited them both.

For wealthy Americans, South Americans, Australians, Europeans, and the British, travel throughout Europe—on the so-called "Grand Tour", a travel experience patterned after that awesome experience afforded the very well-to-do from the seventeenth century on–was a decided mark of status. From the early 1900s, passenger ships—like the *SS Cameronia*–catered to the lavish tastes of the rich by providing extravagant spaces at sea on a par with the finest hotels and restaurants of the world. The United States, Great Britain, Germany, and France, competed to create showpiece "ships of state," and new—ever more grand–steamers appeared every year or so claiming—accurately–to being more spacious, more luxurious, offered more courtesy, were faster, and safer than anything that had sailed before. The style of the Gilded Age was to engage well-known hotel designers to fashion the ship's most elaborate spaces into a mixture of historic styles of the great cities of the world that matched the look of fashionable hotels, clubs, and apartment houses, familiar to the wealthy travelers—as opposed to those lesser mortals who were just casual vacationers.

Alexandra was first introduced to her distinguished looking tuxedoed escort, David Nelson, in the First-Class lounge; and shortly thereafter, they were on a first name basis. The lounge featured skylights—lanterns—which brought filtered daylight into interior spaces, adding elegance. The façades of the elegant walls alternated magnificent hand-made Turkish floor to ceiling tapestries with plaster panels depicting famous early vessels and naval battles. Similar grandeur was featured throughout the dining areas, libraries, and other first-class lounges.

Her stateroom—called "the Aristocracy Suite" and described as "a room Napolean or the Rockefellers would covet"–was an apartment which rendered the illusion of a great hotel suite. Her rooms were–in fact–copied and improved upon from the French jewel Peninsula Hotel located 300 meters from the Arc de Triomphe de l'Étoile. The bed was the epitome of comfort; the furniture was richer and more baroque than actually fitted the room: matching deep red velvet couches, Moroccan leather swivel chair and mahogany desk, French leather wingback chair, and matching gilded silk and damask tapestry carpet, draperies, and bedspread. There was electrical lighting and facilities en suite. She successfully achieved the first wireless communication between ships out at sea and was able to transmit a message to her three children about why and where she had gone and about the provisions of their trusts and her will which would make them richer than anyone they knew; in sum, the amenities created the illusion of not being at sea for a two-week voyage of unparalled luxury.

David rapped on Alexandra's stateroom door precisely at the agreed-upon hour; so, they could make a short orienting tour of the first-class common areas, all decorated differently, and all extravagantly—he in his tuxedo, and she in her most recently acquired and most gorgeous new gown with the daring décolletage. After all, one of the most important reasons for leaving one's stateroom was to demonstrate the level of affluence demonstrated by such magnificent attire. On the way to the first-class dining and theater area, David introduced her to the mens'smoking room, one of two writing rooms, a small private lounge for cards, cocktails, and intimate conversation, a grand curving staircase, and a cosy veranda café that evoked the moist greenery of an indoor winter garden, and at the same time, something of the ambience of an outdoor café in gay Paree or snooty uptown New York.

Alexandra and David walked into the First-Class Dining area at precisely eight o'clock, the dinner hour. The *maî·tre d'hô·tel*–in his perfectly fitting long coat, white tie, and tails escorted them to a cosy table for two with a view of the swiftly passing ocean. The first-class dining saloon was inspired by a mid-17th century French château–Château des Comtes de Marchi–located in all its elegance in Belgium. Above its oak splendor rose a dome dotted with Chinese signs of the zodiac. Creamed Oysters, Creamed Lobster, boiled salmon, boiled live lobster tail, giant prawns, and duck constituted the main course. During the 1920s, buffets and sit-downs had become very popular with an emphasis on "creamed" meat dishes like chicken or fish, hot vegetable dishes, bread rolls, salads, prime rib of beef, and various cakes, and ice creams—all of which were readily available after the massive dinners in the dining room for the passengers with discerning but unwisely over-enthusiastic palates.

David introduced Alexandra to the etiquette and history of champagne.

"The first thing to know, Alexandra, my dear, is that champagne *must* be made from grapes grown in the Champagne region of France and must follow a specific set of production practices. When conditioning champagne for service, the chilling should be slowly and carefully done by placing the warm bottle in a refrigerator for several hours and not packed in ice until shortly before serving. Vintage champagne should be served at forty-five degrees. Upon taking the bottle from the cooler, Alexandra, my dear, it should be well wrapped with a napkin; so, the warm hand of the waiter will not come in contact with the bottle and inadvertently agitate the wine. One should only fill the flutes to within one-fourth of an inch from the brim; and, of course only "solid stem" glasses should be used.

"It is crucial to watch the tiny bubbles rise up the interior of the flute before sipping. The finest way to be served champagne is to create a pyramid of glasses delicately balanced and to pour the bubbly swiftly so as to fill each glass without spilling more than a very few drops. As much as we should love a beautiful champagne flute or even admire plain crystal white wine glasses, neither should be used in the construction of a tower because it is so important that all the glasses—coupe glasses–be identical. Remember that for future reference. Champagne is never gulped or slurped; that is evidence of a low-class and uneducated upbringing. The proper time for serving champagne is during the last meat course of the dinner just after clearing the palate with a lemon sorbet."

Alexandra had to laugh—an easy and companiable sort of laugh—because David took his champagne so seriously. It was part of his charm; but, for her, more than a bit absurd. He liked it that she was so genuine and comfortable to be with.

After the sumptuous and soporific dinner, David escorted Alexandra to the ladies' cocktail lounge–another elegant first-class location; and he went to the smoking room—a restful and inclusive room which evoked a late-Renaissance Italian palazzo ambience. It was *de rigeuer* for men traveling in first class to retire to this room after dinner to drink, to talk, to play games, and to be seen.

By the fourth day at sea, Alexandra found herself becoming rather bored. During those four days, David squired her to every activity that created the magical glamor of life on board known to the ocean cruising elite: shuffleboard, badminton, wooden horse racing across the second-class deck, the gymnasium where he introduced her to free weights, climbing bars, twenty-pound medicine exercise ball, climbing ropes, chin-up bars, stationery bicycle, and punching bag.

He sat for hours with her on the sundeck where the passengers were served by a deck steward in starched summer whites. She woke up to breakfast in bed, more sumptuous than any meal she had eaten in Australia. In the afternoons, she and David joined the other passengers in formal dress to relax and listen to a piano performance, read the ship's newspaper, browse in the many ship's shops, exercise in the swimming pool, play hoopla (ring toss), celebrate birthday parties, and to improve her education of the world around her in the large planetarium and ample libraries. She went trap shooting off the stern with a determination each day to better her record of the day before. Even though she was the only woman among shooters, Alexandra consistently won.

In her favorite library, she began a determined study of financial markets, economics, and how to manipulate the stock markets. Always patient David allowed her to win at card games—whist, bridge, gin rummy, phase 10 card game, train dominoes, and even poker where she was able to contribute some games as yet unknown to the other passengers or the activities directors—games she somehow always won, and by which she considerably enriched herself. Before dinner, she and David went dancing and even started dance classes; so, she could learn the Argentine tango, the Viennese Waltz, the quickstep, the samba, the cha-cha, and the rhumba. She wore him out, but he felt himself to be highly successful. Later each evening, after dinner and a necessary short rest, they enjoyed a ball every night, especially the ship line's balloon dance, costume and hat parades, followed by quiet moonlit strolls on the deck.

Despite this level of frenetic activity, Alexandra felt bored or perhaps more accurately, unfulfilled. For the first time in years she began to think about her two Russian sons, then to be concerned about them, then to develop a determination to find out where they were. Although David tried his level best, he began to realize that Alexandra was drifting away from him. His job depended upon making this rich woman happy and content. As the days passed, he noted that she preferred to sit in the women's library and to research some arcane Russian history and current affairs—for the life of him, he could not fathom why in the world she did so. He had to get her interest to return to him, or she would look unhappy to the ship's activities directors; or, heaven forbid, she might register a criticism.

On the sixth evening at sea, he determined that bold action was required. He walked her to her stateroom after they closed down the dancing with a final request to the orchestra that they play a soft arabesque, then a full orchestral accompaniment to the Charleston and the Shimmy—with a dynamic range from pianississimo to full fortississimo, a tonal range to include the lowest to the highest notes of the piano and everything in between, and speed from legato to staccato. The orchestra loved to share in the skill of the two great dancers and enjoyed improvising for affect. This was an era when dancers moved independently of other couples and created a mood of greater intimacy and sensuality. They finished with one of Chopin's Polonaises, a Baroque English country dance, and one wild ragtime number.

It was a dreamy romantic evening. The moonlight on the water turned it to silver. The thrumming of the engines, and the sound of the great ship's wake—like a troika gliding over show—promoted a comforting sense of lassitude. David said good night to Alexandra and waited until she entered her state room as he always did. An hour later, Alexandra heard a quiet rapping on her door. She squinted through the eyehole in the door and was surprised to see David standing outside, still in his tuxedo, and now holding a bouquet of coral red rose buds in his right hand and a platter with a bottle of Dom Pérignon vin de goutte–first press, using only the weight of the grapes on top of each other—which produced the highest quality wine] champagne and two flutes in his left.

Alexandra muttered to herself, "*Uh, oh,*" and reluctantly unlocked, turned the dogs, and opened the door.

"May I come in, my dear?" he asked with a slight slur in his speech.

As he drew close, she caught a waft of alcohol on his breath which heightened her level of caution.

"Of course, David. What is the occasion–Dom Pérignon and Fragrant Cloud red rose buds? I love its captivating fragrance more than any other rose."

"An opportunity to pay a compliment to you and to provide an opportunity for us to have some private time together without the Aryan Hordes we encounter in the lounges and dining salon."

"That's very nice, David; but I am afraid I am too tired. You wore me out today. This is not a good time."

"Ah, my dear lady," David said, "anytime is a good time for Dom Pérignon and Fragrant Cloud. They create a definite mood, and are the quintessence of romance, don't you think?"

"Perhaps, but; I think you have gotten the wrong idea; or I have sent out signals that were inappropriate. I can't tell you how much I appreciate all you have done, but I do not have such tender feelings for you. I will be frank, and do not wish to give offense; but I am not in the mood for a romantic connection with you tonight or any other time. Our pleasant times together were just that. Please do not make this awkward, David."

"Alexandra, I know you have some feelings for me. Perhaps you are like the rose buds—beautiful but not fully opened as yet."

"David," she said sharply, "you have stepped over the line. I am not a giddy girl struck dumb by heady overtures of romance. The reference to my being 'opened up' is an ungentlemanly and grossly improper inuendo. Please leave."

"I'm sorry, Alexandra. Please let me be completely candid. I have definitely become fond of you. The grandees of the Anchor Line expect—even require–that we escorts make direct overtures—and hopefully—have romantic liaisons with the ladies we entertain lest they think we do not find them appealing; and they are affronted. Please consider me in a positive light and give me a good letter of recommendation."

He was almost in tears.

"David, I will do as you ask if you leave *tout de suite* and never harass me again."

CHAPTER SIXTY-SEVEN

RETURN TO SHANGHAI

To my child's eyes, which had seen nothing else, Shanghai was a waking dream where everything I could imagine had already been taken to its extreme.

— J. G. Ballard

"New York may be the city that never sleeps, but Shanghai doesn't even sit down, and not just because there is no room."

— Patricia Marx

On board the British Passenger *SS Cameronia* from Sydney to Shanghai, from January 28 to March 12, 1913

David did a sharp about face and left the room. Alexander never saw him again for the remainder of the voyage. She was relieved at the gentlemanly departure and absence, even though she felt a mild stirring that she had long believed to be only historical for her. She was mildly put out at herself for having allowed a hairline fracture to insinuate itself into her deeply held defenses. She was disappointed that she had begun to equivocate about her strongly held indispensable desideratum for her life—a life free of entanglements with men and dependence upon outsiders. The idea that her base urges could even momentarily distract her caused her to have a niggling doubt about her resolves and her ability to sublimate her temporary needs to the long-term plan.

The *SS Cameronia* made landfall in the early morning of January 23 and pulled alongside the dock of the huge and extremely busy Port of Shanghai of the Republic of China at the mouth of the Yangtze River. There were tea clippers, ocean liners, steam cargo freighters, treaty power gun boats, junks, and sampans moving about in the crowded waterways. Alexandra and the other first-class passengers were piped off the ship and gathered on a red-carpeted area of the wharf where they were greeted by a Chinese band. The famous musical group was led by Li Jinhui who was regarded by the populace the "Father of Chinese Popular Music". They played spirited Mandopop tunes [Mandarin popular songs that started in the 1920s called *shidaiqu*, meaning "music of the time"—i.e., popular music]

Alexandra and her fellow notables were officially greeted by Sir Francis Aglen, inspector general and director of the port; Sir Martin Frontieriari-Bedford, British plenipotentiary and governor of HongKong; Li Choa Tse, Superintendent of Customs, and Chin Hoy, the Tao-Tai—the senior government official in charge of the district.

The Tao-Tai bowed and spoke for the coterie of dignitaries: "Welcome to the Treaty Port of Shanghai, *Griffins* [Shanghailander term for newcomers to the city], we are pleased to have your presence in the Paris of the East, the New York of the West. The Chinese name for our city means 'City on the Sea' located at the point where the great Yangzi completes its 3,400 mile journey to enter the Pacific Ocean.

"As the young people say, 'Shanghai is the place to be' because— we are proud to say–it has the best art, modern restaurants featuring the foods of the world, the greatest architecture available anywhere on earth, the finest dance halls, international clubs, *Duì jìyuàn de wĕiwăn shuōfă* [selling tofu, or gentleman's clubs–euphemisms for brothels] and—tennis clubs. Of course, we have our great Shanghai Racecourse. We cater to your every whim."

The superintendent of customs gave a short welcome and instruction: "We welcome you to The Chinese Customs and maritime and International Service. Here, we will collect your entrance information and the *likin* [provincial tax on transfer of goods]. After that, safe transportation will be provided to the Richards' Hotel, our city's finest."

Alexandra climbed into a Citroen Landaulette taxi along with a Sikh police officer as a security guard and was taken directly to the venerable old Richards' Hotel and Restaurant on The Bund at 15 Huangpu Lu, Shanghai, near the confluence of the Huangpu River and the Suzhou

Creek in the Hongkou District. It was near the northern end of the *Waibaidu* [Garden] Bridge. They drove at the dizzying speed of thirty-five-miles-per hour—the fastest Alexandra had ever moved. This amazing speed was accomplished despite the presence of thousands of rickshaws, other taxis, overloaded lorries, herds of pigs, sheep, and goats, an infinity of peddlers, and heedless pedestrians. The sides of the streets and the buildings were plastered with advertisements and billboards, making them a blur of Chinese characters as Alexandra's taxi wove its way past the impediments. There was no accident, Alexandra thanked God; but a thousand miracles.

As they got out of the taxi, the officer suggested–as tactfully as possible–that "Missy should wipe the feet after being in the taxi. Is good health practice."

Foreigners had every reason to feel safe and secure. As her taxi moved along Nanjing Road, she watched the Shanghai Volunteer Corps participating in a parade. The Corps was established in 1853 to protect foreigners against the recurring chaos of war. In addition, Sikh policemen seemed to be omnipresent. the Sikh policemen were an indelible part of the landscape of Shanghai in the first decades of the twentieth century. The Sikh branch of the Shanghai Municipal Police had the crucial role of assisting in the governance and policing of the International Settlement in treaty port Shanghai. Their presence showed the power and importance of the British presence in China and on the Indian sub-continent. In all the treaty ports, British power had an Indian face. Alexandra loved the British and all that their colonial development offered.

The development of the "Modern Shanghai" Alexandra was observing, started at the beginning of the 20th century when she was in Australia which was struggling to achieve a modicum of modernity. Shanghai–on the other hand–demonstrated the modern world in full flower when she arrived in 1913. Municipal government and public facilities were of high quality. They were into the booming city by international settlements. In addition, there were technologically up-to-the-moment telegrams, telephones, and movies–Shanghai had 40,000 theater seats with extremely high attendance–with the most popular movies being *wuxia* [martial arts] and family dramas]–dance halls, buildings for society balls, and other Western lifestyles brought in by the technological development collectively to create the unique city.

The needs of the daily increasing volume of trade and commerce, telegraph communications became a necessity. Shanghai's local and world-wide banking business developed quickly, making it one of the Far East's financial hubs by 1910. Alexandra and her Wáng family tong did millions of dollars worth of business in their principle bank in Asia—the HSBC [The Hong Kong and Shanghai Banking Corporation] located on the Bund and used the International Savings Society on Shanghai's Avenue Edward for transactions requiring quicker fluidity.

The Chinese people and the foreign expatriates, along with Alexandra, were the people who were the very first to experience a true modern city: the rampant media, advertisements, films, high-level communication, commerce, and education. During her stay, Alexandra rode on The Shanghai Electric Construction Co. Ltd.'s streetcar line—Shanghai's first—which traveled on trolley rails along Nanjing Road [the business street], from Jingan Temple to the Shanghai Club Building.

Once she was comfortably ensconced in her Richard's Hotel Suite and had a small lunch to tide her over, she hailed down a rickshaw puller to take her to the Shanghai French mansion of the new taipan, James Matheson II, now the master of the entire Jardine-Matheson conglomerate. The taipan served as the best man for her groom, Boris, when they were married. James was "Jamie" to her, even though he had succeeded the recently deceased great Taipan Sir James Nicolas Sutherland Matheson, 1st Baronet.

As the straining puller took her along the Huaihai Road in Luwan, she was brought to remembrance of the city's *lilongs*—old Chinese alleyways where commerce had never evolved; and poverty showed its beaten head. They arrived at the Zhujiajiao Chenghuangmiao Temple–No.69 Caohe Street, Zhujiajiao Town, Qingpu District. Alexandra overpaid the emaciated coolie, then she walked the final two blocks north of the temple to number 71, home of the new taipan. The taipan's home was and the former residence of Soong Ching Ling–third wife and widow of Sun Yat-sen, and a political figure in her own right–was built in the Xujiahui District at the Huaihai Middle road in 1843. Along with several others in the French Concession, the neighborhood drew a plethora of rich families together into a section of the city which became the most affluent and best residential area in Shanghai.

The colonial French officers created a district in 1849 for French people which evolved into the French Concession. Even early on, the

French demonstrated their love of color, precision, tree lined avenues, and unique architecture, making it not only the richest area, but also the most beautiful in the huge sprawling city. There was a mix of races on the street, but the binding thread among them was money. Chinese and Caucasian alike made up the near frenetic bustle characteristic of the Shanghainese.

Alexandra struck the gong on the front gate; and, shortly, a tall, powerful guard with a clean, well-oiled queue opened the gate for her and escorted her to the main entrance.

The two beautiful cypress wood doors–intricately carved to show a finely detailed dragon–opened unexpectedly. Each was held open by a uniformed man. Neither of them smiled or nodded.

A uniformed maid showed them in and had them sit on uncomfortable silk covered settees while she left to inform the taipan's staff of the arrival of the Russian woman. Almost immediately, a tall, powerfully built late-middle-aged man with short cropped hair, a monocle, and a conspicuous scar on the right cheek, walked up to them. Alexander recognized him immediately, having met him when she and her father visited the uncle of the present tai-pan.

"*Kommen sie mit,*" the stern man said brusquely, transmitting a welcome sense of déjà vu to Alexandra.

"*Ja wohl, mein herr,*" the maid said as sternly as the butler.

The butler made a smart about face and started down the parquet hallway without looking to see if he was being followed. Alexandra trotted obediently behind him—another déjà vu experience.

"*Der taipan werden sie jetzt sehen.*"

He said it hopefully, not remembering the considerably changed Alexandra and not yet quite sure that she spoke or understood *hoch deustch.*

Alexandra marched confidently and with an affectionate smile into the much less palatial office than she remembered from her first visit to the city. She walked in and right up to the heavy Philippine mahogany desk that Sir James had passed down to his nephew. Taipan James II had the same sandy hair, bushy eyebrows, and mutton-chop mustache, now beginning to turn to grey ginger. The man she remembered had been a vibrant jocular young man. Now that he was the taipan, he was late middle-aged like her. His eyes were the same robin's egg blue that she remembered, and that his uncle had had. Unlike his uncle, Jamie's eyes were not hard and unfeeling. He wore what Alexandra presumed was the latest fashion from Germany–close fitting tweed morning coat starched white shirt with cufflinks bearing the emblem of the house of Jardine-Matheson, a black bow tie, dark grey unpleated, uncuffed, woolen trousers, and scuff leather brogans.

"Hello, Jamie," she said and gave him her most natural and radiant smile.

He looked up from his work and seemed startled to see her. It took him a moment to recognize who she was, to sweep away the wrinkles and cares on her face.

"Alexandra, what a delight it is to see you."

He said it with none of the Scottish brogue that his uncle Taipan Sir James Nicolas Sutherland Matheson, 1st Baron, used so artfully to his advantage. James II—Jamie–was larger, younger, and more eager than his lordly uncle had ever been in Alexandra's memory of the austere old man.

Jamie stepped from behind his huge desk and strode quickly to stand face-to-face to Alexandra. To her astonishment, Jamie threw his arms around her and gave her a hearty, almost breath-taking hug. She gasped to catch her next breath and laughed, which made him laugh.

"What brings you to Shanghai? You must have good spies, because my plans were to be in Hong Kong this week."

"I do, Jamie, the Wáng family tong."

"Of course. I know about your shipping adventures, but you disappeared after that. You'll have to tell me all about what has gone on since that long-ago time when we last saw each other. Tell me, is the mandarin, Wáng Wen Sheng, still among us? What about Hou Eadric?"

"The venerable mandarin is still very much alive and is active in business although his daughter, Caihong, is responsible for most of the day-to-day affairs of the Wáng Family Tong. As for the old bandit, Hou Eadric, he was hanged in Hong Kong some years ago and his body left hanging from the gates of the city as an object lesson to pirates."

Jamie screwed up his face trying to decide to release his pent-up laughter over Hou Eadric or to remain somber out of respect for Wáng Wen Sheng. He looked to Alexandra's eyes for guidance; and, seeing a twinkle at the corners of her eyes, he gave a short laugh.

"It is very good to learn that the mandarin still prospers. Not surprised that Hou got his just desserts, however."

"Just so," said Alexandra. "I severed business relationships before getting entangled with his last set of schemes."

"You always have had a watchful Chinese golden lion guardian angel, good luck, or good joss, Alexandra. How is that holding up for you these days?"

"Actually, Jamie, that is part of what I came to talk to you about—to seek your good advice."

CHAPTER SIXTY-EIGHT
ADVICE FROM AN OLD FRIEND

Feelings that come back are feelings that never left.
—Dionne Warwick

I was wrong when I said that I did not regret the past. I do regret
it. I weep for the past love which can never return. Who is to
blame, I do not know. Love remains, but not the old love; its
place remains; but it is all wasted away and has lost all strength
and substance. Recollections are still left, and gratitude, but...
—Count Leo Tolstoy, *Family Happiness, Chapter 4*

**Number 71 Caohe Street, Zhujiajiao Town, Qingpu District,
Shanghai, Residence of the Taipan of Jardine Matheson, Ltd,
March 9, 1913**

Jamie spread his arms in a welcoming gesture and directed her to
take a seat in one of the sumptuous arm chairs that faced his desk.
He sat in the other and faced her with an expression on his face that
read, "I'm listening." Alexandra drew in a deep breath and collected her
thoughts.

"I'll be glad to help if I can, Alexandra. Advice usually comes cheap
but may be costly in the end. At least that's what my old uncle used to say."

"I am coming back to you from Australia where I have been living
for the past several years. My original life's plan was to become richer and
richer here in the far east, to have many children, to live happily with my

tall, handsome, rich husband, and to live out our family life together in Vladivostok and sailing around the China seas."

"I take it that is not what happened in reality."

"You are right. What did happen was that I became a rich, adventuresome, risk taking, oceanic entrepreneur. That part of the plan held true. I had two children—that part you already know. What you probably do not know is that I forced Boris to leave me and my two boys because I witnessed him whipping unfortunate deportees from Russia to Balagansk Prison. I was young and rather naïve; and I considered his actions to be unbearable; what kind of a man could do such things? He told me that this action on my part would not stand; and, as I recall, that I would live to regret my decision. That was certainly true."

"How so?"

"Within two days, he sneaked back into my father's house and abducted my two boys, Nikita and Oral Borisovich. I have never seen nor heard from them since. I do not know if they are living or dead."

"Sorry to interrupt, Alexandra; but I can shed some light on that. I, too, have my spies. Boris was first sent by the imperial army to Manchuria for a short stay, and the boys lived in Port Arthur. He was then sent to Novonikolaevsk to teach in the Novonikolaevsk Military Academy School for Boys. Nikita and Oral were enrolled in the prestigious school and achieved ratings of superior for all their endeavors. I lost track of them four years ago. Sorry."

"And Boris?"

"I know that he was actively engaged against rioters, smugglers, and terrorists throughout Siberia, but not exactly where or when. I do not know if your sons were with him."

Alexandra shrugged and went on, a bit subdued, "That is more than I was able to glean with two years of research personally and with all of the Tarasova resources. I feel like I need to find Boris and have the conversation I should have had before our breakup."

"You are still married, I presume."

"I suppose—in name only."

"Have you considered finding a new marital partner, my dear friend?"

"Not for years."

"But you haven't given up entirely, then?"

"I guess not. I do need to tell you why I came to see you. It is somewhat personal, but it is about money and about dealing with conditions in Russia."

She was a bit uncomfortable about where Jamie was heading, although she was flattered. She did want to get his uncluttered advice before any relationship conversations progressed.

"I was rather depressed about my life here in the East; so, I made a major move to Australia, and found it to be a very interesting and promising place. I made money, and I lost money. Perhaps you have heard of the gold rush and bust resulting in the so-called 'Smellbourne' era?"

Jamie laughed, "I have indeed, and was amused by the name for the down-turn in the Australia, especially the Melbourne, economy… 'Smellbourne…how apt.'"

"After some time, with the help of friends in the Wáng Family Tong, I recouped my losses and went on to do very well. For personal reasons I would rather not discuss, I decided to make a clean break from Australia and have moved most of my assets to the far east and parts of Russia. I am asking your advice about the political situation, the incidents of civil unrest, and the long-term financial outlook."

Jamie looked pleased.

"I was afraid you were going to share a sad tale of bankruptcy or some similar devastating financial entanglement. I am proud of you, Alexandra. To tell the truth, I would not have expected anything less from a person as brilliant as you."

She blushed, "Oh, gracious, Jamie," was all she could muster.

"Let me start with Russia. Politically, militarily, economically, commercially, and governmentally, the empire is a mess—a great tottering tree looking for a place to fall. Whatever comes of the internecine strife among the factions—the Bolsheviks, the Menshiviks, the Reds, the Whites, the aristocrats, the peasants, the executive portion of the government, or the legislative–you and I will not live long enough to make investment in that fracturing empire worth any degree of risk."

"More sobering than I had imagined."

"Indeed. Talk of civil war is in the air, and that may be a self-fulfilling prophecy. It is probably too early to panic, but it is not too early to be frugal and sensible about your not inconsiderable fortune. Oh, yes, my spies long ago told me that you were one of the richest people in the world and easily the richest woman. From what you are telling me now, that description has only improved. However, great and powerful men and women, even major industries and nations, have faltered and failed owing to poor, emotionally, or religiously based decision making. It is time posthumous to remove your money from anything Russian and transfer it to London, which is stable, or to Shanghai or Hong Kong, which are rapidly expanding, or to America which I think is the next great power. I can assist you if you will let me. Be assured, I have followed my own advice inasmuch as I can."

"I have always considered you to be level headed and a scientific thinker, Jamie; so, please advise me on investments and security for them. First of all, what should I do with my money in Russia."

"All right. I will be brief and will now speak more as your financial consultant than as your friend. First and most important: as soon as you possibly can, liquidate all your assets in Russia anywhere. If you must remain there for a time, keep your valise packed, and cash money and gold in a satchel you can take with you in an emergency. Send the rest to the Wáng family tong account in their principle bank in Asia—the HSBC [The Hong Kong and Shanghai Banking Corporation]."

She raised a questioning eyebrow.

"Yes, my dear, those pesky spies of mine again. Next, if you must have a connection in Vladivostok or elsewhere in Russia, secretly build a small comfortable dacha somewhere in the forest where no one else knows about it. Stock it with provisions to last you for two or three months. Lastly, carefully plan an escape route out of Vladivostok and out of Russia. Contact me and make your way to me. Allow me to make a suggestion in that regard. Travel overland to Irkutsk and make your way into Outer Mongolia. Stay in Niislel Khureheh–the capital city–until you can contact me in Hong Kong. I will make safe arrangements for you to come to me there.

"I presume you have sufficient funds to make serious investments. Keep your investments in Hong Kong, Shanghai, or in London or New York in America. Your tong family contacts working with mine can ensure your future. Please trust me, Alexandra, I will protect your assets as I would your person. I will help you in any way I can whenever you need my help."

He was so earnest that Alexandra thought she could detect a tear drop forming in both of his eyes.

"I trust you, Jamie. I trust you completely…with my very life. I hope we can continue to be in contact to work out any details regarding transactions that become necessary."

As they talked, two wraith-silent servants brought in platters of food, set them near the two high personages who were talking, and slipped away as anonymously as they had entered. There were eight delicacies in hot sauce, Shepherd's-purse Wonton, and Crystal Shelled Shrimp as starters. The more robust assortment included samplings of Nanxiang Small Steamed Buns, Mini Steamed Buns, Crab Soup Buns, Barbecued Pork Buns and Vegetable Buns. Dessert selections–on a separate serving plate–included Plum Flower, Date Mash, and Chop Rice Cakes, and Osmanthus Cakes, Black Rice Balls, and Eyebrow-like Crisps.

"Absolutely. Perhaps I am about to overstep my boundaries or maybe the limits of propriety. But I must say something to you that I have kept in my heart for years…ever since we sailed together. I refrained from speaking then because first you were too young; then along came dashing Prince Boris; then he left; and you vanished and became a mystery. Now you are back.

So, I will just say it. Alexandra, I have been in love with you for decades. I never married because I had the strange and compelling hope that I would see you, and we could be together—I mean for always. Perhaps you consider me too old or too much of a platonic friend, but I ask you to consider marrying me sometime when you deem it appropriate. I will say it even if it might come to embarrass me later: I love you, Alexandra Tarasova."

She was floored, so much so that a rush of Russian, then Australian, words came to her to describe her initial feelings: *izumleny*, and gobsmacked among them

"Jamie, I never suspected. You have always been a wonderful friend. When I was barely twelve, I was so infatuated with you that I could scarcely sleep. Shortly before I met Boris, I envisioned you courting me, us having a grand Cinderella marriage, and making loads of beautiful children."

"And living happily ever after," Jamie threw in.

"Certainly."

"What happened to all of that?"

"Boris. He swept me off my feet; I was still just a girl, you know. My parents were enchanted by him and by his title and his fortune. I got caught up in the tidal wave."

"That's very honest of you. Dare I ask what your feelings are now?"

"A bit confused. I have to say that something drove me to make land in Shanghai. Maybe I used my need for financial advice as a ruse to get to be near you. I admit fully that, as mature as I am…or should be…that I am all atingle like a shy girl meeting her Prince Charming."

"Then, I may dare to hope?"

"Please do. I will. Let me sort myself out, and soon—very soon—I will get back to you; and we can see how serious we really are. And, I love you, too, Jamie. I suppose I always have, and no one else was ever quite right for me."

He kissed her hand, and assisted her to her ship, the *Imperial Russian Czarina*, which was to set sail for Port Arthur, Tokyo, Seoul, and finally, Vladivostok at dawn the next day.

Jamie was at the dock when the ship began pulling away from its berth. They waved to each other until they could no longer make out their faces in the distance.

Jamie said to himself, "*What a fascinating woman, what a mysterious one! What an enigma.*"

Alexandra went to her stateroom and had a good cry—whether for happiness, or for sadness, or just for release; she could not decide. Perhaps she would never really understand herself. It was mystifying.

CHAPTER SIXTY-NINE
WELCOME BACK HOME

"I think you travel to search and you
come back home to find yourself there."
—Chimamanda Ngozi Adichie

"It's no use going back to yesterday
because I was a different girl then."
—Lewis Carol,
Alice's Adventures in Wonderland, 1865

Tarasova House, No. 71 Svetlanskaya Street, Vladivostok, Far East Russia, March 18, 1913

The stops in Port Arthur, Seoul, and Tokyo, were casual and largely served to ramp up Alexandra's excitement at the thought of returning home. It was going to take two and a half weeks–weather permitting, and no setbacks–so, she had to occupy her mind. She bought trinkets and souvenirs—nice ones—in each of the markets where the *Imperial Russian Czarina* made port. Something for her father Abram, her mother, Irina, her two brothers, Veniamin and Valéry, and for as many of the servants and employees of the Tarasova Fur Company she could remember.

The sturdy ship entered Golden Horn Bay in late morning and was tied up at the wharf of Vladivostok Freeport Harbor by late afternoon. Several dozen stevedores, coolies, clerks, *gruzchiki,* and other cargo handlers, swarmed aboard to off-load heavy boxes, machinery, furs, and the passengers' and officers' baggage. Alexandra had wired ahead; so, an excited party of well-wishers thronged the dock to welcome her back. From the arrival deck, Alexandra could see her parents–Abram and Irina–who now looked wrinkled and stooped—long in the tooth, and grey of pate. Even Veniamin and Valery looked middle-aged.

"*Have I aged that much?*" Alexandra asked herself.

On the wharf, Alexandra was enveloped in powerful loving arms circumferentially and kissed until her cheeks glowed pink. Signs stood haphazardly all around: "Welcome Home," Welcome Daughter," "Welcome Back, Little Sister," "Welcome Princess Yusupov", Welcome Home Mrs. Alexandra," "Welcome, Welcome Lady Tarasova Yusupov." Laughter, tears, shouts of joy, and murmurs of loving endearments formed a cacophonous shell all around her creating a nest-like sense of being back in the bosom of the family, almost back into the womb.

She could not wait to give out her gifts. She directed a Buryat servant to open the gift boxes, and she handed them out with a small personal greeting to each recipient. Everyone—rich and humble, old and young, male and female, servant and master—was touched by the largesse and the genuine feelings of love they all shared together in the cool moist north wind whistling across the dock and up the hillside.

The following week was one long party. Family, friends, and neighbors crowded in and dirtied up the house; but even Irina and her maids paid no mind. They ate until they were surfeited with food and semi-stuporous with drink. They played, and sang, and danced to near exhaustion. By the end of the week, Alexandra felt herself to be fully welcomed home.

Life slowly returned to the world of work, commerce, shipping, and fur trading, and seemed more normal than before Alexandra had even met Prince Boris. Vladivostok seemed to have settled into its long-established routines and traditions, giving the lie to warnings from Jamie Matheson. The great angst of 1905 was becoming a thing of the past, of memory.

The Russo-Japanese war began in 1904 and resulted in a terrible disheartening defeat which spread depression over the land. Sunday, January 22, 1905 unarmed demonstrators in St. Petersburg, were fired upon by soldiers of the Imperial Guard as they marched towards the Winter Palace to present a petition to Tzar Nicholas II of Russia. Those Bloody Sunday shootings provoked public outrage and a series of massive strikes that spread quickly to the industrial centres of the Russian Empire. There followed a terrifying foreshadowing of anticipation of the world coming to an end with waves of political and social upheaval by the masses spreading like a great fire over vast stretches of the Russian Empire.

Several problems long embedded in Russian society contributed to the revolution of 1905. Serfs emancipated by Tzar Nicholas II in 1861 earned too little and were not allowed to sell or mortgage their allotted land. Ethnic minorities resented the government because of its discrimination and repression, such as banning them from voting and serving in the Imperial Guard or Navy and limited attendance in schools. A weak and powerless industrial working class resented the government for doing too little to protect them by banning strikes and labor unions. Radical social and political ideas fomented and spread after a relaxing of discipline in universities allowed a new consciousness to grow among students.

Among the many incidents of the short-lived 1905 revolution were protests and anger from hungry and weary peasants, others were specifically directed at the imperial government. At its zenith, the protestor/would-be revolutionaries included workers of all sorts on strike, crop burning by poverty-stricken peasants, and even several military mutinies. It lasted from January, 1905 to June, 1907. While the revolution failed to topple the government, real changes occurred: Constitutional Reform was instituted which included establishment of the State Duma–a multi-party system–and the creation of the Russian Constitution of 1906; and the empire quieted down.

Vladivostok was briefly governed by rebel military units in early 1906 resulting in unrest in the city which was quelled with diplomacy and judiciously applied force by the imperial army led by General Georgy Kazbek, Commandant in charge of the Vladivostok Fortress. During the period after 1907, the tzarist government wisely garnered the favor of the public by enabling improvements and construction of much-needed facilities: an attractive 17th-century-style railway station, a power station, two girls' schools, a school of commerce, trams, and the Versailles Hotel were built. Business and commerce flourished with a large increase steamship activity in the port, including 477 foreign ships. The number of shops in Vladivostok increased to over three thousand.

In 1913–when Alexandra returned–local publishers produced sixty-one titles in Russian and several other languages.

The Tarasovas resumed their active commercial businesses once the unrest settled down. Alexandra remained skittish; but her parents and brothers became contented that life was back to normal; and the taste of revolution was so repulsive that it would not be considered again. Tai-pan Jamie Matheson II visited on one of his smaller commercial vessels in early June of 1915 when he learned of some minor skirmishes between the supporters of the Bolsheviks and the White Army.

Jamie and Alexandra closeted together and talked "turkey" as he termed it, i.e. seriously.

"Alexandra," Jamie said, as soon as they found an empty room in the house. "I am not an alarmist, but the 'handwriting is on the wall', as the Bible said. Bolsheviks are forming a new regime throughout the country and are making progress in Petrograd and Moscow. My spies have been watching the Irkutsk oblast and especially Vladivostok and Irkutsk cities. The White Army counterrevolutionaries force is weak here, and the Bolsheviks and their supporters are being driven out of the west and are taking hold here in the east. Have you not become aware of the increase in population during the past year and a half?"

"Of course, I have; but I was not aware that the majority of them were Bolshies."

"I hate to sound harsh, especially given my feelings for you; but you cannot stay here any longer. The Reds are going to win when the all-out civil war comes, and come it will. No one can predict when the hammer will fall, but it will not be very long in coming."

"What is your best estimation?"

"A year or maybe two at the most."

"So, I have to move away as soon as I can do it."

"Yes. Have you built your dacha here yet?"

"It's well underway and in a beautiful and secret place."

"Good. Will you transfer your Russian holdings to Hong Kong and Shanghai in the next two or three days?"

"That quickly?"

"Yes. Now, Alexandra, I fear for you. I want you to leave with me on my ship. I can wait until the dacha is finished, but neither of us will be safe after that. I know this is abrupt, but I want you to be safe, and I want you. Would you do me the honor of becoming my wife?"

He actually went down on one knee which made her smile and cry at the same time.

"Yes, I will," she said without hesitation. "Let's get married at Tarasova House the day the dacha is completed. That won't be more than two weeks from now."

"My beautiful and brilliant, Alexandra, you do me great honor. I will scarcely breathe until that moment."

Alexandra was not the least shy or retiring about getting married again. Given the angst that accompanied her absence for such a long time, her mother, Irina, was energized by the idea that Alexandra would be settled, living, and conducting her business in Vladivostok with none other than the Jardine-Matheson taipan. The energy put into the new wedding plans so dominated the energy of the two women, that they paid only scant attention to the dramatic changes in population that were occurring.

Jamie's corporate board began to fear for his safety and for that of his ship and its cargo; so, they unanimously demanded that he return to Hong Kong at next tide. He reluctantly told Alexandra that he would have to leave but would return as soon as the growing unrest quieted down. Otherwise, their fall back escape plan would be put into play.

"Jamie, I don't care about a grand wedding. I just want a marriage with you. I will slow down on the wedding plans and give most of my attention to the dacha. I should be done in a month."

They kissed fervently and promised each other eternity. But he had to set sail that evening to catch a promising tide. They telegrammed each other every day, with a growing sense of ardency and urgency.

Workers fled or refused to work; so, construction of the dacha slowed to a snail's pace. Bolsheviks poured in, and the government run by the counterrevolutionaries began to fail as the White Army proved increasingly unable to keep order. Over the next seven years, Vladivostok's population quadrupled as Whites left and the Reds inundated the city. From 1915 to 1917, the White Army retreated to the east leaving supporters of the old regime to the not so tender mercies of the revolutionaries and all of their internecine struggles for power. The city began to descend into a chaotic mixture of partisan struggles.

Alexandra made numerous but futile attempts to communicate with Jamie. Nothing could get through to him or back from him. Finally,

Alexandra decided that she must join the exodus of the Whites. She told her parents and brothers that they needed to come.

"It will pass, Alexandra. Have faith," her mother said.

"We can't leave our ancestral home, all of our properties and investments, and our people," her father, Abram said. "Besides, Irina and I are too old to begin galavanting around the country or maybe even the world at our age. We will have to weather the storm, as we have always done."

Collapse of the city was imminent. Alexandra asked, begged, cajoled, and even threatened, her family, but to no avail. They were opposed to any change, especially one of such magnitude. The argued that the Bolshies were just like them, decent people at heart; and everything would eventually turn out all right.

Alexandra finally gave up. She made plans to leave with a small cart train of her necessaries and treasures three days from her last urgent pleading with her family, but events moved too quickly for that.

A semi-disciplined Bolshevik armed force advanced to the street before Svetlanskaya Street in the late afternoon and made camp. Alexandra and three of the family Buryat faithfuls took their four horses and four pack horses with hastily gathered crucial goods including rations, firearms, swords, and ammunition, and fled in the night in the direction of General Kazbek and his army of stragglers. Alexandra bemoaned the fact that she could not communicate with Jamie, and in her depression over that; she wondered if perhaps God was punishing her for her bigamies. In lighter moments, she wondered if He were not just saving her from becoming a "trigamist".

Gen. Kazbek's White Army encampment was in disarray. Few tents had been put up; there was no aid station; cooking facilities were inadequate. Discipline was beginning to deteriorate to an every-man-for-himself level with half of the soldiers absent from the camp on hunting trips. The desertion rate was mounting.

Alexandra took stock of the situation and decided that she could best help by working on the mess hall and kitchen facilities to provide efficiently for her estimate of 65,000 men from the garrison and local Vladivostok aristocratic volunteers from among the remaining middle-class citizens, reactionaries, pro-monarchists, non-Bolshevik socialists, socialist revolutionaries, Mensheviks, republicans, and liberals, less some deserters and defectors, and almost that many camp followers. The best soldiers in the camp by far were the members of the well disciplined Ussuri Cossack Host. She relied on them to bring in meat from the hunt and cattle, sheep, hogs, and vegetables largely through forced divestitures from the peasant farmers in the region. She organized the kitchen policing staffs, cooks, servers, and storage managers. In three weeks, she had a well-functioning organization underway.

The success of Alexandra's efforts came to the attention of a young general named Vladimir Kappel. He recognized her value and appreciated her beauty, general healthiness, and ability to endure privation. After watching her for three weeks off and on, he approached her as she finished an all-day shift in the mess hall.

"Mrs. Yusupov, I am Gen. Kappel. I admire your work and accomplishments. I wish we had a few thousand men like you in the White Guard service."

"Thank you, General. It is morale building to know that one's efforts are appreciated."

"I have to tell you that I admire more than just your work, excellent as it is. I admire you and would like you to accompany my army to Siberia when we leave. I trust that you can keep a secret?"

"I can."

He took a moment to decide how far he should go.

"General Kapchek has been recalled to the Southern Front, and I will replace him in command of the White Army in the East, Northeast, and Siberia. I need people of your caliber to be officers under my command. Times are rapidly changing, I hardly need tell you. Old alliances topple; new ones arise. It is difficult for a dedicated officer to know who to trust. I instinctively trust you. I hope you will not be offended, but I also have a rather strong attraction to you personally. I will be most candid; I am bold enough to hope that you and I can march together, live together, and comfort one another as we undertake our massive endeavor for the *Rodina*."

Under ordinary circumstances, in different times, or in pre-civil war society, she would have silenced the man abruptly and told him that he was an unprincipled boor. These, however, were neither ordinary circumstances nor polite society. She had given up her selfish desires to have a "trigamy" with Jamie Matheson or any other man from that long-ago time and far-away place that was "the civilized world".

"You are a great man, General, and likely to go far. You have been pleasant to me in a world that is no longer pleasant. For that I thank you. I am convinced of the righteousness of our cause and think it appropriate for us to help one another and to provide companionship. I would be proud to work with you, but you must know that I cannot be subservient to any man. I will work tirelessly as your partner in all things, but I will not be a *staraya krest'yanka* [old Russian peasant lady, babushka] who dares not speak or show her face."

Knowing she was going against all Russian tradition, and even her best chances to live a decent life in a rapidly deteriorating world, Alexandra looked Gen. Kappel directly in his eyes without giving in to the deep recesses of her traditional mind to look down at her feet.

He gave her a wide grin showing his large healthy teeth—another strong reason to want to be with him. She had long ago learned that good teeth meant good general health, strength, and endurance.

"It is a bargain, Princess," he said and reached out to her.

This was the moment of truth. She decided not to hesitate but leaned in to embrace him without reservation. He kissed her soundly. Later that evening, she moved into his tent, which was five times the size of the one she had been occupying; and light years more comfortable. Despite there being no sort of ceremony, Alexandra Abramovna Tarasova-Yusupov Bradshaw became a "trigamist" enthusiastically.

Vladimir gave Alexandra a brace of ivory handled pistols and a fine newly introduced Italian Cei-Rigotti gas-operated, selective-fire, repeating carbine, with a 20-round magazine as a wedding gift.

"So, you will always be safe," he said.

"Thank you, Vlad," she said, "I can't think of sweeter gift."

They both laughed at the nuanced humor.

Vlad—no one else in the entire army called him Vlad—added, "Another interesting change in the times, Dear Alexandra. Now learn to use it well."

She did, and quickly learned its drawbacks: frequent jams and erratic shooting. She knew better than to complain. She was probably the best armed soldier in the entire White Army.

Kappel's army was in no shape to face a determined and disciplined Bolshevik army at this point. As the Reds drew ever closer, Gen. Kappel made the decisive decision to begin the long march to Novonikolaevsk and the safety of an agreeable populace and a well-fortified military garrison commanded by the most important official in the anti-Bolshevik armed forces, Admiral Alexander Kolchak, who headed the entire eastern front of the civil war and constituted the leadership of the provisional Russian government with its capital in frigid Siberia.

The march from the mountainous area east of Vladivostok to the oblast capital and railhead took an arduous six weeks owing to the rough terrain, the physics of moving a cumbersome and inexperienced army, and the need to proceed in secrecy. In Irkutsk, Gen. Kappel and his army commandeered the Transsiberian train and routed it for Novonikolaevsk [later renamed Novosibirsk].

Alexandra lived up to Vladimir's hopes and expectations when he gave her full charge of the logistics of the railway trip. The Red Army was unaware of White's presence in Irkutsk; so, boarding onto the cramped train proceeded as quickly as possible during wartime. The passenger portion of the train had to be modified to change it to entirely third-class to accommodate the large number of men and their equipment. Cattle cars served to transport the horses, feed animals, and crates of provisions. Like all soldiers throughout history, the enlisted men griped good-naturedly at the bossy woman who had Gen. Kappel's ear. For that reason alone, no one ventured a real complaint or even a comment about the favoritism she enjoyed; but they all recognized that she was performing a crucial service.

The train lumbered out of the Irkutsk station at the tedious speed of twenty miles-per-hour and took more than four weeks to reach the capital of Siberia owing to poorly constructed railroad facilities, inclement weather, and occasional attacks by small units of Bolshevik bandits who were easily repelled but interfered with progress nonetheless. The enlisted men in the third-class carriages with their cargoes of arms and supplies were crammed into the available spaces and were rather severely uncomfortable. After a while, the men developed a Russian fatalistic patience, and realized that complaining was not going to make the journey faster or less uncomfortable. Senior officers—including Alexandra and her general—fared considerably better. For her it was interesting and exciting to see the wild and foreign countryside move slowly past.

Arrival in Novonikolaevsk was gratifying and satisfying. The masses of properly uniformed, well-fed, healthy appearing soldiers, and the absence of cripples, rushing ambulances, and thousand-yard-stares heartened the train passengers. There was a sense of order and stability such as they had enjoyed in their home cities under the tzar's empire. Gen. Kappel left for headquarters and found out that Gen. Kolchak had already departed for the southern front and that he had taken nearly sixty percent of the troops, including all the seasoned warriors. He returned to where his senior officers and Alexandra were waiting.

"We have a problem," he said.

"Just one?" Col. Davidoff commented wryly. "Things are looking up."

CHAPTER SIXTY-NINE

UNSUNG HEROES

"Life is to be lived, not controlled; and humanity is won by continuing to play in face of certain defeat."
—Ralph Ellison, *Invisible Man*, 1952

O great priestess, do not be angry with me; I am going. I shall not fail the roll-call of the shadows.
—Euripides, *Medea*. Translated by C.A.E. Luschnig

Grand Duke Marshal Nikolai Sergeyovich Siberia Military Academy, Novonikolaevsk, Siberia, May 20, 1913

The grim news that the new arrivals would constitute the bulk of the White Army in the Far East and Siberia and that the other troops available would come from military science students, Cossacks, republican bourgeois liberals, social democrats who had no military experience, right-wing Russian Orthodox noviates, *hiero-monks* [priest-monks], ordinary Novonikolaevsk citizens who were champions of tzarism, pro-monarchists of any kind of kingly class, reactionaries, elderly retired imperial soldiers and sailors, deserters from the Bolshevik side, and forced conscripts from among the local men.

Never one to use euphemisms or to shade the truth, Gen. Kappel put the situation into perspective succinctly, "We cannot fight a war with such rabble as our army. In order even to conduct holding actions, we will have to obtain more conscripts from among the healthy young locals and do our best to train them and to give them military discipline.

We will keep a hawk's eye on the Bolshis; so, we can be ready when they come to take our city. I am not inclined to sacrifice my army in some foolish 'fight-to-the-death-for-honor' last stand. We will fight; we will retreat; we will attack as partisans; and when it becomes necessary, we will leave for the South and join forces to keep our cause alive."

Alexandra and the rest of the seasoned soldiers were relieved to know that their commander was a pragmatist as well as a fine and sensible commander. His short speech won him dedicated followers.

Lake Baikal, Russia, January, 1913

The situation was worse than even Gen. Kappel's initial assessment indicated. It was barely two weeks before the first skirmishes with the Reds began in the outskirts of Novonikolaevsk. As inadequately trained and equipped as they were, the hastily organized defenders of Novonikolaevsk acquitted themselves well enough to allow the general and his staff the chance to plan and prepare for a major tactical retreat. All hope evaporated when Czechoslovak Legions stranded in Siberia by the new Bolshevik government, refused to continue what they deemed to be a hopeless defensive position. Kappel and his staff and their newly organized White Army of Siberia held on until late October. The Red Army gained serious ground throughout the month, and Kappel was forced to close ranks again and again until the physical defenses of Novonikolaevsk became so insufficient that no one was surprised when the orders came down for the entire army to retreat to the South in the dead blackness of a misty freezing night.

Thus began what came to be known as the Great Siberian Ice March. Kappel's army retreated to the East then South following the Transsiberian railway towards frozen Lake Baikal with the Red Army in relentless pursuit. The old and weak perished from exposure, frostbite, pneumonia, and inadequate rations, during the three-month trek. The last night–January the twentieth–Kappel had Alexandra and the kitchen crew prepare one final feast. Hunters brought in a wide assortment of meat garnered from the fauna found near the marge of the great lake— reindeer, white tailed deer, elk, moose, musk deer, Siberian roe, wild boar, moose, lynx, wolverine, and wolves. They were not loathe even to harvest polecats, ground squirrels, and handfuls of nasty bite-sized voles.

Alexandra and her Spartan kitchen crew brought out the huge cooking pots and pans, the last remains of her cache of fresh—now frozen—vegetables, and all her spices to make a stew fit for the tzar's family. Scouts reported that the Reds had made camp less than ten miles from the White Army encampment on the edge of the lake. Every movement was calculated for maximum efficiency. Every cooking short-cut that could be taken was employed, and the result was a marvelous eclectic boost for the morale of the nearly defeated White Army.

The quartermaster considered it to be divine providence that allowed the exhausted, frozen, and starving, army to have one last and wonderful meal. Alexandra was queen for the day. It could not last, of course; by midnight, the scouts reported that a significant force of Reds had advanced ahead of the main army to within two miles of the White Army enjoying its last meal.

A whisper order from Gen. Kappel roused the Whites to calm and determined action. They abandoned everything except the tzar's gold and the battle supplies necessary for a last stand and began a forced march across the frozen lake towards Irkutsk and Ulan-ude, Mongolia, capital of the Buryat Autonomous Republic. Their goal was once part of the vast Mongolian empire and that hope for safety was over five hundred kilometers away. Thirty thousand soldiers, their wives and camp followers, and support staff, marched onto the ice where the temperature was below -60°F; and a harsh biting wind amplified the misery. The Whites had scarcely gotten onto the lake before the Reds were upon them. The freezing Whites fought a rear-guard action punctuated with lethal skirmishes and increasingly difficult forward marches. The wounded, dead, and dying, were left to freeze on the surface of the ice.

Exhausted men and women marching dropped to the ice and froze there, scattering corpses in a macabre tableau marking the final throes of a once powerful army. Gen. Kappel and Alexandra Tarasova-Yusupov pushed along arm-in-arm with her mostly holding him up as he began dying from pneumonia. They stopped for a brief rest, and she held his head in her lap. She could not caress him because her hands were frozen to the point that they were hardly better than clubs. He died before she could get him up and going again. She struggled to her feet, alternated putting one hand inside her parka to warm it in her armpit while holding her repeating rifle with the other and began to shuffle on club feet across the ice while unobstructed high velocity freezing winds turned her feet and lower legs into icicles.

She and four men continued to struggle towards the far edge of the lake. Then, the Red Army forward scout unit came out of the icy mists and began firing at them. Alexandra marshalled all her courage, strength, flexibility, and determination to turn and begin firing her Cei-Rigotti repeating carbine at the oncoming relentless rabble. She stood there unflinching with mist and gunsmoke swirling about her. She went through two 20-round magazines until the rifle jammed from overheating. She was defenseless. The world turned white.

> **Both sides carried out atrocities. One journalist claimed that the Red Army received orders on how to behave by the Bolshevik government: "It was proposed to take hostages from the former officers of the Tsar's army, from the Cadets and from the families of the Moscow and Petrograd middle-classes and to shoot ten for every Communist who fell to the White terror.... The reason given by the Bolshevik leaders for the Red terror was that conspirators could only be convinced that the Soviet Republic was powerful enough to be respected if it was able to punish its enemies, but nothing would convince these enemies except the fear of death, as all were persuaded that the Soviet Republic was falling. Given these circumstances, it is difficult to see what weapon the Communists could have used to get their will respected."**
>
> **—Morgan Philips Price,**
> ***My Three Revolutions*, page 136, 1969**

EPILOGUE

After the game, the King and the pawn go into the same box.
-Old Italian proverb

Southern Edge of Lake Baikal, 250 km north of Irkutsk, Spring, 1914

The corpses lay in full view to carrion eaters and any passers-by that might have had occasion to look out at the great lake throughout the remainder of the winter. The arctic winds blew constantly across the lake ensuring that no thawing would occur until the advent of Spring. Admiral Alexander Kolchak—now having the title of "Supreme Leader and Commander-in-Chief of All Russian Land and Sea Forces," and his remaining White Army, reinforced by Czechoslovak Legions, passed through the area to keep ahead of the Reds and to find safe areas to mount ambushes.

Adm. Kolchak ordered General lieutenant Prince Boris Yusupov to organize a graves registry unit to provide Christian burials for their slain comrades. Unfortunately for that endeavor, they were too late. As the hardened—but nonetheless horrified—soldiers watched in dreadful awe, the Spring thaw came early and swiftly. A great fissure opened up across the middle of the lake; and corpses, ammunition boxes, guns, swords, possessions of the men, their wives, and the camp followers slid silently into the open maw and disappeared to the bottom of the nearly one-mile deep lake. Boris had seen too much to be sad, but he did see the body of a woman who somehow—in his overactive imagination—reminded him of his long-ago wife as it was lost to the deep.

The army left no marker and made no record. The identities and histories of the dead were lost with their bodies.

Admiral Kolchak and his senior staff–including Prince Boris–were captured and executed by firing squad and dumped into an obscure river in January, 1920—the exact whereabouts unmarked and lost to history. Boris's two sons died in pointless battles somewhere in Far Eastern Russia that same year and were buried in unmarked mass graves. Since victors write the history, nothing more is known of the once vibrant people who molder in obscurity.

In March of 1921, after a lengthy period of being unable to communicate with Alexandra or to find out definitively whether or not she was alive, Kyle Dewit Herman Bradshaw filed for a declaration of death in the case of his wife–Alexandra Bradshaw–in the State Court of Victoria, Australia in order to obtain access to his wife's presumably very valuable estate. For reasons unknown to later generations, after a protracted legal effort by Mr. Bradshaw, probate was denied in 1931. Bradshaw died of cirrhosis of the liver in 1934.

There is no record of any of the issue of Kyle and Alexandra Bradshaw ever coming into any fortune—or any money at all, for that matter. Perhaps the records are inadequate; perhaps the three offspring made other decisions. There is no information. Searches by missionaries of the Church of Jesus Christ of Latter-day Saints of banking records in Russia, Australasia, and Europe were fruitless; and they lost interest in obtaining more facts once the well ran dry. From their interest, a rather odd thing occurred. Mormons are fond of forming "empty-nester" clubs. Several of the former missionaries who worked on the Victoria Archives Project told a historical fiction writer friend about their quest and asked him to produce a story about the "mysterious Alexandra Tarasova-Yusupov Bradshaw. He agreed.

Alexandra lived. She apparently became wealthy; but beyond that, who knows? And, maybe, it is better left alone to let her rest in peace. She remains the "Mysterious Alexandra Tarasova-Yusupov" of life and fiction.

Konets {Russian}
Jiéshù {Mandarin}
Time to Shoot Through {Strine}
The End {English}